"HE'S TRAPPED," A VOICE SAID.

"Shona, lay down suppressing fire and move up. Zungu, Penga: Flank him."

A blistering barrage of electric-blue plasma bolts screamed over Riker's head. Steam jetted from ruptured pipes, and several pulses per second lit up the walls around him with glowing, half-molten divots. Flashes of light and fountains of sparks illuminated the smoke billowing from the crate as it was peppered with plasma fire.

Riker tried to return fire without losing his cover, but in his weakened state the weapon was too heavy to control. He ended up firing a few futile bursts into the ceiling over his head.

He dropped prone and steadied his rifle. *Have to wait until they get to point-blank range,* he thought. *It's my only chance.*

Current books in this series:

Forthcoming books in this series:

STAR TREK®
A Time to Heal

DAVID MACK

Based on
STAR TREK: THE NEXT GENERATION®
created by Gene Roddenberry

POCKET BOOKS
New York   London   Toronto   Sydney

This book is a work of fiction. Names, characters, places and incidents are products of the author's imagination or are used fictitiously. Any resemblance to actual events or locales or persons, living or dead, is entirely coincidental.

An *Original* Publication of POCKET BOOKS

POCKET BOOKS, a division of Simon & Schuster, Inc.
1230 Avenue of the Americas, New York, NY 10020

STAR TREK is a Registered Trademark of Paramount Pictures.

This book is published by Pocket Books, a division of Simon & Schuster, Inc., under exclusive license from Paramount Pictures.

ISBN: 0-7434-9178-5

First Pocket Books printing September 2004

10 9 8 7 6 5 4 3 2 1

POCKET and colophon are registered trademarks of Simon & Schuster, Inc.

Cover by Zucca Design

Manufactured in the United States of America

For information regarding special discounts for bulk purchases, please contact Simon & Schuster Special Sales at 1-800-456-6798 or business@simonandschuster.com.

We would often be ashamed of our finest actions if the world understood all the motives which produced them.
—François de la Rochefoucauld, *Maxims*

Chapter 1
Tezwa

DUSK SETTLED upon the city of Alkam-Zar. Rays of deep-crimson sunlight flared through the seam of the horizon, casting a fiery glow across the sullen, steel gray clouds. Wind like a mournful cry twisted between the towering husks of buildings both ancient and modern—all sinking now into decay and history.

Starfleet Ensign Fiona McEwan stood on the edge of a rubble-strewn plaza near the center of the battered metropolis. Alkam-Zar, like many other Tezwan cities, was still smoldering more than two weeks after it had been racked by a shock wave from a Klingon torpedo, which had destroyed a military starport several dozen kilometers away from the urban center.

These people probably thought the base's presence made them safer, McEwan mused. *It just made them a target.*

Behind the petite, red-haired young officer, a Federation relief team coordinated the distribution of food, clean water, and medicine to local Tezwans, who had lost most of their basic utilities because of the Klingon barrage. The relief group was composed of civilian workers and physicians. McEwan was one of six Starfleet security personnel assigned to protect them. Some relief groups, working in similarly war-torn urban areas around the planet, had been nearly overwhelmed by Tezwan refugees whose suffering and desperation had led to food riots; other groups had been ambushed by Tezwan military insurgents still loyal to the deposed prime minister, Kinchawn.

Today things had been quiet in Alkam-Zar. Most of its people were still in shock. Tezwan adults and children wandered the streets like gangly, looming phantoms. Their feather-manes were pale with dust and matted with neglect, their arm feathers tattered and scorched and stained with blood. Shuffling footsteps crunched across boulevards dusted with shattered glass and pulverized rock. Broken beams of metal crusted with ancient stone had impaled the ground and dotted the thoroughfares and side streets like monuments to a quiet despair.

So far, the Federation's efforts had focused on providing these people with the essentials of survival—food, water, shelter, and basic medical treatment. Just two days ago the Starfleet Corps of Engineers had arrived, to direct the monumental task of rebuilding this world's ravaged cities.

For her part, McEwan was in no hurry to see the streets swept bare. If a Loyalist ambush were aimed at her squad, she would be grateful for all the cover she could get.

Thirteen more days, she reminded herself. *Then I rotate back shipside.* She had just begun her two-week deployment to the planet's surface and was already looking forward to her return to the *Enterprise*. Because she had risked her life during the commando mission that neutralized Tezwa's ground-based antiship artillery, she had been lucky enough to miss the first, grueling two-week rotation. Danilov had told her the reeking, insect-infested carnage in the major cities had left him with nightmares. Seo had described—in a haunted monotone that made his nauseatingly vivid details all the more unsettling—a guerrilla ambush in Anara-Zel that killed four security officers from the *Republic*. Danilov and Seo were frontline veterans of the Dominion War, so McEwan took their warnings seriously.

A keening cry, anguished and beautiful, cut through the heavy hush. Turning toward its source, McEwan looked up, toward the top of a twenty-story building rendered by war into a gutted frame. Standing like an emperor atop the structure was a lone Tezwan singer, his arms flung wide as if to embrace the sky. Nasal and piercing, his voice reverberated off smashed, hollow edifices painted with the dying light of day. McEwan's heart stirred with his projected grief, ached as it grasped the terrible emptiness of his operatic wails.

Without taking her eyes from the singer, she grabbed the sleeve of a young Tezwan boy who was walking past her. Holding him with one hand, she pointed with the other at the singer. "What's he singing?"

Following her gesture with stunned, distant eyes, the boy seemed utterly unmoved by the singer as he answered. "It's a sorrow-song. We sing for the dead."

McEwan stood, transfixed by the singer. His voice

was like a majestic wolf cry, despondent beneath a shadowy dome of gray, casting on her an enthralling spell of mourning. The boy pulled away from her, and she let go of him. "Who's he singing for?"

The boy glanced up at the singer. As he turned away, he answered with an ominous emotional flatness, "The world."

She glanced at the boy, who plodded off, his daily ration of Federation emergency nutrition packs tucked under one arm. Then the singer's tune crested, pulling McEwan's eyes back to the top of the tower. For a fleeting moment the singer's voice filled every corner of Alkam-Zar. Then his music dropped away like a dying breath. A faint and tragic note rose and vanished into the heavens, like his soul taking flight. He leaned forward and pitched headfirst off of the building.

McEwan's cry of alarm stuck in her throat as she watched the singer plummet. He neither flailed nor cried out, but fell as if it was his destiny to do so. Empathetic dread swelled inside her as the singer's body accelerated.

He hit the ground with a dull, thick, wet crunch.

McEwan's horrified gasp was tangled up in her choking sobs. Burning tears ran from her eyes.

Fighting to compose herself, she turned slowly back toward the plaza. Behind her, the other Starfleet personnel watched in shock. A civilian woman with the relief team covered her mouth and began to weep. Many other relief workers turned away. A young doctor sprinted across the plaza with a surgical kit in his hand, apparently undeterred by the futility of his impending efforts. A Federation News Service reporter ran after him.

But all McEwan could see were the Tezwans, who continued to wait for their food packets and water rations, oblivious of—or indifferent to—the singer's gruesome end. Even more than his suicide, their numb disregard of it frightened her deeply.

Wiping the tears from her cheeks, she counted the days until she could leave this world and never see it again.

Geordi La Forge cinched his parka hood tighter around his face. He hunched his shoulders against the chilly acid rain, which misted, gray and cold, into a blackened and almost perfectly round crater. The circular depression had, until recently, housed one of Tezwa's formidable artillery pieces. A pool of ruddy mud at the pit's bottom grew deeper by the minute.

All around him, once-verdant hills were ragged with skeletonized trees and withering ground foliage. Wafting odors of decaying vegetation tainted the cold, ozone-scented morning air. The catastrophic environmental damage hadn't been caused by the implosion of the nadion-pulse cannon. It was the result of massive quantities of ash, dust, and other toxins hurled into the atmosphere by the retaliatory Klingon bombardment, which had all but annihilated the rank and file of the Tezwan military and obliterated its principal surface installations.

A Starfleet forensic engineering team slogged around the eroding sides of the crater. They scanned the area with tricorders and a variety of specialized devices. Ensign Emily Spitale and Lieutenant Mitchell Obrecht were members of La Forge's staff aboard the *Enterprise*. The other nine engineers were from the starships *Repub-*

lic, Amargosa, and *Musashi.* Judging from their long faces and exasperated sighs, La Forge concluded that this search was proving as fruitless as the twenty-nine others they had already conducted during the past week.

He shared their frustration. Mounds of preliminary evidence had suggested that the Tezwans' brutal weapons might have been based on Starfleet technology. Unfortunately, almost nothing had survived the hastily executed Starfleet commando strike. The six firebases and their antimatter reactors, as well as all thirty-six guns, had imploded. The vaporized facilities had left behind little more than their glowing-hot craters, which had taken nearly a week to cool to a temperature safe enough for on-site inspections.

Along with the physical remains of the artillery system itself, other evidence that had been encountered during the strike missions was now lost or out of reach.

Security Chief Christine Vale had reported discovering, as part of the underwater firebase in the Nokalana Sea, a camouflaged iris composed of chimerium—a rare and restricted material to which only the Federation was known to have access. But when the undersea firebase imploded and sank into the planet's crust, it took the chimerium iris with it, beyond the reach of further analysis.

Assistant Chief Engineer Taurik had shown tremendous foresight in pirating large numbers of encrypted Tezwan military data files from a firebase computer in the Linoka Forest. Immediately after Captain Picard reported the seizure of the evidence, Starfleet Intelligence had exerted its authority and confiscated all copies of the files for its own secret investigation. Two weeks later there still was no word from SI regarding its findings—or lack thereof.

The best evidence that the artillery system had originated in the Federation had come from acting First Officer Data's positronic memory, which had interfaced directly with the Solasook Firebase computer system. After his allegedly "unstable" performance during the Rashanar incident, however, Starfleet Command had expressed grave reluctance to accept the android's perceptions as incontrovertible evidence.

All of which left La Forge kneeling in the mud, a tricorder in one hand and not a shred of proof in the other.

Spitale deactivated her tricorder and turned toward La Forge. Her shoulders were slumped, her expression blank. "There's nothing here, sir," said the athletic young blonde.

"Maybe not on the surface," La Forge said, studying the scene with his cybernetic eyes. "Run a deep-level—"

"—icospectrogram and a dekyon resonance pattern," she said, repeating the instruction he'd issued by rote all week long. "Aye, sir." Reactivating her tricorder, she pivoted away from him and faced down toward the mud pool.

Chasing down one dead end after another aggravated La Forge as much as it did the rest of the team. *We all have our duties,* he reminded himself. His was to search for evidence that would explain how the Tezwans created their armaments. Data's was to serve as the first officer of the *Enterprise* during Will Riker's absence. Vale's was to find Riker—and bring him home in one piece.

La Forge couldn't imagine what Riker must be going through—or perhaps he simply didn't want to. The first officer had been missing for seventeen days so far; if Kinchawn and his allies were holding him, they had yet to demand a ransom or even acknowledge that they were holding him. Worse than any fear of what might happen to Riker was the simple fact of *not knowing*.

By nature and training, La Forge lived for hard facts, for answers to riddles, for certainties. Now he had none. With the *Enterprise* repaired and once again fully operational, he had volunteered to lead the forensic engineering team on Tezwa in order to keep his mind occupied and his fears at bay.

Cycling through another series of tricorder scans, he repeated his silent, reassuring mantra: *Vale will find him. He's gonna be all right. She's gonna find him and bring him home.*

He wasn't sure he believed that. But he was certain that he couldn't stand not to. Slip-stepping across the interior of the slick crater, he held his tricorder at arm's length and continued running scans. "Just keep looking, folks," he said. "Just keep looking and don't give up."

"Relief Group Four-Sixteen Bravo to any Starfleet vessel! Mayday, we need emergency evac!"

The woman's voice squawked from the cockpit speaker. It sounded distant and flat in the rear compartment of the cramped but still antiseptic-smelling runabout. Tenila huddled with four other recently recruited Tezwan peace-officers-in-training and a quartet of Starfleet security personnel. She clutched her phaser rifle and tensed as the team leader, who sat up front next to the pilot, answered the distress call.

"RG Four-Sixteen Bravo, this is Runabout *Cumberland*," replied the confident-sounding young officer, a human named Peart. "We're en route, ETA forty-five seconds. Hang on."

The long, blocky craft banked to starboard and accelerated. Peart rose from his seat and strode into the aft compartment. "Check your weapons," he said. "Make sure they're on light stun. As soon as we're on the ground, wait for my order before you do *anything*." Tenila nodded along with the other Tezwans, then checked her weapon. The four Starfleet personnel seemed totally confident that their weapons were set properly, because they didn't bother to check their settings.

Suddenly anxious at the prospect of leaving the protection of the runabout, Tenila was grimly amused by how much her feelings about the vessels had changed recently. The first time she'd ever seen a Starfleet runabout was only two weeks ago; she had journeyed home to Savola-Cov, one of the great *trinae* cities, to bury her husband, Sangano, and to place her young son, Neeraj, in her parents' custody for a while. Kneeling in the ashes that surrounded the broken memory-stone of her family's ancestral *tava*, she had been carving Sangano's name into the rock with a plasma cutter when she'd heard a faint screech tearing across the darkened sky. Looking up from her sacred task with tear-drenched eyes, she'd decided the Starfleet vessel resembled a sinister bird surveying its new domain.

In the days since then, however, she'd learned of the fanaticism of the former Tezwan government—and how close it had brought her world to suffering wholesale extermination by the Klingon Empire. Realizing the Federation had intervened to save her people, she signed up last week to begin her training as an officer of the law and a defender of the people.

Now she wondered if they might need someone to stay behind and defend the ship. Peart dispelled that fledgling notion with one snapped order: "Everybody—transport positions."

The away team, as Tenila had been trained to call it, moved to the aft of the runabout. They grouped together beneath its recently installed ten-person transporter device. Despite having already survived the "beaming" process a handful of times as part of her training, she was still not comfortable being atomically disassembled, transmitted as energy, and reassembled. Taking a deep breath, she resolved to not dwell on it.

Glancing out the starboard aft window, she saw the smoking ruins of Kuruk-Tau rising from the river plains like a blackened smile of broken teeth. Architecture from twelve distinct eras of Tezwan history all lay in ruins, epic-scale memorials for one of her world's greatest cities. Once a center of commerce and the arts, it vomited black smoke like a volcano, blotting out the daylight. Its millennia of history had been turned into a fine, carbonized dust that lingered like a shadow over the land.

Piercing a dark wall of ashy smoke, the *Cumberland* banked again into a swift dive toward a cluster of Tezwan refugees. Several twisting, irregular columns of people had intersected at a point not too far outside the city, to form a group at least a hundred thousand strong. From this altitude the swarming masses resembled an army of insects converging around a tiny morsel. *I'm not ready for this,* Tenila confessed to herself.

"Look at this," a bald and blue-skinned Starfleet man said to his dark-haired, pointed-eared compatriot. Jabbing a thumb at the view outside the aft window he added, "The Klingons really outdid themselves."

"The damage is extensive," said the pointed-eared one, who Tenila remembered was called a Vulcan. "The city will likely not be salvageable."

Tenila was unsure which she found more infuriating— the blue one's flippant sarcasm or the Vulcan's dispassionate evaluation of a tragedy unlike anything she had ever witnessed before.

Raising his voice to be heard over the suddenly deafening roar of the *Cumberland*'s engines, the copilot hollered back to the away team, "We've got a lock!"

Peart flashed the man a thumbs-up and said, "Energize!"

Paralysis was the sensation Tenila most strongly associated with molecular transport. Some kind of beam held subjects immobile at the beginning and ending of the cycle. It felt to her like being trapped in an invisible, smothering embrace. Next she became aware of a sudden minuscule gap in her consciousness, which the Starfleet people told her was purely psychosomatic—"a physical impossibility," one of them had assured her— but she still felt it all the same, like a miniblackout. Finally, she returned to herself in a tingle of adrenaline, the world reassembling around her, revealing itself in a wash of light and a soft, high-frequency musical drone.

Settling her feet on the dusty ground, she felt relieved to be back on her homeworld. After two weeks living and training aboard the Federation vessel *Enterprise,* she had almost become accustomed to its higher standard gravity.

Her feeling of relief vanished as she saw the six wounded Federation relief workers sprinting awkwardly away from a massive wall of starving, filthy Tezwan refugees.

Peart's voice cut through the angry clamor of the crowd. "Away team! Firing line!" The away team moved forward and formed a half-circle perimeter around the injured relief workers. Peart lifted his rifle, braced it against his shoulder, and stepped toward the rapidly closing multitude. Hesitantly, Tenila pressed the butt of her own rifle against her left shoulder, then held her ground with the rest of the away team. She thought Peart seemed irrationally bold, given the circumstances. Aiming his weapon's muzzle above the crowd, he fired a warning shot that slowed the stampede. More warning shots issued from the other Starfleet soldiers' rifles.

The blue Starfleet man grabbed one of the relief workers, a young human woman. Her forehead and face were streaked with blood. He spoke sharply to her. "Are you all here?"

"Yes," the woman said, terrified and hyperalert.

The away team's defensive perimeter around the relief workers shrank as the refugees pressed in. Their advance was slower than before and more cautious, but no less relentless.

Rounding up the six relief workers into a tight knot, the blue man motioned four of the Tezwan away-team members to join them. The *Cumberland* roared overhead, stopped cleanly, and pivoted to face the oncoming crowd, which recoiled.

Tapping his combadge, the blue man yelled over the

engine noise, "Leet to *Cumberland!* Lock on to Khota's signal—ten to beam up." Stepping away, he lifted his rifle and rejoined the firing line as Tenila's fellow Tezwans beamed up with the rescued relief workers.

Which left Tenila and the five Starfleet security personnel surrounded by a massive throng of hunger-crazed *elininae,* who were quickly gathering handfuls of large stones.

Glaring ferociously at the wall of raging faces, Peart warned them in a tense voice, "Halt, or we will open fire."

The Tezwan refugees crept forward, a slow wave of menace. Choruses of angry shouts overlapped one another, in several major Tezwan languages. Gradually falling back, the away team stood shoulder-to-shoulder in a tight half-circle, weapons held at shoulder height. Billows of hot yellow dust drifted languidly through the horde, propelled by an ominous, low-howling summer wind.

A transport cycle is five seconds, Tenila reminded herself. *Sixty seconds to reset the system.* She had no idea how many seconds had passed since the relief workers had been beamed up, but apparently she wasn't the only one growing anxious. Beside her, the blue man muttered to himself, "What's taking so long?"

From somewhere in the midst of the glowering mob, a single stone catapulted forward and ricocheted off Peart's left shoulder. Like a breaking dam, the sky suddenly filled with airborne rocks. Tenila was certain she'd frozen with fear—until her vision flared white on the other side of a gap in time. She sagged to one knee in the runabout's higher artificial gravity. Already the small vessel was accelerating away.

Peart clapped Tenila's shoulder. "Nice work, but I don't think you're ready to be knighted just yet."

Sometimes he made no sense. "I don't understand," she said.

"Sorry, it's a cultural thing. Knighting . . . kneeling." He looked frustrated. "Never mind." He turned toward the relief workers. The woman with the bloody forehead was being patched up by Khota. The young Tezwan had proved to be a quick study in the Starfleet first-aid course. Peart said, "Are your people okay?"

"I guess," the woman said. "We tried to keep things organized, but then a group of them demanded our portable replicator. I told them we . . ." She trailed off and shook her head. "There was no reasoning with them."

"I just don't get it," said another relief worker, a young man whose face was purpled with fat bruises. A clump of his light-colored hair had been torn out, and his nose was broken. "We're trying to help these people. What's wrong with them? Are they crazy or something?"

"Maybe they are," Tenila said angrily, her nape feathers rising. "They just lost their homes, their families have been killed, and they're starving to death. Wouldn't you be crazy?" She was surprised to hear herself defending the actions of the *elininae*. She knew that Tezwan ethnic differences would likely seem petty to outsiders, but to her, as a *trinae*, speaking out for her tribe's most bitter rivals felt downright surreal.

The battered young man hung his head sheepishly. No one said anything. She thought maybe she had been too harsh—after all, he had just suffered a violent attack and only narrowly escaped being killed. The Federation people she had met really did mean well—they believed in their mission, in laws, and in justice, and in helping people for no other reason than because it was right. That's why she took a chance and believed in *them*.

But her own world's imploded government had taught her that the individuals of a society and the power they served were not the same thing. No matter how hard she tried to believe that Starfleet's presence on Tezwa was lawful, peaceful, and benign, there was a part of her that could never forget that the Federation and its awesome technology had come to her world as conquerors.

Chapter 2
Deneva

NELINO QUAFINA WAS TRYING to be pleasant and focus on the conversation, but he was somewhat distracted by the pistol pressed against the back of his head. "If I might pose a quick question," he said. "Is this quite necessary?"

"It gives me a feeling of security," said Ihazs, a soft-spoken but palpably dangerous Takaran who served as the Orion Syndicate's top boss on Deneva.

After making Quafina wait three days for a meeting, Ihazs and his "entourage" had finally arrived at the door to the Antedean's hotel suite. Seconds later, Ihazs's twin Balduk enforcers had pinned Quafina facedown on the floor.

One of the Balduks kneeled on the gangly official's back, while the other kept the barrel of his weapon snugly against Quafina's skull, just beneath his rearmost cranial fin.

Reclining comfortably on the front room's plush sofa, Ihazs folded his hands across his trim abdomen and said, "Now . . . where were we?"

"I was asking you for an off-the-books shipping con-tract."

"So close. Try again."

It was hard for Quafina to be certain he heard the Bal-duks correctly over their heavy mouth-breathing, but it sounded like they were snorting with painfully sup-pressed laughter.

Intuiting from the context of his predicament what he was expected to say, he offered, "I was asking if I might be allowed to absurdly overpay you for an off-the-books shipping contract."

"Much better," Ihazs said. "No."

That was not the answer Quafina had expected.

"Why not?"

"I have a substantial list of grievances," Ihazs said. "Do you want to hear them all?"

"Could you summarize them? I am on a tight schedule."

Annoyed silence was Ihazs's response for a moment; then he stretched his arms behind his head and crossed his ankles. "All right, then, the short version. We went out of our way to do you a favor, and we don't feel you've reciprocated in kind."

"That was seven years ago," Quafina said, his words garbled by his face being pushed into the carpet. "And five years ago the syndicate helped Dominion agents try to assassinate the Klingon ambassador to Farius Prime. I would say we are even."

Ihazs rolled his eyes. "You shouldn't take things like that so personally. It was just business. And besides, he lived."

"I see. I accuse you of duplicity, and your defense is incompetence. How inspiring."

Ihazs sat up and sharpened his tone. "Let me spell it out for you, Mr. Secretary. We don't want our ships getting hassled anymore in the core sectors."

"That can be arranged," said the Antedean, who only just now noticed that the hotel-room carpet smelled like detergent.

"Tell the trade commission to stop pressing the Ferengi government to release our banking records."

"Of course," Quafina said. "I am sure the Federation Charter guarantees your right to launder money."

"And we want some breathing room on Bajor."

"Only fair," Quafina said. "After all, we promised Bajor a major increase in crime when they signed up."

. Quafina knew he'd have to redeem a great many favors to comply with Ihazs's terms without sparking a major political controversy. But the stakes were high enough that he knew President Zife and his chief of staff, Koll Azernal, would back whatever deal he had to make to get this job done.

"All right," Ihazs said. He motioned to his Balduk strongmen. "Gol, Tuung." The knee that had been putting a near-permanent kink in Quafina's spine lifted, and he felt the tip of the pistol pull away from his silvery-gray scales before he heard the weapon slide back into its holster.

Slowly, Quafina pushed himself up to his knees; then he stood up and tried to pretend he still had a shred of dignity.

"Let's talk money," Ihazs said, making some random gesticulations with his hands. Quafina had known since the day he'd first met the man seven years ago that he was that kind of talker, always afraid his words wouldn't reach his audience unless he fanned them along and poked them forward.

"Half up front, half when all cargo is safely delivered."

Ihazs brushed Quafina's words aside. "Half of *how much?*"

"Ten thousand bricks of gold-pressed latinum now. Another ten thousand after I confirm all my cargo is safely delivered."

The wide-eyed, stupid expression on the Takaran's face was Quafina's reward for having kissed the floor for the past five minutes. After several seconds, he grew impatient waiting for Ihazs to respond. "Shall I interpret your slack-jawed silence as an indication that my terms are acceptable?"

Ihazs nodded. "Absolutely."

"Good. Have a ship and crew ready to fly within the hour. The cargo is ready to travel."

The moment the Antedean asked Captain Trenigar whether the *Caedera* was fast enough to reach Tezel-Oroko in twelve days, Erovan M'Rill had known a tirade was on its way.

Grabbing the awkwardly tall fish-man by the folds of his shimmering blue robes, Trenigar shouted, "Are you calling my ship slow?" The bellowing Nausicaan's voice rebounded inside the *Caedera's* empty main cargo bay. "This is the fastest ship in the sector! I should rip out your eyes and feed them to you!"

M'Rill knew the captain's claim wasn't true. The *Caedera* was more than fast enough to make the forty-nine-light-year jaunt from Deneva to the Klingon border and have a few days to spare, but there were certainly any number of military vessels that could do it faster. Unlike the pompous icthyoid, however, the young Caitian was smart enough not to say that to his captain, whose temper was atrocious, even for a Nausicaan.

Ihazs, the Orion Syndicate boss, was standing next to the Antedean. With exaggerated courtesy, he said to the captain, "It's bad form to kill the client, Trenigar."

The captain grunted at Ihazs. "Did he pay yet?"

"The deposit, yes," Ihazs said.

"Then what do you care?"

"I humbly retract my inquiry," said the Antedean, who hung limply in the captain's grasp. The enormous Nausicaan let go of him. The client collected himself, then reached under his robes.

Trenigar was the first one to draw his pistol and aim it into the fish-man's face. M'Rill leaped forward and pressed his saw-toothed knife against the Antedean's throat a fraction of a second later. Behind the fish-man, First Officer Olaz R'Lash and Chief Engineer Nolram leveled their disruptor rifles.

Ihazs held up his hands. "Stop! Put your weapons down!"

Nobody moved. M'Rill's fuzzy gray tail twitched nervously. His knife slid under the fish-man's neck scales and drew blood.

"If he dies," Ihazs said, "you all die with him."

A low growl rumbled in Trenigar's throat. Slowly, M'Rill withdrew his blade from the Antedean's throat, then sheathed the weapon. The other *Caedera* personnel lowered their guns.

With exaggerated caution, the gangly icthyoid pulled his hand clear of his robe. He was holding a small padd. Handing it to the captain, he said, "These are the ships I have instructed to rendezvous with your vessel, and the coordinates where they will meet you." Trenigar scanned the information on the tiny screen as the client continued. "Once you transfer the cargo and their payment, transmit to the freighter crews the beam-down coordinates for their final deliveries."

"When do we get the cargo?"

"As soon as you can beam it up," Ihazs said.

The Antedean pointed at the display device in Trenigar's hand. "The release authorization is in there."

"Good," Trenigar said. He turned and handed the padd to R'Lash. "Beam it up and get us moving." Looking at Ihazs and the client, he added, "A pleasure doing business, as always. Now get off my ship. We have work to do."

Twelve Days Later

Chapter 3
U.S.S. Enterprise-E

"It's NORMAL for you to worry," Counselor Marlyn Del Cid said. "It doesn't mean you've given up hope."

"I know," Deanna Troi said softly.

Participating in counseling as a patient was common in psychiatric practice, and Troi knew that to refuse the help of a fellow counselor at a time like this would not be healthy or productive. She also genuinely appreciated Del Cid coming here to the *Enterprise,* rather than requiring her to visit her office aboard the *Amargosa.* Despite all that, she didn't feel much like talking.

"Tell me about yesterday," Del Cid said. She leaned forward attentively in the large chair, her legs primly crossed.

"Fairly ordinary," Troi replied with a casual shrug. "A few regular appointments. Some trauma cases."

"You canceled our appointment yesterday."

Troi smiled disarmingly. "I rescheduled."

"At my insistence, yes." Del Cid looked around Troi and Riker's quarters as though she were searching for something. "You put away several of William's things," she observed.

"I straightened up," Troi said. Anticipating Del Cid's follow-up, she added, "I'm not hiding memory triggers."

Del Cid nodded slowly. "Where did you put his trombone?"

"Back in its case."

"And where's the case?"

Troi sighed. "Under the bed."

"I see." Although Del Cid lacked Troi's half-Betazoid empathic skills, the younger woman certainly had a well-tuned sense of when her patients were masking the truth. "Why, exactly, did you cancel—sorry, *reschedule*—our appointment?"

Troi stood up from the couch and walked toward the replicator. "I'm going to make some hot chocolate. Would you like anything?"

"Some straight answers?"

"It was just a long day," Troi said, stepping in front of the replicator nook. "Computer: Hot cocoa." As her beverage hummed into existence, she cast an inquiring glance back at Del Cid. The long-haired brunette signaled with a wave of her hand that she didn't want anything.

Taking her drink back to the couch, Troi sat down again. Del Cid scrutinized her every step and expression with dark, mysterious eyes. Patience was clearly a virtue the *Amargosa*'s counselor possessed in ample quantity. Troi sipped her cocoa, but its familiar, velvety pleasure offered her no comfort.

"Shortly before our appointment yesterday," Troi said, "I checked to see if there had been any update on the search . . . to see if Data had any new leads. That's when the daily security report came in from Lieutenant Peart." Even though she sensed her composure slipping, she continued. "It included a casualty list. I skimmed through it." She put down her mug and was quiet for a few seconds. Brushing a tear from her cheek, she said, "And for a moment, I thought I saw Will's name."

"Was it?"

"No," she said, sniffling loudly to clear her clogging sinuses. "It was similar. 'Riken, W.' "

"Winona," Del Cid said. "She was a doctor on the *Amargosa.*"

"I know," Troi said. "As soon as I opened the file I saw my mistake." Fresh tears sprung from her eyes. "But I realized that for a moment I'd really believed he was gone. It felt *real.* And then I saw the name, and I wondered . . . was I hoping for it? Just to have an answer?"

"I'm certain you didn't," Del Cid said, and she sounded sincere. "But when we spend too long imagining and preparing for the worst, sometimes we look for it first instead of last."

Letting that bit of wisdom sink in, Troi said nothing for a few moments. Maybe she *had* put away Will's things so as not to see constant reminders of him. But on this ship, among their friends, that wasn't possible. It would be impossible anywhere.

"The worst part," Troi said at last, "is that when I thought I saw his name . . . that was the first time I really accepted the possibility that he might not come home. I feel like I lost hope, even if just for a moment—but I know that if the situation were reversed, he would never give up on me. He would never give up hope." The shame welled in her throat and made her feel ill. "Marlyn, I feel like I failed him."

Del Cid got up and sat down next to her on the couch. "You haven't given up hope, Deanna." Taking Troi's hands in her own, she said, "And you *must* continue to believe he'll come home, unless you get irrefutable proof otherwise." She added with a sad smile, "Counselor's orders."

Christine Vale had watched a few newly promoted first officers settle into their roles. It was not at all uncommon for new XOs to feel slightly overwhelmed by the magnitude of the job, especially on a large starship such as the *Enterprise*. But she had to admit, Lieutenant Commander Data was the first one she'd ever seen who overwhelmed the job itself.

Put simply, the android was a quiet dynamo. Unlike many nonsynthetic beings, he could choose to forgo sleep without suffering any ill effects. As far as she knew, Data had been on duty every minute of every day for four weeks. She had read reports from the second- and third-shift tactical officers that described Data's around-the-clock requests for updates on the search for Commander Riker. Wriede, especially, was growing weary of Data's unannounced battle drills.

Vale had suggested to Data that the frequent drills were exacerbating the already high stress and low morale aboard the *Enterprise*. Without taking any offense at her presumptuous advice, he had justified his decision based on what he perceived to be "the credible, mounting threat of an asymmetrical attack by Tezwan guerrilla forces." And so the battle drills continued, at a rate of roughly two per day.

Alpha shift had just begun. Vale had the center seat while Data conferred privately in the ready room with the captain. Sitting in the captain's chair, she reviewed the reports from Tezwa. Hunger-relief teams needed four times as many portable replicators as were available; traveling medical units were using up medicine and supplies as fast as the four Starfleet vessels in orbit could replicate them; engineering teams continued to make little headway in restoring the planet's ravaged public utilities and power.

Because Captain Picard and, by default, the *Enterprise* had been placed in command of all Starfleet personnel in the Tezel-Oroko system, La Forge was spearheading the civic-engineering program and Dr. Crusher supervised the medical initiative. Vale was in charge of the planet's defenses and law enforcement. The sheer volume of information she had to process each day was staggering. Nearly ten thousand Starfleet personnel, including a regiment of Special Ops personnel, were deployed on Tezwa. More than half of that number were armed security forces. Their duties consisted chiefly of protecting their fellow Starfleet personnel and nearly eighty thousand Federation civilian relief workers, and training thousands of newly recruited Tezwan civilian peace officers. Officially, Starfleet's people were here strictly as advisors and peacekeepers. Unofficially, they were the front line standing between the Tezwans and chaos.

Their reward, naturally, was to be regularly ambushed by so-called Loyalist guerrillas, who were allied with the deposed prime minister, Kinchawn. The guerrillas made no discernible distinction between killing Starfleet security guards, unarmed Starfleet medics and engineers, and uniformed Tezwan civilian police. Apparently, the Loyalists also had no compunctions about inflicting casualties on their own civilian population.

During the past four weeks, schisms in Tezwan society had become apparent to Vale. Ethnically and politically, they were split into two major factions: the *elininae,* whose principal political faction was known as the *Lacaam* Coalition; and the *trinae,* who were, by and large, represented by the *Gatni* Party. Former leader Kinchawn was one of the *elininae;* so were the majority of the Tezwan military commanders, who had followed him into exile. Kinchawn's successor, Prime Minister Bilok, was an elder statesman of the *trinae.* Consequently, attacks on Starfleet personnel and Tezwan police were more frequent in *elininae*-dominated urban centers, but the assaults in *trinae*-majority cities tended to be bolder and more likely to cause large numbers of indiscriminate casualties.

Last night's activity reports left Vale shaking her head in dismay: two security officers and one medic killed in Odina-Keh; eleven Tezwan civilians, nine Federation civilian relief workers, and two Starfleet engineers killed in Arbosa-Lo; six Starfleet security personnel wounded and three Tezwan peace officers killed in Savola-Cov; in Anara-Zel, four Starfleet engineers and two Starfleet medics killed, and nineteen relief workers wounded. Less than an hour ago, the Runabout *Samara* had been shot down outside Alkam-Zar by a plasma warhead, killing twelve personnel from the *Musashi.* It had been Starfleet's bloodiest twenty-four-hour period on Tezwa so far.

Complicating matters further, Starfleet personnel on Tezwa were restricted to using nonlethal force, even when attacked by guerrillas who were shooting to kill. The rules of engagement specified by Federation law for a peacekeeping force were quite strict, and Captain Picard insisted they be followed to the letter. "We're here to protect these people," he had reminded Vale last week, during one of her more frustrated moments. "We have nonlethal means at our disposal, and a responsibility to lead by example. We can't be killers and healers both."

She was about to review the latest report from *Musashi* security chief Chiavelli when Data stepped out of the captain's ready room onto the bridge. He walked directly toward her. Stiffening at his approach, she rose from the captain's chair and braced for the inevitable.

"Good morning, Lieutenant," Data said.

Moving toward her station, she said, "Good morning, sir."

"Have you made any progress in the search for Commander Riker?" *The dreaded question,* Vale brooded.

"Not yet. I'm still reviewing the overnight reports."

"Very well," he said with a curt nod. "Keep me apprised."

"Aye, sir." It made her crazy that Data was always so calm and polite each time she confessed that she had no clues to the whereabouts of their MIA first officer. She reminded herself that she had done—was doing—everything possible. In addition to her ordering regular sensor sweeps of the surface, all new Tezwan peace officers were briefed on what Riker looked like, his last known location, and what to do if they saw him. Hundreds of thousands of Tezwan refugees, while being given food and water, had been asked whether they had seen him. His face was quickly becoming one of the most famous visages on the planet.

Tapping commands into her console, she eaves-dropped while Data, with Zen-like calm and perfect courtesy, made the rounds of the major bridge stations. Listening to him, she couldn't remember why she had once thought he would be unsuited to the position of first officer; it seemed to come naturally to him. *It would be nice to see him get the recognition he deserves,* Vale thought—but then she remembered Riker, and amended her inner monologue: *Just not like this.*

As he spoke with Admiral Janeway via subspace com, Captain Jean-Luc Picard decided that bad news always sounded worse when it was delivered long-distance.

"Time is running out, Jean-Luc," she said. *"I don't know how much longer we can afford to wait."*

One of the things he liked about her was that she didn't mince words. Unfortunately, it was a quality that also made it difficult to persuade her to change her mind, since she had already spoken it so plainly. He kept his voice level and his expression neutral.

"All I'm asking for is a few more days, Admiral."

"I admire your loyalty to him," she said, the image of her face framed within the desktop monitor in his ready room. *"But frankly, I was expecting his answer weeks ago. I can't hold up the entire process for one man."*

"You can if you choose to." He knew he was skating along the edge of insubordination, but he couldn't simply sit by and let the admiralty snatch away what might well be Will Riker's last opportunity to have his own command. Protocol and regulations both had required Janeway to inform Picard when she invited Riker to command the brand-new *U.S.S. Titan.* Although Riker had declined many offers of promotion during his early years aboard the *Enterprise,* enough time had passed that there was a strong possibility his answer might now be different. Picard was determined to make certain Riker got the chance to give his answer, on his own terms.

"Jean-Luc . . . I don't mean to sound callous, but there's a very real possibility that Commander Riker is dead."

"I disagree. The evidence my officers found indicates he was captured. Most likely by the Loyalists."

"Yet you have no ransom request, no list of demands—"

"I suspect he's being held as insurance. An asset to be traded in the event that we acquire something—or someone—that they value enough to negotiate for."

Janeway considered that for a moment. Nodding, she said, *"Perhaps. But you're assuming quite a bit—that they have him, that you can provoke them into offering a trade . . ."* She frowned. *"And that I have the time to wait."*

"With all due respect, Admiral, the *Titan* isn't scheduled to launch for some time yet. I know that Will was your first choice to be her captain. Please . . . give him a few more days."

Conflicting emotions tugged at Janeway's face. She wasn't a by-the-numbers bureaucrat; that was another thing Picard liked about her. He trusted her to consider the human element as she weighed her decision. Her expression looked like one of self-reproach as she made up her mind. *"Seventy-two hours, Jean-Luc. After that, I have to name a new captain for the* Titan."

"I understand, Admiral. . . . Thank you."

"Janeway out." Her image snapped off and was replaced by the blue-and-white double-laurel-and-stars emblem of the United Federation of Planets.

Sighing, he got up and stepped over to the replicator. He ordered his customary cup of hot Earl Grey tea, savored a bitter sip, and returned to his desk.

He had three days to find Will Riker. Arbitrary and short as it was, Janeway's extension—the third she'd granted to Picard in as many weeks—was still generous. Any other admiral would have filled the captain's seat of the *Titan* with another officer by now. Sadly, it didn't make the task of finding Riker any less daunting. A month of searching had so far yielded no sign of him; presumably he was being held in a fortified location, something well shielded from their sensors. Passive scans and patience would simply no longer suffice.

"Picard to Lieutenant Vale."

"Vale here."

"Step into my ready room for a moment."

"Aye, sir. On my way."

Seconds later, the door slid open, momentarily letting in the soft hum and low chirps of the bridge. Vale strode in and stopped in front of Picard's desk. "Have a seat, Lieutenant."

She sat down and folded her hands on her lap. Slender and youthful-looking, with strong cheekbones and piercing eyes, she vaguely reminded Picard of Tasha Yar, who had been his first chief of security aboard the *Enterprise*-D.

It wasn't that she looked like Yar; the two women would never be mistaken for one another. Tasha had been tall, and her blond hair had been close-cropped. Vale was shorter, and her auburn hair was shaped into a pixie cut. What she had in common with Tasha was that she didn't look the least bit imposing—a trait that lulled many opponents into underestimating her.

Cutting to the heart of the matter, he said, "We need to adopt a more aggressive strategy to find Commander Riker."

"I agree. Unfortunately, our options on the planet are . . . rather limited."

He nodded. This wasn't the first time Vale had voiced her frustration with the strict limitations imposed on her security forces. Ambassador Lagan, in an effort to smooth some wrinkles in the working relationship with the new Tezwan prime minister, had restricted Starfleet's authority to use force on the planet to defending its own personnel and Federation relief workers. The job of actively ferreting out the Loyalist guerrillas had been left to the nascent Tezwan police force.

"Indeed," Picard said. "Which is why I think we should provide the Tezwan police with additional training."

She replied dubiously, "Training, sir?"

"Small-unit tactics. Counterinsurgency techniques."

Beginning to catch on, she nodded. "Teach them to be proactive, rather than reactive."

"Precisely." He took a sip of his Earl Grey.

"And the preferred method for this training would be . . . ?"

"By example," Picard said. "We'll demonstrate the

tactics in the field. They'll accompany our people as observers."

Vale raised her eyebrows skeptically. "And who would take custody of high-profile targets?"

"We would. To train the Tezwans in proper interrogation methods."

Smirking ruefully, Vale said, "Ambassador Lagan's not going to like that."

"I'll handle the ambassador," Picard said. "Assemble your teams and get started."

"Aye, sir." She stood and turned toward the door.

"Lieutenant," he said, prompting her to stop and turn back. "It's important that we move quickly, but we mustn't give the Tezwans reason to revoke our authority. Take the initiative, but don't let the law become a casualty of our efforts."

"Understood, sir."

"Carry on."

Turning on her heel, she walked briskly out of the ready room and returned to her post on the bridge. Picard took another sip of his Earl Grey while he contemplated how he would present this fait accompli tactical decision to Ambassador Lagan. She was certain to argue that, by aiding the Tezwan government's manhunt for Kinchawn, Picard was meddling in their internal political affairs. He called up a roster of the nearly six hundred Federation civilians and Starfleet personnel who had been killed by Kinchawn's ex-military accomplices during the past twenty-eight days. This was all the justification his new "training program" would require.

Putting down his tea, he stiffened his posture and

fixed his face into a mask of grim resolve. "Picard to bridge. Get me a secure channel to Ambassador Lagan on Tezwa."

"Stop," Vale commanded. The holographic simulation halted, turning the simulated, rubble-strewn Tezwan street into a tableau of people and events suspended in midaction. Her team of eight Tezwan recruits, standing in the middle of it all, turned to look at her. "What are your choices here?"

One of the Tezwans looked bewildered. He asked, "Choices about what?" The rest of the team seemed equally perplexed by Vale's query. During the first weeks of their training, they had all demonstrated an almost intuitive grasp of the diplomatic nature of community policing. Interacting with witnesses and defusing confrontations with suspects were skills that seemed to come naturally to these eight volunteers, especially to Tenila. Unfortunately, the Tezwans were finding the tactical aspects of their new profession more difficult to master.

"Computer, suspend program." The simulation vanished, revealing the gray surfaces and yellow floor-and-ceiling gridlines of the holodeck. The slender security chief looked at the tallest member of the squad. "Sholo, how many people were on the sidewalk on the opposite side of the street?"

He stared at her, dumbstruck. Vale wondered if her universal translator had malfunctioned. Then, with great hesitation, he answered inquiringly, "Six?"

"Don't guess. *Know.*"

Watching him struggle to verify his memory, Vale

wondered if these eight novices really were the best recruits currently available. Then the orange-plumed woman next to Sholo raised her hand. Vale pointed to her. "Tenila?"

"He was correct," she said. "There were six."

"Very good," Vale said. "How many were men?"

"Three. One adult woman. Two children, both male."

Vale smiled approvingly. "Excellent. Good eyes." Pointing at Sholo, she added, "Work on your observation skills." Scanning the group, she continued, "Who can tell me what else you should have noticed?"

Confused looks passed among the eight recruits. Some shrugged, others shook their heads, and not a single one knew what Vale expected them to say. "Positions," she said, and the eight recruits fanned out into four pairs, ready to continue their patrol. "Computer," Vale said, "resume program."

The street reappeared, dingy and smoky. Scorched and dented civilian transport vehicles were parked along its sides. The six civilian pedestrians ambled past on the opposite sidewalk. All eight Tezwan police trainees looked repeatedly toward the opposite side of the street as they strolled toward another pair of dilapidated vehicles abandoned by the side of the road ahead.

A flash of gray daylight off of metal in a fourth-story window across the street was the only warning before the first shot, which left Sholo immobilized in a red restraining field that indicated he had been "killed." Six of the other seven recruits sprinted forward to take cover behind the two derelict vehicles ahead.

The exception was Tenila, who returned fire as she

sprinted across the street toward the sniper's building. Diving over a parked hovercar, she rolled across the sidewalk into a doorway. She leaned out to pepper the gunman's window with more covering fire as she urged her compatriots to follow her.

Then the two junked vehicles exploded, freezing the simulation and entombing all her fellow trainees in protective red energy cocoons. The acrid smell of crude explosive lingered like a pall of shame over the good-as-dead recruits.

"Computer, end program," Vale said. The Tezwans were released from their crimson shells, shaken but unhurt. They regrouped in the middle of the holodeck with her and Tenila. She almost felt guilty about pressing the trainees this hard until she remembered her own training as a peace officer on Izar, more than a decade earlier. Even on a peaceful Federation world, police were trained to see the street as a dangerous place, as an environment that required the utmost respect and attention.

"What you all should have noticed," Vale said, "was the unconcealed bundle of explosives visible beneath the two vehicles in front of you. Always be aware of your environment; the devil is in the details."

"Excuse me," Sholo said. "The *what* is in the details?"

"Never mind," Vale said. "Just remember to stay alert." She looked at Tenila. "Good instincts on your part. I'm promoting you to squad leader, for now."

"Thank you, Lieutenant," Tenila said.

"Don't thank me. I just made you responsible for their lives." Casting a skeptical eye over the others, she added, "I suspect they'll keep you very busy."

Chapter 4
Earth

"YOU KNOW WHY we're here, Mr. President," said Kellerasana zh'Faila, the Andorian representative to the Federation Council.

President Min Zife glumly regarded the three politicians seated on the other side of his desk. Cort Enaren, the newly elected Betazoid representative, sat to the left of zh'Faila. On the other side of the Andorian female—at least, Zife was fairly certain zh'Faila was female—was the Tellarite representative, Bera chim Gleer.

All three visitors squinted at the golden light of the Paris morning, which streamed in over Zife's right shoulder.

The Bolian chief executive had been expecting and dreading this visit for weeks—ever since he had authorized the massive relief and reconstruction effort on Tezwa. Still, that was no reason to make this meeting any easier for his visitors. With caustic faux sincerity he said, "You've come to pledge your continuing support?"

Zife's sarcasm was rewarded by a subtly annoyed

twitch of zh'Faila's antennae. "Hardly," said the Andorian, infusing the word with her patented quiet vitriol.

Gleer elaborated. "At a time when so many Federation worlds are in such dire need, you've committed us to rebuilding a foe."

"Their need is more urgent," Zife said. "I understand that member worlds need help, but I won't play politics with lives."

Suppressing a sneer, zh'Faila replied, "How noble of you."

Enaren expertly suppressed any overt reaction and kept his accusatory stare leveled coldly at Zife. The great hero of Betazed's resistance against the Dominion didn't look at all the way Zife had imagined him; slim and middle-aged, he seemed no more impressive than any other humanoid. Regardless, Zife found him unnerving; after all, the man was Betazoid—who was to say whether or not he was reading Zife's mind?

"Certainly you three didn't come all the way to my office merely to lodge a complaint," Zife said.

"No," Gleer said. "We've come to issue a warning."

"We've cosponsored a bill that I'll be presenting to the Security Council today," Enaren said. "A binding resolution to withdraw material aid and personnel from Tezwa, and redeploy them to Betazed."

So, Zife mused, *it's a direct challenge.* Arching one eyebrow, the president leaned forward. "With all due respect, Councillor, that would be a most regrettable decision."

"I expect it to pass the Security Council with little resistance," Enaren said. "In addition to the votes of my esteemed colleagues here, I've been assured that

I'll have the support of a significant majority on the council."

"Have your colleagues also explained to you that your bill will be subject to executive review? And that I have the option of exercising a veto?" Zife locked eyes with Enaren, who appeared not at all inclined to moderate his position.

"We can override your veto," the Betazoid man said. "It's time for a change, Mr. President. Your aggressive foreign policy might have seemed bold during the Dominion War, but the war is over. It's time to focus on healing the damage at home."

Gleer and zh'Faila jumped in to echo Enaren's sentiments.

"We need budgets, not battle plans," zh'Faila said.

Gleer added, "Our own people have to come first."

Steepling his fingers, Zife knew that zh'Faila and Gleer were letting Enaren do the talking for the same reason they had placed the junior representative's name on the bill: His motives were more sympathetic than theirs.

"I'm sure *your people* will come first, Councillor Gleer." The president looked at Enaren. "How many amendments and provisions does your bill include for development on Tellar?" While Gleer shifted uncomfortably in his seat, Zife glanced at zh'Faila. Returning his attention to the Betazoid, he asked, "Should I presume it also contains provisions for an infrastructure upgrade on Andor?"

Gleer answered before Enaren could speak. "It's a comprehensive proposal, Mr. President."

"Indeed." Zife narrowed his eyes in contempt at Enaren. "What an auspicious beginning for your career in public office," Zife taunted. "Your first piece of major legislation. Your first act of wanton genocide."

Enaren glowered at the charge. "Excuse me?"

Confident that he had all three councillors' full attention, Zife relaxed and leaned back in his chair. "You've all spent so much time looking at budgets and balance sheets, you don't know how to see anything else. I'm well aware of the damage inflicted on Betazed, Councillor Enaren. Your economy is stagnated. Your metropolitan centers require rebuilding. The planetary transporter network is still offline. . . . Are you as well informed about the situation on Tezwa?"

"I know that they built their military bases too close to their population centers," Enaren said. "And I know that they learned the hard way not to antagonize the Klingons."

Zife shot back, "What's the current status of their agricultural yield?" When Enaren didn't respond immediately, the president looked at the Andorian representative. "Councillor zh'Faila. Certainly you're aware that the climatic damage caused by the Klingon attack has obliterated Tezwa's indigenous farming industry? That millions of its people are without food?" While zh'Faila stammered in search of a reply, Zife aimed his finger-pointing harangue at Gleer. "How about you, Bera? Surely you informed your esteemed colleagues that the rapid spike in global temperatures on Tezwa is threatening to disrupt its oceans' thermal-regulation mechanism, posing the risk of an ice age. Or weren't you *aware* that a planet of nearly five billion intelligent beings is in danger of imminent extinction?"

Chastened into silence, Zife's three visitors exchanged irritated sidelong looks.

"You're free to do as your consciences demand, of course," President Zife said. "But before you present your bill to the Security Council, I suggest you ask yourselves whether bolstering your sagging local economies is worth condemning five billion people to slow, terrible deaths. Because that's a question I *certainly* intend to ask when I challenge your bill—and announce my intention to veto it."

Gleer and Enaren looked to zh'Faila, who gave a small nod and stood up. "Thank you for your time, Mr. President," she said, and extended her hand. He stood and shook her hand, then Enaren's and Gleer's.

Watching the trio turn and leave his office, he felt a great surge of relief. His chief of staff—a cunning and almost prescient Zakdorn political strategist named Koll Azernal—had prepared him well for this confrontation. Not only had Azernal foreseen the challenge from Enaren, he also had predicted correctly that zh'Faila and Gleer would be the Betazoid's chief backers. In retrospect, the Zakdorn's recommendation to classify the bulk of Starfleet's reports from Tezwa had also been fortuitous. By preventing anyone beyond Zife's senior cabinet from seeing the daily briefings, Azernal had all but guaranteed that the Security Council's challenge to the Tezwan relief mission would be easily thwarted.

Turning to look out his broad, curving window at the bright cityscape of Paris, Zife knew it would be easy to blame Azernal for creating the Tezwa crisis. It had been Azernal's Dominion War retreat strategy that led to the illegal installation of Federation-made nadion-pulse cannons on Tezwa. Doing so had been a blatant breach of the Khitomer Accords—the Federation's fragile treaty of alliance with the Klingon Empire. Likewise, it was tempting to chastise Azernal for not predicting that Tezwa's prime minister, a hawkish ideologue named Kinchawn, would use the artillery system to militarize his entire economy—or that he would dare to threaten the Klingon Empire. But Azernal, for all his talents, was only a strategist, not a clairvoyant.

Preventing the Klingons from landing a massive invasion force had seemed impossible; if the Klingons had learned that the rogue planet's artillery had been provided by the Federation, war would have been inevitable. As the entire Alpha Quadrant teetered on the edge of a fiery cataclysm, Azernal had counseled patience—and he had been right.

Captain Picard and the crew of the *Enterprise* had done the impossible; against seemingly insurmountable odds, they had conquered Tezwa and halted the Klingon invasion fleet. Even more impressive, Picard somehow defused the crisis between Tezwa and the Klingon Empire. It seemed that disaster had been averted.

Questions lingered, however. Starfleet was investigating the origin of the now-vaporized artillery system. Kinchawn, hiding underground, was no doubt directing the insurgency against the new government. Tezwa's society was fracturing. Azernal's covert effort to lay the blame for arming Tezwa at the feet of the Tholians (or maybe the Romulans—it was hard for Zife to be sure which government the Zakdorn's plan was ultimately intended to incriminate) was still in progress, and at risk of being disrupted by interference from Kinchawn and his Loyalists.

The potential blowback of this debacle was incalculable. If Bilok was deposed, the openly hostile Kinchawn would likely seek to inform the Klingons of Zife and Azernal's cover-up. The result would be a Klingon-Federation war that would slaughter billions and plunge the galaxy into chaos.

Zife felt burdened with dread as he realized that the next few days would determine the fate of the Federation.

"It's been four weeks. Why isn't my cargo there yet?"

Koll Azernal simmered as he stared at the image of Nelino Quafina, secretary of military intelligence, on his desktop monitor. The Antedean had just returned from Deneva, where he'd been doing who-knew-what for most of the month while the future of the Federation circled the drain on Tezwa.

"The arrangements are complicated," Quafina said. The peculiar design of Antedeans' larynges sucked air inward to produce sound, creating the impression that their words were always being pulled away from the listener.

Azernal felt his forehead growing warm as his temper flared. "No," he replied, *"complicated* is justifying the daily casualties on Tezwa when the Council wants us to rebuild half the Federation. All I want you to do is ship some crates."

"I must have misunderstood. I thought you wanted them moved without a trace through unofficial channels. My mistake."

It took all of the Zakdorn's self-control not to indulge in a profanity-laced diatribe against the sarcastic icthyoid. The Antedean's covert mission was to ship to Tezwa several freight containers. They were loaded with contraband that would falsely incriminate the Tholians for arming Tezwa with its now-destroyed artillery. Unfortunately (in Azernal's opinion), since Starfleet had little aptitude or tolerance for morally ambiguous missions such as this, he and Quafina had no choice but to utilize cutouts to get the job done. Collecting himself, he continued, "I can't keep the lid on this mess forever. When will the cargo be delivered?"

"It left Deneva twelve days ago. The entire shipment should reach Tezwa by end of day tomorrow, Tezwan Capital Time."

The tension in Azernal's shoulders eased; this was the first good news he'd heard in weeks. "Excellent. Now, what about those data files La Forge sent from the *Enterprise?*"

Quafina looked puzzled. He blinked his bulbous eyelids, then remembered, *"The ones his assistant chief stole on Tezwa?"*

"Yes."

"I must have misfiled them. I might never find them again."

Azernal nodded approvingly. Quafina could be annoying, but he was so reliable that it more than made up for the heartburn he inspired. Flashing a crooked half-grin, the paunchy chief of staff said, "Well done. Contact me to confirm when all cargo's been delivered."

"Acknowledged. Quafina out." The screen went black.

Azernal felt only slightly more satisfied with the status of the Tezwa crisis than he had been a few minutes ago. Still, it was a start: The Klingon invasion had been prevented; the planet was nominally under Starfleet control; and all the elements necessary to exonerate the Federation of a potentially fatal political blunder would soon be delivered and put in place. For now, however, the matter was out of his hands.

He spied his worried reflection on the darkened monitor. Against his better judgment, he pondered for a moment how many variables on Tezwa were chaotic enough to disrupt his plan and provoke a worst-case scenario for the Federation.

To his dismay, he realized there were too many to count.

Sighing heavily, he opened his desk drawer and took out a small bottle of Aldebaran whiskey and a short glass. He poured a generous double measure of the emerald-green alcohol, then put away the bottle. The potent spirits' fumes teased his sinuses as he took a sip. Sharp and tart, it left behind a pleasant afterglow of warmth on his tongue.

Feeling his years of intemperance and overwork catching up to him, he slouched with a tired grunt and cast his blank stare upon the city outside his window. *It's going to be a long three days,* he mused, and downed his drink in one cheek-swelling mouthful. Plunking the empty glass back on his desk, he opened the drawer, took out the bottle, and poured another double.

Chapter 5
Tezwa

SURVEYING THE GLITTERING CAPITAL CITY of Keelee-Kee from his balcony atop the *Ilanatava,* Prime Minister Bilok heard the whispers of war borne aloft on the wind. His deposed predecessor Kinchawn remained elusive, lurking underground with his partisans, striking at random against Starfleet personnel and Tezwan citizens alike. Together, Bilok's people and the Federation relief workers were exposed, captive targets.

From his office behind him came the voice of his deputy prime minister, Tawnakel. "Prime Minister?"

Bilok turned and walked back inside. He regarded Tawnakel with a sympathetic expression; in just the past few weeks, the man's golden-brown crest and nape feathers had started to show signs of graying. Not that Bilok was surprised—his own gray plumage had begun blanching to a dull ivory color. Placing a hand on Tawnakel's shoulder, he said, "What can I do for you?"

The pair walked together back toward Bilok's desk.

"We've just heard a rumor that Starfleet is planning to go after Kinchawn, but Ambassador Lagan is protesting Picard's plan," Tawnakel said.

Bilok moved behind his desk and sat down. "What *is* his plan?"

"Starfleet troops will conduct hard-target raids and searches, while our peace-officer recruits follow as observers."

Bilok folded his long, bony fingers together as he considered that. "Letting the Starfleet people take the risk of confronting Kinchawn's forces is appealing," he said. "It will give us time to better establish our civilian police force."

"True," Tawnakel said. "But it will also feed the *elininae*'s perception of Starfleet as an occupying force. And it would ultimately undermine our authority."

"Not necessarily. I presume Ambassador Lagan is objecting to Starfleet's plan because it sidesteps the terms of the aid agreement?"

Tawnakel nodded. "That's my understanding."

"Then we invite them." He reached for the pitcher of water he kept on his desk and poured himself a glass of water as he continued. "We broaden the charter of Starfleet's peacekeeping mission to include preemptive defense."

The deputy prime minister looked alarmed by that idea. "Doing so would mean casting ourselves as subordinate to the Federation," he said. "It would set a very dangerous precedent."

"I agree, it would have to be carefully worded," Bilok said. He took a sip of water, and was disappointed to find the chill had gone out of it, leaving it merely room temperature. "We would have to guarantee our right to revoke it at will."

"By the time you know it needs to be revoked, it might be impossible to do so," Tawnakel cautioned gravely.

Setting down his glass, Bilok said, "Risk is a given in our profession, Tawnakel. But who do you think represents the greater threat to our world right now? The Federation and its Starfleet? Or Kinchawn and his army? The Federation has never ruled by force, only by consent. For more than two centuries its behavior in this respect has been consistent. They could have treated our world like a prize of war, but instead they offered us aid and protection. They've earned our trust."

"I agree they've been generous with their help and resources," Tawnakel said. "But let's not forget that it came at the cost of our sovereignty. Our planetary defense artillery was destroyed, our fleet impounded, our army destroyed—"

Bilok cut in, "Until Kinchawn fired the artillery, you didn't know it existed. The acquisition of the fleet from the Danteri was an economic disaster. As for our military, Kinchawn's incompetence slew the rank and file, and his treachery led the officer corps into desertion. Let us place the blame where it is due." Reaching forward, he activated his holographic communication screen. "Computer, open a channel to Ambassador Lagan Serra."

With a thrum of activating holoprojectors, the full-body image of the female Bajoran diplomat appeared in front of Bilok's desk. *"Mr. Prime Minister,"* she said. Unlike off-world transmissions, some internal communications on Tezwa had the option of full holographic representation. Even as a semitransparent hologram, Lagan possessed a stately dignity. Her voice was steady and rich, but the corners of her gray eyes were creased in a manner that suggested she had witnessed more than her share of tragedies.

"Good morning, Your Excellency," Bilok said. "I have an urgent matter I wish to discuss with you."

"By all means."

"I believe we need to amend the aid agreement."

"In what way?"

"I wish to broaden Starfleet's peacekeeping charter."

Lagan bristled visibly at the statement. *"I think that would be unwise, Mr. Prime Minister."*

"I disagree," Bilok said. "The increase in guerrilla attacks is clearly a threat to your relief workers, and my planet's new civilian police force lacks the training or experience to confront such a threat. Under the circumstances, I think the greater good would be best served by empowering Starfleet to enforce the law without restriction."

"Perhaps," Lagan said. *"But what you're asking Starfleet to do is supplant your police and military. Not only does that present a very real risk of political resentment among your people, it's a violation of the Federation charter and of Starfleet regulations."*

Bilok stifled a derisive *harumph.* "Let me worry about the political fallout on Tezwa, Your Excellency," he said. "As for your legal woes, I think they became irrelevant the moment Starfleet personnel conquered my planet."

"You're welcome to request changes to the aid treaty,

if you wish. However, I am under no obligation to approve them on behalf of the Federation."

"Very well. Expect my amendment proposal within the hour."

Lagan nodded her acknowledgment. *"As you wish, Mr. Prime Minister."* Bilok terminated the transmission, and the hologram of Lagan wavered and fizzled out in an instant of static.

"We're back where we started," Tawnakel said. "Even if you and Picard both want to let his people take a free hand, she seems determined to prevent it."

Bilok switched the holographic transmitter to an encrypted frequency. "Computer, open a priority-one secure channel to Earth, the Palais de la Concorde. The following is a diplomatically protected classified communication for Koll Azernal." While he waited for the transmission to connect, he looked at Tawnakel. "Lagan *will* approve the amendment," Bilok said. "She'll have no choice."

Peart adjusted his holographic binoculars and tilted his upper body to get an unobstructed view through the fractured outer wall of the abandoned building. Several kilometers away he spied the target building, which to all appearances was quiet. Switching the field glasses to thermal frequencies, he easily spotted the two Tezwan sentinels concealed on its roof.

Vale stood next to him and reviewed the plan on a padd, whose display illuminated her angular cheekbones with a crimson glow. Milling around in the dusty, debris-filled space behind them was the command team for the impending strike.

Fillion and McEwan finger-striped their faces with hypoallergenic greaseblack. T'Sona and Parminder were fully prepped and waited together near the stairwell entry; side by side, the two women looked mismatched— a pale, willowy Vulcan and a petite, golden-skinned human. Standing watch on the opposite side of the empty, ex-industrial building was Lieutenant Matthew Chiavelli, the chief of security from the *U.S.S. Musashi.*

Clustered together, apart from all the Starfleet personnel, was a squad of eight Tezwan police trainees who had beamed in with the *Enterprise* security chief.

"I count two on the roof," Peart said, lowering the holobinoculars. Broken glass scratched under his boots as he pivoted to face Vale.

"They're probably using hidden lookouts," she said.

"Yup. They'd want relatively high vantage points, clear sight lines to the building's entry points." He pointed out some buildings on the padd's display. "I'd say these two, and a ground-level watcher here."

Vale nodded. "That's where I'd be." She picked up the holobinoculars and replayed the surveillance scan Peart had just completed. "Do we have any readings from inside?"

"About a dozen targets. They come and go, no particular schedule. Looks like they don't plan to stay."

She put down the binoculars. "Why do you say that?"

"Building has no power, no water, no waste removal. It's a shell, just like this one."

"Okay," Vale said. She switched off the padd. Emergency lamps Starfleet had installed on the streets cast angled shafts of pale-blue light through the cracks and fissures in the walls and floors. "Are we positive these are military targets?"

He handed her the holobinoculars again. "Look at the energy signatures. Those are plasma rifles, fully charged. And the scattering field inside the building is state-of-the-art military hardware."

She shook her head. "Looks risky. What's the payoff?"

"If I'm right," Peart said, "the one in charge is General Gyero Minza."

Vale's head snapped up. "Kinchawn's right-hand man?"

"Forty minutes ago, one of our Shadow teams intercepted a low-band pulse transmission," Peart elaborated. "A decryption expert on the *Amargosa* broke the code twenty minutes ago. Data compared the sensor logs from the *Enterprise,* the *Republic,* and the *Musashi* and tracked the signal's origin to that building."

Vale moved to the wall and peered through the holobinoculars. While she surveyed the target, Fillion spoke up in the darkness.

"Excuse me, sirs?"

Peart glanced over, reminding himself to stay calm even though conversations with Scott Fillion had a tendency to be deeply annoying. "What's on your mind, Fillion?"

"I'm as gung-ho as anyone to go in and snag an enemy VIP," Fillion said, "but if they see us coming we'll be dead before we get a shot off—or else they'll be long gone."

"That's right," Peart said. He pointed to McEwan. "Pop quiz: Tell me why we don't just beam in."

Even secluded in darkness, McEwan looked like she was squirming in a spotlight. She said, "The scattering field would kill us?" Her soft voice sounded lost in the cool wind that whistled through the shattered metal-and-stone walls.

"Right," Peart said. "So what do we do now?"

Fillion answered quickly, "Call in a phaser strike from orbit and stun everything in a five-block radius."

Just like that, Peart understood how and why Fillion had washed out of his Special Ops training. "No, Mr. Fillion. That's like using a photon torpedo to swat a fly."

Fillion shrugged. "As long as we get the fly, so what?"

Peart's patience waned. "Imagine that the fly is sitting on a very fragile, very valuable vase. I just want to hit the fly. Your way turns the vase into gravel."

"What's your point?"

Vale turned and interrupted Peart's failed tutorial. "The point, Fillion, is we're trying not to break the damn vase." She put away the holobinoculars. "I'm thinking of a better idea that doesn't involve stunning thousands of innocent civilians for no good reason. . . . Parminder, can you guess what it is?"

Parminder replied with confidence, "A diversion."

"Yes," Vale said. "A diversion. Thank you." Gesturing to the others in the room, she said, "Everyone, c'mon over." The Tezwan recruits hesitated. "That includes you, too," Vale added. The group huddled together around the security chief, who reactivated the padd and called up the street map showing the target building. "We need to plan on a roof entry. Fighting our way up eight flights of stairs has too much room for error."

"We'd need a different weapon to take out the roof guards," Fillion said. "Something silent, with no visible effect."

"A TR-116 should do the trick," Peart said. "Rig it to fire tranq darts, and add an exogenic targeting sensor with a linked, inertia-neutral microtransporter."

"If we incapacitate the roof sentries," T'Sona said in her archly logical tone, "will that not alert the other lookouts?"

Peart nodded. "Yes, which is why we have to cut off their visibility without harming them. Once the roof sentries check in, we replace them with stand-ins while the strike team goes inside."

"Exactly," Vale said. She pointed at the Tezwan recruits. "We'll have two of you hold their positions on the roof."

"I volunteer, Lieutenant," said Tenila, the Tezwan squad leader, whom Peart now recognized as one of his trainees from a mission on the Runabout *Cumberland* two weeks earlier.

"Excellent," Vale said. "Choose one of your people to go with you. Peart, you'll take the strike team inside. I'll ask La Forge to have his people rig up a harmless smoke bomb. We'll beam it into that abandoned truck on the northeast corner."

"Sir," Fillion said to Peart, "will our sniper be able to see the targets through the smoke cover?"

"It's an exogenic sensor," Peart said. "It can look through walls. Smoke won't be a problem."

Parminder spoke up. "What happens if we encounter resistance inside the building?"

Peart shrugged. "If we do our jobs right, we should be able to capture Minza without any shots being fired."

Chiavelli looked skeptical. "And if there's a mistake? Or an accident?" Reacting to pointed glares from Peart and Vale, the rail-thin, blond-haired man held up his hands defensively and added, "I'm just saying."

"We'll monitor signal traffic," Vale said. "If the op goes sour, reinforcements are standing by on the *Enterprise*. We can secure the block in sixty seconds, but those of you inside'll be in for an ugly firefight."

"In other words," Peart cautioned, "don't make a mistake."

"Damn straight," Vale said with a bemused smirk. "Everybody review the floor plan inside the target. Study the dossier on Minza—be able to recognize him on sight. Peart?"

He issued a snap-fast series of orders. "First rule: No fatalities; the whole point is to take prisoners. Two: No phasers, they make too much noise. I want stealth tactics, quiet weapons. Fillion, McEwan, take point on finding Minza. T'Sona, Parminder, watch their backs. Chiavelli, you'll be with me."

"What'll we be doing?" Chiavelli said.

"The fun part," Peart said with a dangerous gleam.

"Braddock to Vale," the sniper whispered over the tactical channel. *"I'm in position, waiting for your go."*

Lieutenant Scott Fillion tensed in anticipation of the order to attack. Ensign McEwan crouched beside him. All traces of her red hair were expertly hidden beneath her black balaclava. She and the rest of Bravo Team were squatting on the roof, staying low and out of their targets' field of vision. No one on the roof moved or spoke. The pair of Tezwan police officers, attired to match the guerrilla sentries on the rooftop, lingered behind Peart, who was leading the strike.

Several meters away, Lieutenant Austin Braddock lay prone on the rooftop, the barrel of his TR-116 sniper rifle balanced on a collapsible duopod. It looked as if he were simply going to fire the weapon into the crumbling battlements in front of him. But he was using one of Starfleet's best-kept secrets: the gun that could shoot through walls.

Too bad it can't see through scattering fields, Fillion groused to himself. *We could've tranqed the whole lot of them and called it a day.*

"Bravo Leader," Vale said, her voice loud and clear over the strike team's lightweight headsets. *"Good to go?"*

"Affirmative," Peart said. "We're five by five."

"All personnel, stand by," Vale said. *"We're about to beam in the smoker."*

The moments before the detonation were eerily serene. A cool wind wafted across the rooftop. White noise from supply shuttles and small ground transports crested and fell like the crashing of waves on a distant beach. The overcast sky gave Fillion the impression that it was draped above the city of Anara-Zel like a comforting gray blanket. In the chill of the wee hours, he imagined he could almost feel the body heat radiating from the other team members.

He tightened his grip on his TR-120. Part of the same anti-Jem'Hadar arms-research program that had produced the TR-116 for snipers, the magnetic pulse rifle was practically silent and had no muzzle flash or other visible effect. Starfleet had designed it to fire adhesive projectiles that would deliver a nonlethal shock strong enough to incapacitate a Jem'Hadar for up to an hour. It was ideal for stealth-combat situations, and Fillion expected it to be exceptionally effective against the Tezwans.

The blast from the street shook the building beneath Fillion's feet and enveloped the target rooftop in a shroud of impenetrable black smoke.

"Stand by," Vale said over the secure com. *"We're getting a lot of chatter on the Tezwans' frequency."*

Fillion reached up and activated his light-intensifying tachyon goggles. The world around him snapped into sharp relief, cast in a monochromatic frost-blue twilight.

"Roof sentries just checked in," Vale reported. *"Braddock, do you have the shot?"*

"Affirmative," the young sniper said.

"Take it."

Two soft thumps accompanied by short, muffled hisses sounded from Braddock's rifle. *"They're down,"* Braddock said.

"Bravo Team, engaging site-to-site transport," Peart said.

Fillion held his breath without really thinking about it. He'd done it ever since his first time being transported, as if it were like swimming under water. Despite knowing it made no sense, he did it now almost as a reflex. The transporter beam grabbed him and washed the dingy, garbage-strewn rooftop from his sight. Then the target rooftop took shape around him. It was like falling asleep in one place and waking up somewhere else.

Moving swiftly under the cover of smoke, the two Tezwans concealed the stunned sentries, grabbed their weapons, and took their places. Peart led the other five strike-team personnel to the roof access door. Parminder checked the minitricorder attached to the top of her rifle and signaled all-clear. T'Sona tested the door, which was unlocked, and opened it. Parminder kneeled in the doorway, weapon ready, covering the entrance. Peart and Chiavelli moved inside and down the stairs to the first landing. Looking back, Peart waved Fillion and McEwan forward while Chiavelli watched the staircase below.

They descended the stairs in a half-crouched crabwalk, Fillion checking for targets ahead while McEwan defended his back. At the landing they traded positions, and he followed her as she took point and moved deeper into the building. The interior of the abandoned hotel was a darkened shambles. Exposed wires dangled from the ceilings. Broken pipes jutted from the walls and dribbled foul-smelling water that pooled in oily patches across the floor. A small atrium reached up through the center of the building, from its subbasement to a shattered skylight whose broken frame sagged precariously inward.

He glanced over his shoulder. T'Sona was only a few paces behind him. Parminder remained a few paces in back of her, and kept watch on their rear flank. Peart and Chiavelli had moved quickly to the lower floors of the building, to neutralize any wandering guards and disable the scattering field that was blocking the *Enterprise*'s transporters from functioning inside the building.

Inching up to the wobbly railing, Fillion gently lifted his rifle and peered through the holographic scope, sizing up the targets on the far side of this floor, past the atrium. Two sentries stood watch in front of a long hallway that extended away from the atrium, toward a secluded suite of rear-facing rooms and the back stairwell. Two more armed Tezwan soldiers walked together, slowly circling the atrium perimeter. Fillion estimated the pair would reach the four Starfleet personnel in a matter of seconds.

He signaled his team to take cover.

The three women pressed into the shadows along the walls. The enemy guards approached the corner behind Parminder and T'Sona. Fillion switched off his light-intensifying goggles and assessed the lighting conditions. He decided that the glow from the one hanging lamp in the corridor on the other side of the atrium was too bright for his team to hide effectively.

He lifted his rifle, sighted the lamp, and fired.

The lamp exploded in a shower of red-hot sparks that faded as they floated to the floor. The two sentries who were closest to it shouted some surprised profanities, and the two patrolling guards halted as the top floor went almost entirely pitch-dark.

"What happened?" one of them yelled across the atrium.

"Stupid light blew out," answered one of the far sentries.

"I told you it was a piece of *zert*," the first one said.

Fillion reactivated his light-intensifying goggles just in time to see Parminder and T'Sona creep from the shadows. T'Sona neck-pinched one unsuspecting guard and lowered him to the floor. Parminder, ever the pragmatist, simply shot the other Tezwan at point-blank range and caught him as he fell. *Easy to do in this light gravity,* Fillion mused.

T'Sona and Parminder split up and circled the atrium to flank the other two sentries. Fillion and McEwan dropped each foe with a single shock-charge, then moved quickly around the atrium and down the corridor to the back stairwell.

Fillion keyed his headset transceiver and whispered, "Checkpoint."

"Next floor down," Vale replied from her secure position across the street. *"Four more bodies on patrol. Floor below that is clear. Target Alpha is in the suite on your right as you get off the stairs. Two unidentified bodies are inside the suite, just past the door on your left."*

"Acknowledged."

Fillion led his team down the rear stairs and paused before reaching the next landing. He peeked around the corner. At the end of the long hallway stood four more armed Tezwans. With a quick flurry of hand signals, he instructed T'Sona and Parminder to monitor the stairwell while he and McEwan dealt with the guards. All three women signaled ready.

He stood up while McEwan crouched in front of him, back-to-front. He gave her the countdown; together they pivoted out and took aim, him high and her low, and squeezed off two clean shots. As the first two guards twitched and collapsed, the second two lifted their plasma rifles. Before they could fire, Fillion and McEwan shot them both in center-mass.

The stunned Tezwans fell heavily to the floor.

Fillion looked over his shoulder at the others and signaled them to follow him. He led them to their next position, on either side of the suite door.

Keying his transceiver, he said again in a hushed voice, "Checkpoint."

"Movement inside," Vale said. *"Target Alpha is in the*

back room to your left, at the end of the center hallway.
Two other bodies, both armed, in the first room on your
right."

"Copy that."

Fillion could see that the door was barely closed, and
that its locking mechanism was not functioning. Cautiously he pushed the door open a few degrees at a time,
peering through the crack and listening intently for any
sign that he had been detected.

He heard a muffled, barking voice issuing orders from
the back room. Muffled conversation drifted out of the
room on the right. The decrepit, decaying suite was full
of broken furniture with torn upholstery, institutional-
looking portable tables, and a few scattered chemical
lanterns burning low. The air was thick with a pungent
odor of rotting food.

Fillion edged his way inside and checked behind the
door while McEwan slipped in behind him and assumed
a covering position. T'Sona advanced past McEwan toward the room on the right. Its door was cracked open.
Fillion gestured to Parminder to defend the door to the
main hallway.

A string of silent commands placed McEwan and
T'Sona in front of the ajar door while Fillion crept into
the suite's center hallway. He gave the two women the
"go" to attack.

T'Sona nudged the room's door open with her foot.
Seconds later, he heard two soft thumps of bodies hitting
the floor. T'Sona and McEwan regrouped behind him
and he skulked forward toward "Target Alpha."

He paused outside the closed door as he heard General

Minza inside, ending a transmission. "Just get it done," the general snapped, then closed the channel and slammed something down. Fillion heard heavy footsteps plodding toward the door.

Figuring he might not get an opportunity like this again, Fillion slung his weapon at his side, peeled off his balaclava, and stood up directly in front of the door.

It swung open. General Gyero Minza stood mute, his hand still on the door lever, as he stared in shock at the grinning, black-clad Starfleet commando.

Fillion punched Minza square on the jaw with a perfectly balanced right jab, followed with a left uppercut to the body. He finished the towering Tezwan soldier with a right cross to the side of his head. Minza fell unconscious to the floor.

"You could have just stunned him," McEwan said.

Fillion looked at Minza on the floor, then squinted at the naive redhead like she was crazy. "Where's the fun in that?"

"Vale to Fillion, heads-up. Peart and Chiavelli are approaching your position."

"Copy that," Fillion said.

By the time Peart and Chiavelli arrived, less than a minute later, McEwan had finished the DNA scan that verified their prisoner really was General Gyero Minza. "Nice work," Peart said, then keyed his transceiver. "Peart to *Enterprise.*"

"This is Enterprise," Data responded.

"Commander, the scattering field is down. Lock on to all life signs inside this building. Have security standing by to take Tezwan guerrilla fighters into custody. Beam us up when ready."

"Acknowledged, Lieutenant. Stand by for transport."

As the transporter beam enveloped Fillion and the rest of the strike team, he grinned at the thought of the look on his son Jason's face when he got home to Mars and told him he got to beat up a general with his bare hands.

Commander William Riker soaked up the melody and basked in its luminous piano solos. The music surged around him, its thumping chords like the rush of his own pulse. He was surrounded by a club filled with reverently listening jazz aficionados. Seated at the best table in the house, Riker and the elegantly attired Deanna Troi had an unobstructed view of the gifted, mercurially dancing fingers of Chicago master Junior Mance.

The pianist enraptured the audience with his virtuoso performance of his own classic standard, "Blue Mance." Behind him were his bass player and percussionist. Riffing masterfully off his cascading runs across the ivories, the thrumming of the bass and the gently brushed tempo wove a tapestry of rich sound that infused Riker with a feeling of bliss. The sumptuous New York club setting, the comfort of Deanna's hand resting on his leg while she savored the trio's graceful improvisations—it all felt like home. He remembered the words she had used to describe Mance's music when she first heard it: Sophisticated. Elegant. Words that immediately made him think of her, his *Imzadi*.

The trio segued into a slow-tempo, rhapsodic interpretation of Johnny Mandel's "Emily." It conjured sentimental memories for Riker, of the days when he and

Deanna had first met on Betazed. Falling for her had been just like Mance's approach to the ballad—uncomplicated, effortless, and as infectious as a grin.

A steel-edged screech sliced through the music.

Riker opened his eyes as the heavy, metal-framed door scraped open above him. The low mechanical throb of the room washed over him as the beloved memories of music slipped away. A dull pain pounded in his temples. His back and shoulders ached from weeks of lying twisted in this cramped space. His hands were secured behind his back with lengths of stiff, naked metallic wire that cut into his wrists. More of the same wire was twisted cruelly around his bare ankles.

He lifted his face from the wet, moldy slime of the corner. Turning slightly, he looked up through the grating and squinted into the omnipresent, harsh white light. The half-dome fixture that hung from the ceiling contained one painfully bright bulb that Riker's captors left on day and night. For several days now Riker had desperately wanted to smash that light to bits.

Three Tezwans stepped into the small room. The door shut behind them. It locked with a pneumatic hiss and the dull thud of magnetic bolts snapping into place. Congregating on the metal grating above his shallow floor-cell, they towered over him like giants. The soles of their boots almost blocked out his view of the rest of them. Their silhouettes blotted out the unforgiving glare of the overhead light.

The one who appeared to be in charge said something that Riker couldn't understand. The man repeated it, angrier, until one of the others who had followed him in interrupted and handed something to him. The leader accepted it, then pointed to the wall. The two subordinates stepped away.

Once again the blinding light stabbed at Riker's vision. He heard the squeaking of a valve being opened, and braced himself.

A jet of cold water raged through the floor grating and stung Riker's skin through his ragged undershirt and torn pants. First the icy spray hurt; then it prickled him with gooseflesh. As the water soaked the short walls and pooled on the filthy bottom of his hole in the floor, it awoke old odors—festering excrement and the charnel perfume of organic decay. It spiraled down the narrow, uncovered drain that he used as a latrine.

As soon as the biting, frigid blast ceased, Riker stretched his lips, cracked and bloody from dehydration, toward the cool drops falling from the metal grating. He inhaled through pursed lips and sucked greedily at the water, which was bitter with chlorine and had a decidedly metallic aftertaste.

Above him, the two subordinate Tezwans laughed while they watched him lick the bars of his own prison cell to quench his terrible thirst. Riker was too badly in need of the water to care any longer about pride, too desperate to survive to care that he was the butt of their abusive jokes.

"Do I have your attention, Commander Riker?"

Sagging back to the bottom of his cell, Riker looked up again. He saw the metallic glint of a Starfleet communicator in the man's hand, and realized that his captor was using its universal translator to bridge their language gap.

Riker said nothing.

"Do you know who I am?" the shadow asked.

Blinking the excess moisture from his eyes, Riker continued to assess his own condition. Slight twists revealed the pain of broken ribs that had set incorrectly for lack of treatment. A short sniff left no doubt that much of the worst odor in his cell came from himself. His legs were covered with bruises and blisters, and a fungal rash had left his feet inflamed and red. His body looked slightly emaciated.

Ducking his head away from the light, he felt the scraggly tendrils of his beard tickle his chest. The hair on his chin and upper lip was flecked with food debris. For the past few days his only meals had been a pasty gruel, which the Tezwans had served on a partitioned tray. With his hands bound behind him, the exhausted Riker had been forced to plunge his face into the sticky rations, devouring them like a wild beast.

"I'm told the poison's effects should be fading by now," the silhouette said. "You are quite fortunate. The bite of the *lokeg* wasp is fatal to Tezwans."

Riker pushed his tongue across his teeth, which were coated with a sticky film. His mouth tasted like sour milk, and his gums were raw and tinged with the salty flavor of blood.

"Look at me, Commander."

It hurt to look toward the light, even when it was eclipsed by the shapes of his enemies. But as his eyes adjusted, Riker began to discern details of the man's face, dim as they were.

"Kinchawn," Riker finally croaked.

"You will address me as Prime Minister."

Riker turned his gaze back down into his own pit of squalor. "The hell I will."

Riker's answer didn't seem to bother Kinchawn. "Very well. It makes no difference, as long as you answer my questions."

"Wasting your time," Riker said. "I won't help you."

"I would not expect you to." Kinchawn squatted above Riker. The Tezwan's long, awkward limbs folded and jutted in a way that reminded Riker of a grasshopper. "Just tell me what you're worth to Picard."

"What I'm *worth?*"

"His people have been very busy looking for you. And now it seems he's raising the stakes. An hour ago, he captured General Minza, my second-in-command. I want him back."

Despite his desire to hold a poker face, Riker grinned. "It's good to want things," he said.

"Will Picard make a deal? Trade his 'Number One' for mine?"

First, Riker laughed. Then he coughed. He spat a bad taste from his mouth. "Forget it. The captain won't be extorted for one man. Not even me."

"We'll know soon enough," Kinchawn said. "If I were you, I would sincerely hope that Picard is not so high-minded as you make him out to be." Kinchawn sprang from his crouch back to a standing position. He turned toward the door.

"I need medical attention," Riker rasped.

Kinchawn stopped in front of the security door. "That won't be possible. Resources are scarce, and my people have to come first." Riker memorized the short series of commands Kinchawn entered into a small device hooked on to the outside of his coat. Loud clacks signaled the release of the magnetic bolts, and the door shifted ajar with a loud hydraulic gasp.

"Captain Picard won't deal," Riker said again.

"Then you will die here," Kinchawn said. One of his two compatriots opened the door for him, and he walked out of the room. The other two followed him out, and the door clanged shut.

Riker sat hunched inside his narrow floor cavity. Overhead the scorching white light beat down, stealing away the promise of night, of solitude, of freedom from the ever-watchful eyes of his captors. Struggling against his bonds, he knew his cramped cell resembled nothing else so much as a shallow grave.

Squeezing shut his eyes and fighting to twist his hands free of the sharp coils of wire, he made a silent vow to himself and his *Imzadi* not to die on Tezwa.

Chapter 6
U.S.S. Enterprise-E

PICARD HAD BARELY REMOVED his cup of Earl Grey from his ready-room replicator when the door chime sounded. "Come," Picard said. The door opened, and Data walked in. Picard sat down at his desk. He didn't have to look at the chronometer to know that the efficient android had reported at precisely 0805 hours, as he had every morning for the past four weeks.

"Good morning, Captain."

"Good morning, Mr. Data." Picard sipped his tea and savored its smooth, gently bitter flavor and soothing warmth.

Data stopped half a meter from Picard's desk and launched unbidden into his morning briefing for the captain. "Security Chief Vale reported fourteen separate attacks on Federation personnel in the past twenty-four hours. She has ordered an increase in runabout support for ground patrols."

"Good," Picard said. "Next?"

"The largest of last night's attacks destroyed the only

functioning hospital in Anara-Zel. Dr. Crusher has requested clearance to set up a mobile hospital and commandeer resources and personnel from the *Amargosa, Republic,* and *Musashi.*"

Picard nodded. "Granted." He gestured for Data to continue.

"The interrogation of General Minza is scheduled to begin today at 0900 hours. Tezwa's minister of justice has demanded Minza's extradition. I have acknowledged the minister's request, but have not responded otherwise."

Picard furrowed his brow and considered ways he might placate the Tezwan minister. "I'll ask Ambassador Lagan to talk to her," Picard said. "Anything else?"

"Commander La Forge has expressed concerns regarding the scheduling of civic projects on Tezwa. He would like permission to schedule a meeting with Ambassador Lagan."

"Do you consider his concerns justified?"

"Yes, sir," Data said.

"Permission granted," Picard said. "Has there been any progress in the search for Commander Riker?"

"Other than the capture of General Minza, none since yesterday, sir."

Picard sighed heavily. "Make the interrogation of General Minza a top priority. He might be our only hope of finding Commander Riker alive."

"Understood, sir."

"I'll be on the bridge shortly," Picard said. "Until then, you have the conn."

"Yes, sir." Data turned and walked out of the ready room.

Watching him leave, Picard noted with somber pride how gracefully Data had risen to the challenges of serving as the *Enterprise*'s first officer. Picard's experience had always been that new first officers needed time to acclimate to the sheer scope of their responsibilities, as well as to adapt to the personalities of their captains. But the learning curve for Data had been surprisingly short. Long gone was the officer who, for all his advanced behavioral programming, would often fail to edit the minutiae from his verbal reports. Now he was calmly masterful; tirelessly efficient; concise, yet specific. The entire crew knew him and respected him, and his reputation, despite the tarnishing it had suffered following the Rashanar incident, still preceded him like a royal fanfare.

He was a splendid first officer.

But whenever Picard paused to acknowledge that fact, he thought of Will Riker, lost to enemy hands on Tezwa, and felt ashamed that he had even dared to imagine replacing him.

Kell Perim loved to watch Jim Peart get dressed. He sat on the end of the bed as he pulled on his boots. His undershirt was taut against his lean, muscled torso. His shock-cut dark hair was still damp, and it seemed to shine even in the dim light of Perim's quarters. He smiled at her as he reached for his jacket.

"I have to be planetside in a few minutes," he said.

The slim young woman sat up against her stack of pillows. "I know," she said, gathering up the sheets to cover herself. Her tawny hair spilled in front of her face, frazzled from the previous night's exertions. "When are you coming back?"

"Not sure." He stood and circled around to her side of the bed. He sat beside her and sighed. His breath was scented with the *café con leche* he'd gulped down after stepping out of the shower and dashing through his morning routine. He gently stroked away a tangle of her hair to reveal her eyes.

The gesture was so casually intimate that it unnerved her. Were they really falling so quickly in love? Could it even happen this soon? They hadn't said the words; maybe she was only imagining that he felt as strongly for her as she did for him. Joining had never ranked high on her list of priorities—not with symbionts, and not with other people. Not romantically, anyway.

Everything had moved at warp speed with Jim. After months of halfhearted flirtation on her part, he'd finally asked her to dinner a month ago, just before the *Enterprise* had been ordered to Tezwa. He had proved as fearlessly straightforward in romance as he was reputed to be in the line of duty. At the end of their first date, he had escorted her back to her quarters; she'd thanked him for a lovely evening; and he'd pulled her into a kiss that left her dizzy with euphoria.

In the weeks since he returned from the hastily planned commando strike against Tezwa's artillery, he hadn't missed a single chance to see her, even if only for a few minutes or a few hours. It was never long enough, in Perim's opinion.

His fingertips traced the path of her leopardlike beige spots, imparting an electric tingle of excitement as they traveled from her temple to her jaw, then lightly down the side of her neck and across her clavicle to her shoulder. She shivered as his hand followed the melanin speckles over her ribs. He stopped and gently pressed his index finger onto one of the brown dermal markings just above her hip.

"That one," he said with a mischievous grin. "That's my favorite spot."

Flashing a lascivious smirk, she said, "Everyone should have a favorite spot. Some place to go again and again . . . and again . . . and again."

"Oh, I intend to," he said. He kissed her softly. As their lips parted, he playfully nuzzled the tip of her nose with his own. "But not right now. I have to go." He stood up. She hated to see him leave, especially when she knew he was going back to that madhouse of a planet.

"I meant what I said last night," she said.

He stopped and half-turned, a thoughtful look on his face. "I don't think I'm ready for that yet."

"It's not an ultimatum," she said. "I'm just saying it's something to think about."

"Kell, leaving Starfleet is a drastic step," he said. "I've been in for . . . I don't know—sixteen, almost seventeen years. Now I'm in line for the command track on the flagship. It'd be a hell of a time to turn in my pips."

"People do it all the time."

"The ones who have no shot at moving up, maybe." He looked anxiously at the door. "Look, I really have to go."

Sinking into an under-the-covers sulk, she grumped, "Go."

Peart hesitated for a moment, as if he were debating

with himself what he should do or say. Then he turned and walked to the door. It opened and he took his first step through into the warm faux-daylight glow of the corridor outside. He halted, reversed himself, and walked back toward Perim. The door closed behind him as he reached the side of her bed.

"Tell me why," he said. "Give me a reason."

"It's not what you think," she said.

"Now you know what I think? Are you a Trill or a Betazoid?"

Ignoring his sarcasm, she said, "I'm not afraid something bad will happen, and I don't have any crazy utopian fantasies about how wonderful life is in civilian clothes."

"Okay, those aren't it. What is?"

"Love and Starfleet don't mix."

Peart chuckled quietly and shook his head. "An oldie but a goodie," he said.

"You know it's true," she said. "How many couples do you know that got split up when one of them transferred to a great new assignment?"

"Like Riker and Troi? They seem to have worked it out."

"What about the horror stories? Can you name one Starfleet couple that didn't feel sick when they heard what happened to the *da Vinci* at Galvan VI?"

"Sure, and they all wept for the star-crossed lovers of the *Excalibur.* But Calhoun and Shelby are fine."

"You're missing my point," she said.

"No, I'm countering it. Look, for every example of a romance that ended in tragedy because of Starfleet, I'm sure there's another that worked out fine. But since gossip only follows drama, we never hear about the happy couples."

"No news is good news, in other words."

"Exactly," he said.

"Sometimes, no news is just no news."

He leaned forward and kissed her on the forehead. It was a dismissive gesture that reminded her of her father.

"Now I really have to leave," he said. "We'll talk about this when I get back." He turned and strode out of her quarters. With a brief glance back, he left. The door closed after him.

Lying alone on her bed, Perim pounded her fist on the mattress. She hadn't meant to push him; she knew how much his Starfleet career meant to him. Until a few weeks ago, she had lived for her work. Absent the touch of a lover or the bond of a Trill symbiont, the closest she had come to experiencing a personal communion was when she sat at the helm of a starship.

But it was a poor substitute for feeling wanted . . . feeling needed . . . feeling *loved*.

What if he was right? What if their time together on the *Enterprise* wasn't so fragile as she feared? Riker and Troi had been shipmates for more than fourteen years, on two successive Starships *Enterprise*. The flagship had a reputation for long-term officer retention; maybe it wasn't unreasonable to think she and Peart would still be serving together aboard this ship ten years from now.

Then she reminded herself that dozens of their *Enterprise* shipmates had been killed on Tezwa in the past four weeks. At the rate casualties were mounting on Tezwa, Starfleet would be forced to send reinforcements in a matter of weeks or else abandon the relief effort entirely.

And Jim had just beamed down there, to a world in

the process of rapidly unraveling into blood-soaked mayhem, because those were his orders. Because it was the duty that came with the uniform they both wore.

That was when she realized she had lied to him.

She *was* afraid that something terrible would happen to him down there. On Tezwa, it would be inevitable.

General Gyero Minza awoke in a small chamber that was as sterile as an operating theater and as cold as the fire of a diamond. He felt ponderously heavy as he lay on the bunk, which consisted of a single undressed mattress composed of an elastic synthetic fabric. The room was bathed in flat white light.

He listened for a moment, trying to determine whether he was alone. All he could hear was the low buzz of a forcefield. Rolling over slowly, he scanned his clean but drab surroundings. They were a far cry from the gritty squalor in which he had been dwelling since following Prime Minister Kinchawn into exile.

Finishing his rolling turn away from the wall, he saw an athletically toned human woman standing on the other side of the invisible energy barrier. She wore a black-and-gray Starfleet uniform; its only splash of color was a golden-yellow shirt collar. She wore two filled-in circular rank insignia, which he recognized as the markings of a midlevel officer. He sat up and faced her.

She nodded to him. "Good morning, General."

He glared bitterly in reply.

"My name is Lieutenant Christine Vale," she continued. "I direct all Starfleet security operations on Tezwa. You're currently in Federation custody aboard the Starship *Enterprise*. Would you like something to eat before we begin?"

Ravenous as he was, he refused to give her the satisfaction of controlling his sustenance. It was a cheap psychological manipulation, used to earn a prisoner's trust. He didn't plan to fall prey to it. He remained silent.

"Suit yourself," she said. "Let's start with the number-one question: Where is Kinchawn?"

Ignoring her, he tried to get a sense of the room beyond his own cell. The other cells all were dark, and the ceiling lights outside his cell had all been deactivated except for the one directly above Vale. The unflattering overhead illumination gave her angular facial features a sinister overtone.

"Maybe you want to start with something easier," she said. "What targets are your guerrillas planning to attack next?"

Minza wondered whether the forcefield to his cell was linked to the ship's internal power grid, or if the *Enterprise* brig had been designed with an independent energy supply.

"How many troops are currently under your command?" Vale asked her questions calmly, quietly, as if she were in no hurry.

While denying Vale the courtesy of eye contact, his own vision adjusted to the dimness beyond his own floodlit cell. Standing in the shadows several meters behind Vale was another figure—a short, slightly built humanoid. Minza strained to pierce the darkness and discern more details, but the glare of the overhead light proved too strong to overcome.

Vale continued talking at him for several more minutes, during which time he found himself growing increasingly curious about the person lurking beyond the edge of the light. Staring at the hazy outline became more unnerving as the one-sided inquisition dragged on.

Minza stretched out on his bunk and rolled away from Vale, once again facing himself toward the blank comfort of the wall.

"You can pretend to sleep, if you want," she taunted. "But I wouldn't count on getting any rest in here."

He nestled his head into the thinning gray feathers of his forearm. *I've slept through worse,* he mused smugly. As far as he was concerned, she could talk all she wanted. He was going back to bed. After a month of guerrilla missions, he needed the rest.

But as he lay there, sleep eluded him. The Starfleet woman ordered the ship's computer to recite a list of attacks made against Federation personnel or *trinae*-dominated civilian population centers. One by one the synthetic feminine voice described each horrific slaughter, identifying each of the dead by name. Each attack took the computer nearly a minute to relate, depending on the number of victims whose names were read. After only the first few citations, the names began to blend together; the details of each attack—whether it was a bombing, or a sniper shooting, or an act of sabotage—fused into a single, muddled narrative. If Vale's goal was to stir up a wellspring of guilt within his conscience, he pitied her. He didn't intend to be shamed for obeying orders.

Nonetheless, no matter how long he kept his eyes closed, no matter how many times he tried to recast the computer voice as background noise, sleep would not come. He wondered whether they had drugged him, or if perhaps they possessed some subtler technological means of depriving him of his easiest defense.

The recitation seemed to drag on forever.

Peeking over his shoulder, he saw Vale still standing just beyond the glowing frame that demarcated the boundary of the cell's forcefield. Behind her, the silent figure continued to hover in the deliberately crafted darkness.

Vale smirked at him. She'd waited more than an hour for him to so much as look at her. Clearly, she was as patient as she was methodical. And if the continuing monotony of the computer's monologue was any indicator, the young woman was also capable of shocking ruthlessness. All of which Minza was prepared to face in stride; a worthy opponent in the open was a challenge not to be squandered.

But the one he couldn't see . . . that one concerned him.

Turning away from Vale once again, he draped one arm over his head in a vain effort to block the light and the droning computer, which continued to voice its litany of bloodshed.

He'd lost all track of time by the time the voice stopped.

When he looked up, he wasn't surprised to see Vale there, standing proud, hands folded behind her back. He'd expected it. He looked her in the eye and waited for her next move.

"If you answer my questions, we can cut you a deal," she said. "Federation custody instead of extradition to Tezwa."

He rolled his eyes in disgust. Such a naked appeal seemed beneath her. He'd hoped for something more oblique. He wanted her to at least make an effort to keep the game interesting. It was all so mundane and disappointing.

"The longer you wait," she said, "the harder this'll get. My way is the easy way. I suggest you take it while you can."

He retreated back beneath his arm. At Vale's order, the computer restarted its recitation from the beginning. It sounded louder to him this time. He shot an irritated glance back over his shoulder, only to discover that Vale was no longer there. But the person in the shadows remained just beyond his vision.

The names of the dead echoed around him, denying him the refuge of slumber as the hours cruelly seemed to grow longer.

Chapter 7
Merchantman Caedera

"M'Rill!" ROARED TRENIGAR'S VOICE over the intercom. *"Get your ass out of bed! I need you on the bridge!"*

The Caitian pilot groaned and rolled out of his bunk. "Aye, Captain," he said wearily. "On my way." The channel chirped closed. M'Rill pulled on his trousers as he danced from one foot to another on the freezing-cold metal deck. His quarters were little more than a closet with a bunk, and he kept everything neatly in its place. That made it easier to get dressed in the dark. He stepped gingerly into his boots, which automatically cinched tight around his feet. Pulling on a loose gray overshirt, he stepped toward the door. It slid open.

He shimmied into the dim corridor, past stacks of sealed provisions and bundled canisters of Saurian brandy, Terran sour-mash bourbon, and real Klingon *warnog*. Living aboard an Orion merchantman one learned quickly to walk sideways. Replicators used too much power for small ships like the *Caedera*—not that the Federation was all that keen on sharing its precious technology—and the main cargo bays were for paying customers. Put those together and the result was corridors full of food.

M'Rill checked the ship's chronometer as he passed a com panel. It was just after 0200, ship's time. Apparently, the rendezvous was ahead of schedule. He reached the forward ladder and grasped a rung with his right hand. Pulling himself forward with practiced ease, he slipped into the null-gravity zone inside the ladder well. His sensitive nose detected the stench of something inedible wafting up from the mess deck. With a gentle push, he glided upward toward the command deck.

At the command deck, he nudged himself out of the ladder well. He let the artificial gravity take hold of him and then stepped smoothly to the door to the bridge, which opened.

A rush of moist heat ruffled the fur of his mane. His whiskers twitched in irritation. He knew that Nausicaans liked it warm, but the captain really took the preference to extremes. He kept the bridge so hot and humid that it felt like a Legaran sauna. Because Trenigar had made a point of disintegrating the last crewman who dared to suggest the heat be reduced a bit, no one was keen to raise the issue again any time soon.

M'Rill walked onto the bridge, which was about as cramped as every other noncargo compartment on this ship. The dark, sweltering little room had barely enough room for Trenigar's chair, a helm console in front of it, and several overlapping banks of small display screens and command interfaces on the walls and ceiling.

Olaz R'Lash, the Barzan first officer, was at the helm.

She swiveled her chair toward the door and looked at M'Rill. "Good, you're here," she said. She stood up. "Sit down." M'Rill walked carefully to the helm, edging slowly past Trenigar's chair. R'Lash stepped aside to let M'Rill pass. She hovered over him as he checked the helm display and assessed their situation.

"Tell the *Cyprus* to drop out of warp," Trenigar said to R'Lash. "Helm, bring us up on her port side. Transporter range and no closer."

"Aye, sir," M'Rill said. He confirmed the position of the Federation freighter and matched its heading and speed. He ducked as R'Lash reached past him to transmit the order to the *Cyprus*. Her long, beaded dreadlocks dragged across his shoulder. Heavy drops of sweat fell from her armpit into his lap. Finishing his maneuver, he said, "We're in position, sir."

"*Cyprus* acknowledges," R'Lash said. "Dropping out of warp in five seconds. Four . . . three . . ."

M'Rill listened to the first officer's countdown, and on her mark he disengaged the warp drive. The *Caedera* dropped back to quarter impulse. "We're out of warp and holding position thirty thousand kilometers from the *Cyprus*," he said.

"Beam over the cargo," Trenigar said.

R'Lash keyed the intership com. "Engineering, bridge. Begin cargo transfer to the *Cyprus*."

Tzazil, the Kaferian engineer's mate, replied, "*Starting transport. Containers one through four dematerializing.*"

Seconds later, an indicator light flashed on one of the ceiling panels. R'Lash jabbed it out with her index finger. "Transfer complete," she said. "The *Cyprus* is hailing us."

"On screen," Trenigar ordered.

R'Lash flipped some switches. The main viewer crackled and switched over to the image of an olive-skinned human man sitting on a nondescript bridge. *"This is Captain Hatrash of the* Cyprus. *Cargo received."*

"You and one member of your crew may come aboard the *Caedera* to collect your fee," Trenigar said. "Make it quick, I have a busy day."

Hatrash looked reluctant to contradict the Nausicaan, but he did anyway. *"I assumed you would bring the payment here."*

"You assumed wrong," Trenigar said. "Be here in five minutes or you're making this delivery for free. *Caedera* out." The captain nodded to R'Lash, who cut the channel.

Trenigar got up from his chair and stomped toward the door. "I have to go pay that *undari*," he groused. "Try and get some heat in here before I get back."

Trenigar hated dealing with humans. Everything frightened them.

Salah Hatrash, the captain of the *Cyprus,* was no exception. He stank of fear the moment he'd stepped off his shuttle into the airlock connecting it to the *Caedera.* Trenigar would swear that the man—and with regard to humans, he used that term only in its broadest possible sense—actually seemed to shrink.

Hatrash's escort, a broad-shouldered Bolian, was probably an imposing specimen among his own kind. But he looked sickly when flanked by the *Caedera's* two guards: Gorul, a black-haired Chalnoth warrior; and

Zhod, a Gorn archosaur who hadn't spoken more than three times in the past year.

"Have your lackey count your money," Trenigar barked. He thrust a disposable data padd at the human. "Deliver the shipment here."

Hatrash reviewed the coordinates while the Bolian scanned the crate of gold-pressed latinum bars. The blue-skinned man looked up at his cowed captain. "It's all here."

"Take it and get out," Trenigar said.

The Bolian sealed the crate of money. Planting his feet on either side of it, he gripped the handles and struggled to lift it. He let out an agonized grunt as the crate lifted slightly. Then the squat box slammed back to the metal deck grating, and the Bolian let out an exasperated gasp.

Trenigar and Gorul laughed uproariously. "Little blue man can't handle his money," Gorul shouted.

The Bolian hid his shamed expression behind a scowl as Hatrash helped him lift the crate of precious metal currency. Working together, they shuffled back through the airlock with their payment, and retreated into their shuttle. Trenigar slammed the side of his gloved fist against the airlock control, closing the inner door and depressurizing the airlock.

"If you can't carry your money, you don't deserve to have it," he declared to his two burly retainers. He thumbed the wall-console com switch. "Trenigar to bridge. Set course for the next rendezvous, maximum warp."

It was Nolram's day in charge of the mess deck, and a collective groan resounded throughout the cluttered spaces of the *Caedera*.

Saff, the Zaldan medic, stood in front of the stewpot. She held her octagonal metal plate in one webbed hand, and the ladle in the other. Peering over the edge of the pot at the bubbling concoction within, she grumbled, "Let me guess. Zibalian chili."

"You want variety, get us a replicator," Nolram said, in between spoonfuls of his lunch. Saff could understand wanting to prepare one's favorite native dishes, but the chief engineer had only one favorite dish, and he would gladly consume it three meals a day, every day. She could even learn to deal with that, except his chili was so murderously spicy that half a bowl would leave her doubled over with intestinal distress for days on end. The only other person aboard who could stomach it was M'Rill.

"Your chili is foul," she said.

"Tastes fine to me," he said, pushing another heaping spoonful into his gray-tattooed, ebony-hued face.

"It deserves to be blasted out an airlock."

"So do you. Eat it or shut up."

She dropped the ladle back into the pot and left her plate on the counter next to it. On her way to the main table, she plucked a canister of fruit juice from one of the dozens of open boxes stacked up in the dining area. She opened it and sat down across from Nolram, who ignored her in favor of focusing on his lunch. Saff drank her juice and said nothing. It felt relaxing to be among people who shared the Zaldans' distaste for social falsehoods, which most species referred to as "courtesy." Some might have called the *Caedera*'s crew unpolished or even rude. To her, they were just honest, hardworking criminals.

Nolram got up, tossed his dirty bowl on the counter,

and moved toward the exit. As he passed by, Saff said, "Want to have sex later?"

"Maybe," he said. "I'll call you if I get bored."

"Whatever," she said, then returned to enjoying her juice.

M'Rill moved quickly between the enormous cargo containers, which were stacked three high in the main cargo bay. Scanning the ID tags on each container, he quickly logged all their serial numbers. The thrumming pulse of the ship's engines masked the soft feedback tones of his scanning device.

His task was simple. See which containers were still here, so he would know which ones were transferred to the *Cyprus*. He had clandestinely recorded all twenty serial numbers the first day the containers had been brought aboard the *Caedera*. A day later he had secretly transmitted the numbers to his superiors. Bundled with that message was a photograph of the fish-man's meeting with Trenigar, and a quick-and-dirty DNA scan of the Antedean's blood, which M'Rill had recovered from his knife.

No doubt the organization was tracking the containers' path to Deneva, and if there was anything to know about the fish-man, his superiors almost certainly knew it. For now, while they worked to determine where the containers had come from, M'Rill's orders were to keep track of where they were going.

He was about to slip the scanner back into a pocket on his trousers when he heard footsteps behind him. He turned to see Tzazil. The slightly built insectoid stopped when he saw M'Rill, and clicked his mandibles. "What are you doing here?"

"Safety check," M'Rill said. "Captain's orders."

"What kind of safety check?"

"He thinks the client might've planted a time-delay bomb in one of the later-delivery items. Told me to do a sweep."

"That's an engineering job," Tzazil said with a buzz.

"Not today," M'Rill said, making a show of continuing his work, moving down the line of stacked containers. He decided to turn the attention back at Tzazil. "What are *you* doing in here?"

"Installing pattern enhancers on the next four containers," he said. "Why would the client pay us all that money just to blow us up?"

"To keep us quiet," M'Rill said. "Wouldn't be the first time someone killed the messenger." He switched off the scanner and cavalierly tucked it in his pocket. "Sweep's done. We're clean." He strode toward the exit. Tzazil reached out and snagged M'Rill's shirt with one viselike appendage.

"Next time, this should be done by engineering."

"Tough talk," M'Rill said. "The day you've got a pair of *jeeloks* big enough to tell the captain how to run his ship, I'll believe it." Looking down at the claw holding his sleeve, he added, "Do you mind?"

Tzazil released him. The feral-looking young Caitian stared hotly at one of the Kaferian's widely set faceted eyes, then turned and walked out of the cargo bay. *If he keeps his mouth shut,* M'Rill thought, *maybe I won't have to kill him.*

Chapter 8
Tezwa

VALE COULD SMELL the smoke even from half a kilometer away. Shuttle wreckage was strewn across several adjacent rooftops on the outskirts of Keelee-Kee. After four weeks of relative quiet in Tezwa's capital city, the Loyalist insurgency had finally come home to roost. Shortly before noon, a portable plasma-warhead launcher had knocked the Starfleet type-10 shuttlecraft *Heyerdahl* from the air and sent it into a fiery spiral that ended in this residential sector of the city.

Starfleet fire-suppression teams rushed to contain the blazes tearing through the buildings. Four officers from the *Republic* had died aboard that shuttlecraft, but they at least had accepted the risk of losing their lives in the line of duty. The same could not be said for the several dozen innocent Tezwan civilians who had perished in the aftermath of the crash.

In the streets below, several uniformed Starfleet security personnel helped three dozen Tezwan peace officers keep a crowd of onlookers safely away from the fire. Standing at the vanguard of that crowd was a tight knot of Federation News Service reporters, all of them hoping to be the one to get an image or a story that would catapult them to the top of the newsfeeds.

Back up on the *Enterprise,* Vale had left the interrogation of General Minza to a fast-talking pair of officers from Starfleet Intelligence. On the other side of town, Peart, her deputy chief of security, was busy establishing a tactical command center inside the Tezwan capital building, which was called the *Ilanatava.* That left Vale with the task of heading up the investigation into the downing of the *Heyerdahl.*

If past incidents were any barometer, she expected not to find any witnesses. As far as physical evidence, she was fairly certain the investigation would yield an exhaustive volume of technical specs that would ultimately add up to what she already knew: Someone shot down the shuttlecraft.

Walking the search grid on the rooftops was an engineering team from the *Musashi.* Clad in bright-orange full-body environmental suits to protect themselves from the heat, they were almost absurdly cheerful-looking amid the scorched debris. The search leader stopped and kneeled down to poke through some smoldering hull fragments from the shuttlecraft.

Vale tapped her combadge. "Vale to Blancaflor."

The search leader glanced up in Vale's direction as he answered. *"Blancaflor here."*

"What've you got, Lieutenant?"

"Looks like the Heyerdahl'*s flight recorder,"* he said.

"Any sign of the crew?"

"Negative. The plasma burst didn't leave much to find."

"Send the recorder up to the *Enterprise* for analysis."

"Will do." The burly Filipino man went back to work exhuming the device from the smoking debris at his feet.

"Vale out."

A warm afternoon breeze mercifully cleared some smoke from the air around her observation point. It also revealed a single FNS reporter crouched between two exhaust towers on the adjacent roof. He appeared to be using his headset video recorder to document the search-and-recovery operation.

With a short whistle and a tilt of her head, Vale summoned *Enterprise* security officers Gracin and Cruzen to her side. She pointed to the reporter, who remained oblivious of the fact he'd been spotted. "Get him out of here," Vale said.

Cruzen glanced at the reporter. Keeping her hand close to her body, she pointed at him. "What about his headset?"

"Confiscate it."

Cruzen and Gracin nodded, then moved swiftly and quietly onto the adjoining rooftop. Stepping lightly, they easily snuck up on the journalist and seized his arms. Gracin plucked the man's headset from his brow while Cruzen tapped her combadge. Seconds later, all three were beamed up to the *Enterprise*.

Under normal circumstances, Vale would not interfere with the work of the press. She knew that their freedom to observe and report to the public helped maintain the integrity of the Federation's actions at home and abroad. But right now, in this place, the last thing she needed was for Kinchawn's guerrilla forces to be encouraged by sensationalistic footage of their successful attacks. Worse, she didn't want them scrutinizing footage of downed shuttlecraft and runabouts for weak spots, or analyzing recordings of standard Starfleet procedures to find tactical vulnerabilities. It put her people at risk while exacerbating an already worsening decline in troop morale.

And, in her most honest moments of introspection, she had to admit to herself that she didn't like seeing daily newsfeeds depicting Starfleet's ongoing failure to stop the Loyalists, find Kinchawn, or protect the Tezwan people. This debacle was unfolding on her watch, and she felt humiliated enough without having to know that her failures were being disseminated across the Federation at two hundred thousand times the speed of light.

Dr. Beverly Crusher had never seen this many patients lined up in one place. She would have sworn the entire city of Anara-Zel had assembled outside the building in which she was setting up her woefully understaffed and undersupplied mobile hospital.

Even twenty meters above street level, the late-morning air was thick with the smell of death and sepsis, the acrid bite of smoke, and the stench of ruptured sewage systems choking the streets with excrement and waste water. Reeling from the assault on her senses, the first thing Crusher did upon beaming in to this empty floor inside a commercial building was ask the Starfleet Corps of Engineers to replace the shattered windows with transparent aluminum sheets. They promised to get around to it "as soon as possible," a euphemism that La Forge sheepishly admitted probably meant "two or three days."

Nurses Alyssa Ogawa and Susan Weinstein were already busy directing triage. In the L-shaped corridor outside the triage room, Medical Technician Brendan McGlynn and a Benzite medical resident named Meldok worked their way down the line of waiting Tezwan patients, singling out the most urgent cases and moving them forward. A chorus of coughs and wheezings mingled with the groans of the sick, the wounded, and the dying. Crusher noted grimly that no matter how many worlds she visited, the sounds of suffering remained the same.

But more disturbing to her than the parade of infected wounds, more troubling than the empty stares of orphaned children and widowed spouses, were the heavily armed Starfleet security personnel and Tezwan police that Vale had insisted be deployed to protect the mobile hospital. It made Crusher feel like she was working inside a fortress. She also distrusted Vale's assertion that the Runabout *Tsavo* had been assigned to the impromptu hospital as an ambulance vehicle. To Crusher, it looked more like a naked show of force masquerading as a humanitarian gesture.

Nine medical personnel, whom Crusher had shanghaied from the *Amargosa* and *Republic*, scrambled to update the mobile hospital's tricorders and biobed software with Tezwan biological baseline data. The five local Tezwan physicians who were still alive and hadn't fled for safer ground did their best to check the Starfleet equipment and verify their calibration.

Crusher wasn't sure whether the city's hospital had been the primary target of attack or had become collateral damage. It made little difference now. Thousands of

Tezwans had been left without emergency care, and with critical personnel and resources already stretched too thin in Tezwa's other metropolitan centers, there simply weren't enough native medical workers available to pick up the slack.

Which meant it was up to Starfleet to get the job done.

From the corridor, she heard a man's voice drawing closer, offering apologies the whole way. "Excuse me, sorry. Pardon me. Sorry, coming through. Oops, sorry. 'Scuse me. Look out. Sorry."

A trim and handsome man in his late thirties rounded the corner into the triage room. Under his arms he carried two large field surgery kits, and clutched in each hand he had a pair of Federation standard-issue medicine packs. Strapped onto his back was a molecular sequencer, which could be called "portable" only if one had a perverse sense of humor and a strong back—which this man obviously did. Sidestepping past Ogawa and Weinstein, he set down the med packs and surgical kits, and shimmied out from under the sequencer. Crusher walked over to greet him.

"Hello," she said, cautiously looking him over.

"Hi," he replied. "The rest of my team's on the way up with more gear. Can I set up over here?"

"The rest of—" She stopped and switched gears. "I'm Dr. Crusher."

"I know," he said with a grin. "We've met." He reached out and shook her hand. His grip was firm and warm. "Dr. Keith Hughes, M.D. I was one of your residents at Starfleet Medical fourteen years ago."

She continued to grasp his hand as she leaned forward and studied his face, searching her memory. Then, *bang,* it came back to her. "Of course! Keith!" She hugged him. "How are you?"

"I'm great," he said, as a group of civilian nurses and technicians filed in behind him. "I just came in on the *Syrinx*. I heard you were setting up shop, so I came right down."

"And you brought friends," Crusher said.

"A little bird told me you could use some extra hands."

"Tell the little bird I said thank you."

Hughes and his team quickly added their equipment to the Starfleet gear Crusher's people had already set up. Watching him direct everyone, Crusher recalled that he had been rather quiet as a resident. Apparently, he'd gotten over that. He seemed comfortable giving orders.

As soon as everything was up and running, the most critical patients were carried in. Doctors, nurses, and technicians swept into action. The singsong oscillations of medical tricorders and bioscanners filled the room. McGlynn ushered a few dozen healthy Tezwans into the serum-collection office, where they would be screened before donating blood, plasma, and marrow.

Cases that involved indigenous viruses and Tezwan-specific maladies were referred to the Tezwan physicians. The Federation doctors restricted themselves, for the most part, to trauma cases. Dr. Shrake from the *Republic* whisked a wounded Tezwan child into surgery, while Dr. Ko from the *Amargosa* suffered the first patient fatality of the day, a middle-aged man who had been hit by shrapnel during the previous evening's guerrilla attack.

After the first hour, Crusher had almost learned to ignore the rifle-toting Starfleet security guards positioned at the corners of the trauma ward.

Then Hughes spoke and called attention to them. "Don't talk much, do they?"

"If we're lucky," Crusher said, as she passed a dermal regenerator slowly over a Tezwan woman's badly scorched lower leg. "Frankly, I'd rather not have weapons in here at all."

"I'll second that," Hughes said. He was busy removing chunks of blast-propelled masonry from a young girl's back. "Part of why I left Starfleet was I got sick of being surrounded by people with guns."

She nodded. "Understandable. I've just about had it with starship life, myself." She adjusted the setting on the dermal regenerator to finish artificially aging the new tissue to match the surrounding epidermis.

He glanced up from his work, just for a moment. "Joining the civilian sector?"

"Not quite." She hesitated, then erred on the side of modesty. "I'm considering a position at Starfleet Medical."

"Which one?"

She felt slightly embarrassed to admit her own good luck while standing in the wake of such misfortune. "The top one," she said, keeping her eyes on her work.

"Not bad," he said. "But if you're looking for a change, don't stop halfway. If you want out, get all the way out."

"Like you did?"

He gave an almost imperceptible shrug. "What can I say? One war was enough for me."

"Yet here you are again."

He put down his laser scalpel and picked up a pair of

miniature forceps. "Well, I couldn't pass up such a perfect opportunity."

"For what?"

"To see you again," he said with a rakish grin.

She looked up at him. He snuck a peek at her, and they locked eyes for a moment. His flirting was shameless. She blushed and patted her patient on the shoulder, and gestured for her to move along to the nurses for a final look-over. Hughes had resumed work, and carefully extracted another piece of jagged stone from the girl's shoulder blade.

"I'm flattered," Crusher said, "but I have to admit, I'm also a little confused. I mean, it's not like we . . . you know . . . we never—"

"I know," he said. "I didn't exactly make my feelings known at the time. But I had the biggest crush on you."

Despite herself, she grinned. "Are you serious?"

"Completely. And when I say this crush was big, I mean it was *huge*. Massive. Any bigger and it would've collapsed into a singularity."

"Sounds serious," Crusher teased as she waved to Ogawa to send over another patient. "Why didn't you say something?"

"How? I was just a resident, and you were the boss. . . . Besides, everyone said you were dating Captain Picard."

Crusher frowned at the mention of the captain's name. She knew that Starfleet protocol had required Dr. Fandau to tell Picard that he had offered Crusher the top post at Starfleet Medical. She had hoped Jean-Luc would ask her not to go; and she felt betrayed when it became clear he wasn't going to.

In the time since she had received Dr. Fandau's offer in writing, she felt as if she and Jean-Luc had been keeping their friendship alive on life-support, barely sustaining it with empty pleasantries and futile gestures. But when she considered their long history of romantic near-misses, she was forced to conclude that her bond with Jean-Luc had been deteriorating by degrees for some time.

During the many years they had served together, there had been times when she almost believed they might be on the verge of breaking new ground. Their first year on the *Enterprise,* they'd nearly tumbled into each other's arms while under the influence of Psi 2000 virus variant.

Several years later, while telepathically bonded on Kes-Prytt, they were finally forced to admit their long-suppressed mutual attraction. That time, however, she had rebuffed his romantic overture. She'd told him it was because she simply wanted to remain friends. But the fact was, she had been deeply concerned by the profound guilt that Picard harbored over the death of her husband, Jack, under his command on the *U.S.S. Stargazer* so many years before. Picard had done nothing wrong, but his obvious discomfort had made a romance feel awkward.

Since then, the emotional chasm between them had only widened. After the death of his brother and nephew on Earth, she'd half-expected him to take her hand and ask her to seize the moment, to make a new kind of life with him before time's fire consumed them as it had René and Robert. That invitation never came. A few years later, when they were rejuvenated on the Ba'ku homeworld, she'd hoped the surge of vitality might also reinvigorate their attraction. Instead, he'd wound up in the arms of Anij, the soft-spoken Ba'ku leader.

And that was fine, of course. Beverly knew she had no claim to Jean-Luc, no exclusive connection. His romantic choices were not her business. They didn't concern her in the slightest. . . .

Ogawa's voice ended her reminiscence. "Doctor?"

Crusher snapped back into the moment. "Sorry. What's the history?" Ogawa read off a string of vital statistics, then handed the padd to Crusher. A Tezwan man whose left arm was barely still attached was carried in on a stretcher and parked in front of her. The major vessels in his arm were already clamped, and a tray of neurosurgical tools on a sterile sheet was placed next to her, within easy reach. Selecting a vascular shunt from the assortment, she set to work repairing the artery in her patient's shoulder.

Hughes watched her work. "Where'd you go just then?"

She took care not to crack the Tezwan's fragile arm bones while she worked. Responding to Hughes, she said, "When?"

"When I mentioned Picard." She could feel him watching her, waiting for a reaction. "Hope I didn't say something wrong."

"No," she said. Then she added, "I never dated Jean-Luc."

"Ah," Hughes said. Weinstein rolled a new gurney in front of him and handed him a padd. He examined the triage report for his new patient, a middle-aged woman whose right leg was so badly mangled and pulverized that it was unsalvageable. Hughes shook his head. "I don't suppose you've developed any prosthetics suitable for Tezwans?"

"Afraid not," Crusher said. "Their bones are too fragile for the composites we use. We're designing some new models, but it'll be at least a few months before we can test one."

"Damn. I hate to send her home without a leg."

"I know," Crusher said. "But you can't fix everything. . . . Some things you have to leave broken and just move on."

Engineer Jodie Goodnough sat down with three of her *Enterprise* shipmates. They had met for lunch in the plaza outside the *Deelatava,* the horseshoe-shaped government administration building in Tezwa's capital city, Keelee-Kee. "At least we got a table in the shade," she said. Glum faces looked back at her.

"There's nothing *but* shade on this rock," Ensign Spitale said, stabbing a fork into her tray of barely edible Starfleet field rations. "I heard Nybakken say that if they don't get the atmospheric processors running soon, there won't be a single indigenous plant left alive on Tezwa."

"We'd have them running if Kinchawn's guerrillas didn't keep blowing them up and shooting down our supply shuttles," Goodnough said. "We lost another one this morning."

"Figures," said Security Officer George Carmona, who sat across from Goodnough. He took a sip of replicated iced tea from a burnished-metal thermos. "This place is bad luck for Starfleet. Always has been."

Next to him, Lieutenant Jan Lofgrin slouched in his chair and massaged his temples. He'd been complaining about his headache all morning long. Flashing an irritated look at Carmona, he said, "What're you babbling about now?"

"When we got here a few weeks ago, I thought the name sounded familiar. I ran it through the history database last night, and I was right."

Lofgrin narrowed his eyes. "Start making sense, or I'm going to shoot you."

"This system's designation is Tezel-Oroko," Carmona explained. "Less than half a light-year from the edge of this system is where the real-life *Kobayashi Maru* was lost."

Goodnough blinked. "Are you serious?"

"Completely," Carmona said.

"Wonderful," Lofgrin said, shaking his head. "Welcome to the home of the original no-win scenario."

Goodnough pushed aside her rations and got up from the table. She walked toward a nearby Tezwan food vendor, whose cart bubbled with steaming foodstuffs that made her sinuses tingle, even from several meters away.

Carmona shouted to her, "Where you going?"

"I want to try the local delicacies," she said.

Carmona and Spitale both laughed. "I wouldn't do that," Lofgrin said.

"You guys need to broaden your minds," the slender brunette said. She stepped in front of the cart and looked over its menu.

"Look at this," Carmona joked. "Jodie's been on Big T one whole day, and already she's going native."

She tossed a good-natured frown back in their direction. "Professor Adara at the Academy always said that to understand a culture, you have to taste its cuisine." She pointed to a skewer of fried vegetables and meats coated in a spice mixture, then handed over a few pieces of local currency she'd been issued.

Spitale raised her eyebrows incredulously. "Eat that, and your mouth'll smell like your feet for a month."

"At least call the *Enterprise* for some antiemetics," Carmona said. "If you think it tastes bad going down, you don't want to know what it's like coming back up."

Goodnough bit into a red-hot chunk of meat. As her vision whited out, she wondered if maybe her compatriots had been right. It was a question to which she would never get an answer.

Geordi La Forge stepped through the door to see Ambassador Lagan standing in front of her office's large, wraparound window, which looked out on the *Deelatava* plaza below. Turning away from the window, she gestured to La Forge. "Please," the Bajoran woman said. "Come in, Commander."

He stepped quickly into the ambassador's office. Her assistant quietly closed the door behind him. Lagan gestured toward a chair in front of her desk. La Forge shifted it slightly aside and sat down.

"Thank you for making time to see me, Your Excellency," he said. She waved her hand as if to dispel the need for courtesy.

"Not at all," she said. Her dark gray eyes looked as hard and cold as untreated duranium. Her thick, chestnut-colored hair was streaked with gray and pulled into a tight knot on the back of her head. She dressed in simple garments. He could easily picture this woman in her past vocation as the leader of a resistance cell on Bajor. "What's on your mind?"

"The work orders you've been giving to my engineering teams," he said.

She folded her fingers together on the desk and leaned forward. "What about them?"

"To put it gently," he said, "they're a disaster."

Her voice rose sharply. "Excuse me?"

"I don't mean any disrespect, Madam Ambassador, but I've noticed a disturbing pattern in the projects that get priority status. Whoever's issuing our work orders is either incompetent, or malicious."

Lagan's brow furrowed into a pinched V above her wrinkled nasal ridges. "Serious allegations, Commander," she said.

He held up a padd. "If I may?"

"By all means."

La Forge opened up a summary of the S.C.E.'s recent work orders and handed the device to Lagan. She looked it over as he continued. "More than half the projects on the roster this week are communications systems," he said. "We've been ordered to dismantle every subspace radio relay on the planet."

"They were probably damaged in the Klingon counterstrike," she said. "Their repair might be a national-security matter."

"No," La Forge said, shaking his head. "I checked. Most of them weren't even scratched. We've been getting orders to rebuild and do core wipes on perfectly intact systems."

"Maybe it was a planned upgrade. Sometimes the old has to be removed to make way for the new," Lagan countered.

"Some of these units are new. At least, they were, until we tore them apart."

Lagan's mouth tightened into a concerned frown. "That doesn't make any sense."

"No, it doesn't," La Forge said. "Especially since critical infrastructure is being neglected for this. Power plants, water supplies, sewage treatment, transit systems—all of them should be prioritized. Instead, they got wait-listed while we were busy wrecking Tezwa's only means of interstellar communication. If I didn't know better, I'd call what we did sabotage."

Glancing up from the padd, she said, "You can prove this?"

"Your orders are the proof, Madam Ambassador. You signed all those directives."

Lagan scrolled through more data on the padd, then rubbed her forehead above her eyebrows. "I should probably read these a bit closer," she said. "But honestly, I sign off on more than two hundred work orders a day. I never realized these were so misprioritized."

La Forge said, "You didn't write these?"

"No," Lagan said, putting down the padd on her desk. "These orders all came directly from Starfleet Operations. I just rubber-stamped them." She shrugged. "Standard operating procedure."

La Forge had hoped his meeting with Lagan would alleviate his concerns. Instead, he was more worried now than when he came in. If Starfleet Operations was issuing these kinds of orders, something must have gone seriously wrong at a fairly high level in the chain of command. In fact, the only entities authorized to make Starfleet Operations issue such orders were the admiralty, the president, or the Federation Security Council.

No matter which one was responsible, pursuing this inquiry any further would be politically ugly and might herald the end of La Forge's career in Starfleet.

So be it, he decided. *I want the truth.*

Speaking carefully, as if risking the wrath of a higher power merely by uttering the words, he asked, "How would I find out who *really* gave these orders?"

She sighed heavily. "You don't." He was about to protest when she held up her hand and added, "I do. They could make your life hell if you push this. Let me kick the asses on this one."

La Forge smiled. "With pleasure, Your Excellency." Figuring his luck had held so far, he broached another touchy subject. "Is there any way I could review the Tezwan relays' com logs?"

"Not without formal permission from their government," she said. She sighed. "I'll talk to Prime Minister Bilok. But I expect his answer will be no."

"Never hurts to ask," La Forge said as he pushed back his chair and stood up. As she rose from her chair, he extended his hand to her. "Thank you, Madam Ambassador."

She shook his hand. "My pleasure, Comman—"

The window that faced the *Deelatava* plaza exploded inward. A hurricane of shattered glass and broken metal slammed into La Forge and Lagan. The shock wave hurled them away from the window. They slammed against the far wall with crushing force as the deafening boom registered in La Forge's shocked ears. Above them, the roof flew away in ragged chunks, revealing a leaden sky flurried with smoke, dust, and scattering debris. Then the floor sagged beneath them and fell away into a yawning darkness.

Flailing around himself, La Forge grabbed hold of Lagan's shirtsleeve. He pulled her to him as they fell. Echoes of the rumbling blast mingled with the roar of the collapsing building. Clutching Lagan in the desperate hope of shielding her with his body, La Forge plummeted inside a maelstrom of disintegrating steel and stone.

His stomach churned with the nausea of free fall. Dust and dirt clogged his mouth and nose. Then he slammed hard into a growing mound of wreckage. As the space around him went dark, his synthetic eyes adjusted automatically to a different wavelength. He just as quickly wished they hadn't.

Watching the oncoming crush of wreckage, he had just enough time to gulp a last, desperate breath before the rest of the building came down on top of him.

Lieutenant Rao called for help. *"Life signs! Over here!"*

Vale scrambled over shifting mounds of dust and shattered concrete. Dr. Tropp ran ahead of her toward Rao. Taurik scanned the area beneath Rao's feet.

Like everyone else working on the rescue operation, Vale was coated from her protective helmet to her insulated boots in charcoal-gray dust. The full-face respirators made everyone's voices sound mechanical.

Tendrils of gray smoke snaked out of the enormous mountain of rubble, which only twenty minutes ago had been the *Deelatava*. The afternoon sky was dark with rising plumes of hot ash.

Hovering overhead were six Starfleet runabouts. Three hundred heavily armed and armored Starfleet security personnel, reinforced by nearly a hundred Tezwan police recruits, formed a defensive perimeter around the blast zone. Inside the perimeter, twenty roving teams of engineers, doctors, and security guards conducted hard-target searches for survivors beneath the smoldering remains of the building.

Monitoring the site from orbit were the *Enterprise,* the *Musashi,* and the *Republic,* all of which had gone to maximum alert the moment the government building was felled.

"Life signs confirmed," Tropp said, after wiping the grime from his medical tricorder. *"Let's get them out, folks."*

"Stand back," Taurik said. He punched some commands into his tricorder, then tapped his combadge. *"Taurik to* Enterprise. *I am sending transporter instructions. Execute on my mark."* Looking around to confirm that everyone had moved back to safe ground, he continued, *"Mark."*

Blocks of violently hewn stone and twisted beams of metal swiftly vanished in bright washes of color and sound. Little by little, the layers of destruction were peeled away. Vale understood the urge to just beam out all the survivors, but she knew this type of rescue had to be done carefully. Beaming out a person from the middle of the mess could destabilize the layers above or beside them, causing shifts that might prove fatal to those still trapped within. For now, they would follow procedure and go one step at a time.

All around Vale, similar efforts were under way. Patches of wreckage rapidly vanished in the flare of transporter beams, and doctors clambered down to extract their patients from the simmering dust. Beyond the perimeter, thousands of Tezwan civilians had gathered. *Any one of them could be working for Kinchawn,* Vale realized. Looking past the smoking footprint of the *Deelatava* to see the sprawl of the capital city, she felt dangerously exposed.

"We are clear to proceed," Taurik said.

Tropp hurtled forward into the carefully crafted cavity, where two Tezwans lay unmoving, coated in dark-gray dust. The Denobulan assistant chief medical officer scanned them both. *"They're stable enough for transport,"* he said. He placed signal pins on both patients, then tapped his combadge. *"Tropp to* Enterprise. *Two patients for direct transport to sickbay. Energize when ready."* Moving away from the unconscious Tezwans, Tropp reached up and took the helping hand Vale offered him. She pulled him up and out of the cavity as the two patients below dematerialized on their way to help and safety.

Amid the shouting and the drone of the hovering runabouts' engines, Vale heard Peart calling her name. She turned until she saw him. He waved her over. Jogging quickly across the ruins, she followed him into another transporter-made excavation. Tangled together at the bottom were La Forge and Lagan.

A female Andorian physician and a Benzite emergency medic from the *Republic* worked on the chief engineer and the ambassador, who were both bloodied, broken, and unconscious. Vale looked nervously at Peart. "Are they gonna make it?"

"I think so," he said. *"Lucky they were on the top floor. We don't expect to find any survivors below the first layer."*

"Do we have an estimated body count yet?"

Peart looked around and wiped the sticky dirt from his respirator mask. *"Best guess? Four hundred. Maybe five."*

Vale didn't like the sound of that. It wasn't like Peart to be imprecise. "Give or take a hundred? Big margin, Jim."

"*We're not sure how many people were in the plaza outside,*" he said. "*Anybody out here got vaporized in the detonation. . . . Witnesses say it was pretty crowded.*"

"Do we know what hit us?"

"*Looks like a hybrid plasma-photon charge. Military-issue.*"

"Small enough to fit in a briefcase," Vale muttered.

"*Excuse us,*" said the Andorian doctor. "*We're ready to go.*"

Vale and Peart helped the doctors climb out of the pit.

She watched as La Forge and Lagan were beamed up. So far, that was the only thing that had gone right today.

In one strike, the Loyalists had wiped out the Federation's central administration on Tezwa. Despite the obvious Tezwan casualties, this strike had been unmistakably directed at Starfleet personnel and Federation civilians.

There was no telling where Kinchawn's guerrilla fighters would strike next, or how. But Vale knew that the best strategy was for Starfleet to stop being a target and to start taking the fight to its enemy on its own terms.

It would be dangerous. Fatalities would be inevitable. But she vowed that next time the casualties would be Kinchawn's.

She looked out across the mountain of dusty, broken concrete and blast-warped steel. "Jim," she said to Peart, who stood beside her. "Get back to the *Enterprise*. Find me a Loyalist target, the bigger the better. Hit it hard."

He looked skeptical. "*How hard?*"

Her jaw tightened with anger. "Hard." She shot him an incandescent stare. "Show these bastards what we're made of."

Chapter 9
An Undisclosed Location

"M'RILL JUST CHECKED IN," Dietz said as his supervisor, L'Haan, entered the signal-analysis center. As always, the slender Vulcan woman's shapely, lean figure was the very paragon of grace and symmetry in her all-black, synthetic-leather uniform.

She joined him in front of the wall of flickering display screens. She never used perfume, yet to Dietz she always seemed to exude a subtle, enticing scent. Watching the changing images, she asked, "Has the *Caedera* commenced its cargo transfers?"

He nodded. "Yes. Two so far. The *Cyprus* and the *Toronto*."

"Where is the *Caedera* now?"

Dietz checked the cross-referenced sensor logs from Xarantine and Ajilon Prime. "En route to intercept the freighter *Venezia* just outside the Tezel-Oroko system. ETA, one hour and eight minutes."

"Have the *Cyprus* or the *Toronto* delivered their cargo yet?"

Dietz called up a traffic display from the Tezel-Oroko system on one of the secondary monitors. "The *Cyprus* just made orbit over Tezwa," he said. "The *Toronto* just signaled the *Enterprise* for approach clearance."

L'Haan shook her head, gently swaying the ends of her Cleopatra-cut raven black hair. "So much effort," she said. "All of it likely futile." Suppressing his unrequited ardor, Dietz forced himself not to gaze for too long in her direction. He knew she would never fraternize with a subordinate, especially not one who was nearly a century younger than her. Her longevity and slower aging process were a constant mental stumbling block for him. He wanted to see her as a contemporary, as a peer, but then had to remind himself that she had been a leader in the organization since before his father was born.

She picked up the padd from the workstation on his right. Reviewing it quickly, she commented, "The situation on Tezwa appears to be worsening."

"Partly because Picard provoked it," Dietz said.

"You are referring to the capture of General Minza," she said. She tended to phrase her questions as declarations.

"Yes," he said. "Picard pushed for a more aggressive strategy, and the Tezwan government supported it. The only person who opposed it was Ambassador Lagan, and she got overruled by Azernal."

"A curious alliance," L'Haan said, her mellifluous voice as coolly neutral as ever. "One wonders whether all the parties are aware of one another's true motives."

"Doubtful," Dietz said.

"Indeed."

Dietz narrowed his eyes as he watched more data scroll across numerous screens. "We're still assuming that Kinchawn will disrupt Quafina's plan to smuggle phony evidence onto the planet, correct?"

L'Haan answered as she surveyed the changing video feeds. "Yes."

"Shouldn't we be preparing a more aggressive response?"

"We have," she said calmly. He was still considering how to diplomatically express his irritation at being left out of the loop on a major strategy initiative when she added, "It is being handled on a need-to-know basis."

There was nothing to be gained from arguing a decision long since made. Dietz put it out of his thoughts and reviewed a summary of ongoing Starfleet deployments being carried out on Tezwa. "Picard's never been an imperialist," he said. "Why is he advocating such an aggressive policy now?"

L'Haan arched one angular eyebrow, then said, "The catalyst appears to have been Admiral Janeway's insistence that she would rescind the captaincy she offered to Commander Riker."

Dietz shook his head. L'Haan's conclusion seemed suspect to him. "That doesn't sound like Picard. He wouldn't risk sparking a major guerrilla war for one man."

"Do not underestimate the chaos of emotions," L'Haan said.

"If you're right," Dietz said, "then Picard's a serious liability. He could destabilize the entire situation."

"I disagree," she said. "Regardless of his motives, he

has spurred Kinchawn's forces into action, possibly prematurely. By taking the initiative, Starfleet might be able to confront its foes directly and restore long-term order on Tezwa."

"If that's the goal, are we going to take steps to help Starfleet achieve it?"

"Possibly," she said. "If Picard and his people capture Kinchawn before he interferes in Quafina and Azernal's clumsy charade to frame the Tholians, we will not need to get involved. But if Kinchawn's guerrillas intercept any of the shipments from the *Caedera* . . . we might need to intervene."

Dietz switched the wall of monitors to a single, segmented image of the toppled *Deelatava*. The telescopic view from the *Musashi* clearly showed the scope of the devastation and the grim toil of the search-and-recovery effort. Glancing from the monitors to L'Haan, he said, "Hopefully before Kinchawn launches another strike like this one."

L'Haan stared dispassionately at the smoking ruins. "Why do you assume *his* forces did this?"

As he pondered the accusation implicit in her remark, he realized that the Starfleet forces on Tezwa might soon face more enemies than they could possibly have imagined.

Chapter 10
U.S.S. Enterprise-E

THE SILENCE WAS BROKEN at the top of the hour, like clockwork.

Federation law was very specific about the rights of a prisoner of war. The detainee was to be provided with properly portioned, nutritionally balanced meals each day. When necessary, the meals would be tailored to accommodate particular medical needs of the prisoner. If Gyero Minza continued to refuse the food offered to him, however, that was his prerogative. By law, he could not be forced to eat.

Deliberate physical harm of any kind was prohibited. Medical care had to be provided. Controlled substances could not be introduced into the food, water, or atmosphere of a detainee, except when prescribed as a matter of medical necessity. It was unlawful to deprive a prisoner of sleep; they had to be allowed their species' normal ratio of sleeping time to waking hours in whatever period of time they considered to be a standard day. For

Tezwans, the approximate ratio was the same as for most humanoids—roughly eight hours of every twenty-four were spent asleep. Consequently, during any standard day aboard the *Enterprise,* Minza was entitled to eight hours of slumber.

Commander Brook North of the Starfleet JAG office, however, had assured Troi that his careful readings of the Federation Civil and Criminal Code and the complete text of Starfleet Official Regulations had found nothing that demanded those eight hours of sleep be granted consecutively.

Troi had listened with calm detachment for two hours as North explained his legal determination, one precedent at a time, to Minza. The general, for his part, had continued to toss and turn on his narrow bunk, always facing himself toward the wall, hiding his mounting frustration. From the side, his feather-maned head looked almost square, like a chopping block. His nose was irregularly shaped. On anyone else, the deformity might have made them look weak by marring their profile, but on Minza it served only to make him look cruder, more aggressive.

An hour ago North had finished his speech and then departed the brig. Since then, Minza had progressed through the early stages of sleep and was on the verge of a REM phase when Commander Rolando Valentin of Starfleet Special Ops walked in, planted himself in front of Minza's cell, and began barking marching cadences of a particularly vulgar nature.

Troi felt Minza's spiking surge of anger and desperation from across the room. Every interruption of his sleep cycle left him that much more shaken, just a tiny degree more vulnerable. Several meals had appeared in his cell's food dispenser slot, only to be automatically reclaimed, untouched, an hour later. She sensed his hunger, his defiant refusal to accept charity from an enemy. Using her padd, she reviewed files describing Tezwan delicacies, and instructed the computer to replicate all the most aromatic ones, at meal after meal.

Listening to Valentin hollering his nonsensical rhythmic chants, she wondered if enlisted recruits really believed the childishly rude limericks' musings on anatomy, patriotism, and the unbridled euphoria of service to Starfleet. She hoped not.

Her padd vibrated silently in her hand. Cupping it to hide its faint glow, she checked the incoming message. Counselor Del Cid from the *Amargosa* was protesting another postponed appointment. Troi deleted the message. She didn't have time to indulge her own fears. Minza was a direct link to Kinchawn, and Captain Picard had ordered her to take every measure within the law to obtain the general's cooperation.

She noticed that Minza was beginning to sweat profusely. Apparently, his room was nearing the peak of its temperature cycle. The law required that his cell be kept within normal comfort parameters; Commander North's interpretation of "comfortable" had equated to "not harmful for short periods." Taking his advice to heart, she had programmed the environmental controls inside the general's cell to vary the temperature, from approximately ten degrees centigrade to thirty degrees centigrade and back again, on a seventy-minute cycle.

And through it all, hour after hour, Troi kept her vigil,

seated here in the shadows. Remaining awake hadn't proved difficult, thanks to a timed-release dermal patch of nonsomnolence medication Dr. Tropp had provided. Rarely used except in dire emergencies, the ages-old hormone-based synthetic compound permitted most humanoids to forgo sleep for up to several days with no deleterious side effects. *I might not be allowed to use drugs to rob Minza of sleep,* Troi gloated, *but there's no law against me using them to stay awake.*

She had been observing Minza since he was brought in more than twenty-four hours ago. The perpetual twilight-level lighting she had insisted upon for the brig was thoroughly disorienting. Twice in the past hour she had been forced to check her padd's chronometer to confirm what time it was. Her prime consolation was that if her sense of time was being thrown off kilter, Minza was certain to be faring far worse.

Minza bolted from his bunk and sprang forward. He struck the forcefield and absorbed its low-level shock, which only fueled his rage. Wide-eyed and ferally disheveled in sweat-soaked tatters, he screamed incoherently at Valentin. Safe on the other side of the forcefield, Valentin continued his taunting cadences without missing a beat. The Tezwan collapsed to the floor and crawled under his bunk, hands over his ears, eyes squeezed shut in furious denial of Valentin's simplistically bellicose, testosterone-inspired oration.

Troi had to concede a grudging admiration for Valentin's success. He had provoked more interaction from Minza in five minutes than anyone else had since he regained consciousness.

Valentin still had one hour and fifty-three minutes in which to continue grinding away at Minza's already frazzled nerves. After that would come a one-hour respite; then it would be Data's turn to command Minza's unwilling attention for two hours. She already planned to follow Data's recital of Gilbert and Sullivan standards with a two-hour excerpt from the prelude to the Klingon opera *Kahless and Molor*. As she watched Minza cower before the former basic-training instructor, she decided to book Valentin for an encore performance at 0100 hours.

Picard sat alone in his quarters. The music of his Ressikan flute was his only company. The instrument's felt-lined, oxidized-copper case lay open on the floor in front of him. His fingers glided across its holes as he breathed out a bittersweet melody imparted to him years before by the Kataan probe.

I played this with Neela, he remembered. So often when he played, memories and connections came unbidden to his thoughts. Today he found himself haunted by questions about what might have been, or by pangs of regret for opportunities squandered.

Mistakes and missteps; slips of the tongue; a moment of misunderstanding—there were so many ways for a life to wander astray. Unjust reversals could exalt the cruel and lay low the righteous, all in the name of a capricious Fate.

Months ago, his command had been torn from him after a tragic moment of mistaken identity had led to the loss of the *Juno* and her crew in the Rashanar Sector. He had been forced into a psychological-evaluation program and almost convinced that he was no longer fit to serve as a starship captain. He had suffered far more heinous abuses at the hands of Gul Madred without breaking. Reflecting now on the past several months, he cursed himself for letting Starfleet shatter his resolve so easily. If not for the courageous intervention of Commander Riker, his career might have ended in ignominy.

But now it was Riker himself who was lost. Years ago, Picard had been misled by a Ferengi named DaiMon Bok into believing he had a son, as a result of a long-ago tryst with the sister of a comrade on the *Stargazer.* When the ruse unraveled, learning that young Jason Vigo was not, in fact, his scion had been a disappointment. But four weeks ago, when Picard thought for a moment that he had lost Riker during the commando strike on Tezwa, he'd finally understood in a single, grim instant what it must be like for a father to lose his only son.

Looking at the sleek, metallic flute in his hands, he realized belatedly that he had stopped playing. His heart was no longer in it. He put the flute back in its case. His fingers lingered briefly on the cold metal; then he closed the case.

He picked up the flute case, stood, and walked over to the shelf to put it away. Tucking it carefully between two short rows of books, he glimpsed the spine of a slender volume of sheet music that Beverly Crusher had given to him as a gift two birthdays ago. He pulled it down from the shelf. It fell open in his hands. Thinking back, he couldn't recall ever trying to play any of the selections in the book. He put it back.

Sitting on the edge of his bed, he gazed out the sloping window that curved across the ceiling over his head. The edge of night prowled across the surface of Tezwa, pregnant with danger. Whatever meager light the planet's wounded cities were giving off was buried beneath its grim shield of ash clouds. Somewhere down there, Beverly was doing everything she could to ease the pain of a people who had suffered for the ambition of a corrupted government.

Melancholy settled over him. Of all the pieces of his life that seemed to be tumbling from his grasp, his worsening alienation from Beverly was the only one that filled him with regret. For the better part of the past eighteen months they had slowly grown apart. At first he had thought it might be for the best; their paths had diverged before, but their friendship had persevered. Now, however, he felt an emotional gulf widening, pushing them farther apart with each passing day. Their friendship had become a pallid mockery of its former self.

He sighed. Romance had never really seemed to be in the cards for them. They had flirted with it, entertained the possibility. It had given their camaraderie a crackle, an undercurrent of easy familiarity. On a few occasions in recent years, he'd seriously considered the possibility of a deeper relationship with her, but the time had never seemed right to broach the subject. *Eventually,* he told himself, *one learns to accept that some things are not to be.*

Regardless, he continued to be stung by her failure to confide in him about her consideration of a transfer off of the *Enterprise.* He picked up a padd from his bedside table. On it was the official communiqué from Dr. Yerbi Fandau, informing him of the written offer Fandau had made to her. The document made it clear that she had been contacted verbally about the job days if not weeks earlier. And she had said nothing—at least, she hadn't said anything to Picard. She had, however, made time to talk over the matter with Data and La Forge, who subsequently mentioned it in casual conversation with the captain.

He reclined on the bed and let the padd drop from his hand onto the end table. "Computer," he said. "Lights off." The overhead lamps faded out quickly. He folded his hands behind his head and shut his eyes. Then, despite his best effort not to replay the scene in his memory, he pictured the horrendous devastation wrought in the Tezwan capital by a single detonation. Hundreds of lives had been lost in a flash, doubling Starfleet's casualty count on Tezwa in an instant. Picard couldn't prove that the guerrillas' destruction of the *Deelatava* had been a direct response to his adoption of a more aggressive tack in the search for Commander Riker. Unfortunately, the specificity of the attack, which had wiped out most of the Federation's civilian relief administration on Tezwa, left little doubt that it had been intended to serve both as payback and as a warning.

With a tired grunt, he sat up and got out of bed. Realizing he needed to be back on the bridge in less than an hour, he considered having something to eat. Searching inside for a clue to his appetite, he was forced to admit that he wasn't hungry.

He looked across the room, to the flute case on the shelf. The instrument's music did not call to him. Standing in the darkness, trapped between sleeplessness and the grim ensigns of command, he decided instead to remain still until it was time again to return to duty. For now, he would enjoy the fragile silence while it lasted.

La Forge had been told not to leave sickbay. His body was still riven with scars, burns, and hastily applied dermal grafts. One of the surgical interns had protested that a chunk of metallic debris was still lodged in the chief engineer's thigh.

"Don't worry," La Forge had said as he limped out of sickbay. "It'll still be there when I come back."

Now, as he shifted his weight, the jagged sliver sent a sharp jab of pain coursing up his sciatic nerve. He and Peart had taken over one of the geosurvey labs and reconfigured it into a sophisticated planetary surveillance center. Signal activity, energy-flow patterns, air and ground traffic—everything of note on Tezwa was being monitored, analyzed, and painstakingly cross-referenced. Data had given their operation top-priority access to all of the *Enterprise*'s sensors.

Of course, Data had been running an almost identical effort for nearly four weeks now, to no avail. The difference with this operation, Peart had insisted to the acting first officer, was that Data's efforts had been devoted exclusively to finding Kinchawn's redoubt, Riker's place of incarceration, or both. Acting on Vale's orders and Picard's broad new tactical policy, Peart and La Forge were simply looking for any sign of guerrilla activity large enough to confront directly.

Peart pointed to a wall monitor that displayed a spike in encrypted data transmissions. "What about that?"

La Forge checked the origins of the signals. "No, those

are legitimate," he said. "Mostly official government business. Lots of items about the *Deelatava* bombing."

Peart said, "Anything suspicious?"

"Hard to tell," La Forge admitted. "I don't think so. The ones that mention it are all after-the-fact."

Peart tapped a finger on his console. "Computer," he said. "Open a secure data link with the *Musashi*, *Amargosa*, and *Republic*. Cross-reference the results of all Starfleet bioscans of major population centers on Tezwa made during the past four weeks. Report any anomalies."

"Working," the computer voice replied, calm and feminine.

La Forge initiated a tachyon sweep of the planet's surface. Once the ten-minute procedure was under way, he paused to check the updated casualty list from the *Deelatava*. Seeing members of his staff listed among the confirmed dead, he sighed heavily. His shoulders sagged. Peart looked up over the chest-high console that separated them. "You all right?"

"No," La Forge said. "Goodnough and Spitale were down there." A dark and sullen mood hung over him. "They were good engineers," he added in a quiet voice.

Looking up, La Forge saw the same look of grim bereavement on Peart's face. "I know how you feel," he said. "I lost two of my guys down there. Lofgrin and Carmona." Peart swallowed hard. "Great guys."

Several minutes passed in silence while they worked, ferreting out new leads from the mountains of sensor logs.

The soft hum of power conduits, the hush of the ventilation system, and the gentle chirping of the computer panels conspired to lull La Forge into a somber reverie.

Part of his mind was still swept up in the vertigo of falling, of tumbling in a storm of broken rock, shattered glass, and twisted metal. Roars and explosions echoed deep in his memory, refusing to be silenced.

Peart's voice snapped La Forge back to attention. "Your tachyon scan's finished."

"Huh? . . . Sorry. What?"

"Your scan. It's done."

"Oh." La Forge scanned through the results. "Thanks," he added. Finding the results inconclusive, he leaned forward onto his hands, to take some of the weight off of his aching leg. "You know what makes no sense?"

"This entire mission," Peart said.

"Exactly," La Forge said.

Peart glanced up, eyebrows lifted. "I was kidding."

"I wasn't," La Forge said. "Seriously, so the Tezwans picked a fight with the Klingons. Why'd we get involved?"

"Orders, I guess," Peart said.

"Sure," La Forge said. "But whose orders? And what's their rationale? I mean, I keep turning it over and over in my head, and it never adds up. We have no treaty with Tezwa. No trade relationship. What are we doing here?"

"Starfleet's been on plenty of humanitarian missions," Peart said.

"Sure," La Forge said. "When we've been asked for help. The Tezwans weren't asking."

Peart rolled his eyes. "What were we supposed to do? Let the Klingons stomp them into paste?"

With a shrug, La Forge said, "Why not? The Klingon Empire is huge. They've conquered hundreds of worlds.

They're doing it even now. We don't stick our necks out to help all of them."

That seemed to bring Peart up short for a moment. La Forge pressed his argument further. "And what about all the stuff we found on Tezwa during the commando raids?"

"Like what?"

"Vale dug up a camouflaged grating made of chimerium, a substance we control as part of our treaty with the Nalori. Or Taurik sending a batch of encrypted Tezwan military data from one of the artillery bases to Starfleet, never to hear another word about it. Or Data reporting that the firebase computers were all using Starfleet protocols."

Peart looked concerned. "Where are you going with this, Commander?"

"I don't know yet," La Forge admitted. "But I'm pretty sure I'm not gonna like it when I get there."

An urgent shrilling tone on Peart's monitor interrupted the discussion. The lean security officer turned off the alert and forwarded his scan results to La Forge's screen. "Looks like the bioscans suddenly show an entire building in downtown Odina-Keh going empty," he said. "Two days ago, it had three hundred residents. Today, nada."

"Hang on," La Forge said. "Let's see if there were official orders to clear the building." The chief engineer tapped in some commands, but found no records regarding the building at all. "It's not in the system," he said. "No utility accounts, no assigned com circuits. It's completely off the grid."

"But two days ago it had power, signal traffic, and

water service," Peart said. "And it was packed to the rafters with bio readings. Now it's empty."

La Forge noted an odd series of null values next to several of the scan frequencies that were now targeted on the building. "Maybe not," he said, his interest snared. "It reads empty to a quick passive scan. But there's a lot of low-level Cochrane distortion—the kind that deflects scanners."

Peart nodded. "Exactly the kind of jamming system you'd use to hide something big."

"I'm calling up a visual," La Forge said. A wall-sized viewscreen behind him flared to life with an orbital view of the building's rooftop. "No roof sentries," he said.

"Wouldn't need 'em," Peart replied. "With a sensor screen like that, the only way for us to get a look inside is to kick the door down."

La Forge thought that the suspicious structure, which was located in the heart of an extremely hostile, *elininae*-dominated city, looked ominously silent. "What's our next move?"

"For you, get back to sickbay," Peart said. He had an intense gleam in his eye. "I have to go kick down a door."

Chapter 11
Merchantman Caedera

"THE *DAMASCUS* CONFIRMS RECEIPT of the cargo," R'Lash said.

M'Rill breathed a sigh of relief. Between the scurrying around the outskirts of the Tezel-Oroko system and the captain's latest increase in the temperature on the bridge, it had been a very long day. The Caitian pilot tried not to let his jaw hang too far open while he panted to cool himself. He glanced at his navigation panel and took note as the *Damascus* jumped back to warp speed, headed to Tezwa.

Captain Trenigar stood and stretched with a growl. His fanged outer jaws spread apart, and then twitched slightly. "Dammit, R'Lash!" he bellowed. "We're flying empty!"

"We just made a fortune," the first officer said. "I think we can afford it."

Trenigar swatted the Barzan woman in the face with his open hand. "Stupid *lovaach!*" She recoiled as he continued, "Never fly empty! It just burns money!"

The enormous Nausicaan's bootsteps clanged heavily

on the deck as he stepped toward the door. "Set course to Ajilon," he said. "Get us a new contract or get yourself another job." He walked out the door, which closed behind him.

R'Lash reached up and reset the environmental controls to their default status. Cool air washed through the room like a wave of forgiveness. "Stupid *liknul*," she muttered. M'Rill watched her fall into Trenigar's seat with a heavy *fwump*. She slumped lazily in the big chair, her elbows propped up on its armrests. "Helm, set course for Ajilon."

"Aye, sir," M'Rill said. He plotted the course, confirmed it, and jumped the *Caedera* to near-maximum warp. All around him, the well-traveled merchantman resounded with the deep, hearty pulse of its well-maintained warp engines. Turning to face R'Lash, he said, "Mind if I get dinner?"

R'Lash waved her hand lazily, as if shooing away an insect. "Go," she mumbled. "Bring me back something."

He activated the autopilot and stood up. "It's Nolram's day running the mess."

"Never mind, then." She aimed her sullen glare at the viewscreen full of warp-streaked stars. M'Rill hoped that her fast might lead to a fortunate accident for Trenigar. *I'm sure all the best mutinies were plotted on empty stomachs,* he mused.

He left the bridge without saying another word. At the end of the corridor, he carefully eased into the null-gravity tube and grasped the ladder rungs. With a push, he glided downward.

As he passed the berthing deck, he heard the savage, animal wailing and frenzied grunting of Nolram and Saff violating each other, not as an expression of affection but as a desperate response to the tedium of shipboard life. Listening to Nolram's steady stream of Zibalian vulgarities, M'Rill sighed dejectedly. If today was Nolram's turn to bed Saff, then M'Rill's turn wasn't for another three days, after Gorul and then R'Lash. Saff's strict schedule of rotation gave their couplings a kind of drab institutional feeling, but its inherent fairness more than compensated for its lack of spontaneity.

With the raging howls of xenocoitus still echoing from two decks above, he bounded out onto the engineering deck. He entered his key code on the door's com panel. It rebuked him with a low, dysfunctional-sounding chirp.

Tzazil changed the code, the Caitian groused. If M'Rill confronted him, the pusillanimous engineer's mate would simply claim he had forgotten to send him the revised code. It was that kind of passive-aggressive nonsense which made the normally even-tempered helmsman lie awake at night, thinking of the slowest, most painful way to kill the toadying Kaferian.

M'Rill entered a security override code he had programmed into the ship's security system, as a safeguard against petty inconveniences such as this. It worked instantly, and the door slid open. He walked into the main engineering compartment and relocked the door behind him.

The noise in the engineering section was louder than on the larger, more comfortably appointed vessels common to Starfleet or even the Klingons. In fact, most military vessels by necessity restricted the acceptable level of ambient noise in an engine room. As a privately owned vessel, the *Caedera* was exempt from such considerations. Consequently, when Captain Trenigar had been informed of what it would cost to equip the engineering compartment with acoustic dampers, he balked and told Nolram and Tzazil to invest in good protective headphones instead.

At the far end of the compartment, Tzazil was splayed atop the primary heat exchanger, basking in its thermal radiance. M'Rill skulked quickly across the narrow gap between the twin fusion relays, and then slipped into a narrow access space that was tucked into a shadowy corner of the engineering deck.

Shimmying past access panels and various protruding components, M'Rill kept his tail tucked cautiously between his legs. The deck vibrated beneath his feet. Despite the vastly powerful energies coursing through the systems around him, the air seemed remarkably cool and fresh after his most recent sweltering shift on the bridge.

At the end of the access crawlspace was a ladder on the rear wall. Next to it was a data-relay repair hatch. He punched in his access code and opened the wall panel. Tucked securely into the tangled web of optolithic cables and glowing isolinear chips was a small, innocuous-looking signal tap that the organization had provided to him. It was designed to be patched into a general relay buffer, from which it would intercept and keep a duplicate record of every sensor reading, subspace communication, and transporter action aboard the *Caedera*. Under Captain Trenigar's command, it was standard operating procedure to wipe all those logs before making port.

M'Rill checked the tap's data log. The past two weeks' worth of intercepts were all there. He triggered its data dump. In the span of just a few seconds, its entire record of the *Caedera*'s activities was sent back to the organization in an encrypted burst of subspace data. Then, just as quickly, it erased any record of its own transmission from the *Caedera*'s communication logs.

His eyes caught a blur of movement from the far end of the access crawlspace. Tzazil was up and moving around, and had just walked past. There was no way for M'Rill to be certain that Tzazil hadn't noticed something amiss a moment ago. The suspicious Kaferian might double back at any moment. With Tzazil up and about, M'Rill decided that going back out the way he came in would be too risky.

He climbed the ladder as swiftly and quietly as possible. By the time he reached the top, he was entirely swathed in darkness. Looking down, he saw Tzazil pass by the crawlspace again. The insectoid engineer paused, leaned back, and peered inside. After a few seconds, he resumed his mindless pacing around the engine-room perimeter.

M'Rill opened the hatch at the top of the ladder, climbed into the auxiliary cargo bay, and carefully lowered the hatch closed behind him.

Soon his latest data dump would reach L'Haan. When it did, she might have new orders for him, or she might simply instruct him to submerge back into his cover identity as if none of this had ever happened.

Until her next orders arrived, all he could do was wait. Which, in his opinion, made this an opportune time to go up to the mess hall and have some chili.

Chapter 12
Tezwa

FOR JIM PEART, the waiting was always the worst part.

Freezing rain drizzled down from a night sky whose dark clouds were edged with the pink glow of city lights. The soft gray patter of falling water seemed to mute the metropolis of Odina-Keh. Deserted streets lay hushed. On the outskirts of the city's main commercial subdivision, a blocky building stood, dark and silent. Its crumbling façade was slick with rain and dangling with gray, stiletto-like icicles.

Peart watched it from across the street, in the darkened lobby of an office building that was ostensibly closed for the night. Grouped behind him in the wide-open, marble-floored space was a platoon of Starfleet Special Ops personnel. They were outfitted in torso armor and protective helmets, and carrying type-3 phaser rifles. No one moved. Everyone breathed shallowly. *It's like being in a room full of statues,* Peart thought.

Waiting in orbit, on the transporter platforms of four starships, were this company's other four platoons of Special Ops troops—more than 130 personnel, all standing by to beam in on Peart's order.

Half a kilometer up the road was a lone, pale-orange streetlamp. Its weak pastel glow stretched across the glistening wet pavement. Every other light along this street, as far as Peart could see in either direction, hung dark and dormant. A dank, low-lying fog crept from the alleyways.

He keyed his headset com. "Peart to *Enterprise.*"

Data responded, *"This is* Enterprise. *Go ahead."*

"Alpha Platoon's in position. What's the holdup?"

"Commander La Forge is making final adjustments to the shaped charges that will precede Bravo Platoon's assault on the roof."

"ETA?"

"Twenty seconds," Data said.

"Acknowledged."

Peart's mouth was dry with nervous anticipation. The adrenaline in his blood gave him a cold shiver. He flexed his fingers around the grip of his rifle. Going into the scan-proofed building was a calculated risk, but it wasn't one he felt good about. Vale's demand for immediate action meant there was no time to tinker with recalibrating the transporters, the tricorders, or the exogenic targeting sights to compensate for the sensor screen protecting the building's interior. Roughly 150 Special Ops troops were about to barge into the target, despite having no idea what was waiting for them.

There could be three enemy troops in there. There

could be three hundred. The only way to find out was to go inside.

"Data to all strike teams. Stand by. Roof charges beaming down in three . . . two . . . one."

The eerie hush of the night felt like a hang-fire. Then came a quick succession of thunderous explosions from the roof of the building across the street.

"Commencing transport," Data said.

It amused Peart that Data made it sound like a simple matter. To beam down four platoons—more than 130 people—to multiple locations around one target, all at the same time, had required all the transporter capabilities of the four starships orbiting the planet. Each of them was beaming in one platoon, while the Runabout *Potomac* had handled the transporter placement of the demolition charges that had just opened a hole in the target's roof.

There were countless variables that could go wrong in such a complicated scheme, but five seconds after saying it had begun, Data reported, *"Transport complete."*

Peart pointed forward as he keyed his com, issuing his order to all five platoons at once: "Go!"

Three men with sonic-pulse weapons blasted out the towering sepia-tinted windows of the office building's ground-floor lobby. Broken glass rained into the street, scattering over the asphalt like tiny fallen stars. It all crunched under the boots of the Special Ops forces who double-quick-timed out of the lobby and across the boulevard, weapons braced for battle.

Once the troops were in motion, Peart didn't have to say anything else. They'd all listened to the mission briefing, nodded almost in unison, and waited for the order to charge. All that remained now was to let them do their jobs.

A phaser blast knocked a heavy door ajar in its frame. Peart kicked it in. A blond female officer raced over it and moved into the target location. Squads of troops surged in behind her. Peart keyed his com before he followed the last Special Ops trooper inside. "Alpha Platoon's in," he said.

"Bravo Platoon, in," came the first reply. In quick succession, the leaders of Charlie, Delta, and Echo Platoons checked in. The Starfleet personnel flooded into the building from three sides on the ground as well as from the roof. Peart heard the whine of runabout engines approaching.

Alpha Platoon advanced single file down a wide central hallway. At stairwells and intersections they split up, dividing into six-person squads as they pushed deeper inside the decrepit, pitch-dark building.

The dim hallways and towering stairwell shafts echoed with the heavy clamor of booted-in doors banging off walls. Pausing at a switchback staircase that ascended to the top floor of the building, Peart listened. Jogging footfalls and splintering door frames overlapped repeatedly.

Something sounded wrong. Something was missing.

There were no voices. No weapons fire.

He motioned to the squads closest to him to follow him. Striding back toward the door to the street, he keyed his com to the master frequency. "Peart to Bravo Leader. Did you engage the enemy yet?"

"Negative," said Bravo Leader. *"We're coming up empty."*

"Echo Leader?"

"Roger that. No one upstairs."

Delta Leader chimed in, *"Delta's got nothing."*
"Charlie's all clear."

Panic swelled inside Peart like the bile in his throat. He broke into a dead run. "Abort! Everybody out! *Enterprise,* get us outta here!" The hallways filled with the mad scramble of running feet. Then the walls between Peart and the exit turned to splinters and flames. A stunning shock wave hit him. His rifle fell from his hands as he scrambled forward toward the night. He ricocheted wildly off the walls, floor, and ceiling. He felt his bones break with dull snaps and brittle crunches.

His body slid and rolled across the rain-soaked asphalt.

Nearly a dozen Special Ops troopers were hurled out of the building behind him, expelled by an expanding cone of fire.

Rolling to a stop on his side, he saw detonations rip through the target building, one floor at a time, ascending toward the roof, which ultimately erupted in a white flash. Expanding mountains of ash and dust jetted out of the building as it began a perfectly choreographed vertical implosion.

Peart tried to scramble away from the collapse, but his left arm was paralyzed. His legs refused to obey his commands. Flailing and twisting desperately, he gulped a breath and shut his eyes. The advancing debris cloud overtook him.

Hot ash seared his already scorched skin. Dust, dirt, and pulverized concrete and rock sluiced over him and turned to mud in the rain. He felt like he was being buried alive. Through the grit clogging his ears, he still could hear the sickening roar of the building flattening

itself and pile-driving its own wreckage past its foundations, deep into the ground.

Deathly silence reigned in the aftermath of the blast.

He coughed roughly. Gasping for air, he sucked dust
into his throat. Gagging and hacking, he didn't dare open
his eyes. He heard the wheezing rasps of the other survivors lying with him in the street. He keyed his com.
"Enter—" Another racking cough shook him. *"Enterprise,"* he said weakly. "Do you read me?"

"Affirmative," Data said. *"Stand by for transport."*

"Enterprise . . . how many strike personnel did you
beam up?"

Peart's already meager hopes dwindled as the silence
grew.

"Fourteen" was Data's eventual reply.

I led a hundred people to their deaths, Peart realized.
Walked them into a trap. His face burned with furious
shame as the transporter beam enfolded him. Before it
disassembled his atoms for the return to the *Enterprise,*
the brash young junior lieutenant questioned, for the first
time in his life, whether he even deserved to wear a
Starfleet uniform.

Beverly Crusher lay on the narrow bed, trying to will
herself to get an hour of rest while she could. Sleep refused to come to her. The dim, oppressively humid recovery ward whispered with the erratic respiration of
sleeping patients.

It was evening, a couple of hours after sunset. Working
a fourteen-hour trauma shift had left her thoroughly ener-
vated, yet she was gripped by a feeling of anxiety that

prevented her from falling asleep. She sat up, sighed, and looked around.

Most of Anara-Zel was still without power. The city outside the ward's empty window frames was a stagger of spires silhouetted against a dark gray canopy of nighttime clouds. Streaking past in the distance was a lone Starfleet runabout, its warp nacelles like a bright blue slash of light across the sky. Crusher watched it appear and vanish from the narrow spaces between the buildings, until finally it sped out of sight.

She walked out of the recovery ward, through a pair of double doors into the L-shaped hallway. She turned right and walked past the serum-collection lab and the emergency ward. Even after a long day and night of non-stop triage and trauma cases, the hallway remained crowded with Tezwan civilians desperate for medical attention. One of the four elevators along the wall to her left opened, disgorging six bedraggled Tezwans. She was dismayed by the number of wounded, sick, or malnourished children who had come in to the hospital alone.

Stepping over patients sprawled lethargically along the floor, she passed the operating room. As she walked past the triage room, she glanced in. Ogawa sat at the desk and supervised the admittance of new trauma cases.

"Alyssa," Crusher said. "How are you holding up?"

Ogawa, her eyes half-closed and dark-rimmed with fatigue, shook her head and replied with a weary shrug.

Crusher knew how her longtime friend and colleague felt. "Take a break soon," she said. Ogawa nodded, then resumed her review of pending trauma cases. Crusher continued walking, past the short bend at the end of the hallway, out the sliding doors to the open terrace.

Nightfall had brought little relief from the muggy heat of the afternoon. A handful of Starfleet personnel and Federation relief workers paced along the wide open-air terrace. Some just leaned against the wall and breathed in a moment of solitude.

A wide, guardrail-bordered catwalk connected the terrace to a large, round landing pad, where the Runabout *Tsavo* descended to a graceful landing. Its running lights spilled blinding splashes of bright color across the platform as it touched down with hardly a bump.

The broad side door of the *Tsavo* slid open with a sharp hiss. Two civilian emergency medical technicians clambered out, then helped a pair of Starfleet medics carry out two stretchers. On one was a young Tezwan woman, on the other an adolescent Tezwan boy. Following them out of the runabout was a handful of other Tezwan patients, who were escorted by Nurse Kristin Jourdonais from the *Republic* and Dr. Dennis Chimelis, the chief medical officer of the *Musashi*.

The procession of patients and caregivers hurried past Crusher, who stepped out of their path. As Chimelis walked past, she nodded to him. "Glad you could make it," Crusher said.

"You called the cavalry, you got it," the fortyish balding physician said with a wink. Crusher chuckled softly. He gave her a fraternal pat on the arm, then continued on his way. As he ushered his patients into the makeshift hospital, Crusher ambled down the catwalk toward the landing platform. A quick gust of wind tousled her red hair. She ran her fingers over her scalp to tame her tresses.

She climbed into the *Tsavo* through its open side door. Almost instantly she felt the change in her weight; she hadn't realized until just now how quickly she'd grown comfortable in Tezwa's lighter gravity.

From the cockpit, the copilot looked back at her. Crusher pointed toward the runabout's rear compartment. "I just want to use the replicator," she said to him.

"Sure, help yourself," he said.

Accustomed to finding comfortable living quarters in the aft section of a runabout, Crusher was caught off-guard by the enormous, ten-pad transporter platform that dominated the compartment. To enable it, the normally roomy craft was packed with extra power modules and control systems. Built into the wall opposite the replicator was a small armory. It was loaded with phaser rifles, photon grenades, and hand phasers. Ignoring the wall of armaments behind her, she ordered a mug of double-sweet *raktajino* from the replicator and thanked the copilot on her way back outside.

Stepping out of the runabout, she noticed Dr. Hughes leaning against the railing on the far side of the platform. Though she had come outside to be alone for a few minutes, she walked over and joined him. He didn't look up as she planted one hand on the railing beside him. "Long day," she said.

"I've seen worse," Hughes said.

"During the war?" She took a sip of her beverage.

He nodded. His eyes scanned the surrounding cityscape as he said, "I was a surgeon on the *Hood*."

Crusher didn't need to ask him to elaborate. The

Excelsior-class starship had been called upon to hold the line in several critical battles during the Dominion War. More than once the ship had barely survived, only to be hastily repaired and sent back into the fray. But its reputation among Starfleet's medical community was one of despair; the *Hood*'s casualty rate during the war had been brutal. More than one *Hood* survivor had spoken in horrified whispers of a sickbay packed with wounded and dying personnel, battle after battle, over a period of two years.

The *Enterprise*-E had played its part in the Dominion War, but its crew hadn't been called upon to make the same kinds of wartime sacrifices as the *Hood*.

"I can understand why you left," Crusher said, after a brief silence.

"I left for a lot of reasons," he said. "But after I got home, I couldn't see myself in private practice, either." A rueful half-smirk tugged at the corner of his mouth. "So here I am." He looked at the mug in her hand. "What're you drinking?"

"*Raktajino.*"

He smiled. "I used to eat at a place on Terra Nova that served Klingon-French fusion cuisine. They had great *raktajino.*"

"You can get one from the runabout replicator," she suggested.

"Nah," he said. "Not in the mood for it right now." He watched her take another sip. "Had dinner yet?"

"Not yet," she said. "Maybe later." With a playful smirk she added, "Why do you ask?"

"No reason," he said, resisting the grin pulling at his

face. "Although . . . now that you mention it, we *could* have dinner together."

"I don't think I mentioned any such thing," she said. Her face was warm. *I can't believe I'm blushing.* She felt flattered by such unabashedly amorous attention from a man nearly twenty years her junior, even if she barely knew him. But she was even more shocked at herself for encouraging him. This was, without a doubt, neither the time nor the place to be flirting.

"No," he said, "I guess you didn't." For a moment it seemed he would leave things at that. Then he added, "Good thing I said something, then. Because in my experience, waiting for dates to happen spontaneously usually doesn't work."

She chuckled and shook her head. "You don't take no for an answer, do you?"

"What kind of cuisine do you prefer?"

She snuck a sidelong glance at him as she took another sip of *raktajino.* Thinking back, she tried to remember the last time she had enjoyed the pleasures of intimate companionship.

There had been Ronin, of course, but he had turned out to be a parasitic anaphasic-plasma being that had survived for centuries by symbiotically attaching himself to her female ancestors. The physical pleasure he had given her had been undeniably real, but upon learning his true motives she had realized he could not possibly have loved her. Nine years had passed since she had broken his bond to her and condemned him to fade into oblivion. His face had haunted her every day since.

Before Ronin had been Odan. *What a whirlwind*

romance that *was,* she reminisced. The dashing Trill diplomat had awakened joys in her that she hadn't felt since her husband Jack had died, during an away mission under Picard's command.

That recollection brought her up short. *Has Jack really been gone for twenty-five years?* A quarter of a century had passed since she lost her husband, and in that time she had only afforded herself two respites from her perpetual loneliness. Yes, her work had been fascinating and fulfilling, and her son, Wesley, had been a source of pride. *But it would be nice to feel wanted once in a while,* she admitted. *To feel desired. . . . And it's not as if Jean-Luc has made me any offers.*

Now here was that gleam of carnal interest, sparkling in Hughes's forest green eyes. He was still waiting for her answer.

"Italian," she said. "I like Italian."

He smiled. "So, is that a yes?"

"I didn't say that," she replied. "I'm just saying—"

"That you like Italian," he interrupted.

"Right."

He nodded and looked around at the city, as if he expected to see thousands of faces watching his ego twist in the wind.

She finished her *raktajino.* "I'm staying on to supervise the overnight shift," she said as she let go of the railing and began walking back toward the entrance to the hospital.

He followed her. "Okay if I stick around?" he asked.

"I won't say no," she said.

He grinned. "That's what I'm hoping."

* * *

"I'm sorry to wake you, Prime Minister," Bilok's aide Leejay said over the com. *"Deputy Prime Minister Tawnakel says he needs to see you right away."*

Bilok blinked and looked at the clock. It was the middle of the night. He hoped this might be just a bad dream.

"Did he say why?"

"No, sir. Only that it was urgent."

He took a deep breath.

"Give me a minute, then send him in."

"Yes, sir."

Times like this made Bilok remember why his wife Kinya had insisted on separate bedrooms since the day he had first been elected to a leadership position in the *Gatni* Party. She had foreseen the endless nighttime interruptions that would come with the job.

He threw off his heavy bedcovers and pushed himself up to a sitting position. By the time he had put on his slippers and found his crimson bathrobe, the knock came at his bedroom door. Tying shut his robe, he called out, "Enter."

Leejay opened the door for Tawnakel, who strode in looking angrily ruffled. He nodded to Bilok. "Mr. Prime Minister." The deputy prime minister glanced quickly back at Leejay, who took the hint and shut the door, giving the two politicians their privacy.

Bilok gestured to some chairs and a plush sofa in the corner of the room. "Shall we—"

"There's no time. One of the shipments was stolen."

Bilok hoped he had misunderstood him. "Shipments . . . ?"

"From your friend, Azernal."

The elder statesman's gray nape feathers stiffened with alarm. "You're certain?"

"Our people at the delivery point are dead," Tawnakel said. "The cargo is gone."

Bilok's legs grew weak. He sat down on the edge of his bed and felt like a frail old man. "When?"

"Lirwon confirmed the delivery was made four hours ago. When he didn't get back on time, I sent Keena to check on him. She found him and his team about half an hour ago."

Rage boiled up inside Bilok. "How did Kinchawn find our delivery points?"

"No idea. Compromised communications, maybe. Or he might have sympathizers inside our ranks."

Closing his slender hand into a fist, Bilok said, "Which components did he capture?"

"We won't know for certain until after we finish inventory on the other shipments," Tawnakel said. "But the engineers think he got the beryllium krellide power cells and some components we needed to refit the industrial replicators." He shook his head in confusion. "What does he think he can do with them?"

"Blackmail us," Bilok said matter-of-factly.

"But those items alone don't prove anything."

"No, but they'll give the lie to the charade Azernal wants us to foist on Starfleet." Sickening waves of dread moved through Bilok's gut. "He'll probably threaten to expose the artillery system's true origins to the Klingons unless we expel the Federation from Tezwa. In exchange, he'll promise us safe passage off of Tezwa, once he returns to power."

"He'd kill us the moment Starfleet left the system," Tawnakel said.

"Of course he would," Bilok said. "And then he'd tell the entire galaxy about the Federation's role in making the cannons that he used to kill six thousand Klingon soldiers. He'd plunge the Federation into a war of attrition with the Klingon Empire, and we'd be sitting smack in the middle of the battle zone."

"There's another possibility," Tawnakel said. "Kinchawn might not make his demands to you. He might go directly to Azernal."

"Try to turn our ally against us," Bilok said, reasoning out his colleague's chain of thought. "Promise Azernal that he'll surrender the evidence about the cannons in exchange for a complete Federation withdrawal from Tezwa."

"And a blind eye when he has us and our families executed."

Bilok nodded gravely. "All too plausible, I'm afraid."

"Either way, we're at a disadvantage," Tawnakel observed. "The moment he strikes a bargain, we're as good as dead."

"Fortunately, some of Azernal's preventive measures have bought us a little time," Bilok said. "He has the Starfleet engineers taking apart the subspace radio system, to help us keep Kinchawn muzzled. And Kinchawn himself did us a favor by blowing up the *Deelatava*. He destroyed the transmitter that Starfleet installed for the Federation ambassador."

"There are still several starships in orbit with subspace-radio capabilities," Tawnakel said.

"True. But most of them are under Federation control.

I don't think Starfleet will help Kinchawn get a message to the Klingons—or to anyone else, for that matter."

"It takes only one transmitter to get a message out," the deputy prime minister warned.

"I know," Bilok said. "If Kinchawn moves against us, we might need to take down the entire system, as a precaution. In fact, since most of the secondary relay centers keep logs of transmission data, we might want to eliminate them now, regardless of what Kinchawn does."

Tawnakel wrinkled his brow as he asked, "How?"

"Nothing complicated. Crude demolitions seem to work well for Kinchawn. Let's imitate his methods. Have a small team of covert operatives destroy the relay centers. When they're done, we'll label the attacks as more of Kinchawn's guerrilla tactics."

Aghast, Tawnakel said, "I'm not sure I can do that."

Rising from his bed, Bilok felt reinvigorated. "Why not?"

"Because there are civilians in some of those facilities."

"Necessary sacrifices," Bilok said. He walked toward the liquor shelf on the other side of his bed. "In a war, I wouldn't hesitate to send a few to die to save the many. If sacrificing one town saves a nation, the dead have not fallen in vain." He took a bottle of *jeefa* down from the shelf, and then grabbed a glass. Pouring himself a drink, he added, "I do not spill blood lightly, my friend. In my heart, I will sing a sorrow-song for every life I sacrifice to save our world." He handed the glass of tart liquor to Tawnakel. "But I will not regret my decision."

He grabbed another glass, filled it, and put the bottle

of *jeefa* back on the shelf. Rejoining Tawnakel, he lifted his glass. "To peace on Tezwa," he said, "at any price."

Lagan Serra limped into her new temporary office. Located on an upper floor of the *Ilanatava,* in the same ring as the offices of many of Tezwa's senior ministers, it was less than half the size of her former suite in the *Deelatava.* Regardless, being invited to reside in so lofty a place felt like an honor, no matter the size of the space. One improvement over the previous office was that this one had far better communications systems.

The middle-aged Bajoran woman lowered herself into her chair with a groan. Outside her window, the capital city of Keelee-Kee was still dark, hours shy of the dawn.

Before she had time to power up her padd and go over her list of unfinished business, someone knocked on her door. "Come in," she said. The antique-style carved wooden door swung open with the squeak of old metal hinges. Kuda, her new assistant, leaned in, his fingers curled around the edge of the door. "Your Excellency, the prime minister is here."

Lagan's eyes widened with surprise. "Send him in." She stood up and moved out in front of her new, barren desk.

Kuda stepped inside the office and moved out of the doorway. He held the portal open for Bilok, who swept into the room. Kuda declared, "Madam Ambassador, Prime Minister Bilok."

The towering Tezwan head of state was garbed in billowing dark green robes over a satin-textured white cassock. His stitched brown leather shoes padded softly across the polished stone floor. He spread his arms wide, and his mane of feathers expanded to resemble an ornate crown. "Madam Ambassador, I'm so relieved to see you," he said. He reached toward her.

Lagan extended her right hand and let him shake it vigorously. "Thank you for your kind wishes, Mr. Prime Minister." As he released her hand, she nodded sideways toward the window. "It's rather early," she said. "I didn't expect to see you for a few hours."

"Sadly, matters of state don't respect the hours," he said. "I was on my way to my chambers when Minister Onoro told me you'd returned. Are you sure you're all right?"

With a wan smile, Lagan said, "No, not really. But to paraphrase your eloquent words, duty calls."

"So it does," Bilok said. "It's been a most terrible day. First the attack on the *Deelatava,* then the trap Kinchawn sprung on your Starfleet personnel in Odina-Keh." He shook his head sadly. "No doubt it was all Kinchawn's retaliation for the capture of General Minza. Perhaps you were right to counsel against granting Starfleet such broad liberties." He sighed heavily. His voice was tinged with dread. "But now the damage is done, and I fear that the violence can only escalate."

"We mustn't think that way, Mr. Prime Minister," Lagan said. "It's important not to give up. There is always hope."

"Indeed," Bilok said. His countenance darkened with a shade of sorrow that Lagan had not witnessed since the Cardassian occupation of Bajor. "There is infinite hope," the prime minister added. "Just not for us."

Lagan wanted to probe deeper into what had made him say that, but before she could inquire he withdrew into himself and turned away. "Best wishes for a speedy recovery, Madam Ambassador," he said over his shoulder as he walked toward the door. "If you need anything, please don't hesitate to ask."

"There is one thing," Lagan said. "Commander Geordi La Forge has requested permission to review the contents of Tezwa's communication logs. If you could expedite—"

"Review the logs?" Bilok sounded suspicious. "Why?"

"I believe he's concerned that recent orders for their demolition might inadvertently result in the loss of critical data. He'd like to review their memory cores to see whether additional safeguards need to be implemented."

Bilok frowned. "I am uncomfortable with that idea, Madam Ambassador," he said. "Confidential data is stored in those systems. I wasn't aware that the Federation was going to ask us to permit monitoring of privileged state communications."

"If these logs are so important," Lagan said, "that's all the more reason to let us make protected backups."

He turned away and walked toward the door. "I will take your request under advisement," he said.

"Thank you, Prime Minister," she said. "Good day."

"And to you," he replied from the outer office as he moved decisively back to the main hallway that ringed the Assembly Forum. Kuda stood beside the door, alternating between watching the prime minister depart and awaiting further instructions from Lagan, who returned to her chair and sat down.

She waved Kuda inside her office. He quickly crossed the room and stood attentively in front of her desk. "Ma'am?"

"I'll need a full breakdown of yesterday's reports," she said. "Get me copies of Picard's briefs to Starfleet Command regarding whatever happened in Odina-Keh."

Kuda tapped the information into his padd. "Understood."

"Next, contact the commissary and see about getting me something to eat. If they have a replicator that can make a breakfast *hasperat,* that would be lovely. And I'll need some fruit juice and something with caffeine—espresso, *raktajino,* whatever. Make it strong and sweet."

"Strong and sweet," Kuda said. "Right."

Kuda turned and walked briskly back toward his desk outside Lagan's door. As he reached to close the door, Lagan said, "One more thing." He paused. She continued, "Contact the *Enterprise* and get me another copy of the report Commander La Forge filed. I want to take a closer look at it. And get me a secure channel to Starfleet Operations on Earth."

He nodded and shut the door. Alone once more, Lagan swiveled her chair and peered through her reflection on the window. Aches and sudden slicing pains from the previous day's attack continued to haunt her. She imagined this window being blasted in, peppering her with jagged shards of transparent aluminum. *So high up,* she observed. *No surviving this fall.* She closed her eyes and pulled in a deep breath. *I could just close my eyes and pretend I'm flying.*

She wondered again why Bilok seemed so nihilistic. His fears weren't unjustified, of course. Kinchawn *was* likely to escalate the violence as Starfleet continue to confront and provoke him. Still, Bilok had, until now, expressed great confidence in the ability of the Federation to secure the peace and contain the Loyalist insurgency.

Had the attack on the *Deelatava* shaken him that badly? Or did Starfleet's stumble into a trap in Odina-Keh rattle his confidence in their prowess?

Lagan hoped that La Forge's report would shed some light on this increasingly chaotic situation. Because the more that Tezwa's politicians said, the less she understood them.

Pretty much like everyone else's politicians, she concluded with an exasperated frown.

Riker awoke to the metallic screech of the door opening above his narrow, shallow pit in the floor. The concrete beneath his face was slick with muck from his last meal, which he had been unable to bring himself to finish. Shifting awkwardly, he lifted himself up from his facedown position to see who was entering the chamber above him. He winced at the blinding light that dangled above him.

A weathered-looking Tezwan man stepped on top of the grating that held Riker captive. He wore a Tezwan military uniform. His pale eyes were bordered by deep wrinkles, which stretched across his temples to his sun-bleached mane of feathers. "My name is General Yaelon," he said.

"You'll understand if I don't get up," Riker said.

Yaelon stepped off the grating and gestured to two guards standing at the door. One of them moved to a control panel on the far side of the room. The other reached down, pushed his long, delicate-looking fingers through holes in the grating, and nodded to his comrade.

Receiving a quick nod in return, he lifted the grating open.

Riker remained silent as the two guards stepped down into the pit. Working together, they lifted him out and deposited him unceremoniously on the cement floor at Yaelon's feet. "Help him up," Yaelon ordered. They each grabbed one of Riker's arms, and then lifted him to a standing position against the rear wall.

He slumped weakly. It was difficult to remain upright. His feet were bound at the ankles, which left him off-balance. Vertigo washed through him as the blood rushed away from his head. He hadn't stood upright for nearly a month, and it had become an unfamiliar sensation.

Yaelon towered over him. "If you cooperate with me, I can make your stay less uncomfortable."

"My *stay?*" Riker almost laughed. "You mean my captivity."

"Call it what you like. My point is, it doesn't have to continue like this."

Can't rush them, Riker decided. *Not with my feet tied. Might as well play along.* "What do you want?"

"Prime Minister Kinchawn already told you about yesterday's capture of General Minza," Yaelon said. "Earlier today we retaliated, in two separate incidents. It would be fair to say that we have raised the stakes by an order of magnitude."

"Congratulations," Riker said poisonously.

"If Starfleet chooses to respond, where will they strike? Will they retreat and continue the fight from orbit, or will their forces continue trying to engage us on Tezwa?"

"No idea," Riker said. He coughed. "I don't know

what you hit or how. Don't know what they know about you."

"Fair enough," Yaelon said. "We could find out what they know if you gave us your command codes."

Now Riker had to laugh, even though it made his ribs hurt. He spat out a half-mouthful of bile and tainted saliva. "Waste of time," he said. "My codes were all voided the moment I got captured. Any common codes I knew were changed."

The general stared coldly into his face. "Are you sure?"

"Positive," Riker said.

Yaelon stepped out of the way just in time for one of the guards to slam a short metal bar into Riker's gut. As he doubled over and fell to his knees, the other guard used an identical weapon to club him on the back of his neck. Riker's face struck the floor hard enough to mash his lower lip into his teeth. He felt the skin tear open. The ferric tang of blood filled his mouth as he writhed on the floor.

The general kneeled next to him, and then grabbed him by his torn shirt collar and the bindings around his wrists. "You really are as useless as Kinchawn says," he said venomously. Riker felt the general sneaking something small into his bound hands as he continued speaking. "No value as a bargaining chip, no usable intelligence . . . I can see why he plans to execute you tomorrow before we abandon the redoubt."

Yaelon stood up and gestured to the guards. "I'm done. Put him back in." One of the guards dragged Riker forward and dropped him next to the pit. The other guard got a two-step head start, sprung forward, and kicked Riker in the ribs.

He fell back into the pit with a loud grunt and gasped to recover the air that had been knocked from his lungs. The metal grating clanged back into position. It was followed by the low hum of its magnetic lock reengaging. White light clouded his vision with dark retinal afterimages. The cell door shrieked and scratched closed as his captors left the room.

Alone again in the dank cavity hewn into the floor, Riker used his fingertips to study the objects Yaelon had given to him. There were at least two separate items in Riker's hands. One felt metallic, and seemed to have some raised features, like device controls. The other was smooth and felt like a synthetic polymer. Examining the metallic item more closely, he deduced that one end contained what felt like a faceted emitter crystal.

Balancing the metallic device between his fingers, he applied a small bit of pressure to one of the controls.

From behind his back, he heard the muffled whine of a charged plasma beam. With great caution, he cut the wires that restrained his hands.

He put away the plasma cutter and looked at the other item.

The device was about the size of his little finger. It was made of a translucent orange material. Its edges were rounded, and one end seemed to have a concavity that reached into the middle of the device. Riker looked inside and saw no indication that it might be a weapon. On a hunch, he lifted it to his ear. He heard it emit a soft, gentle tone.

He placed the device gently into his left ear.

"Commander Riker," its prerecorded message said,

*"This is General Yaelon. I will help you escape. I know
you have little reason to trust me, but you must—because
I need your help as much as you need mine.*

*"Up until the day I followed Kinchawn into exile in
this redoubt, I believed that whatever differences he might
have had with his political opposition, he still would act
in the best interest of our people, and our world.*

*"I was wrong. He pushed us to the brink of civil war
and put us on a path to genocide. This has transcended
politics. Executing billions of our own people in the
name of ideology is madness. He must be stopped. And
so must the rogue elements in your own government who
enabled his rise to power.*

*"Kinchawn captured evidence today that can expose
the entire conspiracy. I can lead Starfleet to it, but I
don't know whether I'll be believed. By saving you, I
plan to show my good faith. Use the weapon I've given
you to stop the executioners. I will help you escape the
redoubt and reach safety.*

*"Be ready when they come for you tomorrow. Do not
try to escape on your own—the tunnels are like a
labyrinth. Keep this device—it will function much like
one of your translators, though only to render Tezwan
languages into your own. Wait for me. May the Maker
preserve you until the morning."*

The message ended. He could not get it to repeat. Its
mention of "rogue elements" in the Federation government, however, lingered clearly in his mind.

He'd already had his last meal for today—and possibly
the last meal he would eat on Tezwa. But it was not, by any
stretch, going to be his last meal. *I will not die on Tezwa.*

His captors would be expecting to find him bound. He picked up the remains of the wires and loosely coiled them around his ankles. Retying his wrists behind his back was harder. Instead he wrapped wire around each wrist individually, then made a loose coil that he could hold taut by pushing his wrists outward. He made sure the wire on his left wrist was loose enough for him to tuck the plasma cutter beneath it.

Lifting the plasma cutter, he shot out the overhead light. He tucked the cutter against his wrist. Then he hid his hands behind his back and pushed himself into the corner. *Time to get some rest,* he told himself. *After all, I want to be my best for my execution tomorrow.*

Chapter 13
Earth and Luna

THE IRATE ZAKDORN barged into Nelino Quafina's office. "I'm running late," Azernal declared. "What do you want?"

Quafina looked up from his work. Even seated behind his fanatically organized desk, the gangly Antedean was still almost as tall as the stout chief of staff was standing up. "Reports from Tezwa," he said. "There could be trouble."

Azernal loomed in front of him and glowered. Realizing after several seconds that Quafina wasn't continuing, he said, "Do you plan to elaborate, or must I suggest everything to you?"

"Nice outfit," Quafina said in his hollow-sounding, inwardly drawn voice. "Going somewhere?"

Azernal inhaled sharply. "Since I know you're trying to goad me, I'll ignore that. What's the news from Tezwa?"

Quafina handed a padd to Azernal. "La Forge is making waves," Quafina said. "Questioning our orders to the S.C.E."

Azernal scanned the official report. The chief engineer of the *Enterprise* had lodged a formal protest with Ambassador Lagan, who in turn had filed a grievance with Starfleet Operations. *Good,* he thought. *They're bogging down in details.*

"It's nothing," Azernal said. He flung the padd back onto Quafina's desk. The device clattered to a stop in front of the inscrutable icthyoid.

Quafina began, "If his protest is investigated—"

"It won't be," Azernal said. "It's a nonstarter. Even if Starfleet gives it a hearing, I can quash it before the gavel hits the bench. Now, if you'll excuse me—"

"Hot date?"

Azernal leveled a withering scowl at the impudent Antedean. "Diplomatic reception," he said.

"Ah, yes," Quafina said. "Say hello to the new Klingon ambassador for me."

"Don't make it sound so pleasant," Azernal said. "It's more like the opening falls of a wrestling match." He glanced at the clocks that were crowded together on the wall in front of Quafina's desk. "On that note, I'd better get up there before someone pins the president with one of his own remarks."

Min Zife didn't mind state functions so much as he loathed the cocktail hours that inevitably followed them.

Lunasphere Artemis was a lovely place for an official function, of course. Beyond its vast and deceptively fragile-looking transparasteel dome, the stars had no atmospheric flicker; they were perfect points of pure light on the glassy black surface of the void. The rising, radiant blue crescent of Earth dominated the vista and overpowered a wide circle of the starfield. Staring at the spacescape, Zife longed for the inviolate silence of the vacuum. His wish was motivated by a growing need to escape the inane chatter of Ferengi Ambassador Derro, who had been prattling on for nearly half an hour about his pet theory for "modernizing" the Federation economy.

At last, Zife reached the end of his patience. "Pardon me, Your Excellency," he interrupted. "There's someone on fire over there. I'll be right back." Zife stepped away quickly, before the stunned Ferengi diplomat could protest the Bolian's brazen exit strategy.

Trailed by a pair of bodyguards in civilian attire, Zife strolled over to one of the many dozens of buffet tables that were scattered around the lunasphere's central plaza. He speared some fruit slices with a fork and unloaded them on to a plate. As he scanned the cheese tray selection, he noticed on the edges of his vision that two persons stepped up to the table on either side of him. To his left was T'Kala, the ambassador from Romulus. On his right, picking through the cold cuts with obvious revulsion, was the Gorn ambassador, Zogozin.

T'Kala nodded to Zife and flashed a deadly smile. "Mr. President," she said in a warm voice that made him shudder.

"Madam Ambassador," Zife replied. Zogozin hissed loudly.

"You seem to have landed Starfleet in quite a delicate situation on Tezwa," T'Kala said. "These must be stressful times for you, and for the Federation."

"We have Tezwa under control," he said, then regretted his choice of words almost immediately. "I mean, we have the *crisis* on Tezwa under control."

"I understood your meaning perfectly, Mr. President."

Zogozin made a noise that was somewhere between a growl and a gurgle, and then he flung a handful of sliced lunch meat on the floor. Zife forced himself to offer the olive-scaled reptilian a crooked smile and a nod of recognition. "Ambassador," he said. Zogozin reciprocated by flashing his jaw full of fangs at the slender Bolian man. Zife turned away from Zogozin and looked directly into T'Kala's eyes. He immediately wished he had continued talking with the Gorn. The strikingly beautiful Romulan woman seemed to take his measure with her gaze alone.

"I understand Ambassador K'mtok is rather hawkish toward the Federation," she said. "Rather a surprising stance, considering he was appointed by Chancellor Martok. You don't suppose the chancellor is souring on the Klingon-Federation alliance, do you?"

"We have no reason to think so," Zife blurted out.

"I just gave you a reason," T'Kala said. "Perhaps the Tezwa debacle is costing the Federation more than you realize."

Wet, grinding sounds of mastication issued from behind Zife. He looked over his shoulder. Zogozin stuffed the last of the table's rare roast beef into his mouth. Zife smiled politely at T'Kala. "Excuse me, Madam Ambassador."

"Of course, Mr. President. A pleasure, as always."

Zife stepped away from the table and dodged through the milling crowd of Federation representatives, Starfleet officers, and foreign dignitaries. Huddled together on the far side of the courtyard were Federation Council representatives zh'Faila, Gleer, and Enaren. The troika seemed to be engaged in a hushed but spirited discussion with two other members of the Federation Security Council— T'Latrek of Vulcan and the infamously irascible Tomorok of Rigel. *That can't be good,* Zife realized.

He stopped in the middle of a wooden bridge. A soft melody of piano music wove through random empty spaces in the low murmur of overlapping conversations. He looked up.

Circling high overhead, near the top of the polarized fourteen-hundred-meter-tall dome, were a pair of recreational fliers. In the featherweight gravity of Earth's moon, almost any ordinary humanoid could strap on an enormous pair of synthetic wings and soar far above the majestic, Brobdingnagian forests of two-hundred-meter-tall trees that thrived in this ersatz paradise. In fact, the only place in the entire lunasphere with Earth-level artificial gravity was this small portion of the central plaza, and even that was a temporary addition for the party. *What I'd give to fly,* he thought. *To not carry all this weight, just for one night.*

One subtle aspect of the place disturbed him, however. There was no wind. The leaves on the trees seemed frozen in time, unmoved by even the slightest breeze.

The rasping voice from behind his back startled him.

"All who dare the heavens must eventually fall."

The president turned to face the imposing countenance of Ambassador K'mtok. The brutish Klingon loomed over the Bolian politician. Zife did his best to keep his expression steady. "Welcome to the Federation, Mr. Ambassador," Zife said.

K'mtok eyed the Federation president like a predator

sizing up its prey. He flashed a jagged-toothed smile. "Thank you."

Zife didn't want to seem rude by looking away from K'mtok, but staring at the hulking Klingon felt equally dangerous. *He might think I'm challenging him,* Zife worried. He permitted himself a brief glance down at the crystal-clear artificial lake that lay below the bridge and surrounded several small rises of grassy land in the bottom of the domed crater. Looking back to K'mtok, he noticed a carved-iron stein in the man's hand. The scent from its contents was unmistakable and overpowering.

"Is the *warnog* to your tastes, Your Excellency?"

The middle-aged, gray-bearded Klingon gave his beverage a disdainful frown. "It is adequate," he said.

For a warrior race, Klingons are remarkably picky eaters, Zife mused. "Has Ambassador Lantar returned yet to Qo'noS?"

"He left this morning on the *vaQchargh,*" K'mtok said.

"Oh," Zife said. "I meant to wish him farewell."

"Chancellor Martok demanded his immediate recall."

Zife wondered aloud, "Isn't it unusual for an appointed ambassador to be replaced so abruptly?"

"Not when they fail the empire."

"I'd hardly say he—"

"He was ineffectual during the Tezwa crisis," K'mtok said. "You ignored him and negotiated directly with the chancellor. You might as well have called him a *vetlh.*"

"Time was a factor," Zife said. His tone became defensive. "There wasn't time to work through intermediaries. As a leader, I made the choice to speak personally with Martok."

"I see," K'mtok said. He took a deep pull of his *warnog*. Its pungent fragrance was heavy on his breath as he resumed speaking. "If only Lantar could have been so effective here as your Ambassador Worf was on Qo'noS."

A nervous tingle traveled up Zife's spine. "In what way?"

"Naïveté does not suit you, Mr. President," K'mtok said. Zife was certain the man's eyes were about to unleash fire upon him as he continued. "Worf was a key tactical asset for you. Assaulting members of our High Council; committing acts of espionage against the Klingon Empire; enabling Picard and his crew to cripple an imperial attack fleet. . . . Most impressive."

Flustered, Zife replied, "Ambassador Worf's duties on Qo'noS are strictly diplomatic. He's never been ordered to violate his diplomatic charge by engaging in any kind of military action."

"I never said he had been ordered to do so," K'mtok said, his faux courtesy thick with condescension. "Only that he *had* done so." He swallowed another cheek-swelling mouthful of his drink. "I suppose I should be grateful that you did not insult me with a denial of Worf's actions."

The president heard hurried footfalls tromping across the bridge behind him. He turned to see Koll Azernal lumbering toward him. The overweight Zakdorn was perspiring lightly and breathing raggedly. "Mr. President," he said. He nodded to K'mtok, his manner the very epitome of a deferential political inferior. "Your Excellency. Please forgive my interruption. Mr. President, I need to relay important news to you, if you can spare me a moment." Shifting his eyes sideways toward K'mtok, he added, "In private."

"Of course," Zife said, recognizing Azernal's time-worn conversational rescue tactic. "Please excuse me, Ambassador."

K'mtok grinned lethally at Azernal. "You arrived in the nick of time," he said. "You're a lucky man, Mr. President." The Klingon let that remark hang fire for a moment before he added, "To have such an effective and well-mannered assistant."

Zife felt Azernal's temper rising to the insult.

"Thank you" was all Zife said to K'mtok. Then he turned and motioned to Azernal to lead the way back to the mingling throng of distinguished guests.

Once they moved out of earshot, Azernal's supplicative expression transmogrified into an arrogant snarl. "What did he say to you?"

"They know about Worf," Zife said. His collar suddenly felt too tight. He tugged on it nervously.

Azernal shook his head. "Everyone knows about Worf. No one can prove anything." A dark thought seemed to flit past behind the Zakdorn's dark eyes. "What did you say to him?"

"It's not important," Zife muttered.

"The hell it isn't," Azernal said. "One badly chosen word with a man like K'mtok can start a war. What did you say?" Zife glared at his chief of staff, who then amended the end of his statement to include, "Mr. President, sir."

"Nothing that will get us into a war." He followed Azernal to the bar. The Zakdorn waved over the bartender—a two-meter-tall Stroyerian man. For a moment,

Zife thought he recognized him, then realized that he had confused him with the once-omnipresent valet to Betazed's most famous ambassador, Lwaxana Troi. He was unable to remember that valet's name, but he recalled that Troi had grieved deeply after the man was killed during the Dominion's invasion of Betazed.

Azernal placed his order. "Kentucky bourbon. A double."

The bartender nodded, and then looked to Zife.

"A *balso* tonic," Zife said. The bartender lurched away to prepare the drinks. The president leaned on the bar and spoke in a low voice. "How are we doing with damage control?" As euphemisms went, "damage control" seemed to Zife like a perfectly apt substitute for "our criminal fraud on Tezwa."

"Everything looks on track so far," Azernal said. "The pieces are where they need to be, and I haven't heard of any problems."

"Good," Zife said. He held back his next remark while the bartender delivered his and Azernal's drinks. Zife sampled his nonalcoholic libation. The lanky Stroyerian moved away to serve other patrons. The president continued, "When can we finish?"

"As soon as tomorrow," Azernal said. "If all goes well." He downed his bourbon, plunked his empty tumbler glass onto the bar, and then motioned to the bartender for a refill.

Zife shook his head. "But then what? I'm beginning to doubt the Klingons will believe it. K'mtok seems like a throwback to the pre-Gorkon days. If that's who Martok's sending us—"

"It wasn't really up to Martok," Azernal said. "He's

getting a lot of heat from the High Council right now. One councillor in particular, a nobleman named Kopek, has been drumming up elitist, anticommoner sentiment against Martok. He's also pushing the High Council to start a war. He'd prefer it be against us, but I think he'll take any war he can get."

"So K'mtok is the High Council's message to us?"

"More like Kopek's personal slap in Martok's face," Azernal said. The bartender poured him another double. "I think K'mtok and Kopek might be kinsmen." He emptied the glass in a single tilt. After a dry-mouthed gasp, he added, "At the very least, they're allies who go back more than two decades."

Now Zife was concerned. He hadn't been briefed on internal developments in Klingon politics for more than a month, and it sounded like matters on Qo'noS had taken a turn for the worse. Leaning close to Azernal, he whispered nervously, "Is Martok losing control of the empire?"

"Not yet," Azernal said in a conspiratorial tone. "But he's definitely in for a fight. And having Worf as a member of his House isn't doing him a lot of good right now."

"Should we consider recalling Worf?"

Azernal grinned. "No! He might not be doing Martok much good, but he's the best resource we've had on Qo'noS in thirty years." He motioned for another shot and chuckled. "The fact that he drives Kopek absolutely crazy is just a bonus."

Chapter 14
U.S.S. Enterprise-E

PEART'S JOINTS made cracking sounds as he eased himself off of the biobed. Rolling his neck, he paid attention to the popping release of every vertebra. He let go of a tired gasp and rubbed his eyes with one hand. Dr. Tropp had patched him up in record time, and then told him to clear out of sickbay to make room for people who needed the bed more urgently. The deputy chief of security looked around for his shoes.

The door swished open. Perim hurried in, scanned the room until she found Peart, then walked directly to his side.

He caught her in a tight embrace. She kissed the side of his neck. The silken texture of her hair against his fingers was a comfort to him. Pressing her forehead against his, she closed her eyes. Listening to her, he realized how rapidly he was breathing. He focused on the rhythm of her respiration, and slowed his own breathing until it fell into tempo with hers.

Peart opened his eyes to see her looking back at him.

She didn't speak. Somehow they both sensed that they were beyond small talk. Some threshold of intimacy had been crossed that made it no longer necessary to fill every silence.

Finally, he said in a somber tone, "I got a lot of good people killed today." Her palm softly brushed his cheek. Self-loathing and shame welled up inside him like a dark fountain. "I might as well have painted bull's-eyes on them." Bitter tears stung his eyes. "They trusted me."

Perim gently stroked her fingertips through the brush-cut hair over his ear. "What did Vale say?"

"She told Picard I was following her orders," he said. "Then she put me back on the *Enterprise*."

"You *were* following her orders, weren't you?"

"She told me to pick a target," he said. "I picked one. I wrote the attack plan."

Perim sounded like she was desperately fishing for a way to salve his conscience. "But she approved it?"

He wasn't letting himself off the hook so easily. "Yeah, but I gave the order to go through the door."

She sat down on the biobed and gently pulled him back down next to her. Placing her arm across his shoulders, she said, "You knew it could end badly when you went in."

"I know."

Reaching over with her other hand, she interlocked her fingers with his. "And you've been sent through doors by people who knew it might get you killed. It's part of the job."

"Listen to you," he said. "The Starfleet apologist."

She sighed. "I'm not trying to give you a pep talk,"

she said. "I'm still serious about wanting out. I'd leave tomorrow. I'd leave today. But I don't want you blaming yourself for a mission that went wrong."

He got up, grabbed his uniform jacket from the foot of the bed, and walked toward the door. "There's no one else to blame," he said. He heard her follow him into the corridor.

"You had your orders," she said, walking behind him. "You went in there with them. And you almost died with them."

He quickened his pace toward the turbolift. "It doesn't change anything."

She matched him step for step. "Name one thing you'd do differently. One thing."

That demand lingered in his thoughts as he pressed the turbolift call button. Replaying the botched mission in the theater of his memory, he honestly couldn't think of anything specific that, if altered, would have yielded a less disastrous outcome. "I don't know," he said. "I wouldn't mind completely altering Starfleet's tactical protocols for urban combat."

"Okay," the slender Trill woman said. "How?"

Several possibilities occurred to him. "Send in non-sentient robotic probes to search the buildings before committing live personnel. Pacify threat personnel with sleep-gas grenades. Better yet, just bombard suspicious structures from orbit with wide-dispersal, heavy-stun phaser blasts." The turbolift doors opened. The pair stepped inside. "Deck six, section four," he said to the computer. With a muted throb, the turbolift shot up, then across as it circuited the primary hull.

Perim leaned against the wall and looked at him. "Would any of those have made a difference?"

"Maybe," he said. "Probably. It doesn't matter. What's done is done." The turbolift doors hissed open. Peart stepped off and turned left toward his quarters. Perim stayed close behind him.

They walked together in silence to his door. He placed his hand over the scanner. The door unlocked and slid open. On the threshold, he turned back to face her. "I've had a long day," he said. "I need to sleep." Judging from the disappointed look that swept across Perim's face, he knew that she understood that he'd meant he needed to sleep alone.

She looked at the floor. "You scared me today." Lifting her eyes to meet his, she added, "I thought I'd lost you."

He took her hand and leaned close to her. Pressing his cheek against hers, he whispered, "That'll never happen. I promise." Breathing in the faint, sweet scent of her hair, he kissed her tenderly on her cheek.

With tears brimming beneath the closed lids of her eyes, she turned her head and kissed him passionately. He hadn't sensed this level of intensity from her before. It was new.

Several seconds later the kiss melted away, but its power lingered between their parted lips like a magnetic force. He opened his eyes first. Her face—delicate and pale and framed by angular brown speckles of melanin from her temples to her collar—looked angelic.

Then she opened her eyes and said, "I love you, Jim."

It was the first time he had ever heard those words.

Perim stood in front of him, waiting for him to speak. She had the demeanor of a person who had just lost her grip on the edge of a cliff and wondered if the person standing on the ledge above would reach down, take her hand, and save her.

More than anything he had ever wanted before in his life, he wanted to be her savior on the ledge.

"I love you, too, Kell."

She shared a bittersweet smile with him, kissed him again, and bade him good night. He leaned against his doorjamb and watched her walk away down the corridor.

After he'd pulled off his uniform and crawled into bed, he realized that for the past ten minutes, all he'd been able to think about was the sound of Kell's voice, the fragrance of her hair, the shape of every mesmerizing cocoa-colored marking on her skin, the grace with which she walked. . . .

Then he remembered the smell of smoke and the gruesome cries of the men and women who had followed him to their deaths.

There was no justice in it. No balance, no logic, no sense of fairness. More than a hundred Starfleet personnel, all with families and friends and bright futures . . . all of them gone, just like that. *And here I am,* Peart lamented, *the guy who got them killed, and I'm up here falling in love.*

Thinking about Kell eased his grief for a moment. Then he wondered about the people who had died in Odina-Keh this evening. *How many of them had someone at home who made them feel the way Kell makes me feel? How many were waiting until they came home to tell someone that they loved them? How many had kids?*

The questions spun like a tempest in his thoughts. He lay sleepless, alone in the darkness and plagued by guilt for having been spared the consequences of his own mistake when so many others had paid for it with their lives.

Bombastic and atonal, Klingon opera for Troi conjured mental pictures of large, ferocious beasts that were trapped in the vast machinery of something that was equal parts pipe organ and metal refinery. *Kahless and Molor,* a classic of the genre if ever there was one, had the added thrill of real battle sounds intermingled with the dueling singers' guttural crescendos.

She hadn't enjoyed it the one time, years ago, when Worf had played it for her, and she didn't like it any better now.

General Minza, for his part, seemed to hate it even more. The last few notes of its prelude lingered, a groaning dirge that faded into silence. Troi knew what was coming, and braced herself by clenching her jaw and closing her eyes before it struck. Then, after a fourteen-second rest, the nerve-rattling, simultaneous crashes of a giant cymbal and a gong shocked the Tezwan prisoner halfway out of his bunk.

Minza tossed aside his blanket and stumbled forward, toward the forcefield. His cell grew brighter. He shivered and his breath huffed in wispy clouds before him. The temperature on his side of the invisible energy barrier was currently at the coldest point in its cycle.

Standing on an angle, his graying feathers crumpled and ruffled, he peered out into the darkness toward Troi. Thirty-two hours had elapsed since his capture. His curiosity and his irritation were unfiltered now. Sleep-cycle interruption was wearing down his temper, if nothing else.

He shouted hoarsely, "Who are you?"

Troi debated whether to grant him a response just yet.

"Why don't you show yourself?"

She lingered in the shadows and allowed the general's tide of emotions to wash over her. She sensed that though he was tired and disheveled, he was merely pretending to be shaken up. Certainly, he was agitated, but he also was looking for any sign of weakness, for a chance to strike back. He was frustrated but not afraid. At his core, he remained aggressive and dangerous.

"Why don't you say something?"

Troi deactivated her padd. "What do you want me to say?"

The statement seemed to catch him off-guard. After nearly thirty hours of people and machines incessantly projecting sound *at* him, he was taken aback by the sound of someone speaking *to* him. Apparently, he had sought a response without really considering what it was he wanted to discuss.

"Who are you?"

Troi stood and walked to the pool of light in front of his cell. Meeting his stare with her own icy gaze, she said, "Troi."

Minza loomed above her. Like most of his species, he was very tall when compared with the majority of humanoids. Troi's own petite form accentuated the difference. His condescension would have been palpable even to a non-empath. "Am I supposed to be afraid of you?"

"No," she said.

"Then why are you here?"

She smirked knowingly. "Why are you?"

The general gave a short laugh, two hard chortling sounds in quick succession. "Because no plan is perfect."

He's getting comfortable, she noticed. "So you attribute your capture and imprisonment to bad luck?"

"Among other factors." His eyes traveled around the edge of the cell's buzzing forcefield perimeter.

"So you don't think that you made a tactical blunder?" His eyes immediately snapped back to meet hers. Troi took some small measure of satisfaction in the ire her comment provoked.

"I don't make blunders," he said. "I don't know how your people found me, but I'm guessing it was some fancy piece of technology."

"Perhaps," Troi said. "It doesn't change the fact that you're here. Or that your only hope of avoiding execution is to cooperate with us."

"Ah, yes, that empty threat," he said smugly. Turning away from Troi, he paced in the tight confines of his cell. "I'm to tell you how to achieve all your objectives in a masterstroke, or else you'll extradite me—deliver me into the hands of my enemies." He sat down on his bunk with a grunt. "I'm a soldier. I've expected to die by the sword every day of my adult life. It didn't frighten me then, and it still doesn't."

Troi narrowed her eyes as she focused all her attention on the ragged Tezwan officer. "What has Kinchawn ever done to earn such loyalty from you?"

"He's my prime minister," Minza said. "I'm loyal to the office, not the man."

"Apparently not," Troi said. "Or else your loyalty to

him would have ended when he abdicated his office and went into exile. Bilok is the prime minister now."

"Bilok is a *Gatni* impostor," Minza said, raising his voice. "Prime Minister Kinchawn ordered a tactical withdrawal when our defenses fell. Establishing a government in exile is a legitimate strategy when one's territory is occupied."

"Your planet isn't occupied," Troi said.

"Ten thousand Starfleet personnel and eighty thousand Federation 'advisors' isn't an occupation?" He waved away her retort before she could speak. "Oh, I'm sorry, of course—it's a 'relief effort.' "

"We're here at the invitation of your government."

"Not our *legitimate* government," Minza said. "Just because Bilok and his *Gatni* traitors sign treaties with our conquerors to make their administration feel like less of a fraud, that doesn't make their actions legal."

"So your struggle is against the Federation."

"Obviously," Minza said.

"Then how do you explain the dozens of indiscriminate attacks on Tezwan civilians your forces have launched?"

"Collaborators are fair targets."

Troi used her padd to trigger a holographic projection inside Minza's cell. The two-dimensional image showed a tangle of Tezwan children, their bodies broken and scorched. Some of them were missing limbs. One had been all but decapitated.

"These don't look like collaborators to me," she said.

"What kind of propaganda is this?"

"Your guerrillas attacked a Federation relief station in Savola-Cov while it was dispensing food and medicine to *trinae* orphans. Seven children were killed, more than forty were wounded."

"Unfortunate," Minza said. "But the station was an obvious target."

"Your troops weren't aiming at the relief station," Troi said. She showed him another image, one of graphic carnage in the street outside the Starfleet-issue temporary structure. "They fired specifically on the *trinae* civilians. The Federation personnel at the scene received only minor injuries."

Minza eyed the image suspiciously but said nothing.

"I think you're actually engaged in a program of ethnic genocide," Troi said. "You're using the presence of the Federation as a convenient excuse to make war against your own people." She turned off the holographic projection. "Does that sound about right?"

"I'm a patriot," Minza said. "A loyal citizen of Tezwa."

Troi kept her voice detached and clinical, but still infused it with a pointedly accusatory tone. "Do patriots undermine their own legitimately recognized government? Do good citizens slaughter children?" Feeling his anger rising, she added, "Do good soldiers follow leaders who've gone mad?"

"Kinchawn isn't mad!"

And the documented Tezwan reverence for authority figures is confirmed, Troi mused. She had studied Tezwan psychology texts for much of the past month, in order to better understand this isolated species. General Minza, apparently, fit the Tezwan cultural archetype of the "loyal vassal." Troi refocused her goading efforts and continued.

"He thought he could challenge the Klingon Empire

and the Federation with two dozen starships and a network of artillery, both of which my shipmates neutralized in a matter of hours. Does that strike you as the calculation of a reasonable leader?"

Minza's bony fingers curled into gnarled fists. "You don't know even half the truth, little woman." His temper smoldered brightly now, but his demeanor remained composed. "It would be simpler for you to think him insane, wouldn't it? Easier to brand him a madman than to consider what might make him think he had the advantage."

No sooner had the words passed from his lips than Troi sensed that he was hiding dark secrets behind his stony façade. She couldn't be certain what he was concealing. Tactical plans? Information about the origin of Tezwa's artillery? Or something even more insidious?

Then he smiled patronizingly at her. His sadistic streak flared brightly to her empathic senses. Without meaning to, she imagined Minza as Will Riker's captor . . . inquisitor . . . *torturer.*

It was only her intuition, but it felt horrifyingly true.

Troi suddenly felt as though she were watching herself from a distance. She canceled Minza's scheduled visitors and changed the length of the temperature cycle inside his cell to ten minutes; six times an hour he would go from roasting to freezing and back again. Next, she increased the brightness of his cell's illumination to two hundred percent of normal. Then she triggered overlapping playbacks of *Kahless and Molor,* Data's most recent performance of *The Mikado,* and Wagner's *Ring* cycle.

The glare was blinding, the din was awful, and she could only imagine the misery of being in a room that swung hot and cold like a thermal pendulum. She wished it could be worse.

Minza shook his head and stared hatefully at her. "I bet you think you're clever," he shouted over the noise. "You think you can break me with your little games." He sat down, folded his arms behind his head, and relaxed against the wall. After a coarse laugh, he said, "If this is your worst . . . I pity you."

Each letter that Picard had written tonight had begun the same way—a brief salutation followed by a boiler-plate expression of condolence: *Please accept my deepest sympathies for your loss.*

In all the missives, he had tried to recount specific details of the deceased, attributes that had distinguished them from their peers. But their service records were often bare of such personifying details. Many had been only just starting their careers. The majority of tonight's letters were addressed to the next of kin of the Special Ops personnel who had been slain in Odina-Keh. Picard had never met most of them.

He reached for his cup of Earl Grey, but he could tell from the chill of its porcelain handle that the tea inside had gone cold, just like the two cupfuls before it this evening.

On his monitor was the list of names for which he still needed to draft condolence letters. Next to every name was a face, all strangers to him. He questioned his ability to write a convincingly heartfelt letter about someone he'd never known, but delegating the task was a luxury he did not want to grant himself. Looking at their images on his screen, he realized that it was his responsibility—

his duty—to acknowledge each of their deaths, one by one. *I owe them no less than that,* he decided.

The door chime to his ready room sounded. Glancing at the clock, he saw that it was almost 0100. *Who would be here at this hour?* Lowering his monitor screen, he said, "Come."

Lieutenant Jim Peart took a few hesitant steps into the ready room and stopped just inside the door. "Sorry to bother you so late, Captain."

"It's no bother, Lieutenant." Picard gestured to the chairs in front of his desk. "Come in. Sit down."

"Thank you, sir." The door hissed closed behind the deputy chief of security as he crossed the room and sat down.

"What's on your mind, Lieutenant?"

"Yesterday's mission," Peart said, reminding Picard that the ship's chronometer had officially marked the change of the day. Forty-one of the seventy-two hours of grace that Admiral Janeway had extended to Picard's search for Commander Riker had passed, and Riker's safe return seemed no closer than before.

"A tragedy," Picard said. Peart nodded. "So many good people, lost in an instant. A commander's worst nightmare."

"Yes, sir."

Picard recognized the tortured look in the younger man's eyes. He had seen it himself, in the mirror, far too many times.

"You blame yourself," Picard said.

"It was my plan, sir," Peart said, staring at the desktop. "I picked the target and the tactics. I led them inside."

Picard sensed that Peart had suffered more than physical injuries at Odina-Keh. Clearly, his confidence as a leader had been critically wounded, as well.

"Part of the reason for the chain of command is to make certain that responsibility falls where it belongs," Picard said. Peart looked up at him. "Lieutenant Vale approved your attack plan. She, in turn, was following orders I had given." Picard sighed heavily as he recalled missions gone fatally awry. "Losing people in the line of duty is always hard. But to lose them like this, en masse . . . it's a very different thing."

Sadness darkened Peart's face. His voice sounded distant. "Yeah," he said. "I imagine what I could've done differently. Ask myself if I should've seen it coming."

"Those are normal responses," Picard said.

"I guess guilt's a fairly predictable response, too."

Picard nodded. "Yes, but in time you learn to accept what you cannot change. And you go on."

"I just don't know how to put something like this behind me," Peart said. "How am I supposed to get over this?"

"In some ways . . . you won't. And you shouldn't."

Peart's hopeful look diminished slightly. "I see."

"I'd be lying if I said that time would eventually wipe this from your memory," Picard said. "We all have moments in our lives that shape us, define us—like the tempering of a blade. But whether you bend or break . . . that's up to you."

Chapter 15
Tezwa

"OKAY, TAURIK," La Forge said with a weary cynicism. "You brought me all the way down here. What am I looking at?"

"In approximately eleven seconds, I will show you," said the slim, archly calm assistant chief engineer.

The two engineers stood together on a high catwalk in an abandoned warehouse. Located on the outskirts of Arbosa-Lo, the vast industrial building was dusty and barren. Dreary gray daylight barely penetrated the grime-encrusted skylight windows that lined the corrugated metal roof. The building's foundation was dotted with holes that once had been used to anchor enormous machines.

Much of La Forge's body still ached from the pulverizing effects of his entombment in the *Deelatava*'s collapse. Taurik had woken him less than three hours after he had gone to bed. Speaking over the com, the Vulcan had said simply, *"I have something of interest to show you."* When pressed to elaborate, he had declined to offer details. Since Taurik didn't make a habit of being either cryptic or mysterious, La Forge concluded that the man must have a reason for imposing such strict secrecy.

But all La Forge saw right now was an empty warehouse.

Then the cavernous room flooded with a rainbow of light and a synthetically melodic ringing. It was a transporter effect on a grand scale, covering almost the entire floor of the building. La Forge shielded his eyes from the prismatic flare.

It faded to reveal a massive mountain of muddy silt and rock. Heliophobic crustaceans scuttled over rocks and burrowed into the wet sand. Judging from the fact that the newly arrived dirt filled the warehouse to within a few meters below the catwalk on which he and Taurik stood, La Forge estimated that it was nearly thirty meters deep.

He looked at Taurik. "That's a whole lotta dirt."

The Vulcan engineer handed a padd to La Forge. "It is a targeted retrieval of the Nokalana seabed, centered on the approximate coordinates at which Lieutenant Vale reported the discovery of a chimerium component."

"Hang on," La Forge said. "Chimerium can't be transported."

"That is not strictly correct," Taurik said. "One cannot maintain a direct transporter lock on a chimerium object. However, if one targets an area, a chimerium component within that area can be beamed in tandem with other matter, provided one is not concerned about introducing quantum errors into any organic material caught in the beam."

La Forge reviewed the information on the padd.

"I won't even ask how much power it took to get this

done," he said. "That's a lot to sift through. What are the odds we'll find the piece we're looking for?"

"Approximately ninety-six point seven percent."

"Okay," La Forge said. Now he understood why Taurik had been so cagey in his message. If they found the chimerium iris from the imploded underwater base, they would have evidence linking Tezwa's cannons to a source in the Federation. If, as Taurik had speculated to him a few days earlier, the analysis of the data files he captured on Tezwa was being suppressed, then there might be elements working against them within the Federation itself. La Forge's own suspicion of the irrational work orders issued by Starfleet Operations to the S.C.E. only made Taurik's suggestion seem more plausible. Even if they were both wrong, he had no doubt that if Kinchawn knew about this clandestine project, he would send his Loyalists to destroy it.

La Forge said, "How many people know this is here?"

"The two of us, and Transporter Chief T'Bonz."

"Keep this strictly need-to-know," La Forge said. "Get Veldon, Porter, Wolfe, and Linder. Nobody else."

"What about a security detail?"

"No, they'll just draw attention," La Forge said. "Work fast. And let me know the *second* you find something."

Chapter 16
An Undisclosed Location

"THAT'S ALL OF THEM," Dietz said. L'Haan stood behind him and studied the wall display, which showed images of five Federation freighters. Next to each one was a bulleted list of data: meeting times, rendezvous coordinates, and the serial numbers of the cargo units that the *Caedera* had transferred to them.

L'Haan said, "What is the *Caedera*'s current position?"

"En route to Ajilon Prime."

Dietz turned slightly to catch a glimpse of her. Bathed in the pale glow of the display screen, her alabaster skin took on the cerulean hues of an Andorian, and her sable hair shimmered with midnight blue highlights. The imperious Vulcan woman glanced back at him, prompting him to avert his adoring gaze.

"Has M'Rill obtained the beam-down coordinates that Captain Trenigar provided to the freighter commanders?"

"Not yet," he said. "But the fifth ship made orbit four hours ago. The cargo's probably already been delivered."

"Almost certainly," L'Haan said. The door opened behind her and Zeitsev hurried in. "Instruct M'Rill to acquire the final transport coordinates," she continued. "We need to—"

Zeitsev's rough-edged growl of a voice interrupted her: "We have bigger problems."

The slightly built, intense-looking man stepped between them, reached past Dietz, and switched the source feeds on the main display. Surveillance images and short loops of crudely recorded video blinked in and out of several adjacent sectors of the screen, almost too quickly for Dietz to follow.

"Activity at the *Ilanatava* went through the roof about three and a half hours ago," Zeitsev said. "Deputy PM Tawnakel woke up Bilok in the middle of the night and convened a senior-level meeting. They've got couriers and cutouts flying all over the planet." A worried scowl added even more lines to his already creased visage. "Something's going wrong down there."

Yeah, that *would be a change,* Dietz thought sarcastically.

L'Haan cocked one eyebrow at the turn of events. "Has Bilok sought aid or counsel from Starfleet?"

"No," Zeitsev said. "In fact, they're going out of their way not to say anything. There's been almost no signal traffic out of the *Ilanatava*."

"Mr. Dietz," L'Haan said. "What conclusion do you draw from this new information?"

For a moment, Dietz was shocked silent that she had asked his opinion in front of Zeitsev. He was a relatively junior member of the organization, and his input was rarely solicited.

"The Tezwans are scrambling to contain a crisis they don't want Starfleet to know about," he said, making certain to phrase it as a declaration of fact rather than an interrogative plea for approval. "Given the timing, the most probable scenario is that Kinchawn's people have intercepted a shipment meant for Bilok, thereby placing Bilok and his allies in grave danger."

"That would be my conclusion as well," she said. "Regardless of how Kinchawn first attempts to leverage his new advantage, his only hope of avoiding retaliation by either the Federation or the Klingon Empire will be to pit the two powers against one another."

Zeitsev shook his head in dismay. "I don't know who deserves more blame for bungling this," he muttered angrily. "Azernal for thinking it up, Quafina for using mobsters as middlemen, or Bilok for trusting any of them."

"Blame is irrelevant," L'Haan said. "This may be our only opportunity to intervene before Kinchawn plunges us into war." She turned to Dietz. Her orders were crisp and quickly spoken. "Forward M'Rill's reports as a priority intelligence briefing to Lieutenant Commander Data on the *Enterprise*. Then order M'Rill to neutralize the *Caedera* crew and ensure its capture."

Zeitsev sounded disappointed. "You aren't serious." He pressed his fingers to his forehead. "Exposing Azernal's scheme to Starfleet? Isn't that what we've been trying to avoid?"

"It is likely they are beginning to suspect the nature of the conspiracy," L'Haan said. "This will simply . . . nudge them in the proper direction—to confirm their theories."

"What if they go public? The Klingon Empire would declare war ten minutes later."

"Azernal's a priori decision not to involve Starfleet was the correct choice," she said. "But now the matter is a fait accompli. What has been done cannot be undone. Under the circumstances, I believe Azernal has underestimated Captain Picard's sense of discretion."

Zeitsev looked unswayed by her reasoning. "Do you really think the way to keep this contained is to reveal the truth to *more* people?"

"If they are the right people, yes," L'Haan said. "Rational minds must be given an opportunity to develop an informed strategy on Tezwa. If Kinchawn alone is permitted to set the agenda, then all is lost."

His face drawn and dour, Zeitsev groused, "And if Picard's conscience gets the better of him?"

"He is not a fool, Zeitsev," she said. "And he will follow the chain of command, as long as he considers its actions to be just." She delicately touched Dietz's shoulder. "Tell Admiral Ross I wish to speak with him."

Chapter 17
U.S.S. Enterprise-E

DESPITE THE MADDENING NOISE, fluctuating temperatures, and blinding glare, Minza sat peacefully on his bunk.

The illumination in his cell was so intense that even through his closed eyelids it was white like desert sunlight.

All at once the deafening music stopped, and the lights dimmed. A cooling draft dispelled the soporific effects of the heat that had just swelled a few minutes ago. He opened his eyes. Troi stood on the other side of the forcefield, watching him with an admirable level of clinical detachment. She hadn't moved since the last time he'd been able to see her.

"A shame," Minza said, his voice rasping from his dry throat. "One of those songs was just getting to a good part."

The replicator slot hummed with activity. Seconds later he smelled the tantalizing aroma of spiced *kessal* meat in a salty broth. He gave Troi credit for being a relentless temptress. With great effort he leaned forward, then pushed himself back to his feet. A few stiff-legged steps later, he stood in front of the replicator nook and picked up the bowl of stew.

Troi flinched as he flung it against the forcefield, which crackled loudly and evaporated most of the liquid. Chunks of meat plopped to the floor alongside the clattering empty bowl.

The general stared at Troi with tired disdain. "What do you really hope to accomplish here?"

"Whatever I can, in our limited time together," she said.

He poked the forcefield and chuckled at the sharp jolt of electric shock that coursed up his arm. "That won't be much."

"It might be enough," she said.

"Just tell me what you want, so I can refuse you and be done with this futile game of yours."

She folded her arms across her chest. "Lieutenant Vale already told you what we want, and what we're willing to offer."

He grunted derisively. "Betray everything I fought my whole life to defend, so that I can rot in a cell instead of meeting the clean, decisive end a soldier deserves." Shaking his head, he added, "You're wasting your time."

Troi remained quiet for several seconds. Then she said, "Why did Kinchawn think he could challenge the Federation?"

"Because you're weak," Minza said. "Your government doesn't have the resolve to maintain this kind of occupation. When the bodies start to pile up, you'll cut and run."

She smiled poisonously. "You're a terrible liar, General." Her expression grew malevolent. "Try telling me the truth."

David Mack

Minza reassessed the petite woman: *Not so gullible after all. I wonder how much she really knows?*

"The truth?" he said. "If you insist. . . . In the course of pursuing its own sovereign interests, Tezwa challenged the Klingon Empire for control of QiV'ol. For some reason, the Federation decided to get involved in our dispute. Now your people swarm like vermin onto my planet."

Troi fixed him with a dark, piercing stare that left him feeling, if only for a moment, utterly dismantled. "That's part of the truth," she said. "But it's not all of it."

Does she know? Or is she misdirecting me, pretending to know more than she does to trick me into admitting something?

"The guns," she said. "Kinchawn's great secret. The military conspired with him in their construction." Minza became increasingly concerned when she said, "You know where the guns came from. You know how Kinchawn smuggled them onto Tezwa. You've been involved from the very beginning."

She talks a good game. But so far it's just talk.

"Yes," he said, weighing his words carefully. "I supervised the building of the guns. I know all about them." Then he turned the burden of explanation onto Troi: "Do you?"

"Starfleet hardware," she said. "Starfleet software. Components too advanced to have possibly been manufactured on your planet. . . . I know more than you think."

"I just built what I was told to build," he said with a dismissive shrug. "Logistics . . . procurement . . . those weren't my responsibilities. If you expect me to tell you where the parts and the programming came from, too bad. I can't."

"Yes you can," she said simply. "I know you can." There was a certainty in her tone that dismayed him. She added, "As I said before, General . . . you're a terrible liar."

So she knows I'm holding out on her, he realized. *Probably another one of their technological tricks, some kind of high-tech lie detector. No matter.*

"Very well, I admit it," he said. "I know exactly where all the pieces came from. I could expose secrets that would shake your Federation to the core and set it on the path to its destruction." He sat down on his bunk and mimicked her folded-arms gesture. "But I won't." He smirked. "How badly do you want the information that I possess? Enough to beat it from me? Or torture me? Enough to set aside your principles and use a truth serum, or a memory-sifting device?"

She glared at him, her fury and frustration well masked but still palpable.

He laughed arrogantly. "This is why you're going to lose."

"All stations secure from red alert," Data said, ending the night's battle drill shortly before 0200 hours.

He closed the intraship com and turned toward Lieutenant Wriede at tactical. "Efficiency rating, Mr. Wriede?"

"Ninety-six percent, sir," Wriede said. "Would you like to run another drill? No one will expect two in a row."

"That will not be necessary, Lieutenant," Data said. Then he noticed the sly grins passing between Le Roy at ops and Magner at the helm. Apparently, either Wriede's inquiry or Data's answer had amused them. He surmised that the slender tactical officer had been speaking facetiously when he proposed repeating the drill. Humor and sarcasm had become more difficult for Data to appreciate since the loss of his emotion chip.

The bridge murmured with the low hum of the environmental system and soft, synthetic bleeps from various consoles. Going over the previous shift's fuel-consumption reports on a padd, Data noticed a sudden increase in power usage. Tracing it to its source, he pinpointed a sudden, massive allocation of energy to the transporter system. Several secondary systems had been taken offline for just under three minutes to compensate.

He got up from the captain's chair and moved to an unoccupied duty station along the bridge's aft wall. Working quietly, he cross-referenced all onboard activities from the time of the power surge and quickly ascertained that it had been orchestrated by Assistant Chief Engineer Taurik. Chief Engineer La Forge had subsequently classified Taurik's orders.

"Data to La Forge."

"La Forge here."

"Please meet me in the observation lounge immediately."

Sounding apprehensive, La Forge replied, *"On my way."*

Data blanked the information from the console and turned back toward the rest of the bridge. "Mr. Wriede," he said. "You have the conn. I will return shortly."

"Aye, sir," Wriede said. The tall, dark-haired tactical officer moved in long strides to the center seat and sat down.

Data exited the bridge through the door to the observation lounge. There he waited silently for La Forge to arrive.

Four minutes and thirty-eight-point-six seconds later, the tired-looking chief engineer entered the observation lounge through the corridor entrance. "What's going on, Data?"

"I have noticed an anomalous pattern of energy usage by the *Enterprise* transporter system," Data said. "It appears to have been executed by Lieutenant Taurik and retroactively approved by you. Have you recently authorized such an action?"

La Forge inhaled sharply and tensed at the question. He acknowledged Data's question with a grudging nod. "Yeah," he said. "I did."

"What was the nature of this activity, and what was its purpose?"

Rubbing his palms together pensively, La Forge said, "I need to ask you not to file a report on this yet."

Data was confused by La Forge's evasiveness. "On what?"

"Taurik had an idea," La Forge said. "He moved a huge chunk of the Nokalana seabed, near where Vale says she found the chimerium vent iris. I've got some people digging through it."

"Attempting to find the missing component?"

"Exactly," La Forge said.

Data tilted his head as he considered this development. "An interesting initiative," he said. "However, protocol requires that such actions be approved by—"

"I know," La Forge interrupted. "Taurik violated procedure. But I agree with his reasons for doing so."

"What are his reasons?"

The chief engineer sighed heavily. "He and I both feel like we're getting the runaround from Starfleet. The S.C.E.'s getting work orders that don't make any sense, and no one at Starfleet Intelligence knows anything about the files we sent them for analysis."

"Starfleet Intelligence is often reluctant to share its findings," Data said. "And disagreeing with the priority of the engineering assignments you receive is hardly evidence of obstructionist intent on the part of Starfleet."

"It's part of a larger picture, Data." La Forge was becoming increasingly agitated. "You interfaced directly with the Tezwans' artillery system. You know exactly what its inner workings were like. So why won't Starfleet accept a download from your memory unit to confirm your findings?"

Data pondered several reasons for Starfleet's reluctance to accept his memory data as evidence. All of them returned to a single root cause: After the Rashanar incident, Starfleet had been reluctant to consider him reliable or credible. Though he knew their fears regarding his emotion chip were baseless, he had acquiesced to their order that he relinquish it.

In answer to La Forge's question, he said, "It is . . . complicated."

"Maybe," La Forge said. "Maybe not. What I'm worried about is Starfleet stepping in and cutting us out of the loop again. I get the sense that there are questions that someone high up doesn't want us to ask, things they don't want us to find here."

"Geordi . . . are you proceeding from a . . . 'gut feeling'?"

"Maybe. But Taurik's a Vulcan—and he arrived at all

the same conclusions strictly through logical reasoning." La Forge shrugged his hands up and apart in a supplicative gesture. "I'm asking for a day to do this search in secret. That's all."

The overhead com gave out a chirp, which was followed by Wriede's voice. *"Bridge to Lieutenant Commander Data. You have a priority signal from Starfleet Intelligence, sir."*

"Acknowledged," Data said. "I will be there in a moment. Data out." Turning back to La Forge, he said, "I will need to inform the captain of your search for the chimerium component. However, I will recommend that he honor your request for discretion."

"Thanks, Data."

He nodded to La Forge, then turned and walked out the forward door back to the bridge. Wriede swiveled the chair, noted Data's return, and moved back to the tactical station. Data sat down in the captain's chair and said to Wriede, "Put the message through to my screen, Lieutenant."

"Aye, sir," Wriede answered as he tapped the command into his console. The Starfleet Intelligence daily briefing appeared on Data's command display.

Immediately, he noticed unusual discrepancies between the report on his screen and every other SI briefing he had received for the past thirty days. The first variance of note was that it had arrived three hours and forty-eight minutes earlier than normal. Second, it had not been approved by Commander Vitale, the chief station officer for this sector. Third, it had been sent to Data personally, rather than sent out as a bulletin.

Suspicious as those details were, it had arrived on the

correct frequency and had used the proper encryption. As he scrolled swiftly through its contents, they revealed a series of events that, if true, would be extremely serious. The *Caedera,* a merchantman suspected of being used for smuggling by the Orion Syndicate, was alleged to have intercepted five Federation freighters en route to Tezwa. At those rendezvous, the *Caedera* had transferred four cargo containers, contents unknown, onto each freighter. There was significant reason to believe the containers held contraband that was being smuggled onto Tezwa.

Data rose from his seat and moved to the aft science console. For discretion and expediency, he used the manual interface rather than direct the computer by voice command. Cross-referencing the confidential report's account of the *Caedera's* meetings with the five freighters, he entered their rendezvous times and coordinates into the Starfleet Perimeter Defense Network. One by one, each midflight interception was confirmed by long-range scans. Within seconds, Data corroborated each scan with sensor logs from the Xarantine Stellar Array, the Poloma III observatory, and the officially filed flight plans for the five freighters in question.

He checked the Tezwa traffic-control system. Four of the five freighters were still soliciting outgoing shipments.

The *Venezia,* a *Paris*-class freighter, had just requested clearance to break orbit.

Data spun away from the console and marched back to the center seat. "Mr. Wriede, put a tractor beam on the freighter *Venezia.* Do not let it leave orbit."

"Aye, sir," Wriede said as he snapped into action.

Vibrations from the impulse engines surged through the deck as Magner maneuvered the ship to give Wriede a clear shot.

"Hail the *Amargosa, Republic,* and *Musashi.*"

Wriede punched a key. "Hailing," he said. He added a moment later, "We've got the *Venezia.*"

The main viewer switched over to a triply split screen showing Captain Craig Engler of the *Amargosa;* the *Republic*'s first officer, Commander Carlos Carranza; and the commanding officer of the *Musashi,* Captain Alex Terapane. Data skipped the customary salutations.

"This is a priority-one directive," he said. "Impound the following four vessels in orbit over Tezwa: the *Toronto, Madrid, Cyprus,* and *Damascus.* Take their crews into custody, and secure their communication, sensor, and transport logs." All three commanders acknowledged the order and signed off. Data returned to the center seat. "Mr. Wriede, have Lieutenant Peart assemble a boarding party in transporter room one."

Chapter 18
Freighter Venezia

ROUSED FROM a deep but troubled slumber, Peart had barely been able to keep his eyes open while he stood on the transporter pad with the rest of the boarding party. His phaser rifle had weighed heavily in his hands. He'd felt almost like a shade of himself, a faint tracing, an empty shell.

Then the transporter effect faded. He was wide awake as his feet settled onto the deck of the *Venezia* bridge.

Hefting his weapon to his shoulder, he sprang into action. "Get down!" he shouted at the captain, a middle-aged Tellarite man. "Down on the deck! Now! Hands behind your head!" The portly captain dropped to the deck at his feet. On either side of him, his pilot and first officer were pinned to the deck by Starfleet security personnel.

"Second squad, secure the bridge," Peart said. He moved quickly out the aft door into the corridor beyond.

He heard the heavy footfalls of the boarding party's first squad following him. He tapped his combadge. "Peart to Cruzen, status."

"Engineering secured," Cruzen said. *"Squad four's heading up to the cargo bay."*

"Acknowledged. First squad's on its way to crew quarters."

At the deck-one ladder, Peart let th'Chun and Parminder descend first and move into covering positions. He slung his rifle and climbed down to deck two. As soon as the rest of first squad regrouped behind him, he took point and moved into the main berthing area. Most of the bunk compartments were empty. *Makes sense,* Peart thought. *They probably had all hands on duty while they were shipping out.*

One crew member was fast asleep in his bunk as Peart and th'Chun opened his door. They pointed their rifles inside. The red-skinned man winced as the light from the corridor hit his eyes. He blinked once. Then he reached for a small phaser on the floor next to his shoes.

Peart and th'Chun fired in unison. Twin beams of blinding blue energy slammed the gaunt, ruddy-skinned man against the bulkhead. They ceased fire. "Get his weapon," Peart said to th'Chun. Turning to Parminder, he said, "Go aft and secure sickbay. Take Liryn and Melo."

A low hum filled the room as th'Chun secured a pair of magnetic manacles on the stunned freighter crewman.

"Cruzen to Peart."

"Go ahead."

"*Cargo bay secure,*" she said.

"How many prisoners, total?"

"*Three engineers,*" Cruzen said. "*One cargo chief, and one mechanic.*"

"Nice work," Peart said. "Peart to Parminder: Report."

He moved back into the corridor while he waited for an answer. A moment later, Parminder responded, "*Sickbay secure. One prisoner, a medic.*"

"Acknowledged," he said. "Peart to T'Sona. Do you have the crew roster yet?"

"*Affirmative,*" the Vulcan woman said. "*Captain Teg has been most cooperative.*"

"What's the complement?"

"*Including himself, nine personnel.*"

"Okay, good," Peart said. "We got everybody. Get the prisoners ready for transport, then have all squads regroup in the cargo bay."

"*Acknowledged. T'Sona out.*"

Peart waited for the channel to clear, then tapped his combadge again. "Peart to *Enterprise*. Target secured. Prepare to receive prisoners, and send over a forensic engineering team, on the double."

"We've almost got it," La Forge said. "Just another minute."

Peart stood in the cramped, sloppily maintained bridge and watched La Forge and Scholz work. The engineers didn't look like they were doing much of anything, but Peart knew that reconstructing deleted transport logs and decrypting communication files was a delicate task. Rather than loom over them and add pressure to their already difficult jobs, he stepped away and tapped his combadge.

"Peart to *Enterprise*."

"*This is* Enterprise," Data replied. "*Go ahead.*"

"We'll have information for you shortly. Can you update me on the status of the other impounded ships?"

"*Affirmative,*" Data said. "*All four have been seized and boarded. Their crews are currently being held aboard the* Amargosa *and the* Musashi. *They will be transferred to the* Enterprise *within the hour.*"

"Were their ships' onboard logs also deleted?"

"*Yes. Recovery efforts are in progress aboard all four vessels.*"

La Forge said to Peart, "We got it. Transmitting now."

"Stand by, *Enterprise*," Peart said. "We're sending over the *Venezia*'s logs."

"*Acknowledged,*" Data said. "*We are receiving the signal.*"

Peart walked back to stand next to La Forge and Scholz. He looked at the information on La Forge's tricorder screen.

If the logs La Forge had retrieved were accurate, the *Venezia* crew had beamed down to Tezwa four containers filled with components that would be integral to the construction of massive directed-energy weapons—devices powerful enough to pose a serious risk to starships in orbit.

"That's not good," Peart said.

"No," La Forge said, watching the same screen. "It isn't."

"Peart to *Enterprise*. I think we'd better wake up the captain and alert Lieutenant Vale."

"I have already done so, Lieutenant," Data said. *"Please report to the* Enterprise *bridge immediately—and bring Commander La Forge with you."*

Chapter 19
Tezwa

CHRISTINE VALE MATERIALIZED in the eastern rotunda of the *Ilanatava*, courtesy of the *Enterprise* transporter system. When she'd heard Data's report of the contraband that had already reached the surface of Tezwa, she had requested immediate site-to-site transport, to the Starfleet Security Command Center in the Tezwan capital building. Because the facility was heavily shielded, she'd had to settle for beaming in to one of the *Ilanatava's* outer ring of domed halls.

She sprinted across its polished marble floors toward the central atrium, which reached up toward the highest levels of the *Ilanatava*, where the Assembly Forum was located. Her running footsteps echoed loudly in the predawn silence of the cavernous space. Whipping around a hairpin turn, she scrambled down the wide stairwell that led to the subterranean command center.

She reached the bottom of the stairs. The six Starfleet guards who were posted at the command center's entrance had, as a precaution, moved behind portable blast barriers and readied their weapons. *Good,* Vale thought. *At least they aren't getting lazy.* "It's me," she called out.

The guards held their fire as she moved to the biometric scanner and let it verify her retinal pattern and DNA signature. *"Identity confirmed,"* it said. *"Please state clearance code."*

"Vale Tango Seven Nine Sierra Foxtrot."

A high-pitched beep and a muffled hiss indicated that the door's multiple safeguard locks had been released. She stepped forward. It swished open, then closed behind her as she entered the bustling room. Overlapping reports intensified the already charged atmosphere. The hundred-plus security specialists currently on duty buzzed around Lieutenant Gracin, whom Vale had appointed the third-shift supervisor for security operations on Tezwa. He looked relieved to see her arriving early to resume command.

"Talk to me," she said, joining him in the center command post, which was elevated slightly above the rest of the room.

"We're getting steady reports from upstairs," he said, using the security team's shorthand jargon for the four Starfleet vessels in orbit. "They just sent down the fifth freighter's set of unauthorized transport coordinates."

Gesturing at the activity on the tactical monitors, she asked, "Who's in motion?"

"Five squads of ours, plus some Tezwan personnel," he said. He pointed in quick succession at different monitors along the wall: "Aboard the runabouts *Ohio, Tunguska, Roanoke, Thames,* and *Cumberland.*"

Vale nodded. "Good. Show me what we have from upstairs."

Gracin handed her a padd. "Looks like someone plans to build more big guns on Tezwa," he said cynically.

She skimmed the reports, then shook her head. "Not on our watch," she said. As she took stock of the components that had been beamed down, she became even more confused. "There's barely enough here to make one or two key pieces of a nadion-pulse cannon," she said. "And some of these components aren't even part of the design."

"Maybe they're building something else," Gracin said.

Before she could dissect the report any further, Ensign Grigsby called out from the monitor station. *"Roanoke's* touching down," she said. "Squad three's moving into the target."

Vale put down the padd. "Gracin, tell the folks upstairs we need fire support on standby, then get everything we've got ready to move. If something shakes loose, I want to hit it before it hits us."

Fiona McEwan took a deep, calming breath. The Runabout *Tunguska* banked into a steep, diving turn toward the city of Anara-Zel.

Squad leader Scott Fillion sat beside her, looking either annoyed or bored, depending upon how the muted afternoon light hit him. Seated on the opposite side of the runabout was Tenila. The gangly, orange-plumed Tezwan woman and her detail of Tezwan peace officers were accompanying Fillion's team on this search for smuggled weapon materials. The two squads sat together in the narrow center compartment of the small craft.

The *Tunguska* leveled out, then finished its descent with a sudden vertical drop. Its side door slid open with a deep rumble, revealing the expansive roof of a squat building.

Fillion was the first one out the door. He gave a sharp, loud whistle and a sweep of his arm to order the deployment. "Let's go!"

McEwan was the second one on the roof, followed by Tenila, then the rest of their mixed unit. Together, they sprinted across the tar-papered roof, moving between ventilation pipes spewing steam, and bulbous shells that contained spinning air-intake fans. The whine of machinery and the hiss of steam drowned out the dull roar of the desolate, blast-torn city that sprawled around them on every side.

A single phaser blast was all it took to open the locked door to the building's main stairwell. Fillion led the way into the building, his eyes locked on his tricorder as they wound their way down the wide switchback staircase.

"Beaming in would have been easier," McEwan complained.

"Sensor screen in the basement," Fillion said. "Cheer up. It's only five flights."

At least we're going down *the stairs,* McEwan consoled herself. The clatter of footsteps echoed and re-echoed in the space between the two sides of the stairwell.

Four flights later, Fillion held up a closed fist. The group behind him halted. Tenila, who had fallen back to the middle of the group, passed on the signal to those who were too far back to have a direct line of sight to Fillion.

"Movement," Fillion said. "Comin' right at—"

A shrieking blast of charged plasma from the floor below his feet cut him off.

The first two shots missed him by centimeters. He pressed himself against the wall. McEwan fired back through the steps. Several more rounds of plasma bolts burst up through the stairs and killed Ensign McPherson behind her. Two stray shots hit Lieutenant Witmer, nearly severing his left arm; another shot vaporized the knee of a female Tezwan officer named Yenliya. She and Witmer collapsed in agony against each other.

For the next several seconds, it seemed that everyone was firing at the steps, drowning out Fillion's orders to hold their fire and fall back. Moments later the stairs collapsed into splinters under their feet, and half the search team plunged wildly into the midst of their civilian-garbed attackers.

McEwan plummeted through the furious crisscross of plasma bolts, hit the ground with her knees slightly bent, and rolled into the fall. The nimble redhead came up shooting, her weapon set for wide-field maximum stun. Her first shot knocked three Tezwan men onto their backs in a crimson flash.

Behind her, Fillion shouted, "Down!"

She hit the deck and covered her head with one arm.

The high-frequency whine of his sustained phaser blast tore around the darkened room in an unbroken line. She heard the heavy thuds of bodies being hurled backward onto the dusty, bare concrete floor. Feeling the firm clasp of his hand on her shoulder, she got up. "More hostiles," Fillion said, pointing toward a corner that led to a narrow hallway. "Take cover."

"There is no cover," she pointed out.

The sound of hushed Tezwan voices drew closer. "Hang on," he whispered, adjusting his tricorder. "I've got an idea."

Looking around, she realized that the two of them were the only members of the squad in the basement who were still standing. Witmer and Yenliya either had been knocked unconscious by the fall or had slipped into shock from their wounds. She had seen Cobbins land on her feet only a couple of meters away from Fillion, but now the wiry young woman with the wide smile lay dead, with a smoking plasma scorch where her upper torso had been.

Above them, Tenila crouched on the edge of the smoldering staircase, her rifle aimed at the basement hallway. The rest of the team had fallen back; only Tenila had stayed in position to try and offer additional covering fire to Fillion and McEwan.

With nowhere to hide, McEwan crawled under one of the stunned Tezwan attackers, set herself in a prone firing position, and waited for a clean shot to present itself.

On the edge of her vision, she noticed Fillion aiming his phaser rifle directly at a wall—in the opposite direction of the approaching enemy personnel. As he adjusted his aim, he watched his tricorder display. He fired a single, deafening shot that was as bright as sunlight. From somewhere else in the building's sprawling basement came a muffled explosion.

The odor of smoke and burnt polymers reached McEwan's nose. She heard a group of Tezwans murmuring just beyond the corner pictured in her holographic targeting sight. She hoped to at least put up a good fight, limited as she was to heavy stun while her foes shot to kill.

Then came the singsong whine of several transporter beams in the hallway, accompanied by a luminous glow. Before the first transporter effect had faded, another began in the room around McEwan. Twelve humanoid and Vulcanoid figures took shape, all of them wearing Starfleet uniforms. At the front of the group was Security Chief Vale, who emerged from the radiant halo of light. Pointing at Witmer and Yenliya, she said, "Get them to sickbay."

Then she noticed McEwan and Fillion.

Vale asked, "Who fragged the sensor screen generator?"

"That would be me," Fillion said, raising his hand.

With a nod, Vale said, "Nice work. We beamed the hostiles to the brig." Noticing Cobbins's body, she added more grimly, "Let's go find out why these bastards shot at us."

"It's not great Italian, but it's all they had programmed into the *Tsavo*'s replicator," Hughes said as he walked into the triage office. He carried a tray on which were two identical plates of watery-looking lasagna and two glasses of synthehol-based red wine. An unusual-looking piece of the local flora was nestled between the plates as a makeshift centerpiece.

Crusher looked up from her padd. She sat behind the triage desk, catching up on her paperwork now that she and Hughes had finished treating the trauma patients and discharged the less serious cases with instructions for follow-up care.

She picked up the lone utensil next to her plate of lasagna. "A spoon?"

"It's practically soup," Hughes said, poking his lasagna. "I can get you a fork, but I think the spoon'll work better."

Scooping up a spoonful of the loose, steaming casserole, Crusher grinned. "I see your point."

They ate for a minute without talking. Hughes washed down a mouthful of food with a generous swig of syntheholic wine. "You know," he said with a sideways nod, "aside from the weird texture and the bland flavor, it's not too bad."

Crusher swallowed a sip of her wine. "Don't be so hard on yourself," she said. "Whatever shortcomings the meal might have are more than offset by the shortcomings of the wine."

She glanced up at the same moment he looked over at her. The grin tugging at the corners of his mouth widened. He chuckled self-consciously. Then she laughed, and within moments they chortled together over what she was certain had to be one of the worst-tasting replicated lasagnas in history.

The laughs abated quickly, and left behind a tense, clumsy silence. He shook his head at the sorry-looking dinner that lay on the table between them. "Okay, this didn't work out as well as I'd hoped." With a sheepish grin, he added, "Sorry."

"Don't be," she said. "It's the most romantic thing anyone's done for me in years."

Oh my God, her inner voice cried. *Did I say that out loud?*

"I find that hard to believe," Hughes said, his tone one of admiration.

She put down her spoon. "I wish I could say the same."

Hughes put down his spoon and waited for her to continue.

"You don't mean to let years slip away from you," she said, making a leap of faith in trusting him with her confidences. "They just . . . pass you by." She picked up her wine but didn't bother to take a sip. "People you thought would be waiting in the wings . . . opportunities you always figured would be there when you were ready for them . . . aren't."

Leaning back in her seat, she slumped with exhaustion—not just from the long day in the oppressive, carbolic atmosphere of the hospital, but from long years of fruitless waiting. "So you learn to take comfort in your routines, in your job, in your friends. After a while, you begin to think maybe it's enough. . . . Then, one day, you realize it isn't. But by then, of course, it's too late."

Please don't let him say something awkward, she prayed.

He pushed aside his own plate of lasagna. "I wasn't really hungry for dinner, anyway," he said, rising from his chair. Then he smiled and held out his hand toward her. "Want to go to the runabout and check the dessert menu instead?"

Taking his hand, she said, "Absolutely." As they walked together out the sliding doors to the terrace and turned toward the landing pad, she said, "Normally, I'd never skip straight to dessert . . . but I think it'll be okay just this once."

"I don't know what the hell to make of this," La Forge said.

He dropped his gravitic calipers back in his portable toolkit and stepped back from the massive machines. Vale stood clear of his team of engineers, who swarmed over the equipment the security personnel had discovered after securing this ramshackle building only minutes ago.

Harsh floodlights had been set up around the perimeter of the room, which buzzed and whistled with the sounds of numerous high-tech devices operating in synchronicity.

"Geordi," Vale said, "tell me anything about it. I lost two people finding this; I can't file a report to the captain that says 'mysterious thing found on Tezwa.' He'd have my head."

"I can tell you what all the pieces are," La Forge said. "What I can't figure out is why someone would put them all in the same device."

"For example . . . ?"

He pointed at a large, angular component. "Take this. Standard-issue Starfleet plasma distribution manifold, right?" He shook his head. "Wrong. We don't use kerrium alloy in our casings." La Forge summoned Lieutenant T'Eama with a wave and said to her, "Brief Lieutenant Vale on what you found."

The Vulcan woman turned and addressed Vale with precise diction. "The force coupler matches all Starfleet specifications except for the composition of its emitter. Its crystal lattice is inconsistent with Federation design."

Vale asked, "Whose design *is* it consistent with?"

"The Tholians," La Forge said. "At least, that's what someone wants us to think."

"Wait a minute," Vale said. "Are you saying that the Tholians made this stuff? Or that someone else wants it to *look like* the Tholians made this stuff?"

"Jury's still out," La Forge said. "But I'm leaning toward calling it a frame-up, based on this." He gestured to Morello and Heaton. The two engineers carefully removed a large panel from the manifold's outer shell, revealing a complex maze of pulsing circuits within. La Forge reached inside the radiantly warm device and removed an isolinear chip. He handed it to Vale. "That's no imitation," he said. "It's the genuine article, right down to its Starfleet nanomarkers." Pointing at Rao, he said, "Open that crate."

Vale looked up from the chip in her hand as the swarthy engineer pried open the lid of a small, metal box. Inside the container was an assortment of circuitry, optronic cables, and various small devices.

"It's an adapter kit," La Forge explained. "Tholian parts, complete with a manual on how to remove the Starfleet systems and replace them with that pile of junk."

"An instruction manual?" Vale's brow furrowed with concern. "In what format?"

"UFP standard data packet—on a padd," La Forge said.

"In what language?"

"Seshto," the chief engineer said.

Vale sighed grimly. "Tezwa's most popular language." She raised one eyebrow with her dubious sidelong glance. "I don't suppose there were any original Tholian-language instructions on the padd they might have translated from?"

La Forge shook his head slowly, his demeanor somber.

She motioned to him to follow her to a spot where they could talk privately. He walked behind her, away from the busy team of engineers, who scanned, measured, and recorded every tiny detail they could detect.

"This could be the file-decryption fiasco all over again," Vale said quietly. "If we alert Starfleet before we know for certain what we've got—"

"I'm with you," La Forge whispered. "We have to play our cards close. For now, we tell only Data and the captain."

"Agreed," she said. "Let me ask you something: Everything we saw during the strike missions—Starfleet software in the Tezwan firebases, the chimerium iris I found, the files Taurik recovered—think it has anything to do with this?"

"I don't know," he said. "But I'd say it's possible."

"Say it *is* connected," she said. "Speaking hypothetically, what would that mean? What would be the logical conclusion?"

La Forge hadn't served with Vale for quite so long as he had with the other senior officers of the *Enterprise,* but he knew her well enough to realize that she rarely posed questions such as this unless she had already formed an opinion. Under the circumstances, he was afraid she might be speculating the same horrible scenario that had just occurred to him.

"If that's the case," he said, "we're in deeper shit than we thought."

She nodded gravely. "That's what I'm afraid of."

"We have a new problem," Tawnakel said.

The crowd of Tezwan ministers assembled around Bilok fell silent. The prime minister could sense the seriousness of his deputy's mood, and curtly said to the room, "Everyone else out."

His visitors departed in a flutter of robes and a shuffle of hurried footsteps. The door closed heavily behind them, leaving Tezwa's two senior elected officials alone.

Bilok tensed as he asked, "What's happened?"

"We've lost another shipment," Tawnakel said.

"Kinchawn's people again?"

"It was—until Starfleet intercepted *them.*"

"Starfleet?" A pained grunt issued from a deep, tired place inside Bilok's aged chest. "How?" Before Tawnakel could speak, he continued, "No, it doesn't matter. At least tell me we'd finished retrofitting whatever they found."

"I don't think we did," Tawnakel said. "But that's not the worst of it. They recovered the bodies of six of our people, including Teelom."

"He was on the civil payroll," Bilok said, horrified. "If they learn who he is—"

"They'll link him back to us within hours."

Anxiety-fueled nausea churned in Bilok's stomach. He bolted up from his desk and tried to walk it off. His panicked pulse throbbed in his jugular. Moving in long strides, he marched toward the balcony door. It opened automatically at his approach; its polarized glass panels parted to reveal the dawn horizon, which stretched before him, red-streaked and hopeless.

The morning air felt thick. He couldn't pull it into his lungs without effort. "Stall them," he said, then gasped slightly. "Shut down the central database. Call it maintenance."

"That won't get us more than a few hours," Tawnakel said.

Bilok nodded quickly. "It'll be enough. He's dead, so we know he won't confess. Rewrite enough of his life history to make him look like a traitor." Noticing Tawnakel's disapproving look, he said, "You have a better idea?"

Tawnakel frowned, but swallowed whatever protest he had been harboring. "Anything that makes Starfleet look at us, even tangentially, could be dangerous," he said.

"Yes," Bilok said. "They'll want to review any com logs that might connect Teelom to this office. How soon can we hit the remaining com relays?"

"A few hours," Tawnakel said. "We should hit the one in Alkam-Zar first. It's the main backup when other sites fail."

"Get it done. And tell your people subtlety won't be a virtue on this mission."

Without further discussion, Tawnakel turned and left Bilok's office. The prime minister stood alone, high above the capital city, and surveyed the world that he'd just led to the edge of annihilation. The next few hours would tell whether he was capable of pulling it back from the brink, or if it would slip from his grasp and into ruin.

* * *

General Erokene Yaelon had run out of excuses and delaying tactics. Now he was left staring into the face of man who he truly believed had, at some point in the recent past, gone mad.

"I'm waiting for an answer, General," Kinchawn said. "Are we ready to strike or not?"

"Our forces are in position," Yaelon said. "I'm still reviewing recon reports on Starfleet's recent deployments."

"A waste of time," Kinchawn said. "The longer we wait, the greater the risk that Starfleet will locate this base. We need to attack while we still have the advantage."

"Several of the battle plans you've approved were created by General Minza," Yaelon said. "If he's revealed any of those plans to Starfleet—"

"Absurd," Kinchawn said, dismissing Yaelon's theory with a roll of his eyes. "The Federation couldn't break the will of a child. Their pathetic laws practically make it a crime to use harsh language. Minza will tell them nothing."

"They won't have custody of him forever," Yaelon said. "Once he's extradited back to Keelee-Kee—"

"I know," Kinchawn said. "All the more reason to strike now, before the *Gatni* inquisitors beat the truth from him. Besides, if we wait much longer, Starfleet will dismantle every com relay on the planet. We need to capture and defend at least one, before Bilok silences our world to please the Federation."

"That will be difficult, sir," Yaelon said. "My troops are already deployed. I don't have time to pull anyone back for a hold-and-secure operation."

"Make the time. Without those relays we'll be cut off from the rest of the galaxy."

Yaelon considered which relay stations would be most vulnerable, then ruled them out in favor of sites that would be more defensible once captured. "The com station at Alkam-Zar is our best option," he said. "If you're willing to forgo a strike against that city's Federation engineering office."

"Very well," Kinchawn said. "When can we strike?"

Yaelon knew better than to admit that he simply didn't want to launch the attack. If he did, Kinchawn would have him killed and another officer would take his place.

"I can be ready to attack in six hours," Yaelon said.

Kinchawn replied, "You'll go in three hours. Start with the *Ilanatava*." A moment later he added, "And kill Riker."

"Yes, Mr. Prime Minister."

Knowing that further debate would be futile, Yaelon turned and left Kinchawn's office. On the other side of the door was a sprawling underground space packed with troops and weapons. All the self-exiled military personnel who now called themselves "Loyalists" had abandoned their uniforms for ordinary clothes. Their weapons of choice were small and easily concealed. The plan in most cases was for them to blend into the civilian population until the appointed time for the attack.

He didn't want to unleash this army of disguised assassins on the people of Tezwa. If the mission profile had been limited to surgical strikes against Starfleet personnel, he might not have ever questioned his loyalty to Kinchawn. Even declaring the Federation relief workers as targets had not broken his resolve; he found attacking noncombatants to be craven, but against such a technologically superior foe, and one with such vast numbers, the only way to wage war effectively was through asymmetrical guerrilla tactics. If that's what it took, he could accept it.

But Kinchawn's orders had also specified intentional collateral damage—targeted strikes against civilian facilities and residential structures in *trinae*-dominated areas. Reading those orders, Yaelon had known that this was no longer a fight for liberation—if, in fact, it had ever been one. This was a crude excuse to commit ethnic genocide against the *trinae*.

Cultural friction between the *trinae* and *elininae* had spiked since the *Lacaami* rose to power. Hatred had metastasized not just within the Assembly but into the roots of Tezwan society. Regions of the planet had split along ethnic lines.

It hadn't always been that way; when Yaelon had been a young man, the future had promised peace, unity, prosperity. He thought that he had seen the beginning of the end of this kind of tribal xenophobia. He recalled the day his fellow officers had learned his daughter had married a *trinae* man. More than one of them had asked, "What do they plan to call the children?"

For years he had savored the looks on their faces when he had answered, simply and honestly, "Tezwans."

Yaelon's children and their spouses didn't make Kinchawn threaten a Klingon colony without provocation. The general's grandchildren weren't responsible for the prime minister's decision to launch a sneak attack that killed six thousand Klingon warriors and brought a Starfleet invasion.

But they all had paid for Kinchawn's actions with

their lives. All of Yaelon's heirs were gone now, squandered by Kinchawn in the name of perpetual war.

Now the general was powerless to stop Kinchawn from robbing more innocent families of their kin, helpless to prevent himself from being the unwilling tool of such carnage.

If only I could get a message out, he lamented. But he knew that was hopeless; all communications since Minza's capture were being done face-to-face, or via couriers. Kinchawn had been adamant that no transmitters be used that could betray their location to the enemy, not even hard-line systems. Sending a warning to Starfleet about the impending attack would be all but impossible—if not tantamount to suicide.

Yaelon prayed to the Maker of All Things to forgive him, and knew that he would spend eternity haunted by sorrow-songs of the lives that were about to be snuffed out on his orders.

Chapter 20
U.S.S. Enterprise-E

TROI SENSED just enough psychic aura from Minza to know that he was still awake. He had ceased responding emotionally to the petty torments she had unleashed upon him. Severe swings of temperature, an earsplitting cacophony of clashing musical selections, and a blinding glare—he had tuned them all out. Oblivious and silent, he lay on his bunk, calmly defiant in repose.

She tapped a few commands into her padd and terminated the program of calculated harassment. Inside Minza's cell, the illumination dimmed back to normal levels, the music ceased, and the temperature normalized. Several seconds later he opened his eyes and sat up. He smirked at Troi. "You're still here," he said. "Have you been standing all this time?"

Now it was Troi's turn not to answer questions.

"Take a lesson from me," he continued. "Some things in life you shouldn't take lying down. This? Not one of those things."

In the absence of any strong emotion from Minza, Troi felt her own anger and disgust welling up to fill the void.

"I'm tired," he said. "Aren't you tired?"

Troi shrugged.

He grinned. "I can't tell you how amusing it is to me to sit here and listen to you pass judgment on my career," he said. "I've lived my life by a code. I know who my enemies are, what my people expect of me. Then you come along and expect me to feel ashamed of doing my duty." He looked at the empty replicator nook. "I still won't eat your food," he said, looking back at Troi. "But could I get some water?"

She entered the command on her padd. A short, thick-sided glass materialized in a swirl of atoms. Minza picked it up, took a large swig, and spat it out. A glaze of rage washed over his face as he doubled over, coughing and spluttering. Wiping his mouth with the matted feathers of his forearm, he laughed. "Hot water," he said, tossing the rest of the glass's contents on the floor. "Nice to know you have a sense of humor." He put the empty glass back in the nook. It vanished with a wash of sound, reabsorbed by the matter reclamator.

The captive general sat back down on his bunk. He regarded Troi with a weary but defiant demeanor. His voice was low and gruff. "I presume you're familiar with Federation history?"

She nodded.

"Imagine this scenario," he said. "Your long-ago border dispute with the Gorn, on Cestus III: How would the Federation have reacted if the Metrons had sided with the Gorn? What if, within hours of your first battle with the Gorn, every Federation world had been occupied by the Metrons?"

"It's an inappropriate analogy," Troi said. "The Federation wouldn't have launched a sneak attack to start the conflict."

"Think of the Organia incident," he continued. "What if, instead of disabling both sides' weapons, the Organians had sided with the Klingons, blown up your starships, deposed your government, and installed rulers of their choosing? Would you have called that justice?"

"I'm flattered you would compare us with the Organians," she said, in a haughty tone intended to irk him.

"Be obtuse if you like—it makes no difference," Minza said. "But I'm surprised that someone who likes asking questions as much as you do isn't asking the *right* questions."

"Why don't you tell me what they are?"

He studied her with the cold gaze of a predator. "Start with this," he said. "Why did the Federation get involved in our dispute with the Klingons?"

"Your world is located on the border between the Klingon Empire and the Federation," she said. "A major conflict on our border might have posed a threat to—"

"Wrong," Minza said, cutting her off. "Next question: Why is President Zife expending resources to rebuild Tezwa when so many Federation worlds need assistance?"

She didn't like the tone of his questions, but she decided to play along, in case his ramblings led to some kind of insight about him. "The Federation has a long history of humanitarian—"

"Wrong again," he said. Troi found his interruptions

almost as annoying as his smug overconfidence. "Zero for two," he continued. "You're not doing so well. Are you ready to hear the last question you should be asking?"

"By all means," she said.

"Here it is," he said. "When will Kinchawn execute Commander William Riker?"

At the mention of Riker's name, the last vestiges of Troi's clinical detachment crumbled. Her face stiffened into a furious, murderous glare. Her own seething emotions—hatred, rage, fear—were so intense that she couldn't have detected even the strongest base emotions from Minza or anyone else. Her mind was aflame with thoughts of all the hideous, excruciating ways she wished to extract from Minza the location of her *Imzadi*.

The counselor's voice was quiet and rich with implied violence. "Tell me where he is."

Minza laughed cruelly, his smiling mouth contrasting with his feathery and maliciously bunched-together eyebrows.

"That's not a question, madam," he said. "That's a demand. And it sounds a lot like the beginning of a negotiation."

"No bargains," she said softly. "Tell me where he is."

"If you refuse to discuss terms, I don't see why I should."

Troi said nothing. Her fury was overpowering her thoughts. She imagined leaving Minza alone for a while with some Starfleet Special Ops personnel. Or replicating a dangerous truth serum that had been proved to work, but only by inflicting severe pain and causing debilitating permanent brain damage.

He seemed to know, perhaps from experience, what she was thinking. With a taunting inflection, he said, "I suppose you could force the information from me . . . if you wanted it badly enough. Such technological wonders your Federation has. There must be some device, some drug, that could break my will."

She knew that such things existed. Staring into his blunt, compassionless face, she wished she could try them all, one after another, and erase his impudent smirk.

The com chirped to herald an incoming message. *"Data to Commander Troi."* At Troi's request, Data knew not to call her by her professional title while she was interrogating Minza. She had thought it best to give Minza as few details as possible about her personal life or the nature of her work.

"Go ahead," Troi said.

"The Tezwan Minister of Justice has arrived to extradite General Minza. Her paperwork appears to be in order."

"Understood. Troi out."

Minza took a deep breath. His thin outline of a smile grew wider and deepened the craggy lines of his cheeks. "A shame," he said, mocking her with his obvious insincerity. "We were finally getting to know one another."

Captain Picard stood slightly removed from the chaos in the starboard brig while Lieutenant Peart tried to rein in the prisoners, who were engaged in a frenzy of finger-pointing. The arrested freighter personnel hadn't been cooperative at the outset, naturally. Most had seemed either smugly overconfident in their ability to navigate the loopholes of the Federation's criminal-justice system, or deathly afraid of crossing their partners in crime. Then Picard had explained to them that the items they had smuggled onto Tezwa were, in fact, weapon components—and that they were all facing charges of treason and espionage against the Federation.

At that point the problem was no longer getting any of the prisoners to confess, but getting them to confess one at a time rather than all at once like a pack of jabbering monkeys.

After several minutes, Peart shouted them into submission.

"We'll go in order of arrest," Peart said. "Captain Teg: What's your story—quickly, please."

"The Orion Syndicate told to meet one of its vessels and let its crew beam cargo onto my ship," the nervous Tellarite said. "I was given a time and a set of coordinates for the rendezvous, and was told I'd be well paid for my cooperation."

Picard interjected, "The ship you were told to meet was the *Caedera,* correct?"

"Yes," Teg said. "Commanded by Captain Trenigar."

On the periphery of his vision, Picard noticed Peart tapping Trenigar's name into a padd. *No doubt checking for outstanding warrants,* the captain reasoned. To Teg he said, "What happened after you met the *Caedera?*"

"They beamed over their cargo," he said. "Then I and my first officer went aboard the *Caedera* and picked up our money. That's when Trenigar gave us the beam-down coordinates for the final delivery on Tezwa."

"So far, so good," Peart said. "Who told you to make the rendezvous? Who organized this?"

Teg seemed to blanch at the question. He withdrew slightly from the two officers, shrinking like a hermit crab from the touch of a predator. "I don't know," he said, in one of the least believable-sounding prevarications Picard had ever heard. "He—or she—scrambled the audio signal. I never saw a face."

Picard spoke calmly: "Then how did you know the order was genuine?" The new query only increased Teg's agitation.

Peart added his questions to Picard's. "Was there a code phrase? Some means of authenticating the transmission?" When it became clear that fear had rendered Teg mute, Peart addressed all the other prisoners instead. "By not speaking Captain Teg is guaranteed to be spending the rest of his life in prison. Would any of you like to answer his question and be eligible for parole someday?"

No one spoke for several seconds. Then one person broke ranks, his quiet voice easily piercing the wall of silence that stood in front of him. "It was Ihazs," the un-seen man said. The prisoners moved apart to reveal Captain Salah Hatrash.

Peart tapped the name "Ihazs" into his padd. Picard stepped toward Hatrash. "Can you tell us anything about Ihazs?"

"He runs Deneva," Hatrash said. "President Otamad likes to think she runs Deneva, but she doesn't have a fraction of the power he does. He *is* the Orion Syndicate on that planet."

Apprehensive glances were volleyed back and forth among the rest of the prisoners as Hatrash spoke. Picard sensed that his statements had the ring of truth to them. Then he glanced at Peart, who raised one eyebrow and nodded, verifying Hatrash's story. Picard turned his attention back to the captain.

"Do you have family who are in danger? Anyone who might need protective custody in order for you to testify?"

"No," he said. "But it wouldn't make any difference. The Syndicate would find them sooner or later. They always do."

Picard hoped that Hatrash was wrong about that.

Peart said to the prisoners, "Does anyone else have any information to share? Or is Captain Hatrash the only one not going to jail for the rest of his life?" The brig was a mural of empty stares and closed mouths. Peart gestured to a quartet of armed security guards. "Move Hatrash to the aft brig. I wouldn't want him to have any 'accidents' while waiting to testify."

As the guards escorted Hatrash from his cell, Picard turned to Peart. "Issue an arrest warrant for Captain Trenigar and the *Caedera*," he said. "Send the *Amargosa*, the *Musashi*, and the *Republic* to lead the search. I want that ship impounded immediately."

The com chirped. *"La Forge to Picard."*

"Go ahead."

"Captain, Lieutenant Vale and I have something we need to show you right away."

"What is it, Commander?"

"I'd rather not say over an open channel, sir."
Picard didn't like the sound of that. "I see."
"And sir? We'd better ask Ambassador Lagan to join us."

Troi turned at the sound of the brig door opening. Dasana, Tezwa's Minister of Justice, strode in. She was flanked by a pair of Tezwan peace officers, who were tall even for their species; they bracketed the slender, youthful-looking minister like a pair of comical bookends. Data walked in behind them. Dasana moved directly to Minza's cell, stopped in front of the forcefield, and lifted a small display device from her robes.

"Hello, Dasana," Minza said. "I'd heard you succeeded Unoro at Justice. Must have been easy with no opposition."

Dasana ignored Minza's remarks. "General Gyero Minza," she said, reading from the device in her hand, "you are hereby charged with the following high crimes against the people of Tezwa: treason, conspiracy to commit treason, premeditated murder, conspiracy to commit murder, acts of mass destruction, dereliction of duty, and desertion."

Dasana turned to Troi. "Commander Troi, in accordance with the order of Prime Minister Bilok, ratified by a lawful vote of the Assembly, and on behalf of the Ministry of Justice, I have presented to Federation Ambassador Lagan Serra and Starfleet Captain Jean-Luc Picard this order for General Minza's immediate extradition to Tezwa. Said order having been duly acknowledged by all parties, I hereby declare him a prisoner of Tezwa and demand the immediate transfer of custody."

"I'm not finished with him yet," Troi said sternly.

"That's not my concern," Dasana said. "Please release him to our custody."

"He has knowledge of the whereabouts of our missing officer, Commander William Riker."

Dasana's impatience was increasingly evident. "With all due respect, Commander, he's been in your custody for nearly thirty-eight hours. You've had enough time to ask your questions."

From the back of the room, Data said, "Counselor, the captain's orders are unambiguous. General Minza must be turned over to Tezwan authorities." After a moment, he added in the same neutral tone of voice, "That is an order."

Troi knew that Data did not need to wait for her to agree to the transfer of custody. As acting first officer, he had the authority to override her and issue the release directly. But he had learned enough about social graces to permit her to save face in front of subordinate personnel by letting her appear to have a say in the matter.

She looked at the serene face of General Minza. Surely he knew that he was being ushered off of the *Enterprise* to face an executioner. Regardless, his mood seemed to be that of a victor rather than one of a doomed man. *Nothing like the zeal of a true believer,* Troi concluded. Minza was her best—and possibly her only—hope of rescuing her *Imzadi*. But he had lived and now would die by a different moral code than the one she knew. Looking into his remorseless eyes, she was forced to concede that her efforts to bend or break his will, constrained as they were by the limits of her conscience and by the law, had been futile from the outset. *He told me about Will just to wound me,* she realized. *He's known who I am the entire time.*

She stepped away from the forcefield. "Take him."

Two Starfleet security guards lowered the forcefield.

The Tezwan peace officers pulled Minza's wrists behind his back and secured them with magnetic manacles. Without a word, they led him out of the brig at gunpoint. A detachment of Starfleet security guards met them at the door, then followed them away, down the corridor. Data nodded to Troi, then left the brig. Minister Dasana and Troi were the last two people in the room. Troi felt hope slipping away from her, and she trembled.

Dasana said, "He might not really know anything about your first officer. He's a skilled liar, after all."

"He knows," Troi said, her voice dark with bitterness. "I can tell. He knows."

Dasana nodded and tucked her display device back into the folds beneath her robe. "Perhaps," she said. "We will ask him again, on Tezwa. If he does know more than he's said, we will find out."

"How can you be so sure?"

"Our methods are not quite so . . . *benign* as yours," Dasana said ominously. "Had you rendered him to our custody when you first captured him, perhaps your missing officer would already have been found." She gave a small bow to Troi. "Good day, Commander." Dasana swept out of the brig in long, fluid strides.

The brig was dim and quiet. Troi drifted, numb and forlorn, into Minza's cell. The desiccated food was still strewn across the floor. The room stank of stale sweat.

She thought of all the horrors that the Tezwans likely had waiting for Minza on the planet's surface below. Drugs. Exquisite tortures. Threats so barbaric that no

Starfleet officer would even consider making them. And for a moment, Troi felt a cruel glee at the thought of Minza's suffering. The grieving, wounded part of her almost wished she could be there, to savor the sweet vengeance of watching the arrogant bastard crumble. . . .

No, she castigated herself. *That's not who I am. Only a sociopath takes pleasure in the pain of others.*

But her desperate wish for revenge kept asserting itself. It gnawed at her, like a hunger that could only grow until it was fed. She reminded herself of Nietzsche's famous warning: "If you gaze into the abyss, the abyss gazes also into you." Had she peered too deeply into the darkness of Minza's heart? In her fervor to ferret out his secrets, had she tainted her own soul with his cruelty, his fanaticism?

Sitting alone on the floor of the general's now vacated cell, she found no answers to her questions. The only truth that she knew was that she had just let her last chance to save Will Riker slip from her grasp. Her only remaining hope of rescuing her *Imzadi* was that crueler hands than her own would be able to find the truth in time.

Picard greeted Ambassador Lagan as she entered the observation lounge. "Thank you for coming, Madam Ambassador."

Lagan shook Picard's hand. "It was no trouble, Captain." She sat down at the conference table with Vale, La Forge, and Data. Dominating the tabletop was a large, irregularly shaped object covered by a blue sheet. Lagan and La Forge greeted each other with silent looks of shared pain. She only vaguely recalled the moments following the blast that leveled the *Deelatava,* but she remembered the doctors telling her that La Forge had saved her life by shielding her with his body.

Picard followed Lagan to the table and took his seat. Looking at La Forge, he said, "Commander, when you're ready."

The chief engineer stood up. "We've done some further analysis of the demolition orders given to the S.C.E. teams," he said. He activated the large wall monitor. It showed a map of the surface of Tezwa. Numerous locations were marked with red dots. A smaller number of blue dots were scattered among the major cities of the planet. "There's no longer any doubt in my mind that we're being directed to obliterate the planet's com logs. Essentially, we're being used to get rid of evidence."

Lagan replied, "Evidence of what, Commander?"

"I don't know," La Forge said. "That's why I need access to the relays' memory cores, so I can review the logs as far back as possible."

"I passed along your request to Prime Minister Bilok," Lagan said. "Unfortunately, he was not inclined to permit it."

Picard spoke up. "Ambassador, if the Tezwan government intends to obstruct our investigation, we will have no choice but to act without their consent."

Lagan didn't like the sound of that. "What kind of action are you planning, Captain?"

The captain gestured to Vale, who said, "We need to secure one of these data cores and send in some specialists to study its contents. We can be discreet if we have time to work. If we don't, we'll have to be brazen."

Damn these gung-ho Starfleet types, Lagan thought.

Always so quick to think the law doesn't apply to them.
"I presume you have more to go on than your educated guess about the Tezwans' motives," she said.

La Forge sat down. Vale stood up and moved in front of the wall monitor. She used her padd to switch it over to a security report. "These five freighters have been impounded and their crews placed under arrest," Vale said. "They met with an Orion Syndicate merchantman, whose captain paid them to smuggle contraband onto Tezwa." She pointed at the screen. "Searches at four of the five beam-down locations have yielded no evidence. However, at the fifth location, we found this." The security chief changed the screen to show a pair of large cargo containers filled with various devices that Lagan didn't recognize. "These components are identical to the ones used in Tezwa's nadion-pulse cannons, with one minor difference—they've been doctored with materials intended to make them seem to be of Tholian manufacture. The components found with the shipment also seem intended to suggest Tholian involvement, and were made to replace several pieces inside the primary device. Pieces that we've confirmed are of genuine Federation manufacture."

The dead-calm certitude of the woman's statement chilled Lagan. "Are you absolutely sure, Lieutenant?"

"I'm positive." Vale handed Lagan her padd. The ambassador reviewed Vale's report. It traced the nanomarker-identified components from their creation and assembly on Earth to their discovery hours ago on Tezwa.

Data stood up and took Vale's place in front of the wall screen. "There were numerous anomalies in the original report that alerted us to the freighters' smuggling," he said. "Although the report's information has proved completely accurate, the truth of its origin remains unknown. Furthermore, data files that were captured last month by Assistant Chief Engineer Taurik and sent to Starfleet Intelligence for priority analysis appear to have . . . vanished."

Lagan felt a terrible, inchoate dread at the tone of this meeting. She turned her chair back toward the table and pointed at the sheet-covered object. "What's that?"

Vale and La Forge exchanged looks, as if unsure who should do the honors. Finally, La Forge reached forward and pulled away the sheet. Resting uncovered now on the table was a bent, filthy piece of metal. Its interlocking curves and small moving parts were crusted with dirt. The four officers said nothing while Lagan eyed it. She looked at La Forge.

"I'll ask again. What's that?"

"It's a waste-exhaust iris," he said. "The outer layers are composed of material from the floor of the Nokalana Sea, and serve as camouflage. What's relevant is the metal inside: It's chimerium."

Lagan didn't need to be told the significance of that fact. Chimerium's status as a legally controlled material was even more strictly enforced than the purity of latinum. So far, it had been discovered on only one planet in all of known space, a world known as Sarindar, in the Nalori Republic. Thanks to a joint venture with the Nalori, the Federation had secured the exclusive right to remove the rare compound from Sarindar. To say the Federation had guarded its monopoly jealously would be a glaring understatement: Lives had been lost and taken to defend this strategically invaluable material.

"This was part of the Tezwans' underwater firebase," Vale said. "I first saw it when I was planting the demolition charges to flood the base. It sank when the base imploded."

"A few hours ago," La Forge said, picking up where Vale left off, "Lieutenant Taurik secretly recovered the component from the ocean floor. We've compared its design against known Federation components. It's an exact match."

As Data deactivated the wall screen, Picard said to Lagan, "I appreciate that our mission on this world is one of diplomacy rather than occupation, but if the Tezwans have participated in a conspiracy to steal Federation military technology, we must take appropriate steps to learn the truth."

"If Bilok sees this as an attack on Tezwan sovereignty, Kinchawn's guerrillas might not be the only ones shooting at us down there," Lagan said. Picard seemed unmoved by her warning.

"Be that as it may, our first duty is to the Federation," he said. "I need to know the truth."

Lagan eschewed the use of violence and subterfuge, but surviving the Cardassian occupation of Bajor had taught her that there were times when such tactics were both necessary and appropriate. "Secure the relays and seize the logs, Captain," she said. "And forward this to all S.C.E. personnel on Tezwa: All demolition orders are hereby suspended, on my authority."

Picard nodded to her. "Thank you, Madam Ambassador." He turned to Vale. "Escort Ambassador Lagan back to her office and start securing those sites." To La Forge he added, "Dismissed." He watched the two officers follow Ambassador Lagan out of the observation lounge. As the door closed behind them, he imagined what could have possessed the current Tezwan administration to collude in the destruction of its own subspace-communications infrastructure. Then he wondered how they would react when Lagan's cease-and-desist order was enacted and searches began.

He turned to Data. "Take the ship to yellow alert."

Chapter 21
Earth

SHOCKINGLY LOUD REPETITIVE BEEPING shrilled from the door chime on the other side of Nelino Quafina's private residence. Groggy and disoriented, the Antedean intelligence secretary rolled over in his bed. He blinked his bulbous eyes to clear away the glaze of sleep. It was just past 0345 local time.

A gurgling groan rattled inside his throat. His webbed feet hit the plush-carpeted floor as he awkwardly flung aside his bed covers. Plodding through the living room and into the foyer, he checked the security monitor screen. The seething face of Koll Azernal stared back at him like a demented gargoyle.

Quafina opened the door. Azernal pushed past him into the room. Beefy and broad-shouldered, the Zakdorn moved with the heavy, opaque manner of a man accustomed to getting his own way. "Shut the door," he said.

"Please, come in," Quafina said. He closed the door.

"Shut up, we've got a situation," Azernal said.

"No need to apologize for waking me," Quafina said.

"Picard just issued a general impound warrant for an Orion Syndicate merchantman called the *Caedera.*"

Quafina's eyes, which had been recessed into narrowly slitted boredom, now bulged as his attention became engaged. "The *Caedera?*"

"He seized contraband that they smuggled onto Tezwa. All three of his support ships left the system to hunt down the *Caedera,* and Ambassador Lagan just suspended the S.C.E.'s work orders on Tezwa. . . . Quafina, you miserable bastard, tell me you didn't use the Orion Syndicate to move our cargo to Tezwa."

"You wanted discretion," he said. "Criminals excel at being circumspect."

"No, they excel at being caught," Azernal said. "Don't tell me whether you hired that ship. But if you did, make it vanish before Starfleet finds it. And when I say vanish"—he punctuated his thought by jabbing his forefinger against Quafina's chest—"I mean *permanently.*"

Chapter 22
Merchantman Caedera

TRENIGAR CLOSED the subspace channel by punching his fist through his monitor screen. As he stormed out of the comforting swelter of his private quarters, his roar of fury echoed through the ship's ventilation ducts and reverberated into every last nook of the *Caedera*.

Sixteen years I spent making this the best ship in the Syndicate, he raged. *Now that* undari *Ihazs wants me to scrap my own ship because Starfleet issued an arrest warrant.*

He stomped down the narrow corridors, swatting aside unevenly stacked boxes that even slightly jutted into his path. Every few meters, another small crate of fruit or sealed provisions was scattered across the deck in front of him. His boots crushed everything with equal malice as he trod toward the null-gravity ladder tube.

It doesn't make sense, he fumed as he glided up the access ladder to the command deck. *We could just leave Federation space. Make our living in Klingon territory, or the Talarian Republic. Why junk my ship?* He considered becoming a rogue, defying even the Syndicate, going into business for himself.

Then he decided it would be faster and less painful to simply put a gun to his head. If Ihazs said to scrap the *Caedera,* then the discussion was over. *The Syndicate gives,* Trenigar groused, *and the Syndicate takes away. Unfortunately, it only "gives" about one time in four.*

Striding through the door to the bridge, he bellowed, "R'Lash, get us—" He stopped as he saw there was no one there. The captain's chair was empty. The helm was set to autopilot, on course for Ajilon Prime. The Nausicaan captain promised himself that First Officer R'Lash would get a worse-than-usual beating for deserting her post. He fell into his seat like a falling tree and stabbed the intraship com with two fingers.

"Trenigar to R'Lash and M'Rill. Get to the bridge, now."

A few moments later, M'Rill responded. *"Captain, there's something going on in the aft cargo bay,"* the Caitian pilot said. *"I think you need to come down here."*

"You don't tell me where to be, you fuzz-faced *lovaach,*" Trenigar hollered. "Get to the bridge! That's an order!"

"Captain, this is important. . . . R'Lash is meeting with Nolram, Tzazil, and Gorul. Zhod's guarding the entrance."

"What the hell are you—"

"Captain . . . I think they're planning a mutiny."

M'Rill lurked behind the corner closest to the aft cargo bay entrance. He heard the soft, approaching footsteps of Captain Trenigar. The hulking Nausicaan crept up behind him. M'Rill motioned to the captain to remain silent, then pointed around the corner. Trenigar edged past the Caitian pilot and noted the presence of the ship's Gorn enforcer outside the cargo bay door.

"They've been in there for nearly an hour," M'Rill whispered. "Saff went in about thirty minutes ago."

The captain eyed him suspiciously. "Why didn't they include you?"

"They did," M'Rill said. "R'Lash told me to guard the weapons locker. She wouldn't say why, but I think it's pretty obvious."

"If she doesn't trust you, why should I?"

"Because I'll kill Zhod," M'Rill said. "Once the door's clear, we can slip inside and put them back in line."

Trenigar grunted. "And what's in it for you?"

"I want to be first officer."

The captain nodded. "Done. Go kill Zhod."

M'Rill walked confidently around the corner and moved in a straight line for the Gorn. Zhod was normally stoic to the point of immobility, so M'Rill assumed the enforcer's lack of reaction to his approach wouldn't seem odd to the captain. Of course, in the shadows of the cargo deck, it was unlikely that Trenigar would be able to tell from several meters away that Zhod was already dead and had been propped against the wall with a rifle glued to his hand.

"The weapons locker is secured," M'Rill said to the glassy-eyed reptilian corpse. Then the Caitian lashed out and thrust his saw-toothed dagger up through Zhod's jaw, behind the chin. He forced the blade up into the Gorn's brain pan. *That should make Zhod's "instant paralysis" believable,* M'Rill decided. For good measure, he grabbed Zhod's head, braced himself, then twisted it until several upper vertebrae splintered with a loud crunch.

Zhod's freshly desecrated dead body sagged to the deck with a meaty *thud*. M'Rill pulled his dagger free and wiped its blade clean on the Gorn's tunic. A moment later he signaled Trenigar to move up and join him at the door. The Nausicaan captain eyed M'Rill's handiwork with the admiration of a fellow craftsman. "Nicely done," he said. "You're less useless than I thought."

"What are your orders, Captain?"

Trenigar ruminated on that for a moment. "The plasma relay will give us some cover when we go through the door. I'll approach them on the main deck," he said. "You go up to the catwalk and cover me. Stun the others, but leave R'Lash to me."

"Aye, sir."

The captain opened the door. He skulked through, his disruptor in one hand and his *sulav* knife in the other.

M'Rill slipped through the door behind him, leveled his pistol, and shot off most of Trenigar's head in a howling flash of light and heat. The Nausicaan's all but decapitated corpse pitched forward and slammed onto the deck.

The Caitian holstered his weapon and used the cargo bay's environmental controls to reduce the artificial gravity to one-fifth of normal. He picked up Trenigar's body with ease, carried it into the cargo bay, and hurled it on top of the rest of the *Caedera* crew's corpses. Carrying Zhod was a bit more difficult. The Gorn as a species were heavily muscled and had very dense endoskeletons. Once the bodies had been gathered, M'Rill left the cargo bay and sealed the inside door. He opened its outer door and jettisoned the dead into the vacuum of deep space.

He took from his pocket a small control device disguised as a common tool, and triggered a tracking beacon that would aid Starfleet's hunt for the ship. Then he signaled his retrieval team. The light on his device changed from red to yellow, indicating they were moving into range to beam him aboard.

I won't miss this job, he realized, *but I will miss Nolram's chili.*

The light changed from yellow to green. As the transporter beam encircled him, he indulged one final pang of regret: *I never got my last dibs with Saff. . . . Damn.*

Chapter 23
Tezwa

"AWAY TEAM, get ready to go," the copilot called back from the cockpit. The Runabout *Tunguska* dove sharply toward the jagged, fractured cityscape, which was concealed behind gray curtains of sheeting rain and drifting mist. Fat droplets pelted the cockpit window and streaked upward in thick rivulets.

Lieutenant Fillion charged his weapon and gave a hopeful nod to Ensign McEwan. She raised her eyebrows and took a deep breath as the *Tunguska* leveled out and sped through the narrow canyons of broken buildings toward the Alkam-Zar com center.

Bunched up in the aft compartment behind Fillion and McEwan were a dozen Starfleet Special Ops commandos and a handful of engineers from the *Enterprise*. Fillion was relieved to be going into friendly territory for a change: The com center was already under Starfleet control—more than a dozen S.C.E. specialists would be waiting to greet them when they arrived. *I've shot my way into enough places for one week,* he decided.

The runabout rolled hard to port. Fillion saw the flash of a glowing projectile racing past the runabout from behind. He heard the wash of its thruster rumble the outer hull.

It hit the com center in a sunlike flash of light, followed by a rippling shockwave. As the building collapsed, the runabout raced into the expanding blast wave. The pilot yelled over the booming explosion, "Shields!"

Fillion shouted to the troops, "Grab on to something!"

Powerful concussions of displaced air buffeted the *Tunguska*. A few panels in the cockpit flickered, then went dark. Just as Fillion realized that one of them was the master control for the runabout's shields, the first blindingly bright blasts of plasma ripped through the deck under his feet.

"Ground fire!" the pilot called out over the high-pitched whine of the plasma blasts. "Evasive, climb to—"

The aft section of the runabout exploded.

Mangled hull fragments tore away in a maelstrom of fire and wind noise. The artificial gravity cut out; free fall took over. Fillion grabbed the edge of the doorframe with his right hand and held on to McEwan's hand with his left. The four engineers and all but two of the Special Ops team were sucked out of the *Tunguska* into free fall, nearly one hundred meters above ground. The female Special Ops trooper clung to a bolted-down table leg, and her male comrade clung desperately to her left leg.

The *Tunguska*'s engines howled wildly as they suffered more hits. The view outside the gaping hole in the back of the ship was a blur. They were spiraling quickly toward the ground.

More blue plasma fire tore through the hull of the runabout. A shrieking fusillade strafed the male Special Ops trooper and tore him apart. His shredded corpse tumbled erratically out of the plummeting ship into the screaming blur of churning rain and fog that spun endlessly around them.

From the cockpit, Fillion heard the pilot and copilot volleying jargon-heavy commands, struggling to regain control, recover altitude, restore main power. Then he heard the copilot's frantic distress call: "Mayday! Mayday! *Enterprise,* this is Runabout *Tunguska!* We're hit! *Enterprise,* do you—"

The nose-first impact hurled Fillion and McEwan forward toward the cockpit. Before they reached it, the front end of the ship collapsed inward, folding over itself like an accordion. The duo slammed against the twisted, crumpled forward bulkhead. Fillion's left shinbone drove upward through his knee, into his femur. Smoke erupted up at them. It stung his eyes. He choked on the thick dust that filled his throat.

McEwan and Fillion collided with one another over and over again as the runabout thunder-rolled through its forced crash landing. The hull broke apart around them. Even surrounded by the groans of twisting metal and the constant percussion of high-velocity impacts, Fillion still heard the distinctively fragile shattering of the warp nacelles' Bussard collectors.

A final collision brought the *Tunguska* to a violent halt.

He looked over at McEwan. Her face was caked with bloody dust, and her right forearm was twisted at an unnatural angle that indicated a horrific break. She was clearly in as much agony as he was, and he knew they were both very likely going into shock. He looked back to see if the female Special Ops trooper had survived the crash. There was no sign of her.

Through the huge open wounds in the side of the runabout, he saw that they had come to a stop amid the rubble of the com center. Walls of billowing smoke enveloped them. Churned-up ash swirled through the shattered hull like snow flurries. Rain spat through the cracks, tepid and filthy.

Squinting his eyes against the stinging dust and rain, he saw the tall, gangly forms of Tezwans in the distance. They were slowly drawing closer. Lifting his rifle, he peered through the holographic sight. He saw in the approaching Tezwans' hands the unmistakable shapes of plasma weapons.

He tapped his combadge. "Fillion to *Enterprise,*" he said, his voice hoarse and desperate. "The *Tunguska's* down! We need some help down here!" The Tezwans closed in from every direction and started flanking the downed spacecraft. Fillion slapped his combadge again. *"Enterprise,* do you copy? Two to beam up!"

"This is Enterprise," came Peart's distressed reply. *"We* can't *beam you up—we're under* attack!"

Chapter 24
U.S.S. Enterprise-E

PEART'S SHIFT ON THE BRIDGE wasn't scheduled to begin for another thirty minutes. Then a muffled explosion shook the room around him. Half-dressed, he rolled out of bed, jumped into his trousers as the red-alert klaxon sounded, grabbed his boots, and sprinted barefoot out into the corridor. He was halfway to the turbolift when he realized he had left his uniform jacket on his bed.

Flickering lights cast the people dashing by on either side of him in staccato, stop-motion poses. Peart dodged through the slalom of bodies and hurtled into the turbolift just before the doors hissed closed. "Bridge, priority one," he called out, trumping any other instructions the five people crammed in the car with him might have given to the computer.

He didn't apologize for bumping into the others as he scrambled into his boots. No one said anything.

The doors opened to reveal the bridge. Picard was in the center seat. Data was next to him, calmly issuing evasive-pattern orders to Magner. The image on the viewscreen rolled wildly. The planet's edge blurred past every few seconds.

Peart strode out of the turbolift and moved to the tactical console, where Wriede was frantically tracking multiple small ships in the immediate vicinity of the *Enterprise.* "Report," he said as he looked over Wriede's shoulder.

"A cargo shuttle overloaded its fusion core inside the shuttlebay," Wriede said. "I dropped the outer forcefield and ejected the ship." Peart noticed that Wriede didn't mention the four *Enterprise* enlisted crewmen who had been working in the shuttlebay at the time, and whose lives he had sacrificed for the good of the ship. Peart understood the horrible choice Wriede had just made, and knew better than to speak of it.

Wriede pointed to the damage-report screen, which flashed with multiple status-critical items. There were numerous outer-hull breaches on decks four and five, and the main impulse-power relays had been damaged. Wriede singled out the most serious problem: "We lost the shield emitters in sections sixteen through twenty-one. There's a big hole in our shield, right behind the bridge."

"Wonderful," Peart said. Dismayed as he was, he knew that the damage would have been catastrophic had the booby-trapped craft exploded inside the shuttlebay. He noticed in the logs that from the first alarm to Wriede's action less than four seconds had elapsed; if Wriede had acted two seconds later, the blast would have destroyed the *Enterprise*'s main bridge.

It was to Data's credit that this sort of attack was one he had anticipated, and against which he had trained the crew for weeks. His relentless battle drills had likely saved the ship.

Another muted blast rattled the bridge's ceiling. Eyeing the ceiling, Peart asked, "What are these cargo shuttles doing?"

"Kamikaze attacks," Wriede said. "They're everywhere. Eighty-nine hijacking reports in the last two minutes."

Edging the younger man aside, he said, "I'll take over here. Reconfigure science one as backup tactical."

"Aye, sir," Wriede said.

As Wriede moved toward one of the consoles along the aft wall of the bridge, Perim emerged from the turbolift and walked quickly to the conn, where she took over for Magner. She sat down and nodded to Le Roy at ops, then cast a quick glance back at Peart. He showed her a fleeting half-smile.

"Helm," Data said. "Set a new evasive pattern. You may proceed at your own discretion."

"Aye, sir," Perim said. As soon as she took control of the helm, Peart noticed a dramatic improvement in the precision of the large starship's high-speed maneuvers. There were a lot of good pilots in Starfleet, but over the past year Perim had proved herself to be one of the best. Clearly, Data had learned that, in a crisis situation, letting Perim pilot by instinct was preferable to directing her every move.

A shrill tone snapped Peart's focus back to his own console. "Someone's hijacking one of our freighters," he said. "The *Palermo*—it's coming right at us."

"On screen," Picard said.

Peart locked the sensors on the approaching freighter.

The ship appeared on the main viewer. It was blocky and

slow, and no match for the speed or power of the *Enterprise*. But with the flagship's shields partly compromised, a ship that size could inflict a lot of damage as a battering ram.

"Helm," Picard said. "Go to higher orbit. Get us more room to move, and keep that ship at a distance."

"Captain," Peart said, "we're getting more hijacking reports. We don't have enough tractor beams to restrain all these ships."

"Reconfigure the main deflector to fire broad-spectrum tetryon pulses," the captain said.

Peart nodded and began executing the command. "Aye, sir." Routing tetryon pulses through the ship's main deflector would normally take hours, but La Forge and his team, acting on Data's orders, had spent the past month retooling the deflector system so that it could be reconfigured for tactical use in less than ten minutes.

It was a good tactic; against small craft such as these cargo haulers, even low-level phaser blasts might accidentally inflict lethal damage. Tetryon pulses would let the *Enterprise* crew neutralize the ships without risking any fatalities.

More warnings sounded on Peart's console. The alerts came in faster than he could sort them. "Captain," he said. "I'm getting reports of attacks all over the planet. Our people are taking fire in every major city." He didn't have time to say that the Starfleet Security forces appeared to be seriously outnumbered, or that casualties were mounting more rapidly than he could track. As each new distress signal was overlapped by two more, Peart realized that the situation on the planet was spinning disastrously out of control. Looking directly at Picard, he said, "They need fire support, sir."

The captain seemed unfazed by the multiplying alarms. "As soon as we've contained our current situation, Mr. Peart."

"Captain," Peart said, struggling to hold his temper in check, "our people on Tezwa need us *now*. Request permission to disable the hijacked cargo ships with phasers, sir."

Data spoke up: "You have your orders, Mr. Peart."

Peart seethed. He wanted to protest the order, to argue that every enemy life they saved in orbit by waiting to use tetryon pulses instead of phasers would likely cost the lives of dozens of Starfleet personnel being attacked on Tezwa. But the bridge was not a place for debate. He focused on his tactical console.

"Aye, sir," he said. "Reconfiguring the main deflector."

A high-pitched beeping on the tactical console indicated that a priority SOS had been received. Peart patched it through to his console's speaker: *"Mayday! Mayday! Enterprise, this is Runabout Tunguska! We're hit!* Enterprise, *do you—"* A scratch of static swallowed the end of the message. Peart switched to another distress call: "Enterprise, *we're pinned down! Request fire supp—"* The transmission ended with the sound of a plasma blast, followed by silence. He had already patched in a third SOS when Data said, "That is enough, Lieutenant."

The third distress call crackled in the grim silence, ratcheting up the tension that gripped the *Enterprise* bridge.

"Fillion to Enterprise," a downed officer said over the com, his pain and fear evident despite the heavy static. *"The* Tunguska's *down! We need some help down here!"*

Peart's throat constricted with rage as he listened to a call for help that he couldn't answer. Pushing aside his aggravation, he checked his console. "The tetryon pulse will be ready to fire in eight minutes," he said.

Picard stared with a clenched jaw at the pitching starscape on the main viewscreen. Grayish silver blurs whipped past as the *Enterprise* rolled and turned in sickeningly swift circles through its flock of tiny attackers. Moments later, Fillion's voice rasped again over the still-open com.

"Enterprise, *do you copy? Two to beam up!*"

Peart's temper got the better of him. He jabbed his finger onto his console's transmitter. "This is *Enterprise*," he said angrily. "We *can't* beam you up—we're under *attack!*"

Data stood up. Peart fully expected to be relieved of duty.

Before Data could speak, Picard commanded with grim determination, "Lieutenant Peart . . . fire phasers."

"Aye, sir." Turning back to his console, Peart set the phasers to ten percent of normal power and started selecting targets. The arsenal of the *Enterprise*-E did not disappoint him. Dozens of controlled bursts every few seconds lashed out and rattled the buzzing swarm of hijacked cargo shuttles. Peart watched as the cloud of would-be suicide attackers thinned.

Then a pair of damaged cargo shuttles collided and exploded. Peart looked back at Picard, who had watched the accident on the main viewer. "Sorry, Captain."

Picard frowned. "How soon until we can provide fire support to our personnel on Tezwa?"

Peart reconfigured his console. "Four minutes, sir."

"Let's hope we're not too late," Picard said. "Fire for effect, Mr. Peart. . . . It's time to end this."

Chapter 25
Tezwa

WITH A SOUND LIKE THE CRY of a gigantic prehistoric raptor, the cell door scraped open across the concrete floor.

Riker confirmed that the tiny plasma cutter General Yaelon had given to him was still concealed beneath the wires wrapped around his left wrist. Moving his hands slightly apart, he pulled the loose loop of wires until it was taut enough to be believed at a glance for real bindings. He turned his head to hide the small translator device tucked into his left ear.

Four Tezwan guards entered the room. Three of them towered over his cell. The fourth one moved to the control panel on the other side of the room.

"Hurry up," said one of the guards above Riker. Squinting to make himself appear less alert, Riker saw that the man who had spoken had reddish plumage. One of the soldiers with him had brownish feathers, while the other was mostly gray. The one working at the control panel had a dark golden hue.

The brownish Tezwan looked at a device on his wrist that Riker surmised was a timepiece. Looking up, he asked, "Where are we taking him again?"

"Waste-processing station five," said the reddish one.

The grayish guard sounded vexed. "Are you kidding? That's on the other side of the redoubt. If we take him all the way over there, we'll miss the last transport."

"We'll be stuck here," the brownish one added.

The reddish one held up a hand toward each of them. "I don't want to hear it. We have our orders."

From the other side of the room, the golden one said, "They might have a point. If we miss the last transport, we'll be picking up every scut detail for the next month."

"Seriously, sir," the brownish one said. "What difference does it make who kills him? Or where it gets done? Why don't we just shoot him here and move out with the rest of the regiment?"

Heaving a defeated sigh, the reddish one said, "Fine. All the same to me. Gorron, release the lock on my order. You two open the grating, and I'll shoot him. Everybody ready?" The other three Tezwans signaled they were ready. "Go," he said.

The brownish and grayish guards hefted open the grating.

Riker rolled against the wall for cover. He lifted the plasma cutter over the edge of the shallow pit and fired.

If he had been aiming for the Tezwan's weapon, he would have called it expert marksmanship. As it turned out, it was just a lucky shot. The narrow blue beam sliced through the rifle's power cell, which flared into a small explosion.

The blast killed the reddish Tezwan, hurled the ones on either side of him against the walls, and slammed the grating fully open against the floor. Searing heat singed the hair on the back of Riker's neck.

He heard the lone remaining Tezwan scrambling to bring his weapon to bear. Barely pushing the plasma cutter over the edge of his narrow trench, Riker kept his head down and fired blindly. He waved the beam in a narrow arc until he heard the guard's pained cry. A few wild shots from the man's rifle scorched the walls and floors all around Riker. Then, a few seconds later, they ceased.

Grabbing the unconscious body of the grayish Tezwan and using him for a shield, Riker sat up and surveyed the room. The golden Tezwan lay unmoving and possibly dead. Several smoldering trails crisscrossed his torso.

Riker pulled himself out of the small rectangular hole in the floor. He crawled over the reddish Tezwan's corpse. Assessing his own condition, he was not encouraged. His movements were awkward and stiff from muscular atrophy. His mouth was thick with a sour taste. Every step shot pain through his improperly set broken ribs, and his spine ached from prolonged sleeping in twisted positions on a concrete surface. The floor beneath his feet felt ice-cold. He felt dizzy and weak, and he was suffering from a terrible sensation of nausea.

But I'm not dead, he reassured himself. *And I'm not going to be. Not today.*

The brownish guard started to stir. Riker pulled the man's weapon from his shoulder, then used it to knock the Tezwan unconscious. Checking the weapon's settings, he stepped back near the door of the cell and shot the two remaining rifles, rendering them useless.

Crouching down, he searched the reddish Tezwan's pockets until he found a device similar to the one he had seen Kinchawn use to unlock the door. Holding the device in his hand, he struggled to remember the code sequence. He thought he had seen it yesterday, but then he realized that it might have been two days, or maybe even longer.

He had no concept of how long he had been here.

Closing his eyes, he replayed the moment in his memory. Kinchawn's hand had partly concealed the device. Making it more difficult, the markings it bore were incomprehensible to Riker. His only hope was to remember the code sequence based solely on the positions of the buttons. He had watched Kinchawn so intently at the time, but now the hunger and the fatigue made the memory hazy and difficult to keep hold of.

Slowly, he entered the sequence he saw in his mind's eye.

The device in his hand emitted a guttural beep.

He sighed and tried again. There were two entries in the sequence he was unsure of. At that point in the sequence, he selected a key adjacent to the one he had first pushed.

The door unlocked with a low hydraulic hiss and the deep metallic clanging of heavy bolts being released.

Riker opened the door. The corridor outside was dim and subterranean-looking. He leaned out to scan the hall for guards or activity. All seemed quiet. The tall but narrow passage stretched away to his left and right for a considerable distance, and many more corridors intersected it or branched away from it at irregular intervals.

There was nothing to indicate what direction might lead out of this place.

With great effort, he hefted the plasma rifle and crept into the corridor. The concrete under his bare feet was rough and gritty, but at least slightly warmer than in his cell chamber. His legs felt unreliable, as if they might falter beneath him without any warning.

A low vibrato hum pulsed through the ceilings. Riker guessed that the sound came from the environmental system. Even with that steady drone to cover the sound of his movements, he was acutely aware of the soft scrape and muted patter of his footsteps as he tiptoed gingerly from one intersection to the next. At each corner he hesitated, checked for enemy personnel, then continued forward, searching for a path to an exit.

At the end of the corridor, he reached the last intersection. Not wanting to backtrack, he chose to turn left and follow a strict pattern of alternating turns—left, right, left—in case he was forced at some point to retreat.

Several minutes later he realized he had lost track of what direction his last turn had been. Or the turn before that. Stumbling into a dead end crowded with exposed pipes and discarded crates, he admitted to himself that he was lost. He turned back to attempt to retrace his steps when he saw harshly bright beams, like the kind from handheld searchlights, dancing in the dusty darkness past the corner ahead of him.

He heard voices. "The footprints lead this way," one of them said, half a second before faint echoes repeated it ad infinitum. Riker leaned against the wall and lifted one foot off the ground. Reaching down, he ran his hand along the bottom of his foot, and felt it slicked with blood. Looking back at the searchlight beams, he saw that they were zigzagging across the floor—following his own bloody trail.

He ducked behind a cluster of pipes running from the floor to the ceiling and crouched low behind one of the crates. The voices drew closer, and the beams became brighter and more distinct as they sliced through the darkness.

"He's trapped," a voice said. "Shona, lay down suppressing fire and move up. Zungu, Penga: Flank him."

A blistering barrage of electric-blue plasma bolts screamed over Riker's head. Steam jetted from ruptured pipes, and several pulses per second lit up the walls around him with glowing, half-molten divots. Flashes of light and fountains of sparks illuminated the smoke billowing from the crate as it was peppered with plasma fire.

Riker tried to return fire without losing his cover, but in his weakened state the weapon was too heavy to control. He ended up firing a few futile bursts into the ceiling over his head.

He dropped prone and steadied his rifle. *Have to wait until they get to point-blank range,* he thought. *It's my only chance.*

There was a sudden doubling of the ferocity of the weapons fire, followed by a stark, shocking silence.

The same voice that had ordered the attack called out. "Commander Riker? Can you hear me?"

Cautiously, Riker replied, "Yes."

"This is General Yaelon. You can come out."

Riker wanted to trust Yaelon, but he couldn't suppress

his fear that this was a trap. He tightened his grip on the plasma rifle. "Tell me what's going on."

"Kinchawn's begun his attack," Yaelon said. "This is your only chance to escape, while most of his troops are elsewhere. Please, come quickly."

The bedraggled first officer of the *Enterprise* stood up.

Three Tezwan soldiers lay dead and smoking with fresh plasma burns on the floor. At the end of the passage was General Yaelon, his weapon lowered, his hand extended. "We have no time, Commander," he said. "Follow me."

Yaelon's long limbs climbed stairs swiftly, three at a time. He moved through the dark, maddeningly generic-looking corridors and intersections with the perfect certainty of a trail guide. The air quickly grew warmer as they neared the exit to the surface.

He stopped and waited for Riker. The human was annoyingly slow, partly because of his shorter legs but also as a result of the injuries he had sustained during captivity. Reaching the emergency exit stairwell had not been terribly difficult, but the climb had proved exhausting for Riker, who had abandoned his borrowed plasma rifle several flights below.

"Quickly," Yaelon urged. He heard the sounds of a large search party closing in from behind them. Riker gasped for breath, his stamina clearly fading. Had the Federation officer been a Tezwan, Yaelon would have carried him to safety. Humans, however, were much denser beings than Tezwans and weighed considerably more. In any event, Riker had made it clear that he would leave the redoubt on his feet or not at all.

The search party's angry shouts were much closer now. They rounded the corner to the exit. At the top of the long, steep flight of steps was the emergency hatch. Yaelon had planned to escort Riker out of the base and usher him to safety, in exchange for Federation protection. Now, hearing the gap between the voices and their crisp echoes diminishing to nothing, he realized that if he insisted on trying to escape with Riker, they would both die. If he tried to leave Riker behind, he might survive to reach the Federation—but would have nothing to show for his efforts.

The last option hovered before him, grimly just in its cruel irony: He could sacrifice himself to aid Riker's escape. Though personally Yaelon would gain nothing, he might die hoping that he had helped rid his world of a maniacal despot who had slain Yaelon's children and those of millions of other citizens whose only sin had been placing their trust in Kinchawn.

Yaelon pressed a data rod into Riker's hand. "Don't lose this," he said. "Get it to Starfleet." Stepping past Riker and back down the stairs, he added, "Go. I'll cover your escape."

Riker nodded, and the general was grateful that the human didn't waste precious breath on speeches or platitudes. The man climbed in hard, heavy motions up the stairs and did not look back. *May the Maker defend you,* Yaelon prayed.

The first guard rounded the corner beneath Yaelon. The general fired and killed the man with a head shot.

More guards followed. Yaelon fired wildly, filling the narrow landing between flights of stairs with a torrent of bright blue charged plasma. He squeezed off burst after burst and relied on decades of experience to know how not to overheat the weapon's magnetic constrictors.

Behind him, he heard the emergency door open, and he felt a rush of warm humid air surge like a river down the stairwell.

A hand jerked around the corner below him and released a plasma grenade. It flew up in a gentle arc toward Yaelon's feet and exploded before it hit the stairs.

In a searing blue-white flash, Yaelon's lifetime of bitter regrets disintegrated.

Riker savored the sweetness of the sultry air. Cascades of rain swept over him like a baptism as he stumbled away from the camouflaged exit of the redoubt. Staggering like a drunkard, he lunged through muddy streets littered with shattered glass, twisted metal, and broken stone. Derelict vehicles lay forlorn along the sides of the road.

The data rod was clutched in his white-knuckled left fist.

Behind him, reverberating from the hidden staircase, came a booming explosion. Jagged debris on the ground sliced into his feet as he scrambled around a corner.

No matter where he looked, he saw no sign of cover; all the buildings were shattered façades and gutted shells. Pits of rubble bounded by their cracked foundations barely retained enough of their shapes to continue defining the edges of the boulevards that had been lain waste by the Klingons. There were no people on the streets.

He had no idea which way to run to seek help. With no sense of direction, he simply ran for his life.

Then a flash of light in the sky captured his attention. A few kilometers away, he saw an explosion engulf a building. One second later he heard the low report of the blast. The structure imploded with a low roar, like a ten-second waterfall. A Starfleet runabout that had been cruising toward it suddenly was racked with plasma blasts from below. A second blinding flare clipped the back of the craft. Smoke poured from the small ship as it spun and tumbled out of sight toward the ground.

Riker forced himself to run toward it. Though there might not be anyone there to help him, he knew that Starfleet would almost certainly send a rescue team to the downed ship.

As he heard the hue and cry of enemy soldiers charging into the streets behind him, he knew that reaching the crashed runabout was his best . . . last . . . *only* hope of survival.

In the security command center below the *Ilanatava,* Christine Vale watched in dismay as the global scale of Kinchawn's attack became apparent. The runabouts *Ohio, Tunguska,* and *Potomac* had all been hit. The *Ohio* had been destroyed in the air, while the *Tunguska* and the *Potomac* had crashed. As far as she could tell, there were no survivors on the *Potomac.* But Fillion and McEwan were still alive inside the wreckage of the *Tunguska* and desperately calling for beam-up.

Unfortunately, the *Enterprise* was the only ship left in orbit, and it was in no position to help anyone. Until it neutralized its kamikaze attackers, Vale and her people were on their own.

A jumble of frantic voices shouted over one another, relaying multiple reports of attacks every few seconds. Loyalist guerrillas were strafing food-and-water-distribution centers with rifle fire; hammering Starfleet security personnel with plasma grenades; detonating improvised explosive devices against hardened targets.

Gracin shouted out, "Runabout down!"

Vale spun toward him. "Report!"

"The *Delaware*," Gracin said. "Took a grenade hit lifting off in Savola-Cov."

"Survivors?"

"I don't think so," Gracin said.

"Then we need to get to the *Tunguska*," she said.

Gracin shook with frustration and rage. "There's no one to send! Everybody's pinned down!"

Ensign Grigsby jumped up from her console and dashed over to the command platform. She leaned under the railing below Vale and Gracin. "They're hitting the hospitals!" she said. "We just lost med teams in Arbosa-Lo and Masheena-Kel!"

"Evacuate the other hospitals," Vale ordered. Turning back to her second-in-command, she said, "Gracin, goddammit, there's gotta be someone in Alkam-Zar who isn't under fire!"

The security officer turned and checked his console. He keyed through several screens of information in less than two seconds. "Just a Tezwan police squad, guarding last night's strike target."

"Send them. Now."

"They don't have any transport," Gracin protested.

Vale exploded, "They have feet! They have eyes! Tell them to double-time it toward the smoke from the crash! Go!"

From another console below the command platform, Lieutenant Peter Davila waved for Vale's attention. "Sir, Ambassador Lagan refuses to evacuate her office, and Prime Minister Bilok and his cabinet won't leave the Assembly Forum."

She let out a frustrated sigh that grew into a growl. "I don't have time for this!" She stormed toward the exit. "Gracin, hold the fort till I get back. Davila, Cruzen, Floyd, with me!"

The three security officers followed Vale toward the door. She snagged a phaser rifle from the wall before exiting the command center. Behind her followed the clacking sounds of three more rifles being pulled from their brackets. Stepping out the door and sprinting up the wide staircase to the eastern rotunda, she armed her rifle to heavy stun. It charged to ready with a reassuring, rising-pitched whine.

She led her team directly into the clear-walled turbolift. It ascended swiftly toward the upper level of the *Ilanatava,* which housed the Assembly Forum, as well as the offices of the senior ministers and the new office of Ambassador Lagan. As they passed through the top of the eastern rotunda's dome, the cold and stately vanity of the building's interior fell away and was replaced by the orderly sprawl of the capital city. Then, just as quickly as the metropolis had been revealed, it vanished again as the lift car passed back inside the *Ilanatava* and came to a halt on the senior ministers' level.

The doors opened. Vale stepped out of the turbolift and proceeded at a quick march down the curving corridor to the office of Ambassador Lagan. Striding through the outer reception area, she ignored the spindly young El Aurian who tried to intercept her, and opened the door to Lagan's private office.

Lagan was seated at her desk. She looked up, alarmed at first, then angry when she saw Vale and the other officers. She asked, "What's going on?"

"We need you to come with us," Vale said. "Kinchawn's launching a coup. You aren't safe up here."

Haughty and aloof, Lagan picked up a padd from her desk and spoke to Vale as if she were merely a minor distraction. "Go away," she said. "I have work to do."

"Davila," Vale said, "take the ambassador into protective custody and escort her to the command center. If she resists, stun her." Nodding to Lagan, she added, "With apologies, Madam Ambassador." Davila stepped past Vale and forcibly ushered Lagan out of her own office. Meanwhile, Vale turned to face the other security officers. "Cruzen, escort the ambassador's attaché back to command. Floyd, come with me."

She led the junior security officer out of Lagan's suite of offices and continued around the outer perimeter of the *Ilanatava* until they turned a corner that led into the center of the tower, and to the entrance to the Assembly Forum. A pair of black-plumed Tezwan guards stood in front of the enormous double doors. They were armed with plasma rifles. The one on the left, seeing that Vale and Floyd were armed, raised his weapon and called out, "Halt! You can't bring—"

Vale leveled her weapon just above her hip and fired.

A wide-field stunning blast knocked both guards backward against the wall. They slumped to the floor, their rifles clattering from their hands onto the gleaming marble tiles. Vale slung her weapon over her shoulder. Floyd did likewise. She pushed open the doors, and strode into the seat of the Tezwan government like a conquering Caesar.

The excited clamor of the room died out like a snuffed candle flame. Every minister turned toward her and Floyd. Together, they walked into the center of the room and stood before the towering tiered platforms of the senior leadership. From high above, Prime Minister Bilok bellowed down, "What do you think you are doing? You have no right to—"

"Shut up," Vale said loudly. "I'm saving your lives. Kinchawn's on the warpath, so if I were you I'd be moving into the bunker. As in, *right now.*"

"That decision is not yours to make," Deputy Prime Minister Tawnakel declared. "As the sovereign—"

Before Vale could interrupt what promised to be a long-winded rant, a massive blast outside the tower did it for her.

The *Ilanatava* quaked from the explosion, which sent a mushroom cloud of orange flame and coal-black smoke stretching into the sky.

Her combadge chirped. *"Gracin to Vale! The south rotunda's been hit! We've got company!"*

The ministers fell over one another as they scrambled from their seats and rushed toward the exits. Bilok, Tawnakel, and a half dozen other senior ministers all slipped away through their private portals. As the flood-crush of bodies raced toward them, Vale slapped Floyd's shoulder and motioned for him to follow her as she got the hell out of there.

They dashed out of the hall and down the corridor, back to the outer ring. As they sprinted back toward the turbolift, a new explosion rocked the *Ilanatava,* and a second pillar of smoke and fire reached into the sky.

"Vale to Gracin, report!"

"Just lost the north rotunda! We're taking fire from the surrounding structures!"

Vale stopped running and pressed her face against one of the windows. She peered down and saw a steady stream of plasma bolts emerging from the windows of several buildings on every side of the *Ilanatava.* They were surrounded, and it was only a matter of time before the capital building was either overrun or destroyed outright. She resumed her run to the turbolift.

"Gracin, is there any word from *Enterprise?"*

"Negative, they're still pretty bogged down up there."

Floyd reached the turbolift first and held the door open for her. As soon as she was in, he pressed the door-close key, leaving the Tezwan politicians to take one of the other lifts.

"We're on our way down," Vale said. "Arm everybody. Don't let Kinchawn's people enter the building."

"I'm not worried about them getting in," Gracin replied. *"I'm worried about us getting out."*

"One thing at a time," Vale said. "Get somebody into the lobby to protect the ministers. They're right behind us."

"Aye, sir. Gracin out."

As the turbolift descended into the open space between the upper levels and the eastern rotunda, Vale watched in morbid fascination as incoming pulses of enemy fire collided with the building's invisible energy shield, rendering small circles of it momentarily visible. If it collapsed, a counterattack was her only viable tactical option.

Floyd was mesmerized by the nightmarish onslaught. "Sir," he said nervously, "we're not really going out there, are we?"

Vale's mouth was dry. "I hope not," she said.

Nurses and doctors scrambled past Beverly Crusher. Everyone was working as quickly as possible to evacuate the hospital.

Patients who could walk with assistance were led to the elevators. Those who could not were lifted onto gurneys and rolled to the extra-wide turbolift car at the end of the hall. The crowd at the bank of elevators was four deep and not moving.

Outside, distant but clearly audible, came the whine of phaser fire and the angry screech of plasma bolts. The fighting was growing closer by the minute.

Crusher carried a Tezwan child who had lost both her legs below the knees. With no way to reach the turbolift, she looked around for another option. In every direction she turned, she saw only more people, trapped and terrified.

It was so maddening—evicting these sick and wounded people into the streets to become fresh casualties struck Crusher as callous and stupid. Being ordered to abandon those who remained too critical to be moved infuriated her. Worse, it felt like a violation of her hippocratic oath.

A hand grasped her arm. She turned to see Ensign Duncan from security. The wiry, dark-haired man nodded toward the landing platform. "Come on, Doctor," he said. "We have to get you out of here."

"I can't leave my patients," Crusher said. "I won't."

"Doctor, the *Tsavo* is waiting. You and the rest of your staff need to come with us right now."

His plea gave her an idea. She handed the amputee child to him. Instinctively, he took the little girl into his arms, then looked surprised that he had done it.

"Get her on the runabout," Crusher said. "That's an order."

Leaving the stunned security officer behind, Crusher pushed back through the wall of bodies until she found other members of the hospital staff. Dr. Hughes was still in the operating room, performing a reparative surgery. Dr. Chimelis was trying to treat as many patients as possible before Nurse Ogawa and Medical Technician McGlynn ushered the ragged-looking Tezwan civilians back out into urban exile.

Crusher shouted to Chimelis, "Dennis!" He looked up from his frantic ministrations. She pointed toward the runabout. "Get the critical cases onto the *Tsavo!*" He nodded, then forced his way back to the intensive-care ward, staying a few steps ahead of Crusher, who stopped to recruit McGlynn and the third-year resident, Meldok. That left only Ogawa to tend to the last-minute medical exigencies of the hospital's expelled patients.

Less than a minute later, the four medical personnel moved their first quartet of critical-care patients out the sliding doors, across the catwalk to the landing pad, and into the *Tsavo*. Looking out from inside the ship was

Ensign Duncan. Beside him sat the double-amputee Tezwan girl.

"We still have room for you and your staff," he said. "Let's go."

"No," Crusher said. "You're taking four more patients."

"Doc, we don't—"

"They're pediatric criticals," Crusher said sharply.

Duncan put up his hands and acknowledged his surrender. Crusher led Meldok, McGlynn, and Chimelis back inside. As they carried four more children toward the sliding doors, an injured Tezwan woman waiting in front of the elevators stopped Crusher. "Kumbayla!" she cried, reaching out to touch the face of the unconscious Tezwan boy in the doctor's arms. The woman wept as she looked at the child.

Crusher asked her, "You know this boy?"

"He's my son," the woman said, her voice choked with grief.

"Come with us," Crusher said. The woman took the child from Crusher and carried him. Crusher led the group out the sliding doors. At the catwalk they were intercepted again by Duncan.

"Doc, this has to be it," he said.

"Fine," she said. "Take these people to safety."

"We can't take this many criticals without a flight surgeon," he said. "One of you is coming aboard."

Chimelis patted Crusher's arm. "It's okay, I'll go," he said with a wry grin. "Most of these were my patients, anyway."

"Good luck," Crusher said. She turned back toward the sliding doors as Duncan escorted the last of the patients to the *Tsavo*. As the doors parted before her, she glanced back at the group, which jogged across the landing pad to the runabout.

She noticed that the woman who had intercepted her in the lobby was wearing Tezwan military-issue combat boots.

As the woman leaned forward to hand the child in her arms to someone inside the *Tsavo,* Crusher saw the hem of military fatigue pants beneath the woman's civilian garb.

Crusher sprang forward toward the promenade railing. Pointing at the Tezwan woman, she shouted over the rising hum of the ship's engines, "Duncan! Stop her!"

Duncan turned and looked at Crusher, clearly confused by her outburst. In that fleeting moment of distraction, the Tezwan woman reached under her robe, retrieved a fist-sized object, and hurled it into the runabout.

The ship exploded.

The first blast filled the small craft with a blistering orange fireball and knocked over Duncan and the Tezwan woman. A second concussive boom fractured the *Tsavo*'s outer hull and hurled a jet of flame out its open side door.

The third detonation tore the ship apart. The conflagration unleashed a shock wave that hurled Crusher backward, through the still-open sliding doors. Massive, burning chunks of the *Tsavo*'s hull slammed against the outside of the building. The landing platform disintegrated beneath the ship and collapsed. It sheared away from the catwalk with a mournful groaning screech of twisting metal. The cloud of fire, wreckage, and bodies rained down on the street, twenty meters below. Tarmac cracked and shattered as the tons of white-hot debris crashed down.

Crusher shook off the initial shock of the blast and

tried to focus. Most of the medical staff had departed earlier, and three of the six who had volunteered to stay behind had just been blown to smithereens. Only she, Ogawa, and Hughes remained.

A thick tower of smoke rose from the street.

Ogawa and Hughes pushed through the crowd and kneeled beside her. Ogawa said, "Are you all right, Doctor?"

"I'm okay, Alyssa." She put out her arms and let the pair help her back to her feet.

Hughes stared past Crusher, at the smoke from the bombing.

"There's gonna be wounded civilians down there," he said.

Ogawa looked at him like he was crazy. "There might also be people looking to shoot us."

"You don't have to go, Alyssa," Crusher said reassuringly. "I won't make you come with us."

Without hesitation, Ogawa replied, "Give me two minutes, Doctors. I'll go refill the medkits."

Rainwater hissed into steam as fusillades of glowing blue plasma tore through the twisted, broken hull of the *Tunguska*.

McEwan balanced her rifle through a narrow crack in the hull and picked off another charging attacker. Beside her, pivoting on his one good leg, Fillion alternated his fire between the starboard side and the wide-open aft section. Their weapons shrieked loudly in the confined space of the wrecked runabout. By her most conservative estimate, they had each felled at least half a dozen opponents. But more kept emerging from the mist, dashing like shadows between smoking hunks of debris from the fallen building. Every few seconds a plasma burst came from a different location and tore past them.

Then one blazing blue shot ripped through Fillion's wounded leg, just above the knee. He screamed as he fell, his body and the lower half of his leg tumbling in opposite directions. His howls of agony were primal, and his face twisted into a mask of horror and pain.

Bracing her rifle with her shoulder, she drew her type-2 phaser sidearm and snapped off three quick shots to aft. One shot hit a Tezwan who had been steadying his aim at them.

Fillion scrambled up against the wall and pushed himself into a seated position. Tears poured from his eyes as he leveled his weapon and resumed firing to starboard.

As she turned to line up another shot to port, an impact from behind slammed her against the bulkhead. Her body went numb from midtorso down. She smelled the charnel perfume of scorched flesh as she collapsed to the deck behind Fillion.

McEwan stared in mute horror at the crisp-edged, bleeding exit wound in her abdomen.

He glanced down at her. The panic burned bright in his eyes. For several adrenaline-stretched seconds, he fought on, fighting for his balance on one foot as he defended three fronts at once. Then a furious barrage from two directions engulfed him. McEwan shut her eyes, but she could still hear the erratic patter of his body falling in pieces to the rubble-strewn deck.

The enemy rushed forward. There were many voices,

jubilant and angry at the same time, infused with the bloodlust and the animalistic thrill of war. They were coming to finish her off, or to take trophies, or to raid the runabout for its parts and its secrets. She didn't plan to permit them any of these things.

With her bloodied left hand, she searched in fumbling gropes for the photon grenade on the right side her belt. She pulled it free and armed it.

Tempering her fear with proud defiance, she waited for the enemy to come. To reveal themselves.

She imagined the faces of the children she would never have. Heard the curses that her father would heap upon the architects of this wanton slaughter. Dreamed of blue summer skies. And she remembered the voice of the Tezwan singer who two weeks ago had mourned his world in the dying light of day. His elegiac dirge haunted her thoughts.

McEwan clutched the photon grenade in her left hand. Her vision darkened as she slipped deeper into shock.

A trio of Tezwan soldiers stumbled through the open aft section and stared down in surprise at the trembling, bloodied redheaded human.

McEwan clenched her fist and detonated the grenade.

"We're losing the last shield!"

Gracin's warning cut through the frightened clamor of the command center. On the room's main viewscreen, Vale watched the nonstop storm of plasma fire dimple the energy barrier around the east rotunda with crackling blue flashes. Behind her, Ambassador Lagan and Prime Minister Bilok observed the barrage with grim expressions.

"We're sitting ducks down here," Vale said to Gracin. "If we wait for them to bring the fight to us, we're dead."

"Just give the word, sir," Gracin said.

Vale pointed at a tactical map of the area immediately surrounding the *Ilanatava*. "We're taking most of our fire from here," she said to everyone present. "Grigsby, Floyd: Take out this building and clear us a path so we can flank—"

"Hold on a moment, Lieutenant," Lagan said. "Did you just order them to 'take out' a building?"

"Ambassador," Vale said, "I really don't have time to discuss this."

"Make the time," Lagan said. "The rules of engagement still apply. Federation law still applies. I won't authorize—"

"This isn't Federation space," Vale interrupted heatedly. "And we're about to start taking grenade fire. If you live, court-martial me. Until then, shut up and stay outta my way."

Vale turned back toward the roomful of Starfleet security personnel. "First and second platoons, we're on the left flank. Gracin, lead third and fourth platoons to the right. Giudice, take over in here. If *Enterprise* gets clear, relay our target coordinates. Everybody grab what you can and assemble upstairs in the rotunda!"

More than one hundred Starfleet personnel filed swiftly out of the command center, grabbing rifles, sidearms, and satchels filled with photon grenades as they hurried through the door. Grigsby and Floyd loaded up their handheld mortars, slung rifles over their shoulders, and followed their comrades out of the command center.

As the last of the personnel double-timed up the stairs, Vale followed them out. Rejoining them in the cavernous and disturbingly exposed rotunda, she was pleased to see they had already divided into platoons and squads. Beyond the narrow, looming archways around the rotunda's perimeter, the shield flickered wildly as the bombardment continued.

I can't believe we're charging into that, Vale thought.

"Grigsby, Floyd," she said. "Take cover behind those statues near the entrance. As soon as the shield falls, I want mortars on that building until it's gone. Go."

The two officers sprinted ahead to their firing position. Vale looked back at the rest of her troops. "As soon as that building comes down, we go. We have to get inside the occupied buildings and clear them, room by room. Any questions?"

A wall of determined faces looked back at her. No one said anything. No doubt they knew that the odds against this tactic being successful were staggering. The only good thing Vale could say about it was that it was preferable to hiding in the command center until the enemy rolled another photon-plasma hybrid charge down the stairs and set it off at their door.

The shield collapsed with a distorted flicker and a low rush of noise from displaced air. Swarms of howling plasma bolts flooded into the rotunda, shearing through the outer pillars and scoring the floor with glowing streaks. A handful of troops in third platoon were hit by ricocheted pulses.

Grigsby and Floyd fired their first two shots. Streaks of white light cut through the blue flurry and punched into the broad, curving front of the twenty-story, black-glass and durasteel building across the street. Muffled explosions blasted a huge hole in the formerly pristine façade. A shock effect spread like a ripple on a pond, shattering its every window.

The chaotic torrent of plasma fire emanating from the target building coalesced and focused on the winged statue behind which Grigsby and Floyd hid. The duo fired their weapons again in quick succession, both aiming at points near the target's foundation, directly below their first targets. As plasma bursts clipped the statue's wings, thunderous fireballs roared through the building's center.

The center third of the building sank into itself, falling away into a pit of superheated fire. Seconds later, the orphaned outer thirds collapsed inward, as if to fill the gap. With a sound like oceans colliding, the entire building imploded and was replaced by a rapidly growing mountain of soot and sulfurous smoke. For a moment, the enemy fusillade halted.

Vale sprang forward. "Charge! Grigsby, Floyd, regroup!"

She ran beside the billowing wall of ash, using it for whatever cover it could offer. First and second platoons kept pace with her. The streets were all but deserted. As the demolished building hurled its smoldering remains into the sky, the dawn was blotted out and turned to night.

Then the enemy troops in the other surrounding buildings resumed fire. The street lit up with deadly plasma flashes that cut like blazing knives through the charcoal-colored smoke.

Bodies fell to the street on either side of Vale, some wounded, some dead. She continued her headlong charge.

The explosion came from behind her, bluish white and blistering. The blast wave hurled her face-first to the filthy ground. Dozens more crack-booms followed it. Rolling onto her side, Vale saw the telltale flashes of plasma grenades lighting up the blackened dawn. Each burst painted its broken, dismembered victims as silhouettes in the smoky fog.

Vale reached out and locked her hand around her rifle. She forced herself back to her feet, took two stunned steps forward; then another explosion several meters in front of her knocked her back to the street.

Though nearly drowned out by the reports of grenade blasts and the whine of plasma fire, the cries of the wounded and dying washed over her. The charge on this flank had stalled. Any moment the smoke would clear, and she and her troops would be easy targets for the Tezwan shooters.

"First platoon!" she yelled into the dusty mayhem. "Second platoon! Go forward!" The only sounds that came back to her were the agonized groans of the wounded. She scrambled back the way she had come, moving in a low crouch. At each body she stopped, checked for signs of life. Half the people she found were dead, most of the others were critically wounded. After a minute of frantic searching, she had rounded up less than two full squads.

They huddled in the sparse cover of fallen statues in the plaza that lay between the *Ilanatava* and the city.

"We're losing our cover," she said. "We have to go now."

A young enlisted security guard shook his head. "We'll never make it," he said. "We can't, it's suicide, they'll—"

"Quiet," Vale commanded. "You will go. You will reach that building. You will follow orders. Is that clear?"

Swallowing hard, the kid seemed to regain at least a tiny bit of his composure. "Aye, sir," he said, but he didn't sound like he believed it.

"Come on," she said, and led another charge toward the enemy-held building on the left side of the *Ilanatava.*

As they emerged from cover, Vale was the first one hit. Two shots slammed into her, one in her right shoulder, the other ripping through her left hip. The impacts reversed her momentum from a dead run to a dead stop. She landed on her back, stunned and breathless. Two of her people grabbed her and pulled her back to cover, barely ahead of the flurry of shots that had clearly been meant to finish her off where she had fallen.

Blast after blast bit holes through the statuary around them. Vale knew the enemy was no doubt targeting a plasma grenade on her position. But as the smoke cleared, there was nowhere to run. She steeled herself for a sudden end.

Then the sky split open. Majestic beams of light pierced the gray blanket of atmospheric ash. With a bright surge of noise, they traced a perimeter around the *Ilanatava.*

Just as quickly as the beams had appeared, they vanished.

All the shooting had stopped.

Her combadge chirped. *"Peart to Vale."*

"Vale here. Go ahead."

"Sorry for the delay, sir. Enterprise is clear."

"Are the com relays secure?"

"Negative," Peart said, his disappointment evident in his tone. *"They're all dusted."*

"What about the other combat zones?"

"We're neutralizing all Loyalist combatants now. What's your status, sir?"

Vale took a breath. Dozens of Starfleet security personnel lay in the streets, burned and bloody, dead or dying. Three of the *Ilanatava's* rotunda domes lay in smoking ruins. A building that minutes ago had been untouched by war now was a smoldering crater. She was unable to move her right arm or her left leg.

"Sir, are you still there? Are you all right?"

"I'm still here, Jim," she said. "But I'm pretty damn far from all right."

Heat spiked through Riker's body like an electric shock. The plasma-rifle shot had struck his lower left back. It exploded out of his gut in a spray of smoke, steam, and blackened blood. Arms flailing in a desperate bid to keep his balance, he lumbered awkwardly around the corner.

He felt himself pitching forward. Acidic bile rose in his throat, and his pulse, which had pounded heavily in his ears, drowned in a roaring wash of muddy storm sound.

Ahead of him, the column of smoke from the crashed runabout snaked skyward through windblown arcs of rain. His tattered clothing, his hair, and his beard all clung to him in wet knots. He sank ankle-deep into some brownish puddles and splashed clumsily with bare feet through others.

A cluster of six armed Tezwans emerged from the intersection ahead of him. Though his vision was blurred by pain and blood loss and fatigue, their tall, gangly, feather-crested shapes were unmistakable. Equally recognizable were the shapes of weapons in their hands. One of them, a woman with bright orange plumage, turned her head and pointed at him. She led her squad in his direction, cutting him off from the runabout.

He turned back, only to see the troops from the redoubt rounding the corner behind him. To his left was a dead-end alley. His thoughts, fueled by adrenaline, reasoned that one of the doors in the alley might be unlocked, might lead to cover, or to escape. He lunged toward it.

Someone fired. A shot tore through his right thigh. He fell to the rain-slicked pavement and was unable to move. Weapons fire erupted around him. He closed his eyes, afraid that his promise not to die on Tezwa was about to be broken.

Tenila and her squad of peace-officer recruits had slogged more than eight spans across Alkam-Zar in the muggy summer downpour, navigating debris-filled streets and boulevards blocked by fallen buildings. She checked her tracking device, and pointed toward the *Tunguska*'s reported crash position. "Turn right up here," she commanded her squad.

They rounded the corner to see the pillar of black smoke belching up from a fresh patch of devastation. On the edge of her vision, Tenila noticed someone running up the street on her left. She turned her head.

It was a human man, ragged and bloody and holding

his right hand over a fresh plasma-rifle wound in his abdomen. His haggard, sallow face was covered by an unkempt beard. He staggered barefoot in the middle of the street, then stopped and stared at her, dumbfounded in the rain.

She had seen his face a hundred times in the past three weeks—in training, at briefings, on news broadcasts, on screens at food-distribution centers. "It's Commander Riker," she called out to her squad, who halted and turned to follow her pointed arm. "Come on!" She jogged toward him.

Then a dozen armed Tezwans appeared behind the human. They moved with the swagger of hunters stalking their prey into a trap. They wore no uniforms, but Tenila knew from their weapons that they had to be Loyalist guerrillas—Kinchawn's men.

Riker seemed confused, unable to decide which way to run. He lurched toward an alley in the middle of the block.

One of the guerrillas lifted his rifle and snapped off a shot that tore through Riker's leg. He fell to the ground.

Tenila lifted her weapon and fired at the guerrillas.

She dived behind a derelict vehicle as she yelled to her troops, "Take cover! Return fire!"

Plasma blasts shredded the vehicle chassis in front of her. Deema and Sholo reached cover half a step ahead of a barrage of Loyalist fire, but Khota froze in the middle of the street while firing his weapon and was hit in the chest by half a dozen blasts. Behind him, Keelas and Izimo ducked back behind the corner and peppered the guerrillas with phaser shots.

Trapped in the middle of the firefight, Riker lay face-down in the street, pelted by heavy rain.

Tenila issued her commands quickly and in a tone that brooked no questions. "Cover me! Keelas, Izimo, move up! Go!" She broke from cover and sprinted toward Riker, firing at the guerrillas every step of the way.

Behind her, Keelas and Izimo charged to take her place behind the husk of the hovercar. Their own phaser beams sliced past Tenila and scoured the Loyalists' cover.

Deema and Sholo laid down as much cover fire as possible. Stray bolts of blindly fired plasma zinged past Tenila as she grabbed Riker, pulled him to his feet, and forced him to move with her into the alley.

From the street behind her came the bone-jarring boom of a grenade explosion. She wouldn't have much time. Pushing Riker forward with her right arm, she fumbled with her left hand to tap the Federation-issued communicator on her uniform jacket. Her voice was ragged with the exertion of running and propelling the incredibly heavy human. "Tenila to Vale, priority one! I have Commander Riker! I need backup! Repeat, I have Command—"

The plasma blast exploded through her gut, stealing her breath. She fell. Without her aid, Riker collapsed on his back in front of her. She landed on top of him. Feeling her strength ebbing away, she fought to lift her weapon one last time. Looking back toward the street, she saw seven Loyalist guerrillas marching side by side into the alley.

"Move aside," one of them said.

She shot him. The heavy-stun beam flung him backward.

The leader returned fire at Tenila. A single shot hammered into her chest. Her vision dimmed. Gravity pulled her into its embrace. She pressed her weapon into Riker's bloody hand. As her last breath ebbed, she thought of her now-orphaned son and prayed to the Maker that sorrow-songs would soothe his grief.

The Tezwan woman lay atop Riker like dead weight. Her weapon was in his hand, but he couldn't move. Rain drizzled into his eyes.

The six Tezwan soldiers were less than fifteen meters away and walking calmly forward to execute him.

The leader raised his weapon.

A blinding flash enveloped the Tezwan troops, who vanished.

Craning his neck, Riker blinked away the water in his eyes. Shrouded in a gray veil of fog, a Starfleet runabout hovered overhead, its nose angled down into the alley.

The melodious ringing hum of transporter beams filled the alley. Suddenly, he was surrounded by six heavily armed Starfleet security officers, two medics carrying field surgery kits, and Dr. Tropp. One of the medics pulled Tenila off of him. The other injected something relaxing into his jugular.

Tropp watched his tricorder readings and nodded. "He's stable, let's get him to *Enterprise,* stat."

Riker reached out and locked his right hand on to the Tezwan woman. "She comes with me," he rasped. "That's an order."

Chapter 26
U.S.S. Enterprise-E

EVEN AS SHE RAN DOWN the corridor toward sickbay, Troi didn't believe the news. She couldn't risk being disappointed if it was false. The door opened for someone who was walking out of sickbay, and Troi dashed through the open door before it could start to close again. Two steps inside she stopped.

In the middle of the room, Dr. Tropp materialized inside the energized shimmer of a transporter beam. He kneeled in front of two soaking-wet prone figures, one human, the other Tezwan. As the transporter effect faded, he stood up and stepped clear.

Lying on the floor, battered and wounded, Will Riker turned his head weakly and looked at her. He mouthed the word *"Imzadi."*

She crossed the distance in four fast steps and knelt beside him. From the other side of the room, every available nurse and medical technician was scrambling to his aid. Troi took his bloody left fist in hers and permitted herself to shed tears of joy. The hiss of hyposprays and the high-pitched oscillations of medical tricorders surrounded them as she kissed his forehead. He smiled weakly at the sight of her.

He opened his left hand and pressed a data rod into hers.

Tropp issued orders to his staff, who gently slid a stretcher under the battle-torn first officer. "Easy," he said to the nurses and technicians. "Get him into OR Two, stat."

Troi stood as they lifted Riker off the deck. His hand slipped from hers. He whispered, "She saved my life."

Safe in the arms of the *Enterprise* medical staff, Riker was borne away to the operating room. Troi turned and looked down at the Tezwan woman who had been beamed up beside him. She wore the uniform of Tezwa's new civilian police force, and had suffered two gruesome shots to her torso.

Nurse Weinstein stood over her. She closed her medical tricorder. Returning Troi's gaze, she shook her head.

Her *Imzadi*'s rescuer was gone.

She looked at the data rod in her hand, then tapped her combadge. "Troi to Lieutenant Peart. I have evidence that requires immediate analysis."

"Captain," Peart said. "Incoming transmission from the *Republic.*"

"On screen," Picard said. He stood up and straightened his jacket. Captain Lisa Del Colle appeared on the main viewer.

"Jean-Luc," Del Colle said. *"We've got the* Caedera."

"Well done," he said. "Are its logs intact?"

"Affirmative," she said.

"And the crew?"

"No sign of them. We found the ship adrift near the Delavan system."

"How soon can you forward the *Caedera*'s logs?"

"Already on the way," she said.

Peart looked up from his tactical console. "Confirmed, sir. They're coming through now."

"Route them directly to Mr. Data's station," Picard said.

"Aye, sir."

"Lisa," Picard said, "have you or your staff reviewed the *Caedera*'s logs?"

"Not yet," she said.

Picard nodded. "I need to ask you not to. I wish I could tell you more, but I'm afraid it's classified."

"Consider it done," Del Colle said. *"We're putting the* Caedera *in tow and heading back.* . . . *How're things at Tezwa?"*

The captain looked at Data, then at Peart. He was uncertain where to begin recapping the bloody events of the past few hours. Del Colle apparently took note of his hesitation, because she added, *"Forget I asked. Del Colle out."*

The screen blinked back to the deceptively serene-looking curve of Tezwa backed by a curtain of stars.

Picard sighed heavily and turned back toward his chair. Data was already reviewing the files from the *Caedera* on the monitor next to his seat. The rest of the bridge crew worked quietly, their panels emitting unobtrusive feedback tones. The captain was about to ask

Peart to open a channel to Admiral Janeway, so that he could relay the good news of Commander Riker's safe return, when an alert sounded on Peart's console.

"Captain, we just decoded the contents of a data rod that Commander Riker brought us," he said. He did a double take, then added, "We know where Kinchawn is."

Chapter 27
Tezwa

STINGING JOLTS OF PAIN replaced the numb paralysis in Vale's right shoulder. The medical technician adjusted the tissue regenerator and continued repairing the deep wound. A nurse was busy working a similar medical miracle on Vale's left hip.

Almost every remaining security officer on the *Enterprise* had beamed down to Tezwa, to help Tezwa's inexperienced civilian police take into custody the thousands of Loyalist guerrillas who had been stunned by the starship's phasers. Medical personnel moved through the streets looking for survivors, while engineers did their part, tagging slain Starfleet personnel with tiny pattern enhancers so their bodies could be beamed up.

A hazy cloud of brownish yellow dust from the destroyed building mixed with inky black smoke from the destroyed rotunda domes. Around the perimeter of the east rotunda, dozens of once elegant statues had been reduced to broken stone. A runabout hovered overhead.

Reflecting on the half-dozen ships just like it that had been shot down in the past hour, Vale wondered whether the craft would be viewed by straggler guerrillas as a deterrent or as a target.

Her hip flared back to full sensation with a hideous, burning pain. She inhaled sharply through clenched teeth while the nurse administered a hypo of pain relievers. As the pain abated, a warbling tone from her combadge preceded the message, *"Peart to Vale, priority one."*

"Go ahead, Jim."

"We've got a fix on Kinchawn. We're moving in."

"Get me a site-to-site transport. I'm coming with you." Poking the nurse's shoulder, she said, "Hand me my rifle."

With a skeptical roll of her eyes, the nurse reached over, grabbed the phaser rifle, and pushed it into Vale's hands.

Peart, filtered through Vale's combadge, replied, *"Locking on to your signal now. Stand by."*

Vale nodded to the medical technician. "Nice work. Bye."

The excruciating pain in her shoulder and hip seemed to fade just a little bit as the transporter beam took hold of her.

Kinchawn sat alone in the conference room of his redoubt. He had gambled everything on a single lightning attack. Success had depended upon many assumptions that had proved to be false.

He had never believed that the Federation would directly ally itself with Bilok's government. Certainly, the cost in civilian lives would prove too high for the pacifist Federation. But then Picard deployed his people as Bilok's de facto army.

Facing his aggrieved field commanders, Kinchawn had assured them that Starfleet would balk at the first sign of serious bloodshed. Yet despite every escalation of the conflict, including the demolition of the Federation's first command center and the laughably easy slaughter of a hundred of its vaunted Special Ops troops, Starfleet had pressed on.

When three of the Federation starships left the system without warning, leaving the *Enterprise* alone in orbit, Kinchawn had promised his generals that a precision surgical strike would easily cripple the ship, leaving Starfleet's planet-based forces vulnerable and unsupported; but the ship's crew had responded more quickly than anyone expected, and the attack had failed.

Regardless, the coup might still have succeeded had his estimate of Starfleet's ground forces not been so erroneous. All his research, every historical abstract he had ever reviewed, had indicated that Starfleet's rules of engagement would leave its personnel hopelessly constrained. But apparently, the experience of its war against the Dominion had changed Starfleet more than Kinchawn—or anyone else—had realized.

They had become hard and dangerous. War had tempered them with its bitter lessons. Once easily intimidated and quick to negotiate, Starfleet was now a formidable opponent.

He had misjudged his enemy. His army had been swept off the battlefield by the *Enterprise*. The sun was setting on his dreams of empire and he was powerless to prevent it.

He sat in his chair. Listened to the furious volleys of phaser fire from beyond the conference-room door. Awaited the inevitable.

The door opened. He saw the barrel of a rifle aimed at him. The weapon pushed into the room, followed by the human woman who held it. A dozen more Starfleet security personnel followed her in and quickly surrounded him. The level of overkill amused him.

"Secure," the woman said.

Captain Jean-Luc Picard strode into the room, followed by a silver-skinned humanoid man and Federation Ambassador Lagan.

Both Picard and Lagan were legendary for their ability to talk any matter to death. Kinchawn braced himself for what was certain to be at least an hour of pontification, moralization, and high-minded sophistry. His only uncertainty was whether the captain or the ambassador would have the last word.

Picard looked at Lagan. "Do you have anything to say, Madam Ambassador?"

Lagan stared at Kinchawn and shook her head.

A frown creased Picard's mouth as he eyed Kinchawn. "You're under arrest," he said, then turned toward a battle-scuffed female officer who was aiming her weapon with great intensity. "Turn him over to the Tezwan authorities," Picard said.

"Aye, sir," she replied. With a wave of her hand, she summoned forward four more Starfleet security officers.

The magnetic manacles snapped shut around Kinchawn's wrists. They possessed a cold finality that he knew would be surpassed only by his imminent execution. The deposed prime minister sneered at the Federation personnel around him. "Aren't you going to lecture me, Picard? Don't you have a speech ready for this occasion?"

"I have nothing to say to you," Picard said.

"Thank the Maker for small mercies," Kinchawn said as he was led out to meet his fate at the hands of his enemies.

"Wow, look at all this stuff," Obrecht said.

La Forge sighed and nodded in agreement with the engineer's sentiments. Deep inside the bowels of Kinchawn's redoubt, hidden in a dim, remote antechamber, was a trove of huge, industrial-looking weapon components of Federation design and manufacture. La Forge, Taurik, Obrecht, and several other engineers from the *Enterprise* were logging in every item that Peart's search team had discovered, and accounting for the provenance of every last chip, emitter crystal, and device housing.

The most intriguing element was what the search team had found in an adjacent storage space. Half-disintegrated and barely buried under the dirt floor were the remnants of a pair of containers whose serial numbers identified them as part of the contraband delivered by the impounded *Caedera*.

Everything had been found exactly where the files on the data rod delivered by Commander Riker had said they would be. La Forge didn't know how Riker had obtained that intel, but it was proving invaluable. In the past hour, nearly every remaining Loyalist cell had been exposed and taken into custody. Including the suspicious matériel that had been captured elsewhere in Alkam-Zar five hours ago, two of the five contraband shipments had been recovered.

What worried La Forge was where the data rod's intel had indicated the remaining three shipments would be found. If its information proved right once again, then an entirely new motive would emerge for the destruction of Tezwa's com relays—one that pointed not at Kinchawn and his allies, but at Bilok's new administration . . . and possibly at the Federation itself.

His tricorder beeped to indicate that it had finished its latest batch analysis. Another selection of random components had all tested as genuine Federation hardware, from their atomic trace elements to their secret nanomarkers. All around him, other engineers' tricorders whirred and chimed with identical noises.

"Obrecht," La Forge said, "do you have a reading on those spare parts yet?"

"Aye, sir," the young engineer said. "Tholian design, but the molecular structures look a little off. I'd say this stuff is supposed to look Tholian after it's been busted up a little."

Taurik motioned to La Forge that he wished to speak privately with him. La Forge stepped off to one side, then slipped out of the room a few steps behind the assistant chief engineer. "What've you got?"

"I have completed my tests," Taurik said softly. "These components are all genuine."

"Okay," La Forge said. "Factor in the chimerium grating you recovered, and the same kind of imitation Tholian replacement parts we found with the other components a few hours ago. Do you see a pattern emerging?"

"It is too soon to say for certain," Taurik said. "But it appears likely that someone is engaged in a program of deception meant to implicate the Tholians for arming Tezwa with its nadion-pulse cannons."

La Forge added, "And if Peart's team finds the remaining three cargo shipments in the *Gatni*-controlled warehouse in Keelee-Kee—"

"Then the new prime minister is our new prime suspect."

La Forge's combadge chirped. *"Vale to La Forge."*

"This is La Forge. Go ahead."

"Have I mentioned lately that I love the S.C.E.? I mean, that I really love those crazy eggheads?"

Taurik arched an eyebrow at La Forge's curious grin. "No," La Forge said. "Actually, you haven't."

"Well, I do, dammit. . . . Ask me why."

Surrendering to the inevitable, he replied, "Why?"

"Two words," Vale said. *"Redundant backups."*

He took her meaning almost instantly. "The com relays."

"Exactly," she said. *"The team at the Alkam-Zar relay had been worried about causing a surge and wiping out the relay's protected core—"*

"So they made a secure backup," La Forge interjected. "Standard procedure. Where is it?"

He could almost hear her ear-to-ear grin as she said, *"On the* Enterprise."

Deciphering the encryption on the Tezwan com relay had posed no real challenge to Vale or to the *Enterprise*'s new cryptography specialist, Lieutenant Adrienne Soranno. Working with Vale, the striking brunette had shredded the Tezwan system's security protocols so easily that she had actually laughed while doing it. "They call *this* security?"

Sitting in Kinchawn's redoubt office, which she had

commandeered, Vale searched through the relay's logs, which dated back nearly two months. Via her tricorder's secure uplink, the *Enterprise* computer displayed the results of its analysis.

She stared at the screen. A grotesque sinking sensation yawned painfully in her gut. Her wildest suspicions were true.

"Peart to Vale." Responding to his voice enabled her to look away from the evidence.

"Go ahead, Jim."

"I've been to all three Gatni-*run locations listed on the data rod,"* he said. *"I hate to be the bearer of bad news, but—"*

"But there's nothing there," Vale guessed.

"No, it's all there," he said. *"The bad news is some of Bilok's people shot at us."*

She tried to hold her dread at bay. "Casualties?"

"Not this time," he said. *"But I thought they were supposed to be on our side."* After a heavy silence, he added, *"I don't know what we're doing here, sir, but it's looking less like a mercy mission and more like a cover-up."*

Vale stared at the cold, hard facts on her tricorder. "Yeah," she said, her throat tight with anxiety. "I know what you mean."

Hughes and Crusher kneeled side by side in the street. They were surrounded by the scattered wreckage of the *Tsavo*.

The explosion had inflicted a wide variety of horrific wounds on the dozens of civilians who had been on the street below when the landing pad collapsed. Some had organs pulverized by the shockwave. Others suffered having their limbs crushed into bloody tangles of splintered bone and torn muscle. Some had been raked with shrapnel ranging from fist-sized to minuscule. All had been scoured with atomized particles of fuel, clothing, metal, concrete, dirt, and each other's flesh.

Nurse Ogawa moved amid the twisted metal debris, using her arms to shield her face from the flames dancing around her. While she carried out her one-woman search for other survivors, Crusher concentrated on stabilizing the most grievously injured Tezwans. An atonal keening rose and fell around them like waves in a growing tide of misery. Wounded men, women, and children writhed and whimpered under the crackling flames.

Crusher knew their efforts would likely be little more than symbolic until help arrived. They had almost no medicine, no whole blood to transfuse, no way to move the wounded into the hospital, and no one to care for them once they got there. The only commodity they had in abundance was trite assurances no one believed. Minute by minute, more patients slipped away. If she was lucky, she might save one in ten of her patients today.

She heard something thrown to the ground. Turning, she saw Hughes slumped against a chunk of the *Tsavo*'s hull, his eyes squeezed hard shut against tears that wanted to escape. At his feet was his discarded medkit, and a Tezwan woman clutching an infant child to her breast. Even from several meters away, without using her tricorder, Crusher knew that the woman and child were dead. On the other side of Hughes, Ogawa had paused her search to witness Hughes's emotional unraveling.

Crusher went to him and put her hands on his shoulders. The effort of holding back his sobs had stretched his mouth into a long, open grimace that showed his gritted teeth. Tears rolled from the corners of his eyes, even though they were firmly closed, and traced paths across the dust on his face.

Speaking through his grief, his voice was pulled taut. "This is why I left," he said. "I never wanted to see this again." He opened his eyes, which were stained red with exhaustion and sorrow. "This is how they looked when I found them." He glanced at the Tezwan woman, then closed his eyes again. "My wife and my little girl," he said. "Just like that."

He pulled in a deep breath, then forced it out. The effort made him cough a few times. He wiped away his tears with the side of his hand.

Crusher placed her hand against his cheek. Tenderly, she pulled him into a comforting embrace. He trembled, apparently coming down from a severe adrenaline overload.

As they parted, he sniffled then said, "They all keep dying in my arms. . . . I just can't keep losing people this way."

"Then don't," she said. She picked up his medkit and handed it to him. "Save one more life today. Keep going till you do. . . . We can't save everyone, Keith. But let's save the ones we can."

He stared forlornly at the medkit in his hands.

"Okay," he said. Crusher stepped away to search for her next patient when Hughes added, "Thanks."

"Thank me later," she said quietly, and returned to work. She looked back at Hughes. He found another patient lying battered and blistered in the flames. Kneeling down, he snapped to work, calmly running standard Starfleet medical protocols.

In that moment, she genuinely saw him. He was no larger-than-life charmer; no mysterious being; no aloof leader of men. Bereft of his flirtations, he was just a man . . . wounded and imperfect, struggling to live with his past the same as anyone else. He toiled with her in the midst of an urban killing field, his emotional scars laid bare beneath a bleak sky.

To Crusher's lonely eyes, he looked like a kindred soul.

Picard barreled into Bilok's office in the *Ilanatava* as if he owned it. An urgent-sounding discussion between Bilok and his deputy prime minister terminated abruptly as the doors swung open. Vale, Peart, and La Forge entered alongside the captain. Ambassador Lagan walked in a few steps behind them.

"Your people destroyed those com relays," Picard said.

Bilok adopted a look of offended innocence. "I don't understand, Captain," he said. "Why would you imply—"

"I'm not implying anything, Mr. Prime Minister," Picard said. "I'm making an accusation."

Tawnakel stepped out from behind Bilok's desk and interposed himself between Picard and the prime minister.

"Captain," Tawnakel said haughtily, "these baseless allegations are an insult to—"

"Your office knew about the S.C.E.'s demolition work orders because you helped to arrange them," Picard said. "Four weeks ago, you transmitted to someone on Earth a list of sites for demolition. Every site on your list was a com relay station. And your list matches the one that was given to the S.C.E. Matches it precisely, I might add."

Bilok said nothing. Tawnakel shifted uncomfortably. "We have no record of any such transmissions, Captain. And since all our relay stations were destroyed in Kinchawn's attack, I don't see how you could, either. . . . Unless you copied one of our memory cores illegally."

Picard frowned. "I'm not going to play these games with you," he said. "Kinchawn had no reason to want the com relays destroyed. But based on the lists you sent to Earth, you do have reasons for wanting them gone. Reasons that I'll wager are connected to the three containers of contraband we found in the safekeeping of your ministry of trade."

This time both Tawnakel and Bilok remained silent.

Picard eyed both men with grim disdain. "Why don't we cut to the heart of the matter? Where did your planet's artillery come from? Who within the Federation government is helping you destroy evidence and cover your tracks?"

The icy glares of Picard's officers and Ambassador Lagan fell upon the two Tezwan politicians. The captain's questions lingered heavily. Picard knew that with each passing moment the likelihood of his receiving an answer grew more remote.

Finally, Bilok stood from his chair. "Ambassador Lagan, Captain Picard: I hereby revoke Starfleet's peacekeeping powers on Tezwa, and demand that you return full authority to this lawfully elected civil government. Pursuant to this amendment to the aid agreement, I also direct you to remove all Starfleet personnel from the surface and orbit of Tezwa, and to withdraw beyond the accepted boundaries of the Tezel-Oroko system."

Picard sighed. He had expected a more noble response from Bilok. He found it hard to believe that this was the same man who had deftly placated the fury of the Klingons only four weeks ago. Looking at Bilok now, Picard recalled the grim adage "Power corrupts."

Bilok sat down. "Regarding your two questions, Captain . . . I invoke my executive privilege and respectfully decline to answer."

The prime minister nodded to Tawnakel, who looked at Picard and his entourage and pointed toward the exit.

"Get out," Tawnakel ordered.

Chapter 28
U.S.S. Enterprise-E

DATA STOOD IN FRONT of the ready-room wall monitor. Outside the room's narrow windows, he saw the *Amargosa* behind the *Enterprise*. The two ships were still in orbit of Tezwa, coordinating the extraction of the thousands of Starfleet personnel who had survived Kinchawn's coup attempt.

Captain Picard sat at his desk. Across from him sat Ambassador Lagan.

"The five shipments delivered to Tezwa by the *Caedera* comprise twenty cargo containers," Data said. He continuously updated the images and reports on the screen to match his statements. "Each container has a unique serial number for tracking purposes.

"The *Caedera* took the containers aboard at Deneva. Their shipment to Tezwa was paid for by an Antedean, seen in this image from the *Caedera*'s external security sensors.

"Notice in this freeze-frame that a member of the *Caedera* crew places a knife to the Antedean's throat.

That weapon was found aboard the *Caedera* by *Amargosa* first officer Carlos Carranza. The Antedean's blood was still on the knife. According to the ship's internal sensors, no other Antedeans had come aboard the *Caedera* since the meeting on Deneva. That blood sample was analyzed."

A large, crisp-focus image of an Antedean appeared on the monitor. "The blood came from Federation Secretary of Military Intelligence Nelino Quafina."

Dismayed looks passed between Picard and Lagan. Data noted their responses, waited an appropriate interval of a few seconds, then continued.

"Though there is no record of the containers being shipped to Deneva, a more detailed search of the Federation's commercial shipping registry indicates that their last registered use took them to Earth.

"A review of all bills of lading for private, commercial, and military shipments leaving Sector 001 revealed seven that were bound for Deneva bearing classified cargo. Five of those shipments continued on to other destinations. One was received by the planetary governor's office.

"One never officially arrived. That shipment has the distinction of being the only one of the seven whose contents were classified by an executive order of President Min Zife."

Lagan leaned forward. "Are you really suggesting that the president conspired with Quafina to ship contraband to Tezwa?"

Data cocked his head as he formulated an answer.

"I do not think it is likely the two met directly," he said. "There is no record of any contact between Zife and Quafina other than two brief meetings at diplomatic functions."

"A middleman," Picard said.

"The most likely candidate for such a role would be Koll Azernal, Zife's senior advisor and chief of staff," Data said. "Our analysis of Bilok's transmissions to Earth indicate that the majority of his encrypted signal traffic was directed to Azernal. It is highly probable that Mr. Azernal personally directed any past or present Federation initiatives on Tezwa."

Lagan sounded confused. "Past or present? I'm not sure I follow your meaning, Commander."

"Zife and Azernal's efforts to conceal the origins of the nadion-pulse cannons on Tezwa make sense only if they were aware that the systems were of Federation origin. The most likely explanation for such knowledge would be that *they* armed Tezwa."

Lagan shook her head. "I just can't believe we're accusing the administration that won the war against the Dominion of engineering a catastrophe of this magnitude," she said. "If not for Azernal, the Alpha Quadrant might belong to the Founders right now."

"With all due respect, Madam Ambassador," Data said, "I do not believe that any of the parties involved sought to create a 'catastrophe.' Nor do I think that is the issue at hand."

"Agreed," Picard said. "Zife, Azernal, and Quafina engaged in a conspiracy to hide their culpability for causing the Tezwa debacle—and tried to shift the blame onto an innocent party. Now they've cast us as their unwitting accomplices." Picard became darkly introspective for a moment. "Thousands of lives were sacrificed here in the service of a lie." Quiet rage infused the captain's voice. "All that we stand for has been betrayed."

Lagan said sadly, "What are we going to do about it?"

"I don't know what I would have done," Troi said. "For a moment, when he stared at me so smugly, all I could think about was how I wanted to break him."

Marlyn Del Cid nodded. "In the heat of the moment, those kinds of feelings are understandable," she said.

The *Amargosa* counselor had insisted upon following up with Troi even though Riker had been brought back safely to the *Enterprise*. The two women sat in Del Cid's office aboard the *Amargosa*. They faced each other from either side of a narrow coffee table, on which rested two untouched cups of *chai* tea. Troi leaned on the arm of the couch, her legs crossed at the ankles. Del Cid perched on the edge of a plush armchair and leaned forward, palms together and fingers steepled beneath her chin as she listened attentively.

Troi got up from the couch and ambled around the room. Outside the slim window, she saw the *Enterprise* in the distance, slipping past the curving horizon of Tezwa. "It's more than that," she said. "I still think about it: Which drugs would have broken down Minza's resistance? How much pain would it have taken to make him talk? When the Tezwans extradited him, I envied the free hand they'd have with him."

"I see," Del Cid replied. "Were their methods more successful?"

"No," Troi said, ashamed of her disappointment with the truth. "He never broke. They executed him this morning."

Del Cid folded her hands across her lap. "So even if

you had resorted to such amoral means, it would have made no difference."

"I would have been able to see him suffer," Troi said. Almost immediately she regretted having said it.

"But you just said that he didn't break," Del Cid replied. "You'd have observed a prolonged torture that yielded nothing but pain. Would that have brought you any comfort?"

Again, the truth taunted Troi. "Probably not," she said. "It's a primal reaction. Irrational. . . . After Will was beamed up from Tezwa, after I saw what they'd done to him. . . ." She let herself trail off while she struggled to suppress her burning desire to exact vengeance upon someone—anyone—for what had been done to Will, and to her. The cruel fantasies she had harbored didn't deserve to see the light of day. Admitting them aloud felt like a failure. "I can't just extinguish my anger."

"It's going to be a lot of work, Deanna," Del Cid said. "For a month you lived with the possibility that he might be dead, or that he was suffering. Bringing him home offers some catharsis, but this kind of emotional trauma can't be treated overnight. It takes time to confront all your feelings and work through them. Give yourself that time."

Troi shook her head sadly.

"I don't think it's as simple as that," she said. "I feel poisoned. Tainted. . . . I spent so much time grappling with Minza's way of thinking that it began to infect my own thoughts. When he was extradited, I thought of Nietzsche's warning about the abyss. It had always seemed too melodramatic to be taken seriously. But I see now that it was no exaggeration."

Del Cid cast a sorrowful glance out the window at the

planet below. " 'Battle not with monsters, lest ye become a monster,' " she said, quoting from the same passage as the abyss reference. "That seems like an apt analogy for a lot of things these days."

"Yes," Troi said. "It does."

It was cold enough in the *Enterprise*'s aft auxiliary cargo bay for Jim Peart to see his breath. It jetted out in front of him like a short-lived, wispy white spectre. The chill in the room was deep enough that after standing in here for less than half an hour, he found that his hands and the front of his thighs were almost numb.

Long rows of tall metal shelves, six layers high, filled the enormous compartment. Every shelf was packed head-to-toe with blue polymer bodybags—overflow from the *Enterprise* morgue. Each bag was labeled in block English characters, a scannable ID tag, and additional information in other languages as necessary. Since the ship had long ago run out of stasis chambers, refrigeration was only other viable storage method.

Peart walked slowly between the rows, eyeing the names on the tags, counting the dead. More than two thousand Starfleet security personnel had been slain on Tezwa before he could use the *Enterprise*'s arsenal to subdue their attackers. In a matter of minutes, a single well-orchestrated assault had killed nearly half of Starfleet's defensive force on the planet. Had the *Enterprise* been incapacitated by the ship in its shuttlebay or even delayed a few minutes longer by the kamikaze attackers, Kinchawn's coup attempt might have been successful.

Pacing among the dead, however, Peart wasn't convinced that the battle's outcome mattered anymore—or that it had ever mattered at all.

Even more disheartening were all the noncombatants who lay beside them: doctors, nurses, engineers, civilians. For the next few weeks, until a convoy of special medical transports arrived to ferry the casualties home to their final resting places, the dead would outnumber the living aboard the *Enterprise.*

His heart sank with every name he recognized on the blue bags stacked around him: Gracin, Thomas A.; Duncan, Richard; Grigsby, Elaine M. Two very small body-bags caught Peart's attention. The names stenciled onto them were Fillion, Scott J., and McEwan, Fiona. Apparently, very little of the two young security officers' bodies had been recoverable. Peart didn't want to imagine what their final moments must have been like.

Grief tightened its choke hold. The names, the service numbers, the KIA dates and locations—they all blurred as hot tears of anger filled his eyes. Fury swelled within him.

All these lives, he raged. His hands closed into fists until his fingernails bit into his palm. *The Klingons, the Tezwans, us . . . all sacrificed to cover up a politician's lies.* He thought of the millions of Tezwans whose lives had been snuffed out by a brutal Klingon counterattack, and the millions more who were left starving or homeless or without medical care.

All because the Federation used this world as a pawn.

Now Starfleet—and the *Enterprise,* in particular—had been used, as well. Used and discarded.

The double doors to the corridor slid apart. A nimbus of vapor formed immediately as warm air rushed into the cargo bay. The doors closed as a female form stepped through the quickly dissipating cloud. It was Perim. She looked around until she saw Peart, then walked slowly toward him. Joining him in the middle aisle between the rows of the dead, she gently took his hand, which was still clenched into a fist. Gradually, patiently, she pried at his hand. After a few seconds he relented, opened his grip, and wove his fingers among hers.

"The computer told me where to find you," she said. "You didn't answer your com."

"I turned it off," he said. "I needed to be alone for a while."

She squeezed his hand gently. He looked at her and was grateful for her company. He had seen and heard things on Tezwa over the past several hours that he could never share with her, or with anyone else. As much as he wanted to explain to her the dark truth about the litany of errors and lies that had led the Federation into the ultimately disastrous occupation of Tezwa, his orders from Captain Picard had been clear: No one could ever know. Peart had become privy to a secret that held the potential to shatter the Federation-Klingon alliance and plunge the two powers into a war of mutual annihilation.

Those were his orders. He had made his vow of silence.

But if he and others like him were willing to lie and kill today to hide the sins of the Federation, how many others before him had done the same? What dark bargains had been made in the name of the "greater good"? How many times had the Federation engaged in atrocities that no one would ever know of?

Perhaps this was the first such crisis of its kind. Perhaps it was standard operating procedure. Peart simply had no way of knowing. All he could know for certain was that the idea that Perim—lovely, gentle Perim—might one day wind up in one of these blue bags, to help mask a conspiracy, sickened him.

"If we left here," he said, "where would you want to go?"

"You mean the *Enterprise?*"

"No," he said. "You and me. Just the two of us."

She seemed to be caught off-guard by the question. Then a look of recognition crossed her face. "Jim . . . are you talking about . . ." Her sentence trailed off. He felt her staring at him. Her confusion turned to shock as she noticed his collar.

"Jim . . . where are your pips?"

His voice dropped to a low whisper. "They're on Captain Picard's desk," he said. "Where I left them."

She let go of his hand. Moving in front of him, she reached up and placed her hands on his chest. "Are you serious?" Her eyes looked up at him with uncharted depths of concern and compassion. "Are you certain it's what you want?"

"I can't do this job anymore," he said. "Don't ask me to explain why, because I can't. . . . Just believe me when I say that if you're still ready to walk away from all this, I'm ready to come with you."

He didn't try to mask the sorrow or the bitterness that filled his heart. He waited for her to say something. Anything.

She kissed him. Softly at first. Then passionately.

Their lips parted. She pulled away from him.

Then she reached up and removed her own rank insignia

from her uniform collar. "I'm ready," she said. "Let's go."

He took her hand. She led him out of the cargo bay.

Guilt gnawed at him as he passed by the dead, stacked six high by ten deep on either side of a dozen rows around him. For years, since his Academy days, he had followed a plan for his career and for his life. He had mapped out a path to his own command. In a moment, that dream had vanished, consumed like parchment in flames, scattered like ashes in a winter gale.

Despair had offered its easy embrace, its inertia. But with Perim's hand in his, life beckoned him to explore new mysteries. He didn't know where their path would lead, but he no longer concerned himself with destination; all that mattered now was the journey, and the hope that it would carry him far from here.

Captain Picard sat next to Lagan, in his ready room aboard the *Enterprise*. Pictured on the display screen were Admirals Ross, Nechayev, Jellico, Paris, and Nakamura. The five flag officers had gathered in one secure location for this conference, at Lagan's request.

"Going public would mean starting a war with the Klingons," Admiral Ross said. *"It'd be a bloodbath unlike anything in history."*

Lagan said, "I understand that exposing Zife, Azernal, and Quafina to the general public will do more harm than good. But we can't ignore the crimes they've committed, or the lives that have been lost as a result."

"Exposing them isn't an option," Nakamura said. *"No matter what action we take, their conspiracy must remain a secret."*

"There's no question in my mind that Zife needs to step down," Nechayev said, *"or that Azernal and Quafina have to be removed with him."*

Paris sighed heavily. *"Getting them out without causing a political meltdown will be tricky. If Zife's going to call for a special election, we'll need to prepare a cover story."*

"Hold on," Jellico said. *"Let's stand down for a moment. Starfleet's charter makes it very clear that we're subordinate to the Federation government. We don't have any authority to give orders to Zife."*

"No one disputes that, Admiral," Picard said. "But absent such authority, how are we to respond to what Zife and his co-conspirators have done?"

The lean, gruff-voiced admiral furrowed his gray eyebrows as he pondered that question. *"I'm not sure that we can."*

"That's not an answer I'm willing to accept," Ross said. *"Starfleet personnel died for his lie. We led our allies into an ambush because of it. . . . I'm sorry, Edward, but Zife and his people went too far. We have to act."*

"Which brings us back to the question of how to keep Zife's resignation from touching off a panic," Paris said.

Nakamura, who had been leaning back with his index finger pressed thoughtfully against his lips, leaned forward. *"Zife has been meeting a lot of resistance on economic issues,"* he said. *"Councillors zh'Faila and Gleer have been his most vocal opponents. We could ask Zife to cite a need for more experienced economic stewardship as his reason for bowing out and calling for a special election."*

"No one will believe it," Jellico said.

"Yes, they will," Paris said. *"Repeat it often enough*

and it'll become the truth. The real trick will be getting Zife to say it."

"He'll need an incentive," Ross said.

"Secrecy," Nakamura answered. *"Zife and his two cronies step down, vow to stay out of politics—here or anywhere else. In exchange, their reputations as war heroes stay untarnished."*

Ross nodded. *"All right. We put them in protective custody. Somewhere nice, luxurious. Give them new identities. Then we finish cleaning up their mess on Tezwa—and dump every last shred of evidence down a black hole."*

"Are you serious?" Nechayev said. *"Clean up their mess? We're actually going to* help *their plan succeed?"*

"We're not going to frame the Tholians," Ross said. *"Or anyone else, for that matter. But we'll make sure no one finds out where Tezwa's weapons came from."*

Nechayev looked disgusted. *"Abetting their conspiracy? I can't believe we're even considering this."*

Ross shot back at her, *"This isn't about moral purity, Alynna. This is about the survival of the Federation. Unless we want to see everything we've worked for get squandered on a pointless war with the Klingons, we need to contain the damage on all fronts. In this case, that means erasing Zife's mistakes."*

"If we're prepared to do that," Jellico said, *"then why ask Zife to step down at all? If we're going to do his dirty work, why compound our sins by acting against our own president?"*

Picard interjected, "Because our president acted against us." The table full of admirals stopped talking and turned their attention to the captain. "Zife betrayed his oath of office when he secretly and deliberately violated the Khitomer Accords. . . . Sending the *Enterprise* and a Klingon fleet to face an enemy that he knew could overpower us—and not warning us of the danger we faced—was an act of depraved indifference tantamount to murder. Committing us to a prolonged occupation of a sovereign planet, then engaging in a conspiracy to plant false evidence . . . these are the acts of a criminal, not a president. But to impeach him would require a public airing of his crimes—and that would lead to scandal as well as to the war we're struggling to avoid."

Paris seemed burdened by the gravity of the discussion. *"Edward,"* he said to Jellico, *"even you have to realize that Zife and Azernal set this in motion. Millions of lives were taken on Tezwa—"*

"By the Klingons," Jellico protested. *"In response to provocation by the Tezwans!"*

"Who would never have dared to challenge the Klingons had the Federation not armed them with its most advanced weapons system," Lagan retorted.

"Ed," Nakamura said. *"Do you honestly believe that Zife, Azernal, and Quafina deserve to walk away from this?"*

Jellico glared back at the other admirals, who had fixed their accusatory stares on him. Finally, he seemed to diminish slightly. With an air of grim resignation, he said, *"No."*

"Then we're agreed," Ross said. *"Zife, Azernal, and Quafina have to be removed as soon as possible. We'll make it clear that they'll be kept safe and comfortable, but also incommunicado."*

Jellico spoke up. *"What if they refuse?"* The conversation halted. After a moment, he continued, *"What if we* present our demands and make our offer, and Zife won't step down? Do we even have a contingency plan? Or are we just bluffing?"

The mood in the admirals' conference room darkened. Everyone seemed to sense that this question was Ross's to answer. *"We can't bluff,"* he said. *"Zife and Azernal will know we want the truth kept secret as much as they do. If we aren't prepared to force them out, they'll have no reason to comply."*

Ross's words raised the hackles on the back of Picard's neck. "Is this to be a military coup, Admiral?"

Nechayev jumped to intercept the question. *"It's not a coup, Jean-Luc,"* she said. *"Starfleet isn't taking control, we're simply removing corrupt elements for the good of the government as a whole."*

Jellico folded his arms across his chest and frowned. *"Leaving a power vacuum. Do you think the Federation will fracture before or after the Romulans cross the Neutral Zone?"*

If Nechayev's temper rose to Jellico's challenge, she didn't show it. *"You know full well there won't be a power vacuum,"* she said. *"When Zife resigns, the council will appoint a pro tem president. Until the election is held, the current cabinet will remain in place—except for Quafina, of course."*

"Still," Jellico said, *"we'll be looking at a protracted period of instability as we change administrations."*

Nakamura retorted, *"Don't be ridiculous, Ed. There are several good people waiting to run. Once the council approves the candidates, we'll have a new president within a month."*

Nechayev said, *"From a political standpoint, the transfer of power will appear seamless. Once we remove Zife and his accomplices, Starfleet won't have any further involvement in the process. The government will remain under civilian control at all times. We're not going to repeat Leyton's mistake."*

As desperately as Picard wished to, he wasn't certain he believed her. "Those are all very fine distinctions, Admiral," he said. "But let's not lose sight of the fact that this might well be the darkest day in the history of the Federation. Let's not give ourselves the comfort of euphemisms; let us at least be honest with ourselves about what we're doing."

"For the good of the Federation, we're going to forcibly remove our president and two of his top advisors from power," Ross said. *"Is that honest enough for you, Captain?"*

Picard frowned. There was no good answer to that.

Nechayev said, *"This matter must be treated as one of utmost secrecy. We're never to speak of this again, either amongst ourselves or with others. . . . For the record, Captain, this discussion never happened. Is that clear?"*

"Perfectly," Picard said.

"Ambassador Lagan," Nechayev said. *"I can't compel you to secrecy as I can the captain. But I must ask you to abide by this pact of silence. Do you agree?"*

Lagan nodded slowly. "Yes. I swear before the Prophets."

Ross sighed heavily. *"I'll make the necessary arrangements,"* he said.

Chapter 29
Tezwa

INTIMIDATING DARK BIRDS ringed the roof of the centuries-old *tava* like glass-eyed gargoyles. Neeraj didn't look up at them.

The human woman named Vale crouched beside him and guided his hand. She helped him control the plasma cutter. He paid close attention as they burned his mother's name into the memory stone, beside his father's recently engraved name.

The majestic slab had been broken during the Klingons' barrage of the planet, and the top half now rested at an odd angle, propped up against the sandstone wall next to its intact lower portion, which remained embedded in the wall of the tribe's ancestral aerie.

The blinding plasma beam glided across the glossy black stone, making white-hot grooves that cooled into smooth, grayish lines. The young Tezwan boy was barely old enough to read simple words and sentences, but he knew his parents' names by heart. It still confused him to think that nothing remained of them now except for their names, scorched into this rock for all time.

His grandparents stood behind him and Vale, whose Tezwan calligraphy was nearly perfect.

"You write good *Seshto*," Neeraj said.

Vale flashed him a bittersweet smile and gently steered his small hands through a delicate curlicue at the end of Tenila's given name. "No, I don't," she said. "I only learned how to write your mother's name."

That didn't make sense to Neeraj. "Why?"

"As a sign of respect," Vale said. "And to thank her."

"For what?"

"She saved my friend's life."

They worked together for a long while, carefully hewing Tenila's matriarchal surname into the memory stone. A moaning wind cut an invisible path across the dusty plains outside Savola-Cov. As they finished the final cut, Neeraj looked up and squinted against the sun while he studied every detail of Vale's face. It was strangely pale and featherless. Despite her round irises, he could tell by looking at her that she was very sad.

He wondered if Vale missed his mother, too.

"Why did my mother die?"

Vale placed her hand on his arm. Her touch wasn't as warming as that of his own people, but the firmness of her grip was comforting. "Some very cruel people were going to kill my friend," she said. "Your mother wouldn't let them. So they killed her."

"Why did it have to be her?"

The human woman swallowed hard, and thought for a moment. "Because she made a promise," she said. "She promised to protect people in danger and make people follow the law. She gave her life to save someone else because . . ." Vale's eyes became wet with tears. "Because only the bravest people can keep a promise like that. Your mother was one of those people. She was a peace officer."

"Are you a peace officer?"

Vale wiped the tears from her cheeks. "I was," she said. "A long time ago. On a planet called Izar." She reached out and traced the path of Tenila's name with her fingertips. "But I was never as brave as your mother."

"It's not much," Lagan said, "but it's home."

Lagan's new office was small and cluttered. Exiled from the *Ilanatava*, she had been tucked into the dustiest back corner of a dilapidated government building on the outskirts of Arbosa-Lo, far away from the capital city of Keelee-Kee.

Unlike her last two workspaces on Tezwa, this one was on the ground floor. The view outside her windows—assuming she could ever wash off the thick layer of grime—was likely to be nothing more than the blank rear wall of another drab building just like this one.

Picard looked around, lips pulled tight beneath a narrow-eyed gaze that swept over the room with unveiled suspicion. "I've never been a fan of ostentation," he said, "but this seems to take utilitarianism to an extreme."

"It'll do," she said. "As long as I'm allowed to do my job, I won't ask for anything else."

Picard nodded. "I'm sorry that Starfleet can't provide you with any security."

"Don't be," Lagan said. "You and your crew brought more stability to this planet's political arena than it's had since I first came here. Thanks to you, there's a real opportunity right now for Bilok and his allies to make some changes for the better."

"He's abiding by the aid agreement, then?"

"For now," Lagan said, lowering herself into her chair. It squeaked like a mouse in a vise as she swiveled toward Picard. "Whatever role he played in Zife and Azernal's little game, he really does seem committed to restoring social justice and repairing his world's environment. I know I'd have to be crazy to trust him, but . . ."

"But what choice do we have," Picard said, nodding gravely. "How often are we presented with only the *illusion* of choice? We came to this world expecting to be peacemakers, but found ourselves forced into the role of conquerors. We confided in the admiralty hoping to find justice; instead, we triggered a coup. I sometimes wonder if all our choices have already been made for us, and we're all simply waiting to be told what we've chosen."

"I know what you mean," Lagan said. "Had it been up to me, I wouldn't have sent Zife and his cronies to live out their lives in luxury. Frankly, I'd have shipped them to Rura Penthe and lost the paperwork."

Picard sighed. Lagan sensed that if the subject had not been one of such gravity, he might have cracked a wan smile at her remark. As it was, he attempted a grin that faltered into a lopsided grimace.

"It is a travesty," he said. "To think that they should be

permitted the grace of anonymity after the hideous slaughters they caused—with their indifference, their incompetence, their self-serving deceptions . . ."

He shook his head, his mien darkly despondent. "But what choice do we have, Serra? The alternative is interstellar war."

Chapter 30
Earth

KOLL AZERNAL WAS ONLY HALF-LISTENING as Admiral Ross finished outlining the terms of President Zife's resignation.

Ross sat on the opposite side of the table, flanked by Admirals Nechayev and Nakamura. Standing with Zife and Azernal was Nelino Quafina, whom the admirals had marched into the war room like a trophy. Dim pools of light spilled across the wood-textured table from recessed overhead fixtures. The walls of panoramic display screens all were dark as the grave.

The admirals had promised everything that they could. Reputations untarnished by scandal. New identities. Protective custody. Lives of anonymous comfort. All as a reward for Zife, Azernal, and Quafina's long careers of faithful public service.

Azernal knew a scam when he heard one. This one wasn't even clever. He glanced at Quafina. The Antedean's slow, tedious blinking of his huge, bulbous eyes made it clear that he wasn't fooled by the admirals' sales pitch, either.

Zife, on the other hand, actually seemed greatly relieved that Starfleet was, for all intents and purposes, terminating his presidency by force.

The president looked up at Azernal with a desperate expression. "Their terms sound more than fair," he said.

Glowering, the brusque Zakdorn weighed his options. If the admirals really could prove as much as they claimed to, then they had to understand the consequences that would follow from exposing the truth. He decided to call their bluff.

"You make an interesting case," he said. "But what if we refuse your offer?"

Stern, dangerous looks were volleyed between the three flag officers. It was Ross who picked up Azernal's thrown verbal gauntlet. "That's not really an option."

That's it, then, Azernal realized. *It's not a bluff.*

Azernal gently rested his hand on Zife's shoulder. "Take the deal, Mr. President."

Zife looked up at Azernal, then at Ross. "Very well, then," he said. "We do it your way, Admiral. When?"

"Now," Ross said. He lifted his arm and spoke softly into his jacket cuff. "You can come in."

The door to the war room opened with a low swish. Three figures dressed in all-black uniforms entered quietly. One was a statuesque Vulcan woman with an elegant haircut. Beside her was a shorter, trimly built middle-aged human man with an intense stare. Following them was a younger humanoid man whose wiry body conveyed a powerful presence.

Gesturing to the three black-clad visitors, Ross said, "My associates will handle the details of your resignation announcement, then see to your travel arrangements. Whatever you require, let them know. They're at your service."

The Vulcan woman nodded at Zife. "Mr. President," she said. Her attention shifted from Quafina to Azernal as she added, "Gentlemen." With a wave of her arm toward the door, she said in a dry clinical voice, "Shall we?"

Azernal and Quafina stepped out from behind Zife. As the president stood, the admirals rose from their chairs. The three soon-to-be-exiles fell into step behind the Vulcan woman, and her two associates trailed close behind them as they moved toward the door. "Mr. President," the Vulcan woman said, "we will escort you to your office, where you will issue your resignation and call for a special election. When that is done, we will proceed to a private transport. Do you understand?"

The Bolian chief executive nodded. Judging from the looks on everyone else's faces, Zife was the only person in the group who didn't know who the officers in black really were, or that after his resignation speech no one would see him, Azernal, or Quafina ever again.

This is the way it has to be, Azernal told himself. *If we're to be patriots, we have to pay the price. Starfleet will finish our work and keep our secrets. All we have to do is die.*

The Zakdorn's broad, rounded shoulders slumped in defeat as they stepped out of the war room and proceeded down the eerily deserted corridor toward the president's office.

Azernal envied the president's cluelessness. *I could*

warn him, he mused. *So could Quafina. But what good would that do? Zife would just panic, say something stupid in front of an interstellar newsfeed. . . . Better that he doesn't know. Maybe if he doesn't expect it, the killing blow won't hurt as much.*

The disgraced trio strode past one empty office after another. Their steps snapped crisply on the hard polished floors; the footfalls of their escorts were ominously silent.

Zife, at long last, adopted a truly presidential bearing as he marched toward the end of his career. He carried himself with the mien of a Roman senator, proud and resolute in expression.

Azernal said nothing as he walked beside his president, prepared to meet his fate at the merciless hands of Section 31.

Chapter 31
U.S.S. Enterprise-E

THE RICH AROMA OF COFFEE wafting out of main engineering was La Forge's first clue that no real work was getting done in there.

"Repair teams, I need you on deck five," he said as he rounded the corner into the main compartment. "The shield grid isn't going to fix itself."

No one responded. They were all clustered in front of a low console monitor, with their backs to him.

He pushed through the group to see what they were all looking at. They all stood transfixed by a live subspace newsfeed of President Zife's resignation. Two days after leaving the Tezel-Oroko system, one-third of La Forge's staff was still on medical leave, leaving every shift short-handed. This was exactly the kind of distraction they didn't need right now.

La Forge shooed everyone away from the center console, which was littered with discarded, half-empty mugs of coffee. Reaching past the monitor to shut it off, he caught a few moments of Zife's unscheduled address to the Federation. Despite himself, and even though he was joining it in medias res, he was riveted by it.

"—because I feel that this resignation is perhaps the greatest of those services that I can now give to the Federation," Zife said in a stately tone. *"While my chief of staff and I were able to serve our nation well in war, we were, it seems, less suited for peace. As the war grows more distant in our past, it has become increasingly obvious that Koll and I need to step down for the good of the Federation. The model by which we survived during the war, and even during the first few months afterward, is no longer tenable as we and our allies attempt—"*

La Forge clicked off the newsfeed. The screen switched to the blue and white emblem of the Federation. Resting his palms on the console, he took a deep breath. Most of the Federation would probably believe Zife's rationales for leaving office. It sounded reasonable enough.

But La Forge would always know the truth, and so would dozens of other officers on the *Enterprise,* many of whom had pieced together countless secondhand accounts into a narrative of death and betrayal. Few, if any, personnel outside the senior staff knew the most damning details, but whispers of scandals and high crimes susurrated through the lower decks of the ship.

Beyond the microcosm of the flagship, however, life seemed to go on as normal. Councillor Ra'ch B'ullhy, the former governor of Damiano, had been elected by the Federation Council to serve as president pro tem until the new elections could be organized. Meanwhile, the Federation Council argued endlessly about one bill or another, and the newsfeeds treated the thousands of dead Starfleet personnel on Tezwa like either a petty statistic or a political travesty, depending upon which reporter was interpreting the "facts."

He wished he could make them all see what a disaster the mission to Tezwa had been from start to finish, and how much more important it was than any pointless debate about which planet's transporter network was more antiquated. But he knew that was a lesson he would never be allowed to share. If the truth were unleashed, the dogs of war would be close behind.

There was nothing left to do but bury his anger and bear the ugly truth like a secret scar for the rest of his life.

With a resigned sigh, he picked up a toolkit and set off in search of something that he could fix with his hands.

Picard strode through the corridors of the *Enterprise,* a bottle of champagne in his hand. He had somewhere to be.

Beverly had invited him to breakfast this morning.

She had said in her message that she had "something important" that she needed to talk over with him. *It must be the offer from Starfleet Medical,* Picard decided. He was relieved that the awkward silence that had reigned between himself and Dr. Crusher for the past several weeks appeared to have passed. It would be nice to be able to sit and talk again. To put the dark cloud of wounded feelings behind them.

He still had no idea what he planned to say to her.

On the one hand, he felt like he ought to be supportive and congratulatory. Wish her well. Offer some sage advice.

The honest part of him wanted to plead with her to refuse the job offer, even though he couldn't—or wouldn't—admit one reason why she should.

Asking her to stay would be the epitome of selfishness, he chastened himself. *How often does such an opportunity present itself? I can't ask her to turn it down. I won't.*

Looking at the bottle of champagne in his hand, he wondered if he had chosen too rare a vintage. *After all, we're most likely going to make mimosas with it,* he reasoned. With a mental shrug he decided it would be fine. *Nothing wrong with a little indulgence from time to time.*

He was still several meters away from Crusher's door when it opened. A thirtyish human man stepped out of the doctor's quarters. His civilian clothing was conspicuously untucked; his short, chestnut hair was mildly disheveled. As he walked past Picard, the captain noticed that the younger man wore a wan smile on his stubbled face; in fact, he seemed aglow with quiet satisfaction. He boarded a turbolift and was gone.

Picard had stopped walking. He stood in the corridor and stared with a slack expression at the turbolift. When he turned back toward Crusher's quarters, it required an enormous act of will to set his feet back in motion. Several dread-freighted steps later, he stood at Crusher's door and pressed the chime.

From the other side of the door, Crusher called out in a lilting, singsong voice, "Come in!"

The door opened. Picard stepped warily inside. He was met by the savory aroma of bacon and eggs and the sweet scent of French roast. The dining table was elegantly set, with sterling service, bone china, and a colorful assortment of fruit and pastries in the center. Delicately cut crystal flutes awaited the mixing of champagne and orange juice.

What Picard noticed was a bouquet of flowers—visible through the doorway, in a vase inside her bedroom.

Crusher looked fresh as the morning itself. Her pastel-hued clothes were crisp and flattering to her trim figure. She greeted Picard with a warm, if oddly reserved, smile. "Good morning, Jean-Luc. I'm glad you could make it."

"As am I," he said. Any other man would have given the radiant red-haired doctor his full attention.

All the captain could see was that the sheets of Crusher's bed were uniformly rumpled on both sides, and that it was unmade. It was a trivial detail, but it obsessed him.

She had company last night was his first assumption.

He countered it instantly. *Or perhaps she had an early visitor, and simply didn't have time to make the bed.*

Before his mind could volley additional scenarios, he cut himself off. *Beverly's private affairs are none of my business.* Looking at her now, however, he pondered whether there might still be time to change that—and came face-to-face with the root of his selfish desire to have her remain on the *Enterprise*.

Then he thought of the young man who had just left her quarters, and he realized that the time for voicing his romantic inclinations had long since passed.

Clearly, Beverly had moved on.

Confronted with that coldly obvious truth, Picard decided that no matter how deeply it would wound him, the time had come for him to do the same.

William Riker felt reborn. Resurrected.

Lying in bed next to Troi, he reveled in all the minor comforts of home, so long forgotten. The satiny texture of their sheets . . . the springy recoil of their mattress. Even the air was a luxurious pleasure, so clean that it smelled sweet to his long-offended nose. To feel whole again, and free of pain, was like the end of a nightmare.

The intricate yet warm jazz constructions of Junior Mance filled their softly lit quarters. Gentle circumlocutions of a musical nature eased Riker's troubled thoughts. He had memorized these beautiful phrases, these eloquent turns in the weeks before the mission to Tezwa. The memory of them had sustained him during his darkest hours in that tiny corner of Hell.

He smiled at the warm touch of his *Imzadi*. She pressed up against him and draped her arm over his torso. His stomach gurgled loudly, apparently quite busy digesting the enormous meal he and Troi had devoured upon his discharge from sickbay. Their living room was strewn with the dirty dishes. He could still smell the garlic in the pasta from here.

Above them, the stars burned with cold fire against the eternal night. Taking in their austere beauty, he remembered the last time he had been able to lie here like this. It had been more than a month ago, shortly after his father's funeral. Everything in his life had seemed so tenuous then.

Now everything was merely in a state of flux.

Looking down, he realized Troi was awake and looking at him. "You're really back," she said in a wistful near-whisper.

"You better believe it," he said, though he was having a bit of difficulty believing it himself. He kissed her forehead.

They lay intertwined, listening to the hum of the *Enterprise*'s engines and their own breathing.

"What're you thinking about?" Troi said.

He sighed. "Change."

She shifted her weight and propped herself up beside him, on her elbow. "About your father? About our engagement?"

"Among other things," he said. "It's funny. When I was younger, I was always looking to try something new. Go someplace I'd never been before. Face some new challenge." He rolled over onto his own bent arm and faced her. "Being the first officer of the *Enterprise* has been the greatest experience of my life."

"You've never made any secret of that," she said with a half-grin. "No other ship was ever good enough to tempt you."

"That was part of it," he said. "But not all of it. I won't deny I liked the prestige of being on the flagship. But the truth is, on some level, I just got too comfortable."

"There's nothing wrong with being comfortable, Will."

"Not in general, no." He shook his head. "But I think

that after a certain point I was just being selfish. It was easier to stay here than it was to take a chance on making my own destiny. And I—" He stopped abruptly and reconsidered what he was about to say.

Troi, her empathy keenly attuned to his emotional state, zeroed in on his discomfort. "What?" He shook his head. "You were going to say something," she said. "What was it?"

There would be no deflecting her inquiry, he knew.

The simplest solution would be to simply come clean.

"I think," he began, his delivery slowed with exaggerated caution, "that a key reason I never accepted my own command was because I knew that I couldn't leave you again."

She didn't say anything. Without a word, she rested her hand on his chest, over his heart.

"I never forgot the look you gave me when I left Betazed," he said. "And I never wanted to see that look again."

"And you never will," she said. "Wherever you go, I'll follow. If you want to stay here, then I'll stay, too."

"I *do* want to stay here. That's what I meant about being too comfortable." He sat up and leaned back against the headboard. He wiped his palms over his face, then let them fall back at his sides on the bed. "I look at the influence one starship captain can have, and I think to myself, 'Who wouldn't want that?' Do I really want to be the second-in-command all my life? Even if I stay here until Picard steps down—and between you and me, I don't think that day's coming any time soon—there's no guarantee Starfleet would let me command the *Enterprise.*"

Troi nodded sympathetically. "There's also the fact

that Captain Picard has been subjected to a great deal of criticism since the Rashanar incident," she said. "I know you were worried that leaving him now could embarrass him and the crew."

"I'm not really worried about that anymore," Riker said. "The captain can take care of himself. The one I'm really concerned about is Data."

"Data?" She seemed thoroughly confused.

Riker shook his head. "He's been an exemplary first officer, Deanna. I read some of his reports today. I talked to Peart, and Vale, and the captain. That suicide attack Kinchawn's men tried with the cargo hauler in the shuttlebay? Data saw that coming a month ago. He drilled the crew day after day for that, and for a dozen other things I never would've thought of."

He pulled his knees up and leaned forward against them. "I don't know if I would've pushed the crew that hard. I might've felt sorry for them, let my emotions get the better of me. Not Data. He saved the ship. It's that simple." He pulled a deep breath into his lungs, held it a moment, then let it ebb. "But the same lack of emotions that helped him do that is also holding him back. He doesn't really have ambition. What that meant to me was I never had to worry about someone gunning for my job. . . . So I got comfortable."

Riker turned away from Troi in a futile effort to hide his shame. He knew that she could still read his emotions; he just didn't want her to see his face right now. "I took advantage of him, Deanna. I knew he'd never push me out, so I just let the years roll by. I indulged my desire for comfort at the expense of his career. If I'd accepted my own command when one was offered to me, or even applied for one after five or ten years on the *Enterprise,* Data would be first officer by now."

He stood up and resolved to do the right thing at last.

Turning to face his *Imzadi,* he said, "It's time I stopped being comfortable, and it's time I stopped standing in Data's way. . . . I'm taking command of the *Titan.*"

Acknowledgments

To begin, these acknowledgments are actually a sequel, of sorts, to the acknowledgments in *A Time to Kill,* the volume that precedes this one. I had managed to thank just about everyone under the sun in that go-around, but, inevitably, some folks got missed. Mea culpa.

First up on the "thanks" roster this time is my agent, Lucienne, who handles the business end of all these labors of mine, so that I don't need to worry about the economics of what I'm writing, while I'm actually writing it.

Next, a big tip o' the hat to John Van Citters from Paramount Licensing. Although his coworker Paula was the one with whom I worked during the story-development phase of these two books, J.V.C. was the person I dealt with after the manuscripts were written. His insights and encyclopedic knowledge of the *Star Trek* universe, both cinematic and literary, were invaluable in guiding these two manuscripts through their final stages.

Pocket Books editor Marco Palmieri also provided

valuable information that helped me keep the events of *A Time to Kill* and *A Time to Heal* in synch with the rest of the *Star Trek* literary universe, particularly the acclaimed *Deep Space Nine* post-finale tomes. And Ed Schlesinger deserves my thanks simply for his patience.

Some people I simply cannot thank enough, so I'll mention them once again. My beautiful wife, Kara, has, with varying degrees of sangfroid, tolerated my closed-door nights apart from her, as I tapped at my Macintosh and drove her insane by playing the same five or six movie soundtracks, *over and over and over.* . . . John Ordover showed faith in my ability by entrusting me with this double-volume debut. My parents, David and Yvonne, have always been close by—in spirit if not in body—with encouraging words. And I genuflect before the Malibu tribe, for not clubbing me with herrings as my complaining about "the books" and my "deadlines" stretched to its twentieth week—and beyond. . . .

On a different note, I feel that I owe a great debt to the composers whose brilliant film scores provide me with inspiration and help my mind's eye choreograph countless key moments in my narratives: Howard Shore (all three *Lord of the Rings* movies); Hans Zimmer (*Gladiator, Black Hawk Down*); Brian Tyler (*Frank Herbert's Children of Dune*); Danny Elfman (his *Planet of the Apes* score is riveting); John Williams (the entire original *Star Wars* trilogy, *Raiders of the Lost Ark, Jurassic Park* . . . the list goes on and on); James Horner (*Star Trek II: The Wrath of Khan* and *Aliens*); David Arnold (*Stargate* and *Independence Day*); Jerry Goldsmith (*Star Trek: The Motion Picture* and *The Ghost and The Dark-*

ness); Vangelis (*Blade Runner*); Alan Silvestri (*The Abyss*); Brad Fiedel (*Terminator 2: Judgment Day* and *True Lies*); Basil Poledouris (*Conan the Barbarian* and *Starship Troopers*—belittle the movies if you must, the music is wonderful); and Cliff Eidelman (*Star Trek VI: The Undiscovered Country*). Honestly, I would be lost sometimes without the music to guide me.

Speaking of being lost, let me express my gratitude to Geoffrey Mandel for his invaluable reference work of *Star Trek* astrocartography, *Star Charts*.

Finally, one item of note I'd like to point out for folks who might not be familiar with quality jazz: In a few scenes of this book and *A Time to Kill*, Will Riker listens to music by a "Chicago master" named Junior Mance. For the record, Junior Mance is a real person, and a bona fide Chicago master of jazz and blues. He is one of the most gifted pianists I have ever heard, and one of the nicest people I've ever met. Treat yourself—go buy and listen to some Junior Mance CDs (particularly *Happy Time* and *Blue Mance*) before you read this book.

That's it, I'll stop now. Read, enjoy. See you next time.

About the Author

David Mack is a writer whose work spans multiple media. With writing partner John J. Ordover, he cowrote the *Star Trek: Deep Space Nine* episode "Starship Down" and the story treatment for the *Star Trek: Deep Space Nine* episode "It's Only a Paper Moon." Mack and Ordover also penned the four-issue *Star Trek: Deep Space Nine / Star Trek: The Next Generation* crossover comic-book miniseries "Divided We Fall" for WildStorm Comics. With Keith R.A. DeCandido, Mack cowrote the *Star Trek: S.C.E.* eBook novella *Invincible,* currently available in paperback as part of the collection *Star Trek: S.C.E. #2—Miracle Workers*. Mack also has made behind-the-scenes contributions to several *Star Trek* CD-ROM products.

Mack's solo writing for *Star Trek* includes the *Star Trek: New Frontier Minipedia,* the trade paperback *The Starfleet Survival Guide,* and the best-selling, critically acclaimed two-part eBook novel *Star Trek: S.C.E.—*

Wildfire (to be reprinted in paperback form in November 2004). His other credits include "Waiting for G'Doh, or, How I Learned to Stop Moving and Hate People," a short story for the *Star Trek: New Frontier* anthology *No Limits,* edited by Peter David; S.C.E. eBook #40—*Failsafe;* the short story "Twilight's Wrath," for the *Star Trek* anthology *Tales of the Dominion War,* edited by Keith R.A. DeCandido; and *Star Trek: The Next Generation— A Time to Kill.* He currently is working on an original novel, developing new *Star Trek* book ideas, and writing a new S.C.E. eBook titled *Small World.*

A graduate of NYU's renowned film school, Mack has been to every Rush concert tour since 1982. He currently resides in New York City with his wife, Kara.

The saga concludes in October 2004 with

STAR TREK®

A TIME FOR WAR, A TIME FOR PEACE

by
Keith R.A. DeCandido

Turn the page for an electrifying preview of *A Time for War, A Time for Peace*. . . .

"Mr. Ambassador!"

"What do you want?" Worf asked by way of greeting.

"Supervisor Vark needs to see you right away, sir." Vark was the head of the kitchen staff.

"Regarding what?"

"I don't know that, sir, I only know that it's urgent."

Worf turned his back on Kl'rt. "I have an appointment that is more urgent. Tell Vark to make an appointment with Mr. Murphy."

"Sir, Supervisor Vark told me to fetch you and not come back without you. He'll kill me if I disobey."

Closing his eyes, Worf thought, *I do not have time for this*. He turned to face Kl'rt. "Then you will die, for I will not see Vark now."

Then he saw it.

All the stewards in the embassy wore the same two-piece white outfit, a simple shirt and pants. They were generally formfitting, though Kl'rt's was a bit loose on him. Too loose, in fact—the quartermaster was generally more competent at getting the sizes right.

Kl'rt's service record, which Worf had just been perusing, along with those of the other new arrivals to the kitchen staff, indicated no injuries or deformities of any kind. Such things were always listed in the records—for example, Vark's record noted that he was missing two fingers from his left hand, which happened either in glorious battle against the Kinshaya or after an accident in the kitchen of the House of K'mpec, depending on how drunk the kitchen staff supervisor was when he told the story.

Yet there was no indication in the records of the bulge Worf now saw on Kl'rt's right hip.

Worf hesitated for only a moment, but that was apparently enough for Kl'rt, who removed the small weapon from under his shirt and fired it at Worf. The life of a diplomat had done little to dull Worf's reflexes, and he was able to duck to the floor to avoid the weapons fire, which he recognized as being that of a Breen disruptor.

Murphy, to his credit, immediately pressed the panic button on his desk—one of many security procedures instituted by Worf. The panic button would alert the security forces throughout the embassy of a breach, and also set off an alarm throughout the building.

That alarm did not sound.

Worf reached into the pocket of his floor-length leather coat and pulled out a small Ferengi phaser and fired it on Kl'rt—

—just as Kl'rt turned his disruptor on Murphy.

Both men fell to the ground a moment later.

"*QI'yaH*," Worf cursed. He ran over to Murphy's desk. Worf had stunned Kl'rt—he would need to be questioned—but the human was quite dead. Carl Murphy was a good man who had served the Federation well. Worf swore that those responsible would pay for his life.

A quick check on Murphy's computer revealed that the security system was down, which tracked with the malfunctioning panic button. Worf then entered the code that only he had—indeed, that only he and Wu knew about—which would reactivate the security system.

The system obligingly came online a moment later. Before pushing the panic button a second time, Worf called up the views from the security recorders in the embassy. He needed intelligence before he proceeded further.

In every room, he saw people in the white shirt-and-pants outfits of kitchen stewards, armed with Breen disruptors, rounding up the embassy staff.

One member of security unholstered her Starfleet phaser and tried to fire it, only to have the weapon fail. In another part of the embassy, two more security personnel, armed with Klingon disruptors, did likewise, and their weapons also failed.

The perpetrators of this assault not only disabled security, but must have engaged a scattering field to neutralize any Federation or Klingon weapons. Worf offered silent thanks to Nog. The first Ferengi in Starfleet, the young lieutenant had given Worf the phaser as a going-away present when Worf departed Deep Space 9 to become ambassador. Nog had promised that it was immune to most known forms of tampering and might come in handy someday. *He was right.*

Growling deep in his throat, Worf examined the security monitors. As unthinkable as it may have seemed, the embassy was under siege and in imminent danger of being taken over.

Worf assumed that the fifteen new members of the kitchen staff were the primary instigators. The security monitors revealed that a dozen Klingons were herding the staff to the large meeting room at the center of the embassy's top floor. With Kl'rt down at his feet, that left three unaccounted for—*assuming that Vark is part of this.* Mag, the head of personnel, apparently was not, as he was one of the ones being walked at gunpoint to the meeting room.

So, Worf noticed, was Alexander, currently being brought to the stairwell on the ground level.

Then the screens all went blank again. *Whoever tampered with security is keeping an eye on those systems.* He attempted his personal reactivation code a second time, but it had no effect.

I will have to make do with the intelligence I have so far.

Running back into his office, Worf retrieved a tricorder and his Starfleet combadge from the drawer of his desk and shoved the former into his pocket. They functioned independently of the embassy systems and wouldn't be affected by the sabotage.

To his total lack of surprise, use of the combadge garnered no reply. *If they are capable of a scattering field to neutralize weapons and of deactivating embassy security, they are equally capable of blocking communica-*

tions. Still, he pocketed the combadge in case he might need it and moved back out into the hallway.

"Kl'rt, respond." Worf recognized the voice as that of Vark, coming from Kl'rt's prone form, indicating a communications device somewhere on the stunned steward's person. *"He isn't responding."*

"All right," said another voice, which Worf did not recognize. *"Gitak, Akor, get to the second level and find out what happened to Kl'rt."*

A third voice, that of Karra, spoke: *"Why send two people to stop a mere diplomat?"*

"He's not a mere diplomat, he's a decorated warrior who served in Starfleet for fifteen years in security and strategic operations. He's the most dangerous person in this embassy."

Vark growled. *"Damn you, Rov, if you had waited until after Worf was gone like I suggested—"*

"Then we wouldn't have our most valuable hostage, would we?"

Worf wondered if Rov knew that they already had their most valuable hostage's son. If he didn't, he would soon—Vark knew Alexander from the latter's many visits.

The ambassador needed to get off this floor immediately.

Checking his tricorder, he saw that the only life signs in the building that weren't in the meeting room were the two on this level—his and Kl'rt's—and thirteen moving about the embassy.

This has been a very efficient operation. Worf knew he had to conceal himself in order to plan a counterattack. *Fortunately, I have the perfect place to go.*

Worf took a moment to find the com unit, which was in Kl'rt's ear. Worf inserted the device in his own ear.

Even as he did, Rov said, *"Close the channel, wait for Gitak and Akor to check in."* Then the device went dead.

Worf kept it in his ear in any case. *It might prove useful.*

The door to the stairwell opened to reveal two more Klingons. Worf snarled, leapt behind Murphy's desk, and fired his phaser, now set to kill. *I need only one prisoner.*

As he crouched behind the large metal desk, he heard the thump of a body falling to the floor, meaning his aim was true and he had only one foe to face.

Two disruptor blasts whined as they went over Worf's head. Then he heard a voice both in his ear and from across the room. The shrill report of the disruptor meant that Worf actually heard the Klingon's words more clearly over his stolen com unit.

"This is Akor. Kl'rt's down, and the ambassador's still here. He took out Gitak. I need backup."

"I'm sending B'Eko and Kralk."

Allowing himself the tiniest of smiles, Worf took out the tricorder even as another disruptor blast fired over his head, this one on a different trajectory. Akor was not staying in one place, keeping Worf pinned behind the desk while he moved closer. Worf would have given him credit for good tactics, save for his breaking radio silence. That meant Worf could use his tricorder to home in on the transmission.

A moment later, he'd done so, backtracking Akor's movements in order to predict where he'd be in a moment.

Disruptor shots continued to fire over his head, even

as Worf crawled around to behind the desk, right under the chair on which Murphy's dead body sat. He aimed his Ferengi phaser through the legs of the chair at a spot just past the other side of the desk.

Five, four, three, two, one.

He fired just as Akor came into view. The shot only glanced his shoulder, unfortunately, and so Akor was able to return fire even as he fell backward. Fortunately for Worf, the shot hit harmlessly on the metal chair. The type of Breen disruptor the stewards were using affected only living tissue, doing no damage to inorganic objects.

Worf fired again, taking advantage of the larger target presented by Akor when he fell. This time, his aim was dead on; Akor got off one shot that fired into the ceiling before he died.

"Akor, what happened?" Rov asked over the com unit. *"Akor!"*

Climbing up from behind the desk, Worf bent over to pick up Kl'rt's unconscious form and slung him over his shoulder in a firefighter's carry. Rov's voice continued to blare into his ear as the ambassador brought Kl'rt to the turbolift doors.

The embassy had only one turboshaft on the lower levels, though there were two turbolifts. As the structure widened in all directions, the shaft forked, providing passage on both the east and west walls from the sixth floor up. At this second level, however, there was just the one, and according to Worf's tricorder, both lifts were stopped at the top level and had been deactivated.

That suited Worf fine. He needed only the shaft, not the lift itself.

Utilizing the manual override, Worf pried the lift doors open, then picked Kl'rt back up. The shaft had emergency ladders inset into the walls on the three non-door sides; Worf grunted from the weight of his prisoner as he clambered over to one of them and then started climbing down.

If one inspected the plans for the Federation embassy, one would see, besides the aboveground portions, an extensive basement level. If one had security clearance above a certain level, one could see a different set of plans, which included a subbasement that wasn't even accessible to all those who had clearance to know about it. Worf was among the latter.

However, there was a second subbasement, which almost nobody knew about and wasn't on any plan of the building that existed. Worf suspected that the number of people who did know of it could be counted on the fingers of one hand.

The ambassador himself was aware of its existence only because of a family connection. A high-ranking member of Imperial Intelligence named Lorgh was a friend to Worf's now-defunct House, and had let Worf know of the secret bunker that had been placed beneath the embassy, under the control of people who seemed to be Starfleet Intelligence, but in fact had a much more shadowy agenda, and no oversight that Lorgh could determine. In order to aid Captain Picard at Tezwa, Worf had gone to that sub-subbasement to ask the commander working there for help. Shortly thereafter, the room was cleared out, with not even subatomic traces of the base that Worf had seen. It was just an empty room that nobody even knew about.

Which made it the ideal place for Worf to begin planning to take back the Federation embassy.

Don't miss

KNOW NO BOUNDARIES

Explore the Star Trek™
Universe with Star Trek™
Communicator, The Magazine of
the Official Star Trek Fan Club.

Subscription to Communicator is
only $29.95 per year (plus shipping and handling)
and entitles you to:

- **6 issues of STAR TREK Communicator**

- **Membership in the official STAR TREK™ Fan Club**

- **An exclusive full-color lithograph**

- **10% discount on all merchandise purchased at
  www.startrekfanclub.com**

- **Advance purchase preference on select items
  exclusive to the fan club**

- **...and more benefits to come!**

So don't get left behind! Subscribe to STAR TREK™
Communicator now at www.startrekfanclub.com

www.decipher.com

D E C I P H E R®
The Art of Great Games®

A VIACOM COMPANY
www.startrek.com
STFC

STAR TREK

ACROSS

1 Bajoran cell
5 Made for a colony of ex-Borg in "Unity" [VGR]
8 Author Boardack
13 Used as energy containment coil
16 Kind of carvings in "Stardoesky" [DS9]
18 God-like computer in "The Apple" [TOS]
17 Arachnid with half-meter-long legs
19 Dax symbiont who succeeded Jadzia
20 Teer on Capella IV in "Friday's Child" [TOS]
21 Be a breadwinner
22 Spanish wave
34 2024 San Francisco problem
28 Science station Tango
29 PC alphanumeric: abbr.
31 Scuffle
33 Taxi
34 Like 17 Across
36 Octopus ___ star system
39 Assault weapon
40 T'Lara governmental envoy in "Armageddon Game" [DS9]
44 Opposite of dep.
46 Whitescreen?
48 ___ Trog (Klingon darkea)
49 Klingon capital
50 Bajoran poet Akorem in "Accession" [DS9]
50 Elevator inventor
52 Homeworld of two assassins sent to DS9 in "Babel"
55 Leader before Laren
56 Aldorian beverage served in Ten-Forward
58 Moss: combo word
59 ___-ising-slug
60 ___ ranee of No'Mat
63 Uniform indigenous to the Oellian crewmamber
68 U.S. Pons agent Boat boss
69 Radiate
58 Freeness commander who offered Kirk leave
69 Klaang escaped from one in "Broken Bow" [ENT]
70 Cape for Scotty
71 Eldaoth: Prefix

DOWN

1 Royal letters
2 Samson fitnect of Jadzia Dax
3 Chess castle
4 Bass where the Magellan crew pod on a beach shore
5 Ndele who played Drex
6 Used a towel pod
7 Restless
8 "Enterprise" succeeding producer Howard
9 Brenner or "Violations" [TNG]
10 Tarkassian imaginary friend of Guinan as a child
11 McGivers who befriended Khan in "Space Seed" [TOS]
12 Saloon vendor
14 Actor Morales
18 "___ and I Love" [DS9]
22 Alpha-currant ___
25 Solver
24 Superstore shoot
26 Member of Klingon intelligence in "Visionary" [DS9]
29 Regions on Bros in "Patterns of Force" [TOS]
30 Genesian creature Korax conspared to Kirk
32 Parent of P'Chan in "Survival Instinct" [VGR]
35 Modernized?

37 Deanna on "Star Trek: The Next Generation"
38 Pascal sounds
40 Warp core reactor output
42 Captain of the U.S.S. Equinox loss in the Delta Quadrant
45 Author LeBlan
47 Tactical officer on night cook in "Rejected Past" [TNG]
48 Bajoran grain-processing center
51 Ken is kidnapped in this planet in "Maridor" [VGR]
52 Tanaroha Bay, for one
54 Shore house
55 Priestly robes
57 "Inter Arma ___ Slient Leges" [DS9]
58 Sect of the Kazon Collective
60 Miles O'Been's coffee-cutoff hour
62 Git aid
64 Gagatone: Abbr.
65 Fight finisher

WARP INTO 2005...

Wall calendars celebrating

STAR TREK

STAR TREK: ENTERPRISE

and

STAR TREK: SHIPS OF THE LINE

plus the

STAR TREK: STARDATE
DAY-TO-DAY CALENDAR

Incorporating the entire
Star Trek universe, with
photos of all of your
favorite characters and
episodes!

NOW AVAILABLE